# THE DAGGER DANCE

*Lady Fan Mysteries*
*Book Seven*

**Elizabeth Bailey**

*Also in the Lady Fan Mystery Series*

The Gilded Shroud

The Deathly Portent

The Opium Purge

The Candlelit Coffin

The Mortal Blow

The Fateful Marriage

# THE DAGGER DANCE

Published by Sapere Books.

20 Windermere Drive, Leeds, England, LS17 7UZ,
United Kingdom

saperebooks.com



ISBN: 978-1-80055-213-5

# CHAPTER ONE

*March 1793*

Childish voices and laughter floated up from the terraced gardens beyond the drive. A weak winter sun splashed colour across the early blooming shrubs, melting the remaining frost.

From the window of the large front withdrawing room, Ottilia Fanshawe watched, with an envious eye, her two nephews playing with the diminutive Pretty, running across the lawn and jumping the little girl between them. Pretty was well wrapped up against the March chill. Her nurse, Hepsie, could be trusted to see to that, although the boys' antics were likely to heat the child unduly.

Hepsie was standing by in case of accident should the boisterous lads prove careless. Not that it needed Ottilia's intervention to keep the little orphan safe. Her every suggestion was met with cool assurance. Hepsie anticipated each contingency and had as little use for Ottilia's notions as Pretty had for her proffered affection.

In the months since Pretty and Hepsie had been staying at Flitteris, Ottilia's tentative overtures to Pretty were spurned. Pretty made no objection to a smile or kind words, but she answered the smile only with a stare from her big blue eyes and she spoke never a word in response. When Ottilia ventured to pick her up, she squirmed to be released, though she did not cry. Unlike her rescuer. Despising herself for the pointless tears, Ottilia tried to be glad the child had taken to Ben and Tom at the first instant.

"Moping again, Tillie?"

Ottilia jumped and turned, perceiving her husband as he entered the room, closing the door behind him. He had shed his outer garments and the sight of his well-beloved features, lean and strong, with his lush brown hair tied back and his deep brown eyes, swept warmth into her bosom. She suppressed her distresses and held out a hand to him. "How did you fare, Fan? Were the cottages as bad as Mr Pether said?"

"Worse." Lord Francis came across to the window seat set around the bay, took his wife's hand and kissed it, holding it as he sat down beside her. "I've sanctioned the expenditure for repairs. Pether is going to put the work in hand immediately."

"What of the occupants? Where will they go in the meantime?"

"I told Pether to move them to those empty cottages down by the West Wood. It's a little far from the village, but at least they are sound."

Ottilia summoned a show of support. "Can we afford the repairs, Fan?"

"We will be obliged to retrench a little, but nothing too onerous."

"Have you thought where we may make savings?"

Francis's smile was wry. "One is in a way to be made already, if Hemp finds a place suitable to his purposes."

Ottilia's discomfort revived. Her Barbadian steward's intent to leave the household now that his patrimony had come through was another thorn in Ottilia's flesh. "Hemp only seeks to reconnoitre for possibilities. It may be months before he finds what he wants. Besides, it is just an idea at present." She fervently hoped he would think better of it.

"For my part, I think it an excellent one. I will allow him to be just the man to run a lodging house."

Francis's eyes followed where Ottilia's gaze had been and Ottilia could not help looking again. Ben was now carrying Pretty piggyback as he chased after his younger brother. The little girl's muted shrieks of enjoyment tore through Ottilia's bosom.

"I wish you will stop fretting, Tillie."

"I wish it too, Fan, but I cannot." She released her fingers from his hold. "Don't scold. I know it is foolish of me but her rejection hurts me, my dearest. Why does she not like me at all? What have I done?"

He did not speak for a moment, but his frowning gaze scanned her face.

"Well, what, Fan?"

An eyebrow flickered. "I could hazard a guess, but you won't like it."

Ignoring a flitter of unease, Ottilia met his brown gaze. "Go on."

Francis reached for her hand again and held it strongly. "You are trying too hard, my loved one."

"Well, but —"

"No, listen to me." His tone softened. "Forgive me, sweetheart, but I believe you didn't want Pretty for herself. You wanted a substitute for the child you lost. Pretty will never be that."

The words hit hard. Ottilia swallowed on the threatening tears, but her voice was a murmur. "Brutal, Fan. But true, perhaps."

"There is no perhaps, Tillie." He took her other hand and held both, as if he might force his message by this means. "Come, use the intelligence I know you possess. You'll smother the child. Let her alone. Let her learn to trust you."

Dropping her gaze, Ottilia struggled for control. It was so near the bone she could barely tolerate hearing it. Yet hear it she must. At length she looked up again. "She must have sensed my desperation, do you not think?"

His hold relaxed and she allowed her hands to lie slackly in his. "I think you want too much from the girl. She has lost everything, Tillie."

"Except Hepsie. She is more a mother to Pretty than I can ever be."

"She is not your daughter. Nor can we be sure she will be left in your care."

The ever-present apprehension rose in Ottilia's breast, together with the tragic events last summer at Tunbridge Wells that had deprived Pretty Brockhurst of her former life as well as her parents. Her grandfather, Viscount Wem, himself doubly bereaved, had been uninterested in the fate of the little girl and so Ottilia had worked upon her husband until he had agreed to take the little girl home with them.

"But Lord Wem has not even troubled himself to enquire after her, Fan. And we know how he meant to serve her, an unwanted granddaughter, for he made himself clear on that score."

Francis released her hands and rose, impatient now. "Be that as it may, you ought to guard against becoming too attached, instead of hankering for the impossible."

"It is not impossible. You have just said, and I agree with you, that I should give her time. That I should not try so hard. I grant you all that, but —"

"Tillie, we have been over this countless times. The child is safe in a family environment here, and that is all that matters. As to the future… Are you listening to me?"

A movement in the periphery of her vision, coupled with the sound of trotting horses, had distracted Ottilia's attention to the window again. She glanced along the drive. "It is a coach. Are we expecting anyone?"

Francis shifted his stance, peering through the glass. "Not that I know of. Splashed with mud too. They have come some distance."

Visitors from afar came rarely to Flitteris. Indeed, Ottilia's brother's recent flying visit, bringing her nephews for a short stay, had been the only one for an age.

The coach was passing out of sight as it took the turn that led to the entrance to Flitteris Manor. Francis moved out into the room, and Ottilia came to join him in the triangle of sofa and chairs set to catch the heat from the fire, still smouldering although considerably diminished from the morning. Francis took his usual stance at one end of the marbled mantelpiece, leaning an elbow upon it and watching the door, a look of expectation in his face.

"Perhaps it is Lizzy after all," Ottilia suggested as she took her customary comfortably upholstered chair to one side of the fireplace. Their niece, Lady Elizabeth Fiske, had threatened to eschew the London Season and batten instead upon the Fanshawes.

*There is scant hope of Mr Maplewood turning up*, Lizzy had written. *Not that I wish for him since he is evidently incapable of making up his mind, but dearest Aunt, I anticipate nothing so dreary as a succession of parties without his acerbic comments and his dreadful tendency to provoke me. I shall be bored to tears.*

An idle threat, as Francis had said, since Lizzy's mother Harriet would infallibly put a spoke in the girl's wheel. Lizzie's suitor, Mr Maplewood, encountered during their ill-fated visit to Tunbridge Wells, had been deemed set to declare himself with a promise to visit Lady Elizabeth Fiske at her home. But Mr Maplewood's arrival had not gone well with Lizzie's parents and no offer had been forthcoming. Mr Maplewood was an aspiring artist allied to a distinctly unpleasant family, and Harriet, as Ottilia surmised, would have no notion of her daughter's escaping the metropolis where a more acceptable parti than a mere mister might be found. Not that Ottilia approved of such prejudice. But since Mr Maplewood had failed to come up to scratch, there was nothing to be done — for this present at any rate.

A knock at the door produced the butler, Rodmell, breaking into Ottilia's reverie. He shut it behind him and, emitting the spurious cough peculiar to butlers, approached the master and mistress of the house. "My lord, a person has called."

Francis's brows flew up. "A person?"

"I should hesitate to stigmatise him a gentleman, my lord. I believe he may be a person of the merchant class."

Mystified, Ottilia exchanged a glance with her husband, who looked to be equally at a loss. She cut in swiftly. "What sort of merchant, Rodmell? Does he have a name?"

"A Mr Madeley, my lady. He asked in particular for your ladyship." Moving to her, Rodmell presented the small silver salver he carried.

Ottilia picked up the card.

"Well?"

She turned it over. "Nothing, Fan. There is only the name."

"Intriguing. Let us find out, then. Admit him, Rodmell."

The butler bowed and retreated, disappearing through the door. A moment later he reappeared, held open the door and announced the visitor. "Mr Madeley, my lady."

A man of middle years walked in and paused, looking across first at Francis and then towards Ottilia. He was of medium height with a spare frame, dressed plainly in dark colours, his country frockcoat and breeches cut for comfort rather than fashion. He wore, oddly, a black cravat and a brown wig, uncurled and tied in a short queue, adorned his head, framing features that were vaguely familiar.

He gave a small bow and spoke, a timbre in his words that struck at Ottilia's earlier unease. "Is it Lady Francis Fanshawe? Also known as Lady Fan?"

Ottilia dipped her head. "I am she, sir. How may I serve you?"

He hesitated, which gave Francis an opportunity to interject. "First of all, who are you, sir? We can do with knowing more of you than your name."

The fellow shifted his glance across, and Ottilia noted a tightening at his jaw. "I am about to inform you of it, my lord, although I am not here in connection with my business affairs. I am the proprietor of Madeley & Son, mercers of the County of Shropshire."

The information set a rapid string of thoughts running through Ottilia's head, ending with the significance of the black neckcloth. The truth struck her like a blow. "You are Isabel Brockhurst's father!"

A keen gaze came back to her. "You surmise correctly, my lady. It has taken some effort on my part to locate the whereabouts of Isabel's child."

Ottilia could not speak. She could only be glad her spouse took up the point.

"No doubt you will be glad to know Pretty is in safe hands."

"Glad indeed, my lord, but I must beg to be understood at once." He turned again and Ottilia braced. "I have come, my lady, for one purpose only. To retrieve my granddaughter."

Of all possibilities, Ottilia had never reckoned on having to deal with the other branch of Pretty's antecedents. Ever since Isabel Brockhurst's untimely death and the subsequent debacle that left Pretty an orphan and set the entirety of her father's family in turmoil, Ottilia had dreaded the advent of Viscount Wem, the only person, as she had thought, with a legitimate claim upon Pretty. Here instead came the little girl's other grandfather, proving to be the nemesis she feared. The thought of how foolish she had been passed through her mind and gave way to urgent need. Her glance swept the merchant and fixed upon her husband. He evidently read her dismay, taking immediate command.

"That, Mr Madeley, remains to be seen." The visitor opened his mouth to speak and Francis held up a hand. "Perhaps you are not aware that Viscount Wem placed the child in our care?"

Mr Madeley's gaze remained steady, his determined air in no way diminished. "I am perfectly aware of his lordship's dislike of his son's connection with my daughter."

"That is not to the purpose."

"Forgive me, my lord, but it is indeed to the purpose. My acquaintance with his lordship is one of long standing, albeit in a capacity of business. I know his temper and I know where his loyalties lie. I do not believe for one moment Lord Wem might welcome such an addition to his household."

Ottilia found herself so much in agreement with this sentiment that it softened her distress and loosened her tongue into the bargain. "You are perfectly right, sir, and it is for that reason we took it upon ourselves to proffer an alternative solution."

Mr Madeley turned in her direction, a frown marring his brow. "Then you cannot object to my removing her to a secure environment."

Rising in swift rebuttal, Ottilia confronted him. "But I do object, Mr Madeley. I object strongly."

"Ottilia, take care!" Francis cautioned.

She gave a brief glance in acknowledgement of the warning, but swept on. "You cannot have considered, sir. Would you disrupt the child all over again just when she is settling?"

Mr Madeley's frown intensified. "Pertesia's place is with her family."

"She has no family, Mr Madeley. No immediate family. What do you imagine it has taken to soothe her after such a loss? After the treatment she received at the hands of the Brockhursts?"

"All the more reason, my lady, to bring her to live with those who may replace what she has lost."

"That is impossible."

"For your ladyship also, if I may be so bold."

The words, spoken without heat, struck at the heart of Ottilia's discontent and she was silenced. To her inestimable gratitude, Francis took a hand.

"Will you not be seated, Mr Madeley? This is scarcely a matter to be decided in an instant." He moved away from the mantel as he spoke, gesturing to the sofa. As Mr Madeley moved towards it, Francis signalled Ottilia to resume her chair. She did so, dismay returning. It was not going to be easy to persuade this man to leave Pretty in situ. She cast about in her mind for arguments with which to convince him as her spouse went to the bell-pull and tugged upon it. "Will you take a glass, Mr Madeley? I can offer you Madeira, or claret if you prefer."

The merchant looked a little surprised, but he proffered thanks and opted for Madeira. He did not wait for the butler's entrance, but resumed the argument at once, addressing himself to Ottilia. "My lady —"

Impatience caused her to cut in. "Oh, call me Lady Francis if you must. Or Lady Fan will do. I abhor excessive formality."

He inclined his head. "As you wish, ma'am."

A thought occurred to Ottilia and she gave it voice. "You said it was difficult to trace me. Did you go to Tunbridge Wells?"

"Among other places. I tried for you in the capital, but I was unable to glean any word of your whereabouts from Lord Polbrook's household."

This was said with a glance towards Francis, whose brows rose as he sat down on the chair opposite Ottilia. "I should certainly doubt of your enquiries being welcomed in my brother's house. Did you explain your need?"

A faint grimace crossed Mr Madeley's face. "I was not granted the opportunity."

"Then where did you learn where to find me?"

He turned back to Ottilia. "From the servants at Lady Wem's residence in Tunbridge Wells, ma'am. Where I also learned of the role you had undertaken on behalf of my granddaughter and Mr Daniel Brockhurst, for which I must thank you."

The tone was grudging, and Ottilia began to think she had a battle on her hands. The man would not readily yield. His determination had carried him thus far. She tried a throw. "Your persistence is commendable, Mr Madeley, but I fear you have made a wasted journey."

The opening of the door prevented the merchant from responding. Rodmell appeared, armed with a tray upon which reposed two decanters and several glasses. Behind him came

Tyler, armed with a separate tray. Ottilia recognised the coffee pot and her spirits lifted a trifle. The servants knew her so well. Her favourite beverage was precisely what she needed at this moment.

"Ah, you have anticipated us, Rodmell, thank you. You've brought the Madeira, I trust?"

"Certainly, my lord."

Francis put in Madeley's request and the butler poured two glasses of the amber liquid, what time the footman served Ottilia's coffee, laced with the precise amount of cream and sugar she liked. She smiled and thanked him as he handed it to her and fortified herself with several sips as the servants withdrew.

"Well now, Mr Madeley," Francis began, "let us discuss this matter without beating our heads together." With which, he threw an admonitory glance at Ottilia. "I imagine we all want what is best for the child."

Ottilia gathered her arguments. There was no question in her own mind what would best serve Pretty's interests, but how to convince the child's maternal grandfather?

# CHAPTER TWO

*Is it Doro?* The first glimpse had kicked in Hemp Roy's gut. After leaving the Fanshawes' home to seek for a potential business opportunity, trying first in Weymouth and now in Bristol, the last thing he had expected was to see Dorote Gabon, transported as he had been to foreign shores. How was she here in England, when he had last seen her under Barbadian skies? He must be mistaken. It had been all of two years. No, three. Yet he knew that face so well. Skin of ebony shot with those blue, blue eyes.

Shock gave way to elation, hope, fear as the memories raced in Hemp's head, his steps taking him ever closer to Doro, the flowered chintz of her petticoats a beacon under the short dull-coloured jacket that looked inadequate for this cold, although a weak sun cast shadows on the buildings along the quay. Doro had always loved bright colours. He recalled the way she used discarded cloth, wrapped about her head like a joyous cap. Here in Bristol — arrived on one of the trader ships? — she was bonneted in the conventional way, causing doubt to dampen the sweeping longings he had believed conquered long since.

She was threading through the persons milling on Broad Quay as one of the ships anchored in the floating harbour disgorged its quota of passengers onto the dock. Doro, if it was she, slipped readily between the weary and harassed travellers, the porters, cabmen and growing mounds of luggage. Hampered by his height and size, Hemp made a wider detour around a pile of barrels close to the harbour's edge, nevertheless keeping her within sight. At length, he drew abreast, though still divided from her by several yards thick with persons he heartily wished at Jericho.

The fixed intent of discovery proved strong. Hemp barged his way through and caught the lithe figure as she passed a pair of porters burdened with a heavy trunk.

"Doro!"

He had seized her arm and she halted perforce, emitting a gasp of protest. Hemp slid in front of her, retaining his hold as those unmistakeable eyes lifted to his face in violent question. And then they changed. She did not speak, but the shock in her eyes mirrored his own. Hemp lost his head and began to babble. "It is you! Doro, Doro, are you real? I knew I could not mistake. Doro, how came you here? Whence this miracle? I never thought to see you again…"

The words died in his throat as he took in her altered state. She was thinner than he remembered, the shine gone from her skin which looked grey, hollowed below the cheekbones, the magnificent eyes dulled, sunken in circles visibly darker than the rest.

As he stared, the unhealed crack in his heart revived, pity coursing through the wasted affection. "Doro, what happened to you?" From nowhere, a thrust of rage welled up. "Did *he* bring you to this?"

Doro shied, dragging back, no longer meeting his eyes as she dipped her head, her altered features now concealed by the bonnet. Her voice came low and ragged. "Release me!"

Hemp's grip held. It was the voice he knew too well, but altered. "I cannot." He dropped his tone. "Doro, talk to me!" The rigidity in her arm increased as she tried to pull away and Hemp became aware of how thin it was. He loosened his hold, running his hand down her sleeve to find her fingers, lifting them. "You still bite your nails."

She did not resist when he turned her hand. That her fingers and palms were calloused came as no surprise. She had laboured long years in the sugarcane fields. Hemp lifted the hand, set a kiss in the palm, closed her fingers over it and released the hand.

She was looking up again. A tiny smile flitted across her lips. "That I remember well."

He caught her gaze and it held. "I remember everything."

Her eyes darkened. "No! I am a slave, Hemp. Long ago it was finished."

"Not so long. And it was not your owner who finished it."

"Now he does." Her tone had hardened and she dipped her head again. "I must go."

"Wait! Where can I find you?"

She backed a step. "It is better you do not."

"Doro!"

The bonnet rose again and her eyes met his. "Pray leave it, Hemp. I am not the Doro you once knew."

She slipped by him and hurried on her way. Hemp hesitated a moment, but a hint of anguish in that last echoed in his head. Without hesitation, he abandoned his plan to look over a house for sale that let directly onto the harbour and followed at a discreet distance.

Her mind in chaos, heart in tatters, Dorote Gabon fled from the man she'd betrayed. The shock of seeing him yet shrieked in her veins, calling to the deeps of guilt and yearning. Hemp Roy had loved her once, truly. Until the devil's snare caught her, where she writhed even now.

She hardly knew what path she trod, crossing the lower Bridge and slipping through the back streets of her customary shortcut to Park Street, from thence making automatically for the Scalloway home in Charlotte Street. The buried memories were flying free. Walks, so late when work was done, under the moon, hidden by the tall canes. His hand, strong about her fingers … the kiss in her palm, every time they parted … times when she felt the hot desire behind the gentleness, the vigour of his wanting held in. An echo filtered in, of that intense jealousy as she watched him, in the distance, caring for his ward, Tamasine. Never could she rival the mad beauty in Hemp's heart. And Tamasine was gone now. Cuffy, who had accompanied Hemp to England with Tamasine's entourage, had told them how it was when he returned at last to the island, told them of Hemp's inconsolable grief. Had he grieved also for Doro?

She must think no more of that. Though she had, even as the ship drew ever closer to the land where he walked, she had thought of him, wondered, dared to hope in some secret pocket of unwisdom. She felt again the first shock as he grasped her arm and stood before her, large as life. A vision? It *was* he. She hardly knew what he said, what she replied. Instinct made her run. Had she conjured him, all unknowing, with whispered incantations vaguely recalled from the witch doctor's mutterings in her half-forgotten beginnings? If she had, she must banish him again. There was no pathway to the past.

Her steps took her back to Hades before she knew it. Doro clattered down the area steps and slipped into the narrow hallway leading through to the pantry and then the kitchen.

Stout Peg, busy stirring a pot on the range, her round face already sweat-stained, saw her first. "Back are you, Doro, my dear? Been ringing like the fiend, she has."

Quin, lounging at the table, dug his knife into a hunk of cheese. "No rush, Doro girl. Jenny's gorn up. Sit. Here, have a bite." He held out the speared knob of cheese on the point of the knife.

Ordinarily, Doro avoided the sly little man. He was apt to touch and squeeze, catching her in dark corners. His position in the household, officially the boots but in reality that of general factotum, afforded ample opportunity to slide about the house more or less as he chose. Doro suspected the errands upon which the master sent him were as dubious as those upon which the mistress sent her, if for different reasons. But today, with Hemp Roy's presence in the town ringing in her bosom, caution flew to the winds.

"It is kind, but not now, Quin. I must go to the mistress."

Surprise flickered in his eyes, but he gave her a leering smile. "Later then. I can wait."

Doro was glad of Peg's intervention as she untied her bonnet and made for the inner door.

"Have you nothing better to do, Lazy Bones? Sitting around my kitchen like the King. You can peel them potatoes for me."

Quin's truculent response was lost as Doro hurried up the stairs, making first for her little room in the attics to put away her bonnet, don her apron and make sure her cap was straight. The resumption of normality served to settle her shattered nerves a little, the encounter at the quay taking on an aspect of unreality. This was her life, her truth. Hemp Roy was but a buried dream.

Nevertheless, the memory of his physical vigour lingered in the recesses of her mind as she ran down the stairs, heading for the front parlour where Mrs Scalloway was apt to spend her days. The maid Jenny met her halfway along the corridor.

Doro detained her. "What does the mistress want? Peg said she was ringing for me."

"She didn't have no chance to tell me. *He* come in, didn't he?" Jenny, a plump youngster, rolled her eyes. "At it again, they are. If I was you, Doro, I'd stay out of there."

As if she had that luxury. Doro thanked the girl and went on her way. The raised voices reached her as she approached the parlour and her heart sank. Wrangling again? If the master's temper was roused, she was as much at risk as the mistress. She still had bruises from the last occasion. She was obliged to banish a fleeting thought of what Hemp might say or do did he know how ill she was used. He was not her champion now, never could be, not after —

Doro cut off the thought. There she must not go. Her duty lay before her. Tugging on resolution, she opened the parlour door and slid inside, closing it behind her.

Neither combatant noticed. Mistress Scalloway was over by the windows, conveniently shielded from assault by the intervening sofa set between her and the area before the fireplace where the master stood, his face blotched with furious red in contrast to his wife's countenance, pallid against the dark of her hair.

"You've done naught I asked of you. You say you spoke to Radcliffe; where is he, then? Where's the draft to appease that fellow Harbury?"

"Why should you pay? He was your partner. He should take the loss as well as you."

The master's eyes took fire. "You are quoting Radcliffe. How dare you throw his words at me?"

"He said the same to you? Then why are you badgering me? It is none of my affair, after all."

A sneer crossed the master's face. "None of your affair? Harbury has your note of hand."

The mistress flared up. "You said you would destroy it!"

"How could I do so? He has it in his possession."

"Then on your head be it, Marcus. There is nothing I can do. Lord Radcliffe —"

"Nothing, is it? I'll go bail you told Radcliffe not to grease me in the fist, didn't you?"

The mistress sighed in a way Doro had heard all too often. "I did try, Marcus. I begged him, for my sake, for the sake of my mother's memory, but he is adamant. Lord Radcliffe will advance you no money against my inheritance. I even mentioned the note, but he says it will not hold. If Harbury takes it to court, he will claim I was coerced. And I was, Marcus. Can you deny it?"

All at once, the master's ire collapsed. He sank back, half falling against the mantel and throwing a hand to his head. "I'm finished, then. Might as well blow my brains out." His hand dropped and he threw a glare at his wife. "Not that you'd care. You'd welcome my death, wouldn't you, eh? Wouldn't you?"

Mrs Scalloway's pale features, once exceptionally lovely, now marred with discontent, went whiter still. Her voice came low, but on a vicious note. "If I had the courage, I would kill you myself."

Doro let out a gasp, drawing the master's attention. To her consternation, ignoring his wife's words, he strode in Doro's direction, the look she dreaded in his face.

"What the devil are you doing here?" As he reached her, his arm went up and Doro cringed away. "Breathe a word and I'll flay you, witch girl!"

Before the blow could land, Mrs Scalloway flew across the room, barging between them to confront her husband. "Touch her and I *will* kill you! I mean it, Marcus!"

He eyed her, the avenging hand poised to strike, withheld for the moment. Over the mistress's shoulder, Doro saw uncertainty in his expression. As he paused, Mrs Scalloway drew an audible breath and spoke again. "I am leaving you, Marcus. I will be gone by tonight."

Shock enveloped Doro. The mistress was her only protection. If she were gone, the master could do as he willed, Doro powerless to stop him.

Mr Scalloway's shock was clearly equal to her own. "You can't leave. Where will you go? An empty threat!"

"It is no threat. I am leaving you," she repeated.

His hand dropped. "Elinor!" Was it a plea?

Doro could feel the mistress trembling, so close behind her she stood. But there was determination in her voice.

"I was going to go without telling you. It is all arranged."

"But where will you go?" His expression changed. "Culverstone! You mean to run off with that low-born rogue?"

Was that what had been in the note Doro delivered? Surely the mistress would not take a step so drastic?

"I am going to Lord Radcliffe and his lady. They will help me arrange for a deed of separation."

Doro saw panic spread across the master's countenance, no less than that rising in her own bosom.

"Elinor! You can't! Think of the scandal." He seized her hands. "Stay! I will change. It will be different between us."

She tugged her fingers out of his. "You won't change, Marcus. You only want me for what I may bring you when my father dies, and that is too long away for me."

Desperation sounded as he began to beg. "It's not true. I care for you, you know that. Don't go! Not yet awhile. Give me a day or two. What use in going at once? We have Sunday before us. Let us talk of this. We can come to some arrangement."

"What arrangement? Marcus, this is useless."

"You are my wife!"

"Yes, and you've used me ill. I can endure no more of it."

"One night only. Two nights. You have an engagement tonight, do you not? Let us talk tomorrow. Another chance, Elinor. You owe me that much."

"I owe you naught!"

"Please, Elinor! You've taken me by surprise. You give me no opportunity to — to change, make amends. Give me tomorrow at least, I am begging you."

The heavy sigh came again. "Very well. I will give you tomorrow. But on Monday I leave this house."

He seized her hands, kissing the fingers. "You won't regret it, Elinor. I will prove myself to you. You may not see me today, but tomorrow we will talk."

He was at the door, but the mistress stayed him. "Where are you going?"

"To find a way out of this difficulty so that we need not trouble Radcliffe."

The door closed behind him and the mistress sank into the nearest chair.

Doro went to her. "You are shaking, madame. May I fetch you a drink? Coffee?"

Mrs Scalloway grasped Doro's hand and squeezed. "Presently." The breath shuddered out of her. "I did not think I had the courage to tell him."

Doro let her hand lie slackly within the hold, her apprehension rising. "You truly mean to go, madame?"

Mrs Scalloway looked up and smiled, though her lip trembled. "Don't you believe me either? Are you afraid?"

Doro felt the prick in her eyes, but she must not let the tears fall. "I am afraid, yes. For you. For myself also."

The hand tightened. "There is no need. We will be well taken care of."

Hope leapt. "We, madame?"

Mrs Scalloway shook the hand she held. "Of course, we. Did you think I would leave you to his mercy? You will come with me, Doro."

"But I am his slave, madame. He bought me."

"He bought you for me. You are mine, if you are anyone's. Once I am free of him, I will set you free too."

Elation rose up, mingling with fear. Doro knew the master too well. He was cunning. She spoke her thought aloud. "Madame, he will never let you go. Nor me neither. We will be free only when he dies."

# CHAPTER THREE

Loitering in the street felt out of place to Hemp, but he could not bring himself to leave his post opposite the establishment in Charlotte Street. He rubbed his hands together, feeling the cold after standing motionless for too long. He had chosen the shadowed side of the street where the sun did not penetrate, able thus to observe the building opposite without himself drawing attention. It was not substantial, but of a respectable size, rising two stories above the roadway. The porch, under a pillared portico, was attained by a short stone stairway, but Doro had slipped between the railings on one side where an iron stair ran down to the narrow area. How could he depart without seeing her again? She was in that house, and unhappy. Mistreated by the devil who had stolen her away from him? What had she said? Her owner finished it between them, now not then. Brief words, reviving the agony.

Finished? No, Doro, he would not have it so. To find her again, here, like this? It was a new beginning rather.

The front door opened and a man came out. He was dressed for the street in a double-caped great-coat, unbuttoned as if he had shrugged into it in haste, a round black beaver hat crammed onto his head. He turned back towards the still open door before Hemp could see his face, talking to someone within. Then he moved towards the steps and a rat-like fellow came out behind him and closed the door. Small of stature and wearing the garb of a servant, he slunk down the steps behind his master, nodding as the latter, his back towards Hemp, gave some instruction. Then he slipped by the man and hurried off along the street.

Hemp's gaze reverted to the master, who turned, affording a good view of his countenance. Recognition jolted in Hemp's chest. *Marcus Scalloway, the devil himself!*

He began to walk in the same direction as his servant, towards Park Street. Then towards the harbour? Instinct bade Hemp to follow, but Doro was still inside. He could not go. Not yet. But he made the best of the brief time he had to take in the condition of the loathed face.

It looked older than it should have, deteriorated like Doro's, if differently. Scalloway was fleshier than Hemp remembered, his once lean cheeks now bloated. His eyes, that could flirt warmth with spurious sincerity or, with more frequency, gaze out in calculating cynicism, were set now in dark shadows and puffiness below. Both discontent and dissipation were rife, by the look of him. The latter was no surprise. Hemp had taken his measure at the outset. Devil looks, devil heart. But Doro had been dazzled, flattered, duped. Too young, too innocent to see the man for what he was.

A demon voice in his own breast whispered that she had been well enlightened, but he crushed it, saddened by the change. Was it Scalloway who owned her now? If so, Hemp could not doubt she had been punished enough. The thought of what she might have endured at the villain's hands lodged like stone in his gut. Scalloway had crushed her spirit, that was clear. His Doro, his queen, the bright, engaging light of his life, gone like the dream he had cherished. Until the advent of a callous, philandering brute, who no sooner caught a glimpse of those mesmerising blue eyes in the dark features than he turned on that fatal charm.

The memories flooded his mind and he strove to beat them out, seized with a resurgence of the violence that had beset him then. If his mentor had not tamed him, he might have slain his rival — and hanged for it as Matthew Roy had pointed out.

Movement on the area steps caught his attention and the images in his head faded as he watched. *Doro!* His vigil was rewarded.

She did not see him, turning at the top of the steps for the main street, hurried and hunched in to herself. Hemp crossed the road and caught her up in a few swift steps, taking his place beside her. She shied and halted, staring up at him.

"You! What do you here? Did you follow me? What do you want?"

He matched her tone. "Did you think I could walk away from you? Not again, Doro."

Under the bonnet, her gaze flickered away and back again. "It is useless. I am occupied. Leave me be." She began to walk again, faster, head down.

Hemp kept pace. "Tell me you will meet me and I will leave you in peace."

She did not look up. "I have a message I must deliver."

"Afterwards? A few moments of your time, Doro. Can you not grant me that much? You would have done so once."

At that, she cast him a raking glance. "That time is gone. It is over. It was over long ago."

"Then it begins again."

She stopped dead. "No! I cannot. Not now. Let me alone, Hemp."

He paused as she set off once more, prey to resentment. Could she not give him even this? But his feet moved again, almost without benefit of his will. He did not take his place again beside her, but remained behind. That she was aware of him was evidenced by the shift in her shoulders and a sideways motion of her head.

Silence held for the length of the street. Doro crossed the road and turned for a lane leading off Park Street. At the entrance she halted again and half turned her head, though she did not look at him. "If you will follow me, you had best walk by my side. You make me look particular."

There was less vehemence in her tone and Hemp rejoiced, moving to join her in the lane. He said no word, hoping by compliance to lessen her discomfort. They traversed Frogmore Street and Doro took another small lane leading to the harbour. Hemp realised they were retracing her earlier steps, but she did not cross at the first bridge this time.

The Cathedral side of the harbour proved to be as busy as the Quay. Doro weaved easily through the press of persons. *Long practice?* His tongue loosened. "How long have you been in England?"

"Near six months."

She did not look at him and Hemp suspected the response was automatic as she volunteered no more.

"All the time here in Bristol?"

"He has acquaintance here."

"Scalloway?"

A flash of those strange eyes came his way. "How did you know?"

"I saw him leave the house." Hemp paused, the words hovering on his tongue striking unwise in his head. To remark upon the man's looks could only alienate her. He changed them. "You serve him, Doro?"

"Never in this world!" The tone was vicious, though spoken low. "I serve his wife."

Married! Had he not known the blackguard had no honourable intent? Had he then made Doro his mistress? His guts kicked. There he must not go. "Who is she? Do I know her?"

"She was a Carey."

The name was known to Hemp. One of the sugar barons, an acquaintance of Master Roy, who visited sometimes at Flora Sugars. And Scalloway had married his daughter? "He did well for himself there."

"But ill for my mistress." The vicious note again.

"No surprise to me, Doro." It was out before he could stop it. A scorching look was cast up at him and she hunched in again, quickening her pace. He caught up. "Forgive me. I did not mean it for a reproach."

"It is what you think." Low and tense. "Do you suppose I do not know? I wish you will leave me be."

"When I have only just found you? How can I?" He stopped, seizing her arm to halt her and holding it fast. "Doro, look at me!" Her head came up and her eyes met his, pain in them. Hemp lowered his voice, the tenderness reviving. "I see you wretched and ill, Doro. Do you think I can bear to recognise how you are situated and just walk away? You will haunt me, Doro, just as you have haunted me these three years. I beg you, meet with me so we may talk. Not like this. Will you? Tomorrow?"

"I cannot get away on Sunday. I have to attend my mistress to church."

"Monday, then?"

"I do not know where I may be on Monday."

Yet she made no move to pull away, and Hemp was encouraged.

"It makes no matter. I will meet you wherever you are. Appoint a place and I will be there."

She wavered, her gaze flicking away and back again. Then her head dropped. "Let me think on it. I must go. My mission is urgent."

He released her. "Then I will accompany you."

"I cannot prevent you."

The faint hope died. But at least she was shifting ground. He kept up as she hurried on, crossing Stone Bridge at the upper end of the way known as Under the Bank, and taking the left lane into Quay Street, heading away from the docks and the banks of warehouses. Was this from where she had come when he met her earlier in the day? She had not taken this exact route, which indicated she'd had more than one errand to run. From his role as a footman, prior to his employment with the Fanshawes, Hemp understood the work of a lower servant. He could not help wondering what could be her purpose this time, especially considering her attitude.

"You are carrying a message for your mistress?"

She did not answer and a spurt of irritation seized him. He suppressed it, unwilling to jeopardise the possibility she would agree to his request.

She halted before a house about halfway along Nelson Street, turning to face him. "Stand off. My business is private."

Hemp was obliged to bite down on a sharp retort. She was giving no quarter. His sense of justice came to his rescue. Whatever she had to do here, she did not need a conspicuous escort. Accordingly, he retraced his steps until he was effectively out of earshot, aware Doro watched him. He took a deliberate pose of inattention.

Apparently satisfied, she approached the door of the house and knocked. It opened shortly and she entered.

Hemp was left to kick his heels. His mind roved over the few exchanges, grudging on her part. Her words struck him anew.

Why should she not know where she might be on the morrow? His concentration had been on her reluctance, but on review he realised there was more. Distracted? Anxious? Both of those. Urgency also.

It betokened something other than Doro's dismay at his worrisome presence. She was less dismayed than impatient. What was afoot?

Before he could further examine the question, a man came out of the house, Doro following. A youngish fellow, well dressed and pleasant of feature, who looked to have partaken of Doro's anxiety. The two conversed, the man evidently questioning her in a tone too low for Hemp to hear the words but loud enough to show eagerness and anger both. Doro's responses were swift and brief. He nodded, turned and set off towards the harbour, Hemp taking care as the man passed him to look in the opposite direction as if he was engaged in finding his bearings.

Doro watched him away and then her gaze shifted to Hemp. He started forward.

"There is something amiss, is there not? What is it, Doro?"

"I cannot tell you." She avoided his gaze, setting out immediately back towards the harbour.

Hemp reached out to halt her. "Wait! Give me a moment only, Doro."

She paused, raised her head, fixed him with those blue, blue eyes. "It is not possible to appoint a meeting. I cannot make any arrangement."

His heart lurched. "You won't even give me that? Do those years mean nothing, Doro? Can you not even grant me the friendship we shared?"

An agonised look flared for an instant and was gone. "It is not… We were friends, yes, more even. But the time is not right, Hemp. I cannot say more."

A faint hope surfaced. "You do not hate me, then?"

"Hate?" Was that a fleeting smile? "Never that."

"Then I will wait outside that house on Monday. Come out when you can. I will be there."

Her gaze held on his face. A look in her eyes that took him back. For one precious moment she was the Doro he remembered, before the breach. She seemed about to speak, but no word came. Then she dipped her head and left him, her booted feet striking a tattoo on the cobbles that echoed in his breast.

# CHAPTER FOUR

Only the knowledge Mrs Scalloway meant for her to accompany her mistress when she left the house served to quiet Doro's thrumming nerves as she fulfilled her latest errand. Past incidents when the master had spent the night outside of the house ran through her mind as she hurried along the street, huddling in her jacket against the chill wind this early in the day. Mr Scalloway's temper under the influence of a night of debauch was liable to erupt. She had protested to the mistress in vain.

"Why do you not leave now, madame, while he is gone?"

Mrs Scalloway, still in bed and drinking the morning chocolate Doro had brought, spurned the suggestion in no uncertain terms. "Steal away in secret as if I am at fault? I will not give him the satisfaction. Especially after he failed to put in an appearance at church yesterday, returning home only for dinner, saying scarcely a word and going straight out again afterwards. How dare he treat me shabbily after begging me to remain? And all for naught. Besides, I can hardly remove in such a scrambling way. There is no saying what Marcus may do if I do not take a proper leave of him. No, we will take time to pack all that I require and value and I will leave him with my head held high."

"Then let me begin the packing, madame. What matters it if he chooses to absent himself?"

For her part, Doro would much prefer never to see her master more. Not that there was much hope of such a wish coming to pass. A deal of to-ing and fro-ing was bound to ensue once the mistress carried out her threat to leave her husband. Truth to tell, Doro's deepest fear lay in the expectation Mr Scalloway might induce his wife to change her mind, to give him yet another chance to redeem himself. That must make Doro continued prey to his assaults.

The mistress proved adamant. "I dare say he has stayed away in a bid to test my mettle. He does not believe I meant what I said. I dare say he spent the night in that lowly Pyg & Whistle only to spite me. A fitting tavern for a ruined man. You will likely find him there, having drunk himself into a stupor, left with no choice but to fall into the nearest bed."

There was venom and scorn in Mrs Scalloway's tone. Doro knew only too well how accurate was the likelihood of these predictions. How many nights had she striven to comfort madame's distress? At least in the days before Elinor Scalloway learned to loathe her spouse. Latterly, anger had been uppermost, such that the mistress had been driven to accuse the master on his eventual return and berate him, only to be abused for her pains. Marcus Scalloway had not scrupled to lash out with his hands as readily as with his vile tongue. But when his wife began to fight back, using any weapon that came to hand, he opted instead to vent his ill temper on Doro.

"You must fetch him, Doro. Tell him I am readying to leave, but will await his presence before I go. I have much to say to him."

"What if the master stops you from leaving?"

"He cannot, Doro. Lord Radcliffe is coming to fetch me and will protect us both. The message I sent with you to Mr Culverstone on Saturday was to beg him to intercede with his lordship on my behalf, to tell him what has transpired and to come for us with his carriage at noon today. He intimated when he met me in church that all is in train."

The reassurance of this arrangement sufficed to make Doro do her bidding, but it failed to quiet her alarms. She must first find the master and beard him alone. Who was to protect her from his wrath? If he had indeed imbibed freely as was his wont, the resulting headache and lack of sufficient sleep were enough to throw him into fury at being disturbed. Let alone hearing his wife intended to abide by her decision and was merely awaiting his coming to be gone forever from his house.

Unpleasant memories of the master's violence towards her persisted in Doro's head as she passed along the quiet of Park Street towards the harbour, overlaid with the nearer recollections of Hemp's appearance and pursuit.

Why had she not succumbed to his desire for a meeting? He had divined her unrest, as of course he would. The man she remembered had ever known instantly when she was distressed. Doro yearned all at once for that forgotten past. Forgotten? Never entirely. Hemp Roy had occupied a place in her restless dreams for many a long year. In the busy days she might consider him gone forever. But the nights over which she had no control brought him back time and again. Then he had appeared in person.

The shock of it trembled once more in her bosom. His presence had proved too unsettling, too reminding of the consequences of her rash conduct. Shame alone made her reject his overtures. Would he try again? Would he take the trouble to find her once she left the Scalloway home with her mistress? Or had she driven him away? Again. To her cost the last time.

She brushed the thoughts away as she turned in to The Butts, the harbour already busy despite the early hour. Passing St Augustine's charity, she slipped readily between a porter carrying a trunk on his back and a group of sailors winding rope, hurrying her steps towards the little lane that led her within sight of the disreputable Pyg & Whistle tavern. There she slowed, reluctance catching at her breath. Yet she had no choice. She was wholly dependent upon her owners, upon the goodwill of her mistress. Slaves who ran fared ill, especially in an unknown land. Besides, she had no real desire to run, just when fate looked to be offering a turn for the better. If the mistress succeeded, if Marcus Scalloway did not dispute her hope of taking Doro with her…

The heart of her fear struck anew. Marcus Scalloway had bought her, claiming she came as a bride gift to his then unsuspecting new wife. Doro knew better. She was under no illusions, for he had shown his hand all too soon. Legally, she was his property. If he chose to exert his right, madame could not save her. She could not even buy Doro unless her husband agreed to sell.

A fleeting thought of escaping in the company of Hemp Roy crept through her mind. She dismissed it as swiftly. There was no route out that way. No route at all without she did her mistress's bidding.

With a breath for courage, she stepped up to the tavern door and pushed it open. The stink of stale beer and tobacco assailed her nostrils as she walked into the fuggy entrance hall, its walls dark with years of stains, the wood floor dusty, the stair at the back worn with the passage of many boots. She was no stranger to the place. This was by no means the first time she had been obliged to come here to find out the master's whereabouts. This time was different, however. She had not previously been called upon to fetch him home. Mrs Scalloway had merely desired to know if he was there with the object of preparing herself for his probable condition.

Crossing to the door to the taproom, Doro leaned in and glanced around. The room was low-ceilinged, poky and long, short benches forming intimate corners before and behind a dominating bar. Walls once white were yellowed, soot-stained over the fireplace where last night's ashes had not yet been scraped out. The place was deserted but for a young lad Doro knew by sight who was sweeping the floor with a desultory air, yawning the while.

"Hey, you boy!"

The lad's broom stilled and he looked over. "Aye?"

Doro took a pace into the room. "Can you tell me, if you please, whether Mr Scalloway was here last night?"

"Aye," said the boy, leaning on his broom as his sleepy gaze appraised his questioner. "You bin here afore."

She ignored this. "Did you see him leave?"

The boy emitted a snigger and pointed upwards with his broom. "Left with Cherry, he did."

A little of Doro's alarm left her. If the master had taken the barmaid to bed with him, there was a faint chance he would be sufficiently satisfied to refrain from pawing at Doro. "Which room?"

Surprise flickered in the lad's face. "You goin' up there?"

"I have a message for him. Which room?"

He told her the location and Doro went back out into the hall and headed for the stairs. There were sounds coming from above which indicated people were stirring: footsteps along the corridor beyond the gallery, a hacking cough from one of the nearer chambers, and voices speaking low from another as she made her way through a dim passage to one of the rooms at the front situated above the street outside. She hesitated a moment to gather herself for the coming scene, and knocked.

There was no response. Doro knocked more loudly and waited. No sound came from within. Had he risen already and left? Had she missed him? No, that was unlikely. The landlord was not even in evidence for him to pay his shot. Nor would he go without at least throwing water over his aching head.

She tried the door. It proved to be unlocked. Doro pushed it open just wide enough to be able to slip through. She left it ajar and moved into the chamber, her gaze seeking the bed. It was curtained, half open on this side and in the light seeping from about the closed shutters at the window, she could see the bump under the covers that indicated the presence of the master.

A small sigh escaped her. He was still asleep. To wake him would prove foolhardy, but she must do it. Poised for retreat, she called out from where she stood.

"Master! Master Scalloway!"

No answering grunt came from the bed. It was instead eerily silent and her voice echoed around the room as she called again.

"Master Scalloway, wake up!"

An odd chill enveloped Doro and her mind froze. Only half realising what she did, she moved quickly to the bed, seized the curtain and wrenched it back towards the bedhead.

The soundless scream died in her throat, held there by sheer terror. Marcus Scalloway lay dead, a dagger in his heart.

Hemp watched the comings and goings at the Scalloway home with puzzlement. On Saturday, the only visible signs of life had been the appearance of the man himself with his servant before Doro came up the area steps and went off on her errand. Today, Hemp had seen several persons entering and others leaving before he had been at his post for a matter of half an hour. Moreover, it was not yet ten of the clock.

No sign of Doro. The gentleman she had approached with a message when Hemp followed her had gone inside and was not yet come out. An older gentleman, accompanied by a female, had arrived in a carriage. He had left again, but the female was still within. For the rest, the man carrying a bag looked to be a doctor, and the other two were obviously servants.

The bustle indicated a situation out of the ordinary. Would he get a sight of Doro? Or was she too busy to take a moment to come out to him? What had she said? She did not know where she might be this day. Was there point in waiting or should he leave and try again tomorrow? He dug his hands into his pockets, the cold March wind tempting him away.

Yet another person hurrying along the road caught his attention. Recognition hit. Was this not the same ratty little man who had come out upon the previous occasion along with the master of the house? Hemp watched his approach, the intention forming to accost the fellow if he proved to be one and the same.

Sure enough, the man swung into the gap between the railings and headed down the area steps. Hemp crossed the road and went after him. By the time he reached the area, his quarry was disappearing through a door into the nether regions of the house.

"Hi, you there," Hemp called, and leapt for the entrance before the door could close.

The little man swung about, staring up at him in obvious shock. "What the deuce? Who are you? What do you want?"

The passage was too dim to see the man's face clearly, but Hemp noted both belligerence and fright in the voice. He tried a soothing note. "No need to be afraid. I'm a friend of Doro's."

Hemp sensed an immediate change as the man paused, his head tilting in a bird-like fashion. A short laugh came, mirthless.

"You'd best come in, friend of Doro."

The man turned on the words and led the way through a pantry into a large kitchen where a stout woman was stirring a pot on the open-fired cook stove. She spoke as she turned, her tone querulous. "That you, Quin? How come it took you…?" Catching sight of Hemp, she faded out, releasing her hold on the wooden spoon. "Who's this now? We've enough strangers in the place already, I'd 'a thought."

"Keep your hair on, Peg. None o' my doing." The fellow Quin tugged out a chair and waved at Hemp. "Best you sit down."

Hemp did not avail himself of the invitation, a sense of unease invading his breast as the man Quin turned to the cook.

"He says he's a friend of Doro's."

Was there significance in the way the man said it? The glance exchanged between him and the woman Peg deepened Hemp's growing alarm. "What is afoot, if you please? I take it there is something amiss in the house?"

Another bark of mirthless laughter escaped Quin. "You could say that."

The cook bustled forward, a touch of wariness in her broad face, which she wiped with her apron where she was sweating from the heat of the fire. "Doro never said nowt about no friend."

"We only met again a couple of days ago. I ran into her in the harbour. I am also from Barbados."

Quin squinted up at him, grinning. "Could have guessed that." Then his mouth twisted. "Won't find her here today, friend."

"Why not? What has happened?"

Quin opened his mouth to speak, but Peg thumped his arm. "Not so fast." She squared up to Hemp. "How do we know you're one to be trusted? She's got trouble enough has our Doro, without adding no more."

"What trouble? Take my word, I mean Doro nothing but good. My name is Roy. Hemp Roy. I have known Doro from a child. We were both workers at Flora Sugars. I knew Scalloway and I know the Carey plantation. Your mistress was a Carey, was she not?"

"Was she, Quin? You were there when the master married her."

The little fellow was eyeing Hemp in a considering way. "Aye, I was. I might've seen you, now I think on it."

"If you were with Scalloway in Barbados, that is only too likely. But I beg you won't keep me in suspense any longer. What has happened to Doro?"

Peg emitted a heavy sigh and plonked down into a chair at the kitchen table. "You'd best tell him, Quin. You seen it all."

Quin indicated the chair he'd pulled out earlier. "Sit down then, Hemp Roy. Don't want a big feller like you falling down with shock and wrecking Peg's kitchen."

He laughed at his own joke, and Hemp was obliged to tamp down a strong desire to seize him by the throat and choke the life out of him. Instead he took a seat, masking his impatience as he repeated his question. "What has happened to Doro?"

Quin folded his arms and nodded in a manner as infuriating as it was frustrating. "More like what's happened to the master is what it is."

"Scalloway?"

"The same. Dead as a doornail."

The blast hit Hemp and then subsided. The fellow's insouciance belied the words. Had he no feeling for such a shocking event? His master too. Even as Hemp realised the death must account for the unusual activity, he was conscious of disbelief mixed with foreboding. "Dead how?"

"Murdered. Stabbed with a dagger."

Peg shuddered and covered her face with her hands, but Quin was clearly relishing his tale. If he had hoped to shock, Hemp was glad to disappoint him. The fellow little knew how much he had encountered of murder. Besides, he could not be dismayed to hear of Scalloway's demise. The man was a blot on the human race. All he cared for was Doro's role in the story. Please God she was not killed too!

"Where is Doro in all this?"

"Ah, there's the rub, ain't it?"

"What do you imply, Mr Quin?"

Peg dropped her hands and looked up at that. "Give over playing games, Quin." Her gaze shifted to Hemp. "It's a crying shame, sir, and I don't believe it for a moment, but they're saying as Doro did it."

This time there was shock, a kind of numbness, under which Hemp realised he had been expecting it. Doro hated Scalloway. A fiery wench she was, or had been once. It was why they had parted with such violence of feeling. For the first time in an age, he recalled the last quarrel that had made the final goodbye so awkward. But that was in the past. Right now, he was needed, even if Doro did not know it.

# CHAPTER FIVE

As a last resort, Francis had invited Pretty's grandfather to stay instead of taking a room in the inn in Knights Inham, obliging Tillie to desist from the argument and make arrangements for his accommodation. Not much to his surprise, she took him to task as soon as they had a moment alone prior to changing for dinner.

"What ails you, Fan? Why did you not send him packing?"

Francis was already at the bellpull to ring for Joanie and his valet, but he stayed his hand. "For one thing, it is scarcely hospitable to be turfing the fellow out on the eve of the Sabbath. For another, if you want to win this, Tillie, you must be prepared to take your time about it. Madeley won't give up without a fight."

She plonked down on the bed. "I don't want him in the house."

"Now you are being ridiculous." Francis tugged on the bell. "Put on your best hostess face, my dear one, and use the charm I know you possess."

A great sigh came. "It won't work on that man. Besides, I cannot endure the thought of him taking that poor infant out of all she has come to know, disrupting her all over again."

"You said as much and it failed to move him from his purpose." Francis began to strip off his coat. "You would do better to let him come to know her a little."

"I don't want him to know her."

"Let him see how comfortable she is in her present environment," he pursued, ignoring the interjection, "and he may come to the same conclusion himself."

Tillie was clutching the bedpost, but she released it, an arrested look replacing the agitation in her face as she caught his regard. "Will that work, do you think?"

"Well, it has a better chance than putting up his back every time you open your mouth."

She gave a giggle and his heart lifted. Too prone to brooding had been his darling wife these last months. Joanie and Diplock arriving at that moment, there was time for no more words on the subject. Instead, Tillie elected not to change her dress.

"I dare not suppose Mr Madeley has come properly equipped and I would not care to embarrass him. I will wash, Joanie, and you may dress my hair again."

"Yes, my lady. Would you wish to wear the Paisley shawl?"

By the time they were both presentable again, Tillie was looking thoughtful. She greeted the visitor, who was indeed still wearing the same clothes, in a warmer fashion than she had used hitherto. "You will not object to the presence of my two nephews at the dinner table, I hope? We do not stand on ceremony here."

Madeley was visibly relieved and Francis noted how he relaxed a good deal as soon as the two Hathaway boys bounced into the parlour adjacent to the dining room, where it was the custom at Flitteris to foregather before going in to partake of the main meal of the day.

"We've had a capital notion, Auntilla," announced Tom, the younger of the two boys. "We're going to —" He broke off upon receiving a dig in the ribs from his brother, who had evidently noticed the presence of a stranger.

Ben, a year older and at twelve about a foot taller than his sibling, had ever been the more observant of the two. Both boys were blond like their mother, although Ben's hair showed signs of darkening. His features were beginning to sharpen out of the deceptively angelic looks that still characterised the younger Tom.

Francis made them known to the visitor and Ben gave an awkward bow.

"How do you do, sir?"

Tom stared. "Are you Pretty's grandpa, then?"

Madeley frowned. "How did you know?"

"Hepsie said. She recognised you. She said you came once to the cottage where Pretty used to live with her parents."

"Tom, that will do," said Tillie, although she threw a glance at Francis which spoke volumes. If Madeley had only once visited the Brockhurst ménage, his claim upon Pretty became a trifle thin. "What is this capital notion of yours?"

Tom turned back to his aunt. "We are going to teach Pretty to ride."

A startled silence greeted this triumphantly uttered pronouncement. Ben cut across it. "Not on a real horse, Auntilla, so you need not look so forbidding."

Francis laughed. "Your aunt has never looked forbidding in her life, Ben."

"But she will forbid this," Tillie cut in. "Have you both run mad? Pretty is only three."

"Papa put us both up before him when we were small, Auntilla."

"Yes, when you were five or thereabouts, Ben. Besides, you were always rambunctious little beasts and you plagued Patrick's life out until he took you up."

"Pretty wants to ride," said Tom, unheeding. "She says gee-up when we carry her piggyback."

"We only mean to put her on a pretend horse, Auntilla."

"You mean a rocking horse? We don't have one, Ben."

"We're going to make her a hobby horse," put in Tom.

"Well, we aren't going to make it, but we asked Williams and Ryde and they said they could make one easily."

Before Francis could object to his coachman and groom being commandeered in this fashion, Madeley himself chimed in. "It is a simple enough thing to fashion, I agree. But you must tell them to pad out the seat well so that the child does not injure herself. I remember I made one for…" He faded out, the sudden animation dying out of his face.

Francis was seized with a tug of sympathy for the man. He was feeling the loss of his daughter. Before an awkward pause could lengthen, Tom moved to Madeley, full of all his usual eagerness and oblivious to the man's distress.

"Could you help us make one for Pretty, sir? Williams says there is plenty of wood and they have leather in the stables for the seat."

Ben joined him. "We were thinking of straw for stuffing the seat, or is that not suitable?"

Madeley produced a smile, but Francis noted the sadness still present in his eyes. "Hessian is better. Unless you have horsehair."

The ensuing discussion was pursued at the dining table until Tillie called a halt. "Pray cease pestering poor Mr Madeley, boys. He is not here to make hobby horses."

Madeley looked across. "But I should like to do it, ma'am, if you permit. It is for my granddaughter after all."

Francis gave an inward sigh as Tillie's face closed. She contributed little to the conversation for the rest of the meal, confining her remarks to necessity. She rose after the accustomed cheese and fruit had been consumed. "Come, Tom. You too, Ben. We will leave Mr Madeley and your uncle to their port."

As Francis did not usually sit over his wine when he and Tillie were alone, during their visit the boys had not previously been told to leave the table and he half expected a protest. But their habit of minding the wishes of the aunt who had virtually brought them up through their early years prevailed. He was left alone with the mercer, Rodmell instructing his junior to set a few more coals to the fire before both servants departed.

Francis poured port for the man and sat back with his own glass filled. Was Tillie expecting him to take the opportunity to press her claim upon Pretty? He hoped Madeley did not mean to resume his own demands. Had they not had enough of the business for one day?

After a few moments of silence, during which the visitor sat in a brown study, Francis tried for a neutral topic. "Do you find much change in your part of the world, sir? With War now declared with our French neighbours, I mean. Will it affect your business at all?"

Madeley looked up, seemingly puzzled. "Should it?"

"I wondered if you imported goods from the continent, perhaps?"

"From India, if anywhere, my lord. Moreover, if I had been in the habit of such, I should certainly cease. I cannot have truck with a country guilty of regicide."

Francis refrained from reminding him that England had itself been guilty of this same crime in the previous century, and indeed could scarcely blame the man. The execution of Louis XVI a few weeks since had rocked English sensibilities. Bad enough to have destroyed the better part of their aristocratic landowners, as well as countless blameless commoners. The newspapers had been full of outrage, as well as fears for Louis' unfortunate imprisoned Queen, Marie Antoinette. Britain expelled the French Ambassador and in retaliation France declared war upon the country within days of the killing. Francis, with friends from his soldiering days still in the armed forces, was following proceedings with a high degree of interest.

Not so Mr Madeley. He rejected the promising topic. "However, I am not here to talk of the War, nor of my business interests. Unless you seek to discover if I can afford to keep Pertesia in a suitable manner?"

Francis raised his brows. "The thought had not crossed my mind. I must suppose you are successful if you are patronised by such as Lord Wem."

"Was so, sir. No longer."

"What? Do you tell me people are so prejudiced?"

Madeley sipped his port. "I do not suffer from any such. I meant the Brockhursts. The late Lady Wem did not set foot in my shop after my daughter married her son."

"But she did visit the couple, for we learned as much when my wife was investigating the deaths." Realising what he had said, Francis backtracked. "I beg your pardon. It must be painful to you to be reminded of it."

To his surprise, Madeley gave him a straight look. "No, my lord. In fact, I would be exceedingly gratified to hear a round tale. What exactly happened to my girl, sir? What happened in Tunbridge Wells last year? Pray do not beat about the bush, but tell me straight."

It was the last thing Francis had expected. Truth to tell, it was not a story he wished to revive. But had not Madeley a right to the truth?

At the end of a swift and somewhat expurgated recital in which Francis explained how he and Tillie had happened upon the mystery of the deaths of Pretty's parents, through which the visitor remained remarkably calm and quiet, except to request enlightenment on one or two particular points, Madeley surprised him yet again.

"I begin to see why your lady wife has taken this intransigent attitude, my lord."

Francis doubted the man could have a true insight, being wholly unacquainted with Tillie's loss of their own son, but he seized the chance to build upon this view. He offered to refill his guest's glass as he spoke, but Madeley waved the decanter away.

"My wife conceived a strong feeling of sympathy for Pretty. Especially as Lord Wem's intentions towards the child were ambivalent at best. I do not wish to distress you, but the truth is Pretty received even less welcome among the Brockhursts than did your daughter Isabel. Lady Francis could not endure to think of the child being left in such uncaring hands."

Madeley gave a long sigh. "I had no knowledge of any of this. None of that family would tell me more than that there had been a tragic accident. I gleaned a little from common gossip, but one cannot set store by such whisperings." He lifted his glass and tossed off the remaining wine. "I see that I have cause to be grateful to her ladyship. I will thank her."

But there was no opportunity for him to do so. By the time they entered the drawing room, Tillie had already retired. Francis determined to make it his business to introduce Madeley to his granddaughter as soon as he could.

# CHAPTER SIX

Bucketing rain on Sunday had not deterred the Hathaway boys from venturing into the stables to procure the materials required for their hobby horse. Once the whole party had returned from the service at St Michael's and All Angels in Knights Inham village, arriving home just ahead of the downpour, Tom and Ben had commandeered Madeley's services and dragged the poor fellow out to oversee their activities. Ottilia, however, had made objection to her nephews risking their health in the freezing stables and obliged Francis to send a servant to fetch them back. Madeley perforce returned with them, and seeing their disappointment proposed concentrating instead upon the design, which would make it a deal easier to build the hobby horse upon the following day.

Francis could not but warm to him for this evidence of kindness, although his wife was not similarly softened, despite hailing the decision with relief.

"At least it will keep him from plaguing me about Pretty."

Tom was despatched to the nursery to take Pretty's measurements while Ben found paper and pencils and, commandeering a vacant parlour on the second floor — "Auntilla won't object to it if you don't, Uncle Fan!" — set himself to drawing under the tutelage of his new mentor. Tillie retired to her personal parlour, leaving Francis free to peruse the weekly journals in pursuit of further news concerning the straining of credit following the declaration of war. The cottagers' roofs were going to cost a pretty penny and if the banks were to refuse to accommodate a loan, it might become necessary to retrench further.

Monday dawned reasonably fine and there was no keeping the Hathaway boys from pursuing their intent, in complete disregard of the puddles dotting the way to the stables. Madeley was thus kept busy for the better part of the day, rather to Francis's relief since Tillie had shown signs of wishing to resume the argument about Pretty's future.

"How long are we to have him on the premises, pray? Cannot we be done with this nonsense? It is not as if he cares for Pretty."

"You've not given the poor wretch an opportunity to show whether he does or does not."

"No, and I don't intend to. To my mind, the less he sees of her, the better. How can he possibly suppose she could be happy to be dragged from pillar to post with a virtual stranger?"

"He's her grandfather, Tillie."

"So also is Lord Wem, and we have seen how much he cares for Pretty's welfare."

Francis held his peace. There was no arguing with his wife in this mood. But he was not to be deterred from prosecuting his design to allow the unfortunate Madeley at least some acquaintance with the child.

Come Tuesday morning, notwithstanding the apparent urgency of constructing a hobby horse, Francis seized his chance while Tillie was occupied with the housekeeper, catching the merchant before the boys could monopolise him yet again, and escorting him up to the rooms which had been given over for nursery use.

The accoutrements were not wholly new, for a good deal of preparation had been done under Tillie's supervision to accommodate the child who should have occupied the place two years since. Hepsie had not made many changes. The nursing chair, never used, had been consigned to a position by the wall along with the infant's cradle. A child's cot had been procured for Pretty and put into the adjacent bedchamber, although Francis knew from Tillie that the child often spent her nights in the nurse's bed set alongside.

The playroom boasted a cabinet of toys and books, a set of small chairs about a suitably sized table, and a huge open carpeted area where a child might spread their playthings with impunity.

When Francis entered with the visitor, Pretty was seated on a rug before the cheerful fire, engaged in building a complicated monument with wooden bricks. Blonde locks tumbled about her capless head and a pair of little feet, shod in soft blue leather, poked out from under the baby gown. The nurse, who was seated nearby, no sooner saw who entered than she set aside her sewing and rose. She moved forward, putting herself between the visitors and the child, her challenging gaze going to Madeley, though she addressed herself to Francis.

"My lord?"

"This is Pretty's grandfather, Hepsie."

She threw an unmistakeably inimical glance at the visitor. "I know, my lord." She bobbed a curtsey. "Mr Madeley."

The merchant regarded her from under lowering brows. "Have we met?"

"Not officially, sir."

Aware of hostility in the nurse's voice, Francis intervened. "Mr Madeley wishes to learn a little of his granddaughter."

Hepsie's gaze burned. "She won't know him. How could she? He never cared before."

"Hepsie, that will do. You forget yourself."

The nurse closed her lips tightly together, bobbed another curtsey and withdrew a step.

Madeley chose not to react to the radiating resentment. Instead, he nodded. "You are protective of Pertesia and I understand that. I mean her no harm. I am here to offer her a home with her family. You too, of course."

Seeing a look of alarm cross the nurse's face, Francis cut in swiftly. "As to that, it is not as yet decided. Her ladyship does not want to see Pretty uprooted again just when she is settling." He looked across at the child as he spoke and saw Pretty had ceased her labours with the bricks. She had evidently heard her name spoken and was looking from one to the other of the adults, blue eyes big with puzzlement. Fear too? Francis lowered his voice. "We must speak more quietly. It will not do to make the child aware of our dissension."

Madeley was watching the little girl, a softened expression on his face. He spoke in a ravaged murmur. "She is the image of her mother."

Francis seized on this. "That must be hard for you, sir. Do you think it wise to have such a reminder about you all the time?"

Madeley's voice grew thick. "I owe it to Isabel. I did not do well by her."

"Atonement?" Francis had difficulty keeping the rising savagery out of his tone. "I hardly think it is in the child's interests to become the instrument of assuaging your guilt, Madeley."

The merchant turned a violent look upon him. "Not that. I wish only to do right by this child. She ought to be with her family."

"Wem might say the same, but my wife would resist him as strenuously."

"Lord Wem has a lesser claim."

"On the contrary. Your daughter, sir, became a Brockhurst upon her marriage. In law, he has the upper hand." He continued as Madeley looked daggers, "But this is not the place to be arguing the point. I brought you here only to make better acquaintance with Pretty. Let us stick to the business in hand."

Madeley subsided with a sigh. "You are very right, my lord." He eyed the little girl for a moment in silence. She stared back, grave and quiet, but the instant he took a step in her direction, Pretty leapt to her feet and ran. Not, as Francis expected, to her nurse who sprang towards her, but to him.

The small body attached itself to his booted leg and clung. Astonished, Francis could only stare down at her, aware of some shocked sound from the nurse and Madeley shifting away. Instinct made him bend to the little girl, prising her arms loose. He lifted her up. A pair of luminous big eyes met his. A treble voice piped up, "Papa! Papa!" Then two little hands were clutching about his neck, the face disappeared into his chest, blonde curls tickled his chin and his heart was racing.

It felt an eon as he stood thus, the babe in his arms and a riot of speculation in his mind while a constriction lodged in his throat and his chest became taut with feeling.

The child was confused. He had no look of her father. She must have forgotten in all these months. Who could have thought she would seize upon him for a substitute? Tillie would hate this. She longed to be taken for a mother. He'd had no notion of becoming a surrogate papa. Yet this scrap of a girl had chosen him. What was he to do? He could not deprive her of yet another parent. Repudiate her overtures? Unthinkable.

It came to him that he was already holding her close, cradling her against himself as he had only previously cradled Tillie. A wave of affection swamped him. Love had no barriers. This little girl might also be his, never mind that she was not of his body. The determination was settled in him almost before he realised it. There could be no releasing Pretty to Madeley now.

With the gentleness previously reserved for his wife, Francis eased the child back. "Pretty?" She raised her head and the smile she gave was half the world. Francis was reluctant to let her go, but needs must. "Go to Hepsie now, sweetheart."

The endearment came out without thought and Francis heard the echo of it in his head with a sense of wonder. He felt changed, oddly distanced from the world as if a small miracle had taken place inside him. And then Tillie's voice cut across it, throwing him back to reality.

"There you are, Fan. I have been hunting for you everywhere."

A streak of dismaying guilt went through him. All in a moment he had achieved what Tillie longed to have, without effort or desire. She could not know it, although she looked strangely to see the child in his arms. He made haste to pass Pretty across to the nurse. "Take her, Hepsie." He turned to face his wife. "I brought Madeley to meet his granddaughter properly."

Tillie's gaze scorched him, but her words belied the look. "Never mind that now, Fan. I need to speak with you on a matter of urgency."

Did she mean to ring a peal over him? Well, if so, he had his answer ready.

Madeley got in ahead of him. "Do you go on, my lord. I will take a little time with Pertesia, if I may." He gave a laugh. "Until those boys of yours want me again for the construction of this hobby horse. I set them to smoothing down and polishing the wooden shaft, which ought to keep them busy for a while."

"Very well. I will tell them where you are." Francis moved to where Tillie was waiting by the door. She did not look best pleased, but he had means to placate her. Pretty was not going anywhere.

He followed Tillie out of the nursery door and closed it behind him. She turned to confront him before they reached the stairs. Francis threw up a hand. "Before you say anything —"

"No, Fan, this cannot wait. It is a complication we did not need at this precise moment, but I cannot fail Hemp."

Bewildered, Francis blinked. "Hemp? What has he to do with all this, pray?" There was grave trouble in her face and his loyalties clicked in. "What is it, my dear one?"

She set a hand to his chest in the way she had and his affection reanimated. "Hemp sent an overnight express. He is asking for my help. Not for himself. For a slave girl he knew in his past life."

A horrid presentiment attacked Francis. When Tillie was called upon, it could mean only one thing. "Don't tell me. She is arrested for murder."

Tillie gave a smile. "Just so. In Bristol where he met her. I must go at once to his aid, Fan, you know I must."

"Oh, dear Lord, here we go again!"

# CHAPTER SEVEN

The pass-room stank. Odours of sweat and urine mingled with the unmistakeable stale tang of female effluvia. Under the meagre light from high, barred windows, women prisoners lay or sat on palliasses, some boxed in, others like Doro, on a mere pile of dirty straw in a dark corner. Turned into the wall and huddled, she was only recognisable by the colourful flowers in her chintz gown.

Hemp's bosom burned with remorse. He ought to have come yesterday, instead of wasting his time in useless attempts to find out the truth of the business at the Pyg & Whistle and elsewhere. Primed by milady's past actions, he had tried, and failed, to rout out the doctor who had certified the death. Pucklechurch, the constable who had made the arrest, was unhelpful, referring him to the magistrate. Mr Belchamp, however, was adamant there could be no doing anything until an inquest had been held.

Despairing, Hemp determined to beg milady's help. By the time he had procured suitable accommodation for the Fanshawes, written and despatched his letter by fast post-boy on horseback, it was too late. The Bridewell gates were firmly shut against him. Today, before he tried what else he could to garner such information as he guessed milady might need, he betook himself to the prison. Seeing the pitiful condition in which Doro was placed, he regretted his tardiness with some degree of bitterness, which erupted and burst upon the turnkey he had bribed to bring him here.

"Is this the best you can do? She's not even been put to question by an inquest and this is where you house her?"

The man sniffed. "There ain't nowhere else fer the likes of her."

"The likes? Because she is a negro, is that it?"

"No use a-blaming of me, mister. Ain't my doing. They all comes in here less'n they got means ter ask fer different."

Resisting the urge to throttle him, Hemp seized on this. "Then there is somewhere better. I have means. I will pay. Move her at once."

A shifty look entered the turnkey's eyes. "Ain't up ter me."

Hemp slid a hand into his pocket and brought out his purse. "Then fetch me whoever is in charge here." He fished within for a silver coin and held it up. "Take this and bring me your master. Now."

Shrugging, the fellow snatched the coin and turned for the door. As Hemp slid the purse into his pocket, his attention on getting to Doro, he became aware of several pairs of eyes watching him. Glancing from one to the other, he noted the avaricious gleams. Hell's teeth! He should not have flashed coin in here.

Two women shunted to their feet and made a move in his direction. Hemp thrust up to his full height, set his feet apart and his arms akimbo, and faced them down. "I shouldn't try it, if I were you. Unless you want to start a riot."

Both women hesitated, exchanging looks of question. Alone, he knew they could not take him, but he could not fight off a score of them. There did not look to be enough in sufficiently good condition to give an account of themselves, especially against a big man with solid experience when it came to a rough and ready fight. But women were apt to bite, scratch and tear, disconcerting to the average male. He clinched the matter, raising his hands and showing clenched fists.

"I don't want to hurt anyone, but I will if you force me."

The would-be antagonists subsided. Not worth the risk? Good. Hemp had no wish to waste his time and energy. All he cared for was getting Doro out of here.

He crossed to where she lay. She had not moved. If she had noticed his presence, she was not acknowledging it. Hemp suspected she had heard and seen nothing. In hard times, Doro had ever been apt to sink back into the despair that had gripped her when she was first brought to the slave compound at Flora Sugars. Had she given herself up for lost already?

He dropped to his haunches beside the greasy straw on which she lay and put a tentative hand on her back.

She flinched, huddling the more.

Hemp let his hand run down her back, stroking. "Doro? Doro, it's me. Come, turn. I'm getting you out of here."

The hump she made shifted. She pushed up on an elbow and looked round. "Hemp?"

Misery in her eyes. He tamped down the rise of emotion. "Come, I'll help you up."

She let him raise her, but when he went to let go, began to sink. Hemp picked her up bodily and held her close against him. She was a featherweight and his heart burned the more. Her head sank against his chest but she did not speak.

Hemp carried her towards the door, ignoring the interested observers, and reached it just as the lock clicked and the turnkey opened up.

"Hey, you can't just take her out, mister. Put her back."

Hemp stood his ground. "Stand aside and let me through."

To his surprise, the man did move aside, revealing another behind him. By his clothing of respectable coat and breeches against the turnkey's short jacket and greasy breeches, this was his superior.

Hemp nodded to the fellow. "Allow me to come out, if you please, and we will talk."

Either his size or his manner proved effective, for the fellow gave place and Hemp was able to manoeuvre his burden through the aperture and into the small lobby beyond. He found the new man's gaze on him as the other was locking the door on the women inside.

"Speeton says you've a fat purse."

Hemp eyed him. "I take it you are the gaoler here? What is your name?"

"Wichenford. I'm in charge of this section, yes."

"Good. A private room for Miss Gabon here, if you please."

The fellow's brows rose. "Ah, so you aren't trying to get her out of the place altogether."

"I will see the magistrate for that. Meanwhile, she is not a convicted felon and I am certain she did not commit the murder of which she is accused."

A sour smile came. "That's for the judge."

Hemp lost patience. "Have you a private room or not?"

The gaoler's mouth twisted. "If you think she's worth it."

Mentally, Hemp damned the man to hell and back. "Just lead me to the room, Wichenford."

His inner attitude must have communicated, for with a short laugh, the gaoler turned to lead the way through a warren of corridors. The room he opened at length was small enough, but the window was unbarred, letting in sufficient light to show the place was at least relatively clean, if poorly furnished. In one glance, Hemp took in a rickety table, a single upright chair and a bare bedstead set against one wall. He set Doro down on the one caned chair and held her about the shoulders to steady her. She straightened and looked about in a vague way.

Hemp turned his attention back to the gaoler. "I want a decent mattress for the bed and proper bedclothes. Find a more comfortable chair too." He swept another glance about and spied an object in a corner. "And get rid of that disgusting bucket. Fetch a proper chamberpot. She's to have a jug and basin for washing and someone must bring hot water daily. Hot, do you understand?"

Wichenford was open-mouthed. "Anything else, your lordship?"

Hemp allowed his triumph to show. "I am not a lordship, Mr Wichenford, but my employer is Lord Francis Fanshawe, the son of a marquis. I dare say he will take it kindly in you to adhere to my request."

The fellow seemed both nonplussed and sceptical. "He would, would he? But he's not here, if so be it's as you say."

Hemp gave an elaborate sigh and dug out his purse again. He shook it in a suggestive fashion, making the coins inside jingle. "How much?"

With his purse somewhat lighter and Wichenford out of the way, hopefully gone upon the errand to fulfil all his demands, Hemp was able at last to embark upon his mission here. He perched on the wooden edge of the cot bed and took Doro's hand, holding it enclosed between both his own. She stirred, the blue gaze flicking up to his face and down again. "Doro, what happened? That fellow Quin told me there was a commotion at the inn. Some maid screaming murder, the constables called and then you were arrested."

A hysterical sort of laughter bubbled in Doro's chest. Whether it sounded or not she did not know. Such a matter-of-fact description of the nightmare was typical of Hemp. Had he not ever made little of disaster? But he had come. He had rescued her from that terrible place.

For a few blessed moments she had felt safe again, cocooned in his embrace, all the intervening horror of the years apart vanishing in his strength. She had forgotten.

"Doro?"

She forced herself to look at him, beset with the weight of her shame. "I must thank you for…"

"Don't thank me. Did you suppose for one moment I could leave you to your fate?"

Her heart clutched tight within her. "Not that. If I had thought … but I could not think, Hemp. It is all such a blur."

"What happened, Doro?"

He would ask again and again until she answered. He always had persevered. Except that one last time…

"Doro?"

She withdrew her hand from his hold. She could not speak freely with his touch pricking at the guilt. Haltingly, she told him of the mistress's plan to leave, of the errand she had run and the hideous discovery she made in the room at the Pyg & Whistle. She was weeping by the end, jerking out the words. "It was my dagger in his heart. Mine. The one you gave me, do you remember?"

"I remember." His deep voice soothed, though she recognised the timbre of sympathy. It gave her strength.

"I was afraid, Hemp. I did not know what to do. I did not think beyond the horror that it was my dagger and he was killed. I seized it. I pulled it out. And then the blood all over it, all over him…" She threw her hands over her face as if by that she could blot out the memory.

She felt his hands take hers and draw them down, but again she could not face him. His voice was gentle.

"Then what happened, Doro? Tell me it all."

Doro shuddered, feeling again the sick disgust at the blood on her dagger, the rising terror, the panic. What to do? What to do? "Before I could think how to act, that girl came in. A barmaid. Cherry, her name is. I know her for one of the master's doxies. I knew it was her because they said her name when it all began. Over and over they said it. She screamed. She yelled for help. She cried out, 'Murder, murder!' I knew then I was lost. She thought I had done it." The injustice of it burst out and time rolled back. "But I did not. I did not, Hemp! You must believe me, *mon roi.* It is just as I said. If only I had not taken the dagger…"

She was in his arms, his voice murmuring soothing words that made no sense, all but those she had not heard in an age.

"*Ma reine, ma belle reine…*"

The horror of the present died away in Doro's mind. For a brief little moment, she was back in the canes, cradled in his strength, queen to his king.

It did not last. Rough voices in the corridor outside impinged upon the dream and the shame and guilt returned. Doro struggled free, pushing him away. Unthought words escaped her, born of regret. "Let be. It is too late. It is over. More so now."

Hemp's countenance showed his disappointment and she cringed inside. But he did not refer to her rejection. "I will get you freed, Doro. Take heart."

She gave a shaky laugh. "How? Are you the witch doctor? A magician?"

With a sense of unreality, she saw him give the oddest smile, like a cat after cream.

"Not I, my queen. But I know one who has magic in her mind. She will free you. And she will find out who did the deed."

A jab of unexpected jealousy thrust into Doro's bosom. "She? What she is this?"

He laughed. "What, is that suspicion, Doro?"

Had he divined her thought? "What is she? How can she do these things?"

"You will find she can. You have no reason to be anxious about Milady Fan, Doro. I have already sent to her, asking her to come here as soon as she may. I work as her steward, but she is also a friend. She will not fail me."

# CHAPTER EIGHT

The Fanshawes' journey to Bristol occupied the better part of two days, even though they travelled post for the sake of speed. Using their coach would have meant long delays to rest the horses, besides having to accommodate both coachman and groom in addition to the footman Tyler, who was able to travel on the perch seat behind the post-chaise.

Ottilia had started out later in the day than she would have wished, due to the necessity to pack, leave instruction with Mrs Bertram to ensure the needs of her nephews and the visitor were looked to and she fretted every time she had to request a stop to make use of the bordaloo, her pressing need annoyingly more frequent than usual.

Anxious both for Pretty's fate and the plight of Hemp's friend, the slave girl Dorote Gabon, she tried not to plague her spouse with her worries, finding alternative subjects for discussion. "I must say that I am relieved Lizzy did not descend upon us as well, with all this excitement."

"Don't even raise that spectre, Tillie! If she had an inkling of this fresh adventure, I would not put it past that wretched child to post down to Bristol to make one of the party, a prospect that fills me with horror."

Ottilia had to laugh. "She is very persuasive. However, for my part I need no assistance other than yours to settle the business."

He had thrown her a rueful look. "If indeed you need mine."

"Come, Fan. You know very well I cannot manage without you. Especially in a City with which I am wholly unfamiliar."

He agreed to it and the matter was allowed to rest. However, when she expressed regret at being obliged to leave Pretty, Francis was oddly reticent, even though she refrained from referring to the child's future being still unresolved. She could withhold herself because he had taken steps to ensure the child's security beyond what Ottilia had dared to suggest. She tackled him on it at length when they were dining in a private parlour at the Lansdowne inn at Calne where they broke the journey after some four hours on the road.

"What made you extract that promise from Mr Madeley, Fan?"

He looked up from a plate piled high with ham, a substantial chop and a wedge of pigeon pie. "Aren't you glad I did?"

"Very much so. Especially as you sent me into panic when you said he might remain at Flitteris in our absence."

Francis took a pull from his mug of ale. "He'll keep the boys occupied making this hobby horse, which looks likely to take some time. The fellow is most meticulous and insists everything is done to his exacting standards."

Ottilia gave a perfunctory smile. "I dare say it will be for the first time in their lives that they do anything other than in a slapdash fashion."

"Furthermore," her spouse went on, "as I have already observed more than once, Madeley deserves at least to get to know his granddaughter. It's unfair on the child to prevent her from acquaintance with her true family."

She eyed him as she ate, aware he was avoiding her gaze. At length the question pressing on her heart could not be withheld. "Pretty did not protest when you picked her up?"

He did not look up. "Fortunately not."

Ottilia laid down her fork. "Fan, what is it? Pray don't keep me in the dark. You know well how troubled I am over that child."

That last brought his head up, a flash of dismay in his gaze. "Well, that's why, Tillie. I didn't want to tell you." He hesitated and she waited. A sigh escaped him. "She mistook me for her father, called me 'Papa'."

The pang was inevitable. It was succeeded by a gleam of hope. "But that is excellent, Fan. A huge step forward, do you not think? If she has accepted you, then it is only a matter of time before…" She faded out, balked by the expression on his face. "What?"

He grimaced. "My dear one, I don't know. It's possible she has lost the inner visage of her real father. She's seen little of me."

"You mean that is why she might well confuse your face with his? But I have been too much in evidence to be mistaken. Yes, I see."

"My darling heart, don't look so downcast. It is early days. Pretty is part of our family now, so —"

"Our family?" Ottilia's heart leapt. "Here's a new come-out. To be truthful, I thought you were angling to let her go with Mr Madeley. You have always told me to expect her to be removed."

Francis's tone was flat. "Well, she won't be. I'll see to that."

Marvelling, Ottilia watched him as he resumed eating. Had this about-face come from Pretty's acceptance? An echo sounded in her head. *Go to Hepsie now, sweetheart.* Fan's voice? Just as she spied him with Mr Madeley in the nursery. She had forgotten it, unnoticed in her conscious mind in the press of the needed response to Hemp's urgent missive. Light dawned and she spoke without thought. "You fell in love with the child!"

He spluttered over his food, reddening. "What the devil are you talking about?"

"You did, Fan. She called you Papa, you said." A somewhat hysterical giggle escaped her. "Oh, that is priceless!"

Francis was coughing. He seized up his ale and took several gulps before setting down the tankard and regarding her with a fulminating eye. "I'm hanged if I see what you find to laugh at."

Ottilia's mirth subsided and she picked up her fork. "You, my darling lord. Cannot you see the irony? Here have I been struggling to make headway with Pretty, all the time fearful she would be torn away from me, and in but a single instant she captures your heart and that is the end of it. Bravo, Pretty! Now I have all the time in the world to win her over."

A sheepish look overspread his features. "Well, if you put it like that, I am relieved."

"Did you suppose I would be jealous?" Ottilia let out a tiny sigh. "I am a little. But that is far outweighed by the advantage of Pretty attaching you."

He threw up his eyes. "Unscrupulous is what you are, Tillie."

She laughed. "I know. Will you give me a little more of that ham, if you please, Fan?"

He complied, carving a couple of slices and setting them on her plate. "Is this increase of appetite also to be put to Pretty's account?"

"I admit to being hungrier than usual, but I feel as if we have been on the move for an age."

"Yet you ate well at our last stop."

"Did I? I don't recall." Was this a good moment for confession? "I did not tell you, Fan, but I gave Ben and Tom a mission."

He gave her an amused look. "You need not trouble to tell me. I heard you. Not that two schoolboys could have prevented Madeley from taking the child."

"You underestimate my enterprising nephews, Fan. They would kidnap Pretty before they allowed him to spirit her away. If only we are not too long about this business of saving Hemp's slave girl and can get back before Patrick sends for the boys to go home again."

Francis appeared unperturbed. "I will do Madeley the justice to say he was adamant I might trust his word. He won't attempt it."

Relieved, Ottilia allowed her attention to turn on the reason for this journey. Quite apart from the need to procure the release of an innocent woman — if she was innocent — Ottilia was intrigued by the strength of her steward's involvement. "She is clearly of great importance to him."

"Pretty?" Francis paused in eating, his full fork in the air. "To Madeley, you mean?"

Ottilia had not realised she spoke aloud. She glanced across. "This Doro."

"Doro?"

"Dorote, but he calls her Doro. The woman Hemp is asking me to rescue."

His frown cleared. "You have a mind like a grasshopper, Tillie. What of it?"

"Only consider, Fan. Hemp went off to Weymouth, intent upon discovering a possible house to purchase —"

"You said he might look elsewhere."

"Yes, but why Bristol? Can he have heard Doro was there?"

"He may have thought it offered better prospects for a potential landlord than Weymouth. It's a busy port all year, and popular for shipping to and from the West Indies."

Ottilia accepted this. "Then he met her by chance. I wonder if the Roy family arrived by that route?" She dug her fork into another sliver of ham and chewed for a moment in silence.

"Well?" A note of impatience sounded in her spouse's voice. Ottilia looked a question. "You said she was important to him."

"Because he is so anxious. I have long suspected there was some bitter disappointment in his past concerning a girl. This Dorote must be she."

"A slave girl?"

"What could be more likely? He may have been free himself but he lived among slaves. His mother, one assumes, was one of Matthew Roy's slaves. Much as I despise the practice of slavery, one cannot avoid the reality of Hemp's situation."

Francis set his utensils down upon his empty plate and took up his tankard. "What if she did kill her master?"

"That is yet to be determined. But I trust Hemp's judgement. He believes her."

"Tillie, you've just said he's prejudiced in her favour."

"But he knows her very well indeed, that is clear." Ottilia became brisk. "Be that as it may, we cannot discount the possibility she is indeed guilty of stabbing the man. Hemp's informant will have it the weapon belongs to her and Hemp believes that is likely. He says he gave her one that is quite distinctive."

"Ha! Well for her she'll have you in her corner, my dear one. If I know these magistrates, that will be quite enough to convict her."

The Ship was crowded and noisy. Although it was not a large establishment, its situation on Marsh Street gave on to the quay behind, rendering the place subject to the shouts, general stir and noise from vessels coming and going, with dockings, disembarkations and the lively paraphernalia of a busy port.

Ottilia was too fatigued by the journey to care. From Calne, they'd had only a matter of some thirty miles to travel to Bristol, but the chaise had encountered roads bogged with mud and the slowed pace had delayed them by several hours. She was uncomfortable, tired and chilled, wishing only for food and rest.

Her spouse, on the other hand, made immediate objection as Hemp Roy ushered them into a snug parlour. "For pity's sake, Hemp, could you not have found a quieter establishment?"

"The better inns are at a distance, milord." Hemp threw Ottilia an apologetic glance. "This one is right in the centre. The Assembly Rooms are just along the road in Princes Street."

"I hardly think we will be attending any Assemblies under the circumstances."

"True, milord. But this place is within a stone's throw of Queen Square and King Street, where all the business of the City may be said to occur. The Custom House and Excise Office are in the former, and in the latter both the Merchants' and the Coopers' halls, as well as the library. Even the theatre, my lady, although I do not know if —"

Francis cut in. "If we are to save this woman of yours, Hemp, I can't see us having time for theatres either."

Ottilia intervened. "Peace, Fan. I suspect Hemp has chosen this situation because we can readily meet with all the persons involved. Is that it, Hemp?"

Hemp looked gratified. "That is so, milady. The Scalloway house is not far, nor the tavern where the murder took place. One or two other venues also, milady."

"Excellent." Without troubling to remove her cloak, Ottilia had sunk into a chair by the fire. She smiled at her steward. "Thank you, Hemp."

Francis had taken off his hat and great-coat and cast both aside, going over to the window. "We certainly appear to be in the thick of it here. We seem to be overlooking this famous floating harbour." He turned on Hemp. "I am glad you managed to get us a private parlour at least."

"I can secure accommodation elsewhere if you wish it, milord, but this is the best I could find to be handy for everywhere milady may wish to visit."

"Let's see how it goes. I presume there are chambermaids enough to assist her ladyship? For the sake of speed, we chose to travel post and could bring only Tyler."

"I met him, milord. I will direct him where to take the luggage."

Hemp headed for the door but Ottilia called after him, "Don't be long, Hemp. I am eager to hear your account of events."

"I am as eager to give them, milady, but not until you have rested and partaken of refreshment. I have arranged for a meal to be served in here within the hour." Hemp gave a small bow and departed.

Ottilia looked across at her husband, still occupied in watching the comings and goings in the harbour below. "You will admit he is efficient, Fan. He thought of everything."

Francis turned his head. "I should think he might well, since he demanded your presence."

"That is unfair, Fan. There was no demand. We must expect him to be anxious. Only think how affected you are when I am in trouble."

"True enough." He turned fully and crossed to join her, leaning an arm along the mantel. "You think this Doro is that important to him?"

"I do, yes. The whole tone of his letter indicated as much."

"How so?"

"He gave nothing away. He did not say who she was beyond her name and that he knew her as a slave in Barbados. Yet his conviction of her innocence was total and he showed an inordinate desire to procure her safety and release."

Francis quirked an eyebrow. "You're the expert, my love. I'll take your reading of it."

"Which means you don't believe it."

"It hardly matters, does it? We are here and that must serve his purpose."

Ottilia sighed. "Let us hope so. I must see Doro first and hear her tale."

Francis became brisk. "Yes, but Hemp is right. You need rest and I am as hungry as a hunter. Up you get, my loved one, and we'll find this bedchamber."

Within a short time, Ottilia was able to remove her outer garments, wash away the stains of travel and tidy up a little. She opted to do without the proffered assistance of a young chambermaid, brushing out her hair and dressing it herself as she had been accustomed to do before her marriage. Her spouse, contenting himself with a wash and a fresh neckcloth, was likewise ready in short order.

"Shall we go? At least the parlour is on the same floor. We may thank heaven for small mercies."

Ottilia preceded him out of the room as he held the door. "It will do well enough, Fan."

"If you can stand the noise. I hope to heaven the place settles down at night or we shall neither of us sleep a wink."

Ottilia suppressed a rise of irritation as she traversed the galleried corridor. "You will feel better after you have dined, Fan."

"Supposing there is anything fit to eat."

She did not answer. Her spouse was apt to become testy when hunger drove him. She was in need of sustenance herself, but her appetite for Hemp's information was stronger.

Hemp did not reappear until a passable meal had been consumed, consisting of pea soup, followed by steaks — wolfed by Francis while Ottilia contented herself with an omelette accompanied by fried mushrooms — with cheese and fruits to come.

"That was better than I hoped for," Francis was saying with satisfaction when a knock at the parlour door was followed by Hemp's entrance. "Ah, there you are. Let's have it, then. What is this all about?"

Ottilia, partaking of her favourite coffee at the table, added her own urging. "Yes, do sit down, Hemp."

But this he would not consent to do. "Let me see to having the table cleared, milady, and then we may talk uninterrupted."

Impatience began to invade Ottilia's bosom. Having achieved his object, was he reluctant to embark upon the business? It argued an even greater disquiet than she had imagined. At length, however, a waiter having cleared everything except Francis's wine, the promised bowl of fruit, a platter of cheese and the accoutrements for Ottilia's coffee, Hemp took a stance to one side of where Ottilia sat.

"I have done what I may, milady, but I fear my influence will only reach so far."

"That's why you needed us?" Francis asked.

"That, milord, and the hope milady's skill will procure both freedom and vindication for Doro." Hemp turned his attention back to Ottilia. "I managed to better her accommodation, milady, but I could not get the magistrate to see reason, though he granted me an interview. He may be reached in Baldwin Street, which again is not far." This said with a flicker towards Francis. "Doro's mistress has a friend with some influence, one Lord Radcliffe, who lives in Queen Square. I could not get in to see him, and Mrs Scalloway likewise is reluctant to see anyone. I sent a message by a servant, but she is said to be inconsolable."

Ottilia's interest quickened. "She is the widow?"

"Yes, milady, and Doro's mistress."

"Why *said to be*, Hemp?"

Her steward's features registered discontent. "Before the man was killed, I accompanied Doro when she took a message to another gentleman. He has been to the house since. Laurence Culverstone is his name. Rumour has it there is some kind of liaison between he and Mrs Scalloway."

"Aha! More to this than meets the eye, eh?" Francis cut in.

Ottilia chose not to acknowledge his amused glance. "What says Dorote, Hemp?"

Hemp's frown became almost a scowl. "Not a word, milady, beyond telling me what occurred that morning. I told her you would come, but she asked me to intercede with Mrs Scalloway. She believed her mistress would intervene on her behalf, perhaps put up bail. When I returned to her with no result, she clammed up."

"Did you tax her with the rumours?"

"You may be sure I did. She would neither confirm nor deny them, except to insist Culverstone is a family friend."

"I suppose you did not think to approach this Culverstone directly?"

Ottilia threw a smile at her spouse. "Just what I was going to ask, Fan."

Hemp blew out a breath. "I have not had an opportunity. I believe the gentleman has been daily closeted in the widow's house since the murder. When I tried to find him at his lodging, I drew blank."

"Which argues for this liaison, don't you agree, Tillie?"

"It would appear so. Just what has Dorote told you, Hemp?"

He shrugged. "Not much, as I said. Nothing to mitigate her apparent guilt. The dagger is definitely hers, one I gave her as I told you in my letter. She hated Scalloway. Quin overheard her telling the mistress that neither of them would be free until the master was dead."

"Who is Quin?"

"The boots, though I gather he was wont to perform a number of other tasks for his master. A wily little braggart I found him, but a useful source of gossip. He was at the Pyg & Whistle when Doro was taken, waiting on the master, he says, on Scalloway's orders. The man was in the habit of drinking and debauchery. Quin had left him there the night before and returned in the morning. One of his duties, he claims, was to be at hand to help get his master home so he might nurse his morning head."

Noting an edge to Hemp's voice whenever he spoke of Scalloway, Ottilia made a mental note to enquire into a possible past association. But this was not the moment.

"What did Quin tell you of that morning's events, Hemp?"

His inner agitation showed in the compression at his jaw and his tone was stiff. "His account seems to be accurate, for I took care to verify all he said for myself at the tavern. Not that I was able to get much sense out of them for the uproar. That was on the day of the murder."

Francis broke in with impatience. "Well, what said the fellow, for pity's sake?"

"Your pardon, milord. Quin heard a chambermaid screaming of murder. He followed the landlord upstairs, along with half the inhabitants of the inn, as far as I can make out. Quin managed to see into the room, though he could not at first make out that the dead man was his master. He saw Doro holding a dagger, the chambermaid backed against the wall, screaming her head off. The landlord sent someone for the constable. It was chaos, Quin said, people shouting, scrambling. The landlord laid hold of Doro and seized the dagger. Quin took it off him and —"

"Did he now?" Francis's tone was decidedly sceptical. "For what purpose?"

"Did he not think to aid Doro? Did he talk to her?"

Hemp's rage began to show. "I asked him the same question, milady. He claims she was too dazed even to see him, let alone understand what he said. That at least I can believe, for she was still in a stupor when I found her in the Bridewell."

"What did he do with the dagger?" Francis persisted. "That seems more pertinent to me."

"He says he gave it to the constable, which Pucklechurch verifies. Quin recognised it for Doro's, as I told you, milady. All I know further is that the magistrate has it now."

A point worth pursuing. Ottilia pushed for more. "The thing must have been bloodied. Did this Quin leave it as it was found?"

"That I don't know, milady. I did not think to ask." Hemp's shoulders shifted. "I admit his failure to act for Doro infuriated me. He might have disposed of the dagger, but no. Instead he handed it to the authorities."

Francis made an exasperated noise. "Talk sense, Hemp. That would have made him an accessory."

"Nor would it have helped your friend." Ottilia softened her tone. "To be rid of the evidence cannot be other than foolish, Hemp. It argues an admission of guilt."

Hemp sighed. "I know it, milady." A reluctant grin showed. "In my more rational moments."

Ottilia let out a gurgle. "Well, we will do what we may to help you to keep your head. Meanwhile, I think my first task tomorrow must be to persuade your Doro to talk. Her account is vital."

# CHAPTER NINE

Ottilia's first thought was that Hemp had done well by Doro, assuming the accoutrements of the cell were of his providing. The second was a momentary astonishment at the startling beauty of this Dorote Gabon, enhanced perhaps by a shaft of sunlight penetrating the casement window. From out of a complexion of deep ebony, a pair of exquisite blue eyes stared at Ottilia, their expression wary. Upon further examination, as Hemp made the introductions, even darker rings about those eyes and a suspicion of greyness to the visible skin above the neckline of a colourful chintz gown gave notice of inner suffering.

Producing a smile, Ottilia extended a hand. "I am sorry to meet you under these difficult circumstances, Miss Gabon."

The slim-fingered hand that briefly touched itself to hers was calloused and worn, throwing the reality of a life of slavery into sharp relief. Ottilia felt a wave of compassion. Guilty or not, Doro had been hardly used.

"May we sit?"

Doro had not spoken but she gestured to the chair and waited for Ottilia to take it before herself perching on the edge of the bed. Ottilia looked up at Hemp. "I believe we will do better alone, Hemp."

He hovered a moment, casting worried glances from Doro to Ottilia and back again. Then he addressed Doro. "Doro, you may speak freely with milady. She will not judge you, I promise."

Ottilia caught his eye and gave a tiny jerk of her head towards the door. Hemp's lips tightened but he contented himself with throwing one more anxious look at Doro before retiring from the room. Ottilia waited until the door had closed behind him and footsteps indicated he had shifted out of earshot.

She leaned a little towards Doro and lowered her voice to a conspiratorial murmur. "Men can never see when they are not wanted, do you not think?"

A low little laugh escaped Doro and her teeth flashed white against the dark skin. "He is adept, milady."

"At refusing to recognise when he is *de trop*? Only with you, I fancy." Ottilia smiled again. "There is no need for milady, my dear. I am known as Lady Fan. May I call you Dorote? Or do you prefer Doro?"

"I am used to Doro. No one calls me Dorote."

"Perhaps they ought. It is a pretty name."

"It is like the French. I think it is. I do not remember well."

Come, this was promising. Doro was relaxing a little. "Do you speak French at all?"

A tiny smile came. "Only when I sleep. Or when I am angry."

"You mean you do not realise when you use the language?"

"It is so. But more, I speak the language of my people, though I no longer remember it well. The master —" An indrawn breath as Doro broke off. Then her head came up in a little gesture of defiance. "Master Scalloway believed I spoke incantations because I mutter. He called me witch girl. He thinks I have knowledge of the witch doctor's art."

"And do you?"

Doro's shoulders shifted. "I was a child when they took me. I know only what I learned in Barbados, in the canes, in the distillery. Also, I know what Hemp taught me."

Ottilia pursued it. She would get further with Doro if she encouraged her to talk. "What did he teach you?"

"My letters. Stories of the world beyond our shores. He opened my eyes." A sobbing breath escaped her. "I never thought to see him more."

Reaching out, Ottilia closed a hand over unquiet fingers. "He has your interests at heart." She waited a moment, but Doro had no answer, her head dipped to hide her face. Ottilia let her go and sat back. "Will you tell me what happened?"

Haltingly, it came out. Ottilia listened, interpolating a question here and there, but allowing Doro to relate the story in her own time. How her mistress had planned to leave her husband that very day; how she refused to leave in his absence — surely an oddity for one intent upon departure? — and insisted upon Doro going to find him at the tavern, this last eliciting a shudder and a telling piece of information.

"I did not want to go. I knew he would have been out of his senses the night before. If you wake him in that state, he is angry. Or worse, amorous. Either way it is penance for me."

Is, not was, Ottilia noted. She had not yet come to terms with the death. "Go on, Doro."

Tremors began to shake the young woman's frame. "I found which room and I went there. He was sleeping, I thought. When I moved closer, I saw the dagger. I saw blood." Her fingers came up, quivering at her lips as if she might wish the words unsaid.

Ottilia persisted. "What did you do?"

The startling gaze came up, anguish in its depths. "I was frozen at first. I cannot tell you all that passed through my mind. I know I did not think of who had done this. I thought of madame's freedom. And mine. And mine! But the dagger — " Her hands came up, covering her face as a deep groan sounded. "Mine too! The dagger I kept hidden in my room. How came it there? How?" Her fingers dragged down her face. "It was my lifeline, always. I used to think of using it should he try again to force me … and there it was. In his heart. And he was dead. Dead, dead! With my dagger!"

Ottilia's heart wept for her but she had to make her finish. "What did you do, Dorote?"

Her breath was gasping now. "I pulled it out. What else could I do? I wanted to throw it away, far away in the sea where no one would ever find it. But that girl came in…" She faded out, shivering as with cold, clearly beset with the memory of the hideous moment of discovery. Ottilia could no longer doubt her innocence. The truth had broken out. Doro was no actress or she would have used the ploy before now.

Swinging over to the bed, Ottilia set an arm about Doro's shoulders and held her until the tremors began to abate. She was surprised when Doro's fingers found hers and clung. No word was spoken for several minutes. At length, the clutch on her hand loosened a trifle and Ottilia sensed the storm had passed. She released herself, patting the hand. "Well now, my dear, I think our task must be to find out who stole your dagger."

"She was, I think, relieved to know I believed her version of events," Ottilia told Francis later, as she sipped at the welcome coffee thoughtfully ordered by her spouse. The prison atmosphere had depressed her spirits, despite the flicker of fascination with the object of Hemp's devotion. Traversing the Bridewell corridors and hearing the locks click to behind her as she passed could not be other than dismaying. Coming out into a sunlit street had been a relief. She looked up at Francis, who had taken his customary stance at the mantel, leaning his elbow on its convenient surface.

"She is exquisitely beautiful, Fan. It is those eyes, I think."

An eyebrow quirked. "What of her eyes?"

Ottilia set her cup down in its saucer. "An anomaly. Hemp says it happens sometimes if there is a mixed ancestry. Dorote has bright blue eyes."

"Good God!"

"You can have no notion of their effect in a countenance so very dark."

"I should think it must be startling at least."

"That, and perfectly mesmerising. It is no great wonder Hemp became enamoured of her."

Her husband's lip quivered on a tease. "Then I take it you are moved to put forth your best endeavours."

Ottilia laughed. "Oh, I believe it will be no great matter to procure her release."

"You jest! When she was caught with the weapon in her hand?"

Ottilia put up a finger. "Ah, but that is a mere coincidence."

"Coincidence? The thing belongs to her, Tillie."

"Yes, and someone stole it with the purpose of shuffling off the guilt upon her shoulders." She received a disbelieving stare and lifted her brows. "You don't agree?"

Francis threw up his hands. "How in Hades can I? You can't possibly know that for a fact."

"No, but it is a valid surmise."

"How so?"

"Figure to yourself, Fan, how it must look. Here is a slave, a female devoid of rights and one who allegedly hates her master. With reason, I may add, for he was plainly a brute, especially in his cups."

"All very well, but you are arguing for the prosecutor."

"Just so. Who better for a scapegoat?"

"Very well, my woman of wonder. Convince me." Francis dropped into the chair opposite, sitting back with all the air of one prepared to be entertained.

Ottilia eyed him in some amusement. "You think to confound me, Fan, but you won't."

He grinned. "Well, go on."

She fortified herself with a few sips of the warming beverage. "Why don't you tell me why a slave, whose mistress was planning to leave her husband, and to take Doro with her — with, mark you, a promise of freedom — should jeopardise such a future by killing her master. It makes no sense, Fan."

"Well, if you put it like that..."

"Moreover, this wife is involved with another man."

"What, you think he did the deed?"

"I don't know, but both he and the wife must be suspect. Why did she insist upon Doro going to find her husband that morning when she could well have carried out her intention to leave?"

"She wanted her to find the body?"

"It is possible."

Her spouse let out a snort. "So, you will have it this female steals her maid's dagger and creeps out in the dead of night to slay her husband with it? Hardly credible, Tillie."

"But more credible that the maid crept out at night? Come, Fan, let us be clear. There may be any number of people who could have done it, for all we know. We have no information as to when exactly Scalloway was stabbed, which might be pertinent. I must hope the magistrate will be better informed."

"Assuming a doctor was called."

Ottilia waved a dismissive hand. "Hemp will know, but I imagine one was. The death must be certified, even if the cause is obvious."

"I was forgetting that. What of this host of potential suspects, then?"

"That is yet to be determined. As yet, we have no information about Scalloway's activities. Who were his associates? And why was his wife taking the drastic step of leaving him?"

"If he was a brute, as you say, the reason is not far to seek."

"But a woman does not lightly seek a separation, Fan. Only think of the scandal. No, there must be a more cogent motive."

"There is. This fellow she fancies. What did Hemp say his name was?"

"Culverstone. I say again, a woman does not lightly plunge into that sort of scandal. Leave her husband for another man? She would be disgraced, a social outcast."

He was frowning now, clearly turning it over in his mind. Ottilia waited, a trifle of anxiety rising. If she could not convince Francis, what hope had she of persuading the magistrate? At last he looked up and smiled.

"What is in your mind, my ingenious one?"

She had to laugh. "Thank you, but I will admit to a trifle of doubt myself. I cannot rule out either the wife or the lover."

"But you think it may well have been another."

"The man was wont to frequent taverns, for one thing. For another, it is his wife who has the expectations. Hemp says she is another of these sugar heiresses. If he married her for her money —"

"Which is all too likely."

"— it may well be that he squandered it and found himself in debt."

"Feasible."

Ottilia smiled. "Almost certain. I have been holding out on you, my darling lord. I omitted to tell you one pertinent thing Dorote let fall. The quarrel that pushed Mrs Scalloway into revealing her intention to her husband was about money."

"You wretch, Tillie. I don't know what you deserve." But his lip quirked nonetheless. "I ought to have guessed you had an ace up your sleeve." He sat up, setting his arms along his knees. "I take it my task is to enquire into Scalloway's associates?"

"If you please, Fan. I will set Hemp to question this boot boy Quin, who must be pretty well informed, and find out some names for you. But I suggest you begin at the tavern where the deed took place."

Francis groaned. "I am yours to command, of course."

A gurgle escaped her. "You are a prince among husbands, my dearest."

"And don't you forget it. Where will you be?"

"I must cultivate Mrs Scalloway and contrive to search Doro's room. Once we are satisfied there is no other dagger in the case, I will tackle the magistrate."

# CHAPTER TEN

The Pyg & Whistle was noisome, smoky, and full to bursting with individuals of many shades, mostly labouring men or sailors by the look of their garments. Francis shouldered a way through to the counter, reflecting that Hemp Roy would not be out of place in this port. Darker-skinned fellows rubbed shoulders with Englishmen, seeming very much at home. He received a belligerent look from an individual he had pushed past, which turned respectful as the man's gaze ran up and down his person. He touched his forelock.

"Begging yer honour's pardon. Didn't see you."

Francis nodded. "Thank you, but it was I who disturbed you, I fear. I am trying to get to the landlord."

A porter from the docks, by the cushion strapped to the back of his hat and the belted smock he wore, the fellow clicked an impatient tongue. "Waste of time, yer honour. I'll get him for you." Upon which he turned towards a knot of men engaged in heated conversation over by the fireplace, set his hands either side of his mouth and bellowed, "Hoy, Pymoor! Bustle, man, you're wanted!"

With difficulty Francis refrained from covering his ears, determining to extract the landlord to some less crowded place or he would never be able to put his questions.

A thick-set individual in his shirt-sleeves, sporting an apron spattered with brown stains, detached himself from the group, who were all now staring towards Francis, and pushed his way across.

"His honour here wants you, Py."

Francis thanked his benefactor and turned his head to meet a pair of somewhat bloodshot eyes in a balding head, the sparse remains of grey confined in a ragged queue at his neck.

"Aye? Was it ale you was wanting?"

His manner was not encouraging. Francis lost no time in establishing his credentials. "I am Lord Francis Fanshawe, Pymoor, and I would be glad of a few moments of conversation. Elsewhere, if you please."

A pair of heavy brows lowered over the eyes, which showed both suspicion and puzzlement. "For why?"

"For a purpose which I shall make plain to you in private."

The sharpened tone had an effect. The landlord straightened, lessening the belligerent stance. Before he could speak, however, the first man cut in.

"If so be he's a lord, Py, you'd best do as he wants, ain't yer?"

Pymoor threw him a look of scorn. "My place is this. I says what I'll do, thankee, Robbo." And to Francis, "There's a parlour empty, me lord, if you follow me."

Turning, he forced a path with a deal more ease than Francis had done, much to his relief as he stuck close behind. The taproom negotiated, the landlord passed towards the back of the square hall and opened a door, jerking his head at Francis to precede him. The parlour was small and ill lit by its single window, but it would serve.

Francis removed his hat and set it on the table that took up most of the space. He pulled out a chair. "We may as well sit down, Pymoor. This may take a while."

The landlord did not avail himself of the invitation conveyed by the second chair Francis shifted with his foot. Instead he stood behind it and gripped the wooden back. "A few minutes, you said."

Francis raised his brows. "Do you have some objection to answering questions?"

Pymoor thrust out his lower lip. "That's depending."

Growing weary of his recalcitrance, Francis cut line. "I am enquiring into the death of Mr Scalloway."

Clearly taken aback, the landlord released the chair and blinked. "I told that there Mr Belchamp all I know already. 'Sides, Pucklechurch took off the black girl straight. She'd the dagger in her hand. I took it off her meself."

Francis seized on this. "You saw it all? You were there?"

"Course I were there. With that Cherry screaming the house down, I ran up double quick. Only just gone down to the tap when I heard it."

"Did you see a fellow by the name of Quin? A servant of Scalloway's?"

"Him?" Pymoor emitted a scoffing sound. "Him I know of old. Always sneaking in, hanging about and nursing his ale for an hour or more, saying he'd to wait his master out. Wait him out? Oft I've told him he could sleep in the ashes for all of me, for he'd be waiting all night for that one."

Glad the fellow's mouth was running off at such a great rate, Francis took advantage to prise out what he might know. "You were well acquainted with Scalloway? Was he a frequent visitor?"

"Him and his set, aye. Not to my wish, for as he held his purse tight shut. 'Cept as buying what he wet his own face with. Never a groat by way of vails for no one, 'cepting Cherry, and he took her cheap."

Noting this, Francis probed further. "Did he take Cherry that night?"

"Have to ask her. I dunno. Likely as he did. The missus would have me rid of her, but she's a comely wench and she brings the customers in."

Changing tack, Francis recalled the main reason for his mission. "You said Scalloway came with his set. Who were they, do you know?"

Pymoor made a sour face. "None of mine. Only come with him, they did, or to meet him here. One Mawdesley were used to come most often."

"Who is he? A gentleman?"

"Not him. Messenger, more like. Works for a feller who deals in merchanting and shipping and such, name of Harbury. He come hisself a few times, but mostly it were that shifty messenger of his."

"Mawdesley. Why shifty?"

Pymoor's lip curled. "He's another of them little squealers. Like that Quin. 'Tis my belief he don't care what he do, long as it gets him a silver bit."

"Are you talking of Quin or Mawdesley?"

"Naught to choose between them if you ask me. Seen them two with their heads together an' all."

Interesting. It began to look as if Tillie was on the right track, setting Hemp on to question the man Quin. Were he and Mawdesley cronies, or was the association merely due to the acquaintance between their respective masters? Recalling the landlord's earlier words, he backtracked. "You said you took the dagger from Doro's hand. I understood the fellow Quin had it from you. Did you see what he did with it?"

Pymoor shook his head with vehemence. "Nowt to do with me. I told the missus to see to Cherry and went down to send young Dandy for the constable. By the time Pucklechurch come, which were nigh on a quarter hour, the girl were locked in one of the spare chambers and I ain't seen Quin until she were took."

Then there was no saying what Quin had done with it in the intervening time. There was not much profit in continuing to question Pymoor, but one thing persisted. "Was it only Mawdesley and this Harbury that Scalloway met with here?"

The landlord shrugged. "Far as I know." Then his gaze brightened and he smote his forehead. "Wait a bit. A gennelman come looking for him one time. Maybe more'n once."

"Do you remember his name?"

"Aye, for he's a feller well known hereabouts. Mr Ackworth, it is. Lawyer, he is. I noticed him particular for as he's more like to drink at the Llandoger Trow. In King Street, it is. Strange as he'd come looking for Scalloway here is what I thought."

"Ah. He came especially to find him?"

"Aye, and it were news to me as he knew him. 'Cepting as it might be through my lord Radcliffe, what Scalloway boasts is a friend."

"And he isn't?"

"Don't know that. Nor I wouldn't think he was friends with no lords." A frowning glance came Francis's way. "Unless it be as he's a friend of yourn."

Francis raised his brows. "Mine? I didn't know the fellow." He answered the puzzlement in the landlord's face. "I am acting for Miss Gabon." Let him make of that what he would. A name mentioned earlier surfaced. "You spoke of one Beauchamp, was it?"

"Belchamp. Walter Belchamp, it is. He's one of they justices."

"He questioned you, you said."

"Aye, and I tell him what I see is all."

Evidently the Justice of the Peace had not asked about other potential suspects. Small wonder, with one caught apparently in the act. Remembrance of his wife's earlier cases prompted another line of enquiry. "Where is the body? Was a doctor called?"

"Pucklechurch brung in old Doc Varley. Doc took and had the undertaker come. Good riddance, says I. Not as it didn't bring in the customers all day and night, clamouring to see what weren't there to be seen."

Francis rose. He had ammunition enough for Tillie for the present. He dug in his pocket for a coin and dropped it on the table, retrieving his hat. "I must thank you, Pymoor. It is possible I may need to speak with you again, but for the present I have all I need."

Pleased at the ease with which her title gained her entrance into the Scalloway home, Ottilia took care to proffer spurious sympathies to the widow before embarking upon her mission. Elinor Scalloway was correctly attired in black silk, a pretty black lace cap doing virtually nothing to conceal her hair. Indeed, it enhanced its attraction, disappearing into the dark of the curls flowing down her back. She was composed, if a trifle pale. Or did her pallor owe something to white powder? Her voice was rich and cultured, with just the trace of an accent on certain vowels that Ottilia recognised from Hemp's tones. It struck her that Dorote's speech had a different ring. Was it an African sound?

"It is kind in you to visit me, my lady." Elinor cast a glance across the other two visitors, one a good-looking young gentleman whom Ottilia took to be the lover in the case (if he was one), the other a dame of middle years who had been presented as Lady Radcliffe. "My dear friends have been my constant companions." Her gaze returned to Ottilia and an appraising look entered in.

Ottilia took the bull by the horns. "I dare say you are wondering why I am here."

Elinor gave a little laugh. "I confess, my lady, I am at a loss to understand what prompted this visit."

Excellent. Straight to the point. Ottilia smiled. "Then let me be frank. My steward is a friend of Doro's from Barbados. I believe he did inform you of this fact via your footman?"

The widow looked a little conscious. "I do recall hearing some such tale. I regret I was distrait at the time. It has been a severe shock, you must know."

"I do not doubt it, ma'am. Nor can I suppose you are not in sympathy with the plight of your maid."

Elinor made play with a lace handkerchief she had lying in her lap. "Poor Doro! I little imagined she would go to such lengths."

Ottilia's ire rose but she suppressed it. "You believe her guilty, then? Without question?"

Elinor fluttered the handkerchief. "What else am I to think? She was found with that horrid dagger in her hand, as I understand it."

"As you understand it. Yet you made no attempt to discover whether this was indeed the case, even though Dorote had none but you to speak for her?"

The shaft went home. Elinor Scalloway vanished into her handkerchief, to all appearances dissolved in tears. A hasty motion from the young man brought Lady Radcliffe to her feet in a rustle of modish lilac silk. Her long face pinched in disapproval and framed in the veils of a hat with a sloping crown, she waved him down.

"For shame, Lady Francis! Have you forgotten poor Elinor is but lately bereaved? How might she be expected to turn her mind from such a tragedy? Especially when the girl was clearly guilty."

Ottilia hit back strongly. "Indeed, ma'am? Clearly so? Have you any notion at what hour Mr Scalloway was actually stabbed?"

A cry from Elinor proved too much for the young man. He burst from his chair and sprang to her side, setting an arm about her. "Don't heed her, my dear Elinor! There is nothing you could have done. Have I not told you so over and over?"

Ottilia lost patience. "Oh, come, Mr Culverstone, that will not fadge." She met his gaze as he threw her a look of recalcitrance, which did little to spoil the even planes of his pretty features. He wore his own hair, as fair as Elinor's was dark, tied at the neck with a black ribbon, but a couple of escaping curls looped into his cheeks, lending him a devil-may-care aspect. Ottilia was neither beguiled nor intimidated by his patent disapproval. "You are Laurence Culverstone, are you not?"

"I am, but what that has to do with —"

"Let us cease this pretence, if you please. You too, Lady Radcliffe. Did any of you suppose Doro would not speak of what has been happening here?"

Her attackers exchanged a glance — of consternation? Well might they! Elinor's head came up and she eyed Ottilia with all the air of one confronting a venomous snake.

"Yes, Mrs Scalloway, I have spoken with your maid and I know that not only were you planning to leave your husband, but that you, Lady Radcliffe, were complicit in the plot. Your husband was to fetch Elinor and Doro at noon that day. And Doro herself took that information to you, Mr Culverstone, a couple of days prior. Now tell me, if you please, why Doro should take it into her head to slay the man from whose malevolence she was only too happy to know she was to be freed? I can think of two far more cogent motives." She took time to look from one conscience-ridden face to another. "It does not look well for either of you, do you not think?"

The widow was the first to recover. She tucked the handkerchief into her sleeve and fixed Ottilia with a bland stare. "If it does not seem valid for Doro to have killed Marcus, you might impute precisely the same reasoning to me."

Ottilia smiled. "I might. I likely shall. But it does not excuse your ignoring Doro's predicament. One might also suppose you welcomed the solution, for that suspicion might not then fall upon you."

Elinor gave a gasp and Lady Radcliffe intervened again. "You are offensive, Lady Francis."

Ottilia did not flinch, instead turning her gaze upon Culverstone, who half shrunk away from it. "What of you, sir? Had you no reason to wish to be rid of Mr Scalloway?"

The protests became voluble.

"How dare you say so?"

"This is the outside of enough!"

"You go too far, my lady!"

This last, from the young man himself, urged Ottilia into speech again. "It is not so convenient when the tables are turned, is it, sir?"

The widow burst out at this. "Don't say that! It is not — it was not a matter of convenience. I couldn't help Doro, don't you see? How could I take her part when everyone supposes me to be prostrate with grief?"

"Everyone outside your household and these few friends, I take it?"

"Yes, if you must have it. Marcus was murdered! Even if I meant to leave him, such a horrid taking off was a terrible shock. I could not think straight, I promise you. If I was not stricken with grief, I assure you I suffered a good deal of remorse."

"But not on Doro's account."

"I thought she had killed him! I swear it. I knew she hated Marcus. She had reason enough, for he was cruel to her. It would have been worse if I had not saved her time and again." The passionate outburst ended in a riot of sobs. Genuine this time, Ottilia decided.

She watched as both sympathisers fussed over the widow, waiting in some degree of impatience for the performance to abate. It began to look unlikely that Elinor was any more guilty than Dorote, but she had expected that. The jury must be considered still out on Culverstone. He had failed so far to convince, except of being hopelessly enamoured of the widow. As for Lady Radcliffe, it was plain she and Elinor were as thick as thieves and she would back the woman to the hilt. Might there be profit in bearding Lord Radcliffe? He at least must be au fait with such monetary dealings as Scalloway indulged in, by Dorote's account of that final quarrel.

As the cacophony abated, Ottilia picked up the thread again. "Make yourself easy, Mrs Scalloway. I have no immediate intention of making any formal accusations."

Lady Radcliffe turned upon her. "By what right do you seek to accuse anyone, Lady Francis? Who are you to interest yourself in this affair?"

Ottilia regarded her with interest. "You have not heard of me, then. I am relieved to know I may still claim anonymity in some quarters."

The other stared, her amazement echoed in the widow's reddened eyes as she straightened, her ruined handkerchief clutched within the fingers of one hand. Her cavalier either had not heard or chose to ignore the comment, his gaze fixed upon the pallid countenance of his evident adoration. Mrs Scalloway found her tongue first.

"I do not understand. Ought we to know of you? We have all but lately come from Barbados, you must know."

Ottilia could not but be amused at the anxious hint that a faux pas might have been committed, eliciting the excuse of necessary ignorance. She prevaricated. "Well, it is of no importance. I have had a little success in this line in the past, that is all."

Lady Radcliffe, looking intrigued now, moved across the room to resume her former seat. "In what line, Lady Francis?"

"Murder, ma'am," said Ottilia with guilty relish.

The effect was all she could have wished. Both ladies emitted gasping breaths, while Culverstone, who had taken a chair next to his inamorata, at last took notice.

"What can you mean, ma'am?"

"I mean, Mr Culverstone, that I intend to find out precisely who killed Mr Scalloway, because Dorote Gabon most assuredly did not."

# CHAPTER ELEVEN

Doro's attic room was quite in the general run of servant accommodation. A narrow cot bed with a small dressing commode to one wall and a simple washstand in a corner comprised the entirety of the furnishings. A rug covered part of the floor alongside the bed, which boasted only a couple of blankets and a worn quilt. Doro's prison accommodation was almost better equipped, Ottilia reflected, thanks to Hemp's purse.

"Well, it should not take us long to make a search in here. Do you take the bed, Hemp, while I look in the dresser."

The maid Jenny, who had accompanied them to show the way, hovered in the doorway. "Shall I stay, my lady?"

"Yes, do, if you please." Ottilia smiled at her. "You may serve as a witness if we should find anything."

Hemp was already on his haunches, pulling out a battered portmanteau from beneath the bed. Ottilia turned her attention to the top drawer of the dressing commode and began to work systematically through the maid's meagre clothing, taking care not to disturb its neatness too much.

Taking advantage of the dismay engendered in the party downstairs, she had asked to see Doro's room. No one thought to enquire her reason, the widow instructing Culverstone to ring the bell.

"My maid will show you up, ma'am."

"I thank you. I wonder, Mrs Scalloway, if you will be so kind as to grant me a private interview upon my return?"

Ottilia caught Lady Radcliffe's swift shake of the head, and noted the lover's look of consternation. But the widow saw neither, or else she chose to ignore them.

"Certainly, Lady Francis."

"But, Elinor —"

"Hush, dear Caroline. I am minded to assist her ladyship, if I can."

Ottilia thanked her, forestalling any further objections, although she had no doubt many were raised the moment she had left the room with the girl Jenny. Hemp was awaiting them in the corridor, having been primed ahead that this was her object.

The drawers were soon gone through, yielding nothing. Ottilia had half hoped to find the dagger, which would at once obviate any argument with the magistrate in the case. She sighed. "No luck, Hemp?"

"Nothing, milady."

"You looked under the mattress?"

"Short of turning it over, milady, yes."

"I do not think we need to go that far. If she hid it under there, it would be within reach."

He said no word and Ottilia was pained to note tightness in his face. Did he find it hurtful to be going through Doro's belongings? Or was the procedure churning up memories? On impulse, she turned to the maid. "Thank you, my dear. You must have a great deal to do, so we will not keep you longer. I believe we may find our own way back."

The maid, looking relieved, bobbed a curtsy and left them. Ottilia moved to the door and closed it, turning to look at Hemp. "What happened between you, Hemp?"

Agony flitted across the dark features. He looked away and his voice came low. "A man with those devil looks lured her."

"Away from you?"

"We had an understanding … I thought."

"She betrayed you?"

He winced. Ottilia had chosen the word with deliberation. Better for him to confront the truth of it. Would he find excuses for her? "Doro was young. Impressionable. I was too … comfortable."

Yes, he could not endure to blame her. Ottilia softened her tone. "She is very beautiful, Hemp."

Light came into his face. "From a girl, always. She could not have been more than ten, eleven, when I saw her first, when she came with a consignment of slaves. Skin of velvet midnight, eyes like twin skies, that magical blue, deep with fear and loneliness. She captured my heart in an instant."

Ottilia could not speak. How many times had he relived this, only to re-experience the pain, of loss and rejection both?

Hemp was silent for a space. Lost in the memory? Then he blinked, seeming to come to himself again. He lifted a hand and ran agitated fingers across his face. "I have never spoken of these things."

"Then I am privileged, Hemp." Ottilia moved across and laid a hand briefly on his arm. "We will rescue her for you."

A great sigh escaped him. "I think she won't be grateful. Not to me."

Ottilia shifted back, the better to look at him. "But why, Hemp? Does she not love you?"

"She is ashamed."

"Of hurting you? Of mistaking his character? It was Scalloway, was it not?"

Hemp's jaw tightened. "It is hard not to be glad he is dead."

Ottilia eyed him. "Were you tempted to kill him yourself?"

A laugh came, his expression startled. "Shrewd, milady. Master Matt kept me from the deed."

"Well, thank heavens for that." She paused a moment. "Did you think Doro had done it?"

Hemp blew out a breath. "Until I spoke to her, I did. She was ever a fiery little thing." Sadness came into his face. "That has gone now."

Ottilia felt for him. "It will return, Hemp. Once she is free and a new life awaits her, she will recover her former self."

He shifted in obvious discomfort. "I wish I might believe it. She is chary of me now. I do not know if…"

He faded out and Ottilia had no difficulty in filling in the blanks. "Dear Hemp, don't despair. There is hope. You have forgiven her, have you not?"

His tone was bleak. "Doro cannot forgive herself."

Ottilia made a mental resolve to work upon Dorote, if she would allow it. It was to Hemp's credit, and must make the task easier, that he understood his love so well.

It was plain Elinor Scalloway had recovered her composure. She was alone in the parlour when Ottilia returned, and she greeted her with an offer of refreshment.

"My footman brought up tea, ma'am. May I persuade you to a cup?"

A show of complacence might well serve. "Thank you, that would be most welcome, Mrs Scalloway."

Ottilia waited for the tea to be poured, added a lump of sugar and took a seat opposite the sofa where the widow was ensconced. She stirred it and set down the spoon, looking up to find the woman regarding her in an expectant fashion. Ottilia withheld a gurgle of amusement. "You are no doubt wondering why I wished to speak with you alone."

Elinor surprised her with a smile. "Oh, I think I can guess. My companions are a little over-protective." Was there a challenge in her gaze? "I can hold my own."

"I don't doubt it. The wonder is, I suspect, that you endured the difficulties of your marriage as long."

The widow gave her a straight look. "Doro has been tattling, has she?"

"By no means. She told me only what happened that day and your intentions formed a part of that story. It is a fair inference, do you not think?"

Elinor pouted. "I dare say. I might endure the inevitable gossip while Marcus was alive. Now, however…"

"You would prefer not to sully his reputation? Or do you merely hope to retain the illusion of inconsolable widowhood?"

A shrug. "Either, or both. I care not. I see no reason for the world to become privy to my personal affairs."

"I fear there is scant hope of keeping them — some of them at least — from public scrutiny."

"Because he was murdered?"

"Just so. These events are accompanied by inquests, hearings and trials. You will likely have to stand witness in court."

A little shiver shook the woman. "Horrible."

Ottilia relented. "But perhaps less so than the consequences of a legal separation and divorce, supposing Parliament was disposed to grant one."

Elinor's lips parted in a tiny smile and her eyes twinkled. "You are frank, Lady Francis."

Despite her first impressions, Ottilia warmed to the woman. It was evident she could be engaging when she chose. "To tell you the truth, I am not always so. In this instance, however, I am anxious to secure your co-operation. I will not do that by using subterfuge."

The more friendly tone vanished. "You wish me to exert myself to help Doro. Since we are using candour, ma'am, you must see how it would look for me to champion her."

Ottilia was obliged to damp down a sharp retort. She was making headway. Why ruin it for a scruple? "You need have no fear. I will champion her."

Yet her better opinion of Elinor Scalloway lessened. She was, after all, a slave owner and likely shared the common belief that those in bondage were lesser beings. Was Doro dispensable in her eyes? She was obliged to remind herself not to make prejudiced judgements before she could crush an inevitable disgust. She took refuge in sipping her tea until she could command a natural tone again. "Nevertheless, you can help me if you will, Mrs Scalloway, without compromising your reputation."

The woman had the grace to look a trifle shamed and colour came into her cheek. "What do you need of me, ma'am?"

Conciliating at best, but it would serve. "I wish you will tell me of your husband's business dealings. I take it he was in debt?"

Elinor's hand jumped a little and liquid spilled from her cup. She set it down with an exclamation of annoyance and rubbed at a stain on her black petticoat.

"Oh, I beg your pardon. Did I embarrass you?"

Elinor looked daggers. "Embarrass? No! How in the world did you know? Pray do not tell me Doro said so."

"But she did. Oh, not directly. Doro's relation of the last argument you had with your spouse told me so. You sued to Lord Radcliffe on his behalf and he refused to support Mr Scalloway further. Is that not correct?"

Elinor's countenance was aflame. "Yes, if you must know." Defiance crept in. "But I lied. I would not ask his lordship for one penny to help Marcus."

"You asked instead for his aid in assisting you to leave your husband?"

"What else could I do? Impossible to depart without sanctuary, I knew that. Besides, Lord Radcliffe is my trustee. Without him at my back, I would be penniless."

Ottilia digested this. "Your fortune is secured, I take it?"

Elinor let out a sigh. "For which I may thank my father. Until he dies, my inheritance is tied up. But Lord Radcliffe has power to advance me funds should I need them. That is what Marcus was counting upon. Only I told him his lordship would not budge."

Ottilia shifted her focus. "The matter is now clear. Pray what dealings had your husband that resulted in his falling into debt?"

Elinor gave a spurious spurt of laughter, redolent with scorn. "He sought to make his fortune. Marcus bought into a shipping venture, one which Lord Radcliffe assured me was both risky and running upon extremely shady ground."

"Shady how, ma'am?"

"His partner, for one. Lord Radcliffe had no opinion of this man Harbury. Nor was he satisfied that Marcus was competent to choose a satisfactory crew to man the ship."

As indeed was proven if he was ruined. "You consulted him ahead of these arrangements, then?"

"Naturally. Without capital, Marcus could not have done it. He broached the matter to me, in hopes I would advance him the needed funds." Elinor fidgeted with the silky material of her black skirts, looking down. "It was foolish of me, but I thought — I hoped that if he was successful, it would make it easier for me to leave him."

"You intended this for long, then?"

Elinor's tone became bitter. "Almost from the first days of our marriage when his true character became clear to me." She clenched the hands in her lap. "I never wanted the contract, but I had no choice in the matter. I begged my father for release, but he would not listen."

"It was an arranged marriage, then? What virtue had Mr Scalloway that induced your father to accept his suit?"

Elinor scowled. "Birth. My father supposed his handsome looks, his charm and his address must win my affections."

"Except that your affections were already engaged, is that it?"

A secretive little smile came upon the woman's lips but she did not answer. Ottilia could not avoid the thought that fate had played nicely into Elinor's hands.

Walter Belchamp Esq was a jolly individual, given to laughter by the crinkling lines at the edges of his eyes, which were nonetheless keen. He was of average height so that a protruding stomach gave him a portly appearance. His bow had creditable grace, but he no sooner grasped Ottilia's identity than he was moved to proffer his hand.

"You are the female known as Lady Fan, or I am much mistaken."

Ottilia took the hand, aware of her spouse's ironic eye upon her. "You are correct, sir. I had not expected to be recognised here, I admit."

A hearty laugh greeted this. "My dear Lady Fan, if I may so address you, we magistrates are apt to confer with each other, you must know. I have an excellent correspondent in my colleague in Dorchester, for example."

Before she could answer, Francis intervened. "But my wife had no dealings with that fellow. My friend Colonel Tretower reported to him."

Mr Belchamp twinkled and laid a finger to the side of his nose. "Yet old Shellow knew who in Weymouth had uncovered the culprit, for he told me the whole story."

Ottilia received a comical look from her husband and had to laugh. "Well, I will count myself fortunate in your knowledge of me, sir, for it must save me a good deal of tedious explanation."

"Indeed, indeed, I hope so. Will you not be seated, my lady? And you, my lord, of course." He moved to the bell-pull. "You'll take a glass, I hope. I have an excellent sherry, not too dry to the palate."

This air of bonhomie was promising and Ottilia did not hesitate to take the chair indicated, Francis moving to one nearby in the neat parlour. The house in Baldwin Street was small but had an appearance both inside and out of freshness. Ottilia suspected the building was of recent date. Within, the washed walls were plain, apart from a couple of portraits in the hall and a large landscape in the parlour, which looked to have been furnished for convenience rather than taste, with a distinctly masculine feel. Armchairs were upholstered in leather and two large bookcases set either side of the fireplace bore tomes that had seen better days. Mr Belchamp was clearly a great reader. A desk covered in papers and set in an alcove indicated that this was where the magistrate conducted his business affairs. He came back from ringing the bell and sat down in a chair opposite to Ottilia's, becoming brisk.

"Now, my lady, I take it you are come to persuade me that the female we took into custody did not in fact commit the deed?"

Ottilia had to laugh. "Just so, sir. How came you to guess that?"

Mr Belchamp leaned a little forward. "I had my doubts, my dear lady, I had my doubts."

"Then why," demanded Francis, cutting in ahead of Ottilia, "did you arrest her?"

Mr Belchamp sat back again. "She was the only suspect, my lord. Moreover, that little fellow who knew her — now what was his name?" He rose and began heading for his desk.

"Quin, you mean?"

Mr Belchamp halted and came back. "Quin, that's it. A snivelling little fellow. I did not take to him at all. However, he knew Doro, worked with her at the dead man's residence, you must know, and he gave Pucklechurch the dagger, the weapon that was used. Of course, you must know that already, my lady."

"Indeed I do, sir. Also that Doro was found with the dagger in her hand."

"Which she admitted was hers," added Mr Belchamp, wagging a finger.

They were interrupted by the entrance of a servant, who was carrying a tray. A little delay was occasioned by the serving of the sherry. For form's sake, Ottilia accepted a glass, but the moment the door closed to leave them private again, she set it aside and cut directly to the nub. "What made you doubt Doro's guilt, Mr Belchamp?"

He touched the side of his nose with his free finger. "A little thing, but pertinent. By Varley's account — ah, the doctor who certified the death, that is. By his account, the stabbing must have occurred in the night hours, not in the early morning."

Her spouse forestalled Ottilia's question. "At what time, does he know?"

"Between one and three by his best guess." Mr Belchamp's gaze sought Ottilia again, accompanied by an expectant little smile. "You would no doubt have said the same, my lady, had you been able to inspect the condition of the body."

Ottilia spread her hands. "Possibly. It is the one thing I find most difficult."

Mr Belchamp rubbed a closed fist on his knee in a little show of glee. "I am so glad you chose to approach me, my lady. That is just Varley's dictum. One cannot hope to be strictly accurate, he says. Your knowledge of medical lore is remarkable, ma'am."

Ottilia brought out her time-honoured excuse. "I learned from my brother, sir. He is a medical man." She turned the subject. "I must suppose then that you have reached the conclusion, Mr Belchamp, that for Doro to remove the dagger at the time she went to wake her master makes no sense at all if she had indeed murdered him at an earlier hour."

Delight leapt on Mr Belchamp's face. "There!" He turned back to Francis. "Your lady wife, my lord, has struck right at the heart of my thinking. Why leave the dagger in situ at all?"

"Just so. May I ask where the weapon is now, sir?"

Mr Belchamp regarded her with a lurking smile. "You wish to see it? Why, I wonder?"

"I understand it is distinctive."

"That is all your reason?"

Ottilia could not forbear a smile. "Do you have it, Mr Belchamp?"

He gave a bark of laughter. "I see I can't prise out your secrets."

An answering laugh came from Francis as Mr Belchamp rose and headed for his desk again. "Few can, sir. My wife is nothing if not discreet."

"An admirable trait, my lord." Belchamp opened a drawer in the desk and brought out a wicked-looking blade, bearing about the handle a label tied with string. He held it up by the handle. "A lethal little thing. One wonders that a slave girl had possession of it."

Ottilia was up and moving to join him at the desk. "She was given it for the purpose of protection." She held out a hand. "May I?"

"By all means. I shall be interested to hear what you make of it."

Ottilia took the dagger, handling it with care and laid it in the flat of her palm. It was small but eminently serviceable, with a vicious point at the end of the thin blade and a distinctive twist and curl design at the hilt. She found her husband at her side, subjecting the object to inspection.

"Nasty. I should not care to have any of my servants in possession of such a thing."

Ottilia threw him a glance. "Hemp may have one for all we know. After all, he gave this one to Doro." She proffered the dagger to the justice. "Thank you, Mr Belchamp. It is my belief it was stolen from among Doro's effects. There was certainly no dagger when we searched her room."

Mr Belchamp was putting the dagger back in the drawer, but he glanced over his shoulder at this. "You have been busy, my lady."

"I have, and so has my husband."

Mr Belchamp looked from one to the other. "Well, my lady?"

Ottilia smiled. "It will not be well, sir, until Doro is free. You have spoken of your doubts. Will you release her?"

Mr Belchamp's face fell. "Ah, there you have me."

Chagrined, Ottilia could not but be grateful to her spouse for taking up the gauntlet. "I don't see how you can well do other, Belchamp. If it is bail you need, I will take care of that."

Mr Belchamp shook a sorrowful head. "Alas, my lord, if only it was as simple."

"I see no difficulty."

"I am tied, my lord, by my duty to the Law." He regarded Ottilia with an apologetic air. "I regret it, my lady, but unless and until you can furnish me with other potential suspects in the case —"

"But I can! Two with strong motives, and two more who may at least bear investigation. My husband will tell you of those."

He looked surprised, but his brows drew together. "You have such already? Who is it you would name, my lady?"

# CHAPTER TWELVE

Armed with the information provided by Lord Francis, Hemp returned to the Scalloway house to beard the fellow Quin once more. His advent was not uniformly welcome, although the cook was friendly enough when she opened the door to his knock.

"Oh, it's you, Mr Roy. Sit you down, do. I'm ahead of myself with the dinner and can take a moment. Ale or coffee?" Hemp opted for coffee. "Have you seen our Doro, then? Must be miserable, poor girl."

"I have not seen her since yesterday, Peg. I hope to go later today, if there is good news to give her."

Peg left her bubbling pots, wiped the sweat off her face with her apron and came to the table with the coffee pot she apparently kept always filled and ready, pulling out a chair and sitting opposite. "I'll never believe as she done it. Will this Lady Fan of yours get her out of there?"

Hemp crushed his inner doubts, born of anxiety as he knew too well. "She will do her best. It is possible Quin may be able to help."

"Him?" She emitted a sound of scorn as she poured the black liquid into two cups. "Don't help nobody but hisself, does Quin. Now if you told me he done it, it'd be different, only he wouldn't. Not the master. Knows which side his bread is buttered, and the mistress don't like him above half."

This was grist to Hemp's mill. "That is just why I think he can help. He ran errands for your master, did he not?" He drew the sugar jar towards him and added several lumps to his brew. "I saw him given an instruction the first day I met Doro."

The cook glanced towards the inner door and then lowered her voice. "He'll be in any minute, so I'll tell you quick. If there's any havey-cavey goings-on to be found, be sure as Quin knows it all. Often and often I've thought as he were a sight too knowing. Nor he didn't keep hisself to his proper work." Indignation entered Peg's voice and her eyes sparkled with sudden wrath. "I'll tell you summat more and all. Didn't think nowt of bringing a feller into my kitchen and giving him my fresh baked pies or cakes, not to mention the master's best brandy. I'd have spoken if I didn't know as Quin had the master's ear. No use telling the mistress neither, for Mr Scalloway wouldn't pay her no mind." She drank from her cup, set it down and sniffed. "I shouldn't say it, but I can't help but think it. Good riddance! And if Doro had done it, I wouldn't blame her one jot."

Hemp warmed to her, treasuring up the tidbits of information. "She didn't do it, that much I can tell you with confidence. Do you happen to know the name of the man Quin brought here?"

Peg wrinkled her nose, her hands cupped around the vessel. "Not as I remember it full. Muddy? Maudy? Summat like it."

"Mawdesley?"

Peg brightened. "Aye, that'd be it."

"Excellent. That is just who I wanted to ask Quin about."

Peg set aside her cup and rose. "Well, you take care, Mr Roy. A cunning one is our Quin. Out for hisself." Upon which, she moved back to her pots, taking up a wooden spoon. Just in time as it transpired, for the footman walked in on the back of her words, Quin on his heels. The latter greeted Hemp with a surly frown.

"Back again, are you? Don't know what you hope to get by coming here day after day. The mistress ain't best pleased you brought that ladyship of yourn here."

Before Hemp could respond, the footman cut in. "You get along on your errand, Quin. The mistress won't wait all day for those buttons."

Quin snorted. "Buttons! That's for Jenny to buy, not me."

"Jenny's too busy serving the mistress now we've not got Doro. Get along, do."

Hemp rose as Quin made reluctantly for the door. "I will accompany you."

The fellow paused, the doorknob in hand. He threw an insolent look up and down Hemp's tall person. "Can't stop you, can I? But if you're snooping again, I'm mum."

He slipped out and Hemp paused only to thank Peg. He glanced at the footman. "We've not met before."

"Saul. I know who you are. Wish you luck, friend. I liked Doro."

Hemp nodded. "I hope to restore her to the household very soon."

He then left and made his way up the area steps, where he paused, looking both ways for Quin. He caught sight of the wiry little figure just as he turned the corner into Park Street. The harbour again? Hemp set off in pursuit.

It did not take him long to overtake the man. Quin threw up one scorching glance and then put his head down and walked doggedly on in silence, much as Doro had done on that day that now seemed far off. Hemp reflected that even the brief encounter in the gaol when he'd changed her situation had altered his concept of their meeting in this way. Perhaps milady was right and there might be a future? But not, he reminded himself, if he did not do his part to procure her release and vindication.

He set a hand to Quin's shoulder, forcibly bringing him to a halt. Ignoring the man's glare, he kept hold. "It's of no use to try and avoid me, Quin. You have information I need."

The fellow stared up at him, expressionless. "Have I now?"

Hemp suppressed a sigh. "We can have this out here in the open street. Or we can repair to a tavern at my expense. You choose."

A grin dawned. "I'd not say no to a jug of something warming."

"I thought as much. You know the town. Where to? Not the Pyg & Whistle. Somewhere quieter."

Quin led the way, veering off Park Street before they reached the harbour and fetching up at the Hatchet Inn in Frogmore Street. Hemp had heard of the place, which was likely only a degree less disreputable than the Pyg & Whistle. It was less quiet than he might have hoped, but when he had procured a jug of ale, he was able to appropriate a settle in a corner away from a couple of elderly men with pipes, who had the look of old seafaring dogs, a not uncommon phenomenon in this City. He obliged Quin to get in first and sat down, his bulk effectively blocking any possibility of escape.

Quin accepted his ration, downed several gulps, set it on the table conveniently situated in front of the bench, and sat back, regarding Hemp with a gleam in his eye. "Haunted is this place, did yer know?"

"I did not." Nor had he any belief in the supernatural, but he did not think it worth his while to mention it.

"Want to hear the legend?"

Hemp sighed. "I see that you wish to tell me."

Quin leaned in a little, lowering his voice. "'Tis said as under the paint and tar on that there front door, there's a layer of human skin." He sat back, a challenge in his gaze. "What do yer think of that, eh?"

"If I told you, I dare say we would fall into dispute."

"Don't believe it, then? And you from the West Indies? I'll wager it'd make Doro shudder a bit, what with her witch doctoring an' all."

Hemp lost patience. "Enough! I did not bring you here to listen to nonsensical tales."

Quin blew out his cheeks. "No pleasing you, is there?" He jerked up his chin. "What's the story then, friend of Doro?"

At last. Let them waste no more time. "Mawdesley." Quin gave no sign, merely waiting. Hemp pursued it. "You know him, Quin, and I need to know what was his business with Mr Scalloway."

Quin snorted. "Not so well informed, eh, friend? Mawdesley didn't have no business with the master. He were a go-between is all."

"Between Scalloway and Mr Harbury?"

Surprise flickered in the shifty eyes and was quickly veiled. "What d'you know of him?"

"Harbury? In shipping and merchandising, is he not?"

Another snort. "You know so much, what do you want with me?"

Hemp brought his hand down flat on the table, making Quin's tankard judder. He was glad to see the fellow flinch. "Details, Quin. Don't pretend you don't know all about it. I have your measure. I saw you take a message from your master the day of his death. Was it to Harbury?"

The other raised his chin in a defiant gesture. "What if it were?"

"Was this Harbury involved in the shipping venture? Is that how your master came to be in debt to him?"

"In debt? They was partners. Harbury had ought to have taken the loss just as the master did. Only he had that there Mr Ackworth after the master, arsting him to come down with the Derbies."

Now they were getting somewhere. "Ackworth is Harbury's lawyer?"

"Not as I know. Seems to act for all sorts. All I know is my master put his share in and if that dang ship hadn't sunk and lost 'em all the merchandise, he'd have been rich, and me too."

"You?" Hemp eyed him. "How could you benefit?"

A discontented expression entered Quin's face. "Master said he'd see me right, long as I kept me mouth shut." He then dipped his head, seized his tankard and dived into it, gulping noisily. But his expression had given him away. Clearly he had said more than he ought.

Hemp put a hand about the man's arm and forcibly brought the tankard down, keeping an iron grip. "Keep your mouth shut about what?"

Quin squirmed in his hold. "Nowt."

"Don't try me too far, man. Talk."

"Let go!"

"And have you make your escape? Talk, I said." Hemp twisted his hand as he spoke and a yelp escaped his victim.

"Hey! No need of that."

Hemp did not speak, but kept the pressure on his wrist.

"All right, all right." Quin looked away, hesitating, and then back again. "Well, see, it were like this. Ship were master's part and the cargo were Harbury's part, got on behalf of my master, for as he'd agreed ter pay it back after sale. When the ship went down, Master tells Harbury he'll get it off the mistress. Only

Ackworth says in law they was partners so as both has to take the loss, so master say he won't pay after all. But Harbury won't have none o' that for as he blames master, don't he? Said he got proof and all, and Ackworth turned agin master. Master then says Harbury will have to wait 'til mistress's pa dies 'cos he'll get his hands on it then."

It all began to make sense, assuming this was the truth. Or even what Quin had clammed up on. He had told it glibly, but what was there in this history to keep silent about? Hemp pursued it nevertheless. "Was Harbury making threats against Scalloway?"

But Quin had shot his bolt. He turned surly. "Told you all I know."

"Have you? Are you certain there is no other matter you have failed to mention?"

Quin threw him a glare. "You going to let go my arm?"

If there was more, it was not forthcoming. "After you tell me where I may find Mawdesley."

Quin let out an exaggerated sigh and named both street and number. Hemp released him and the fellow rubbed his wrist, looking decidedly aggrieved. "Weren't no need of that, mister. I'm a peaceable man."

Hemp eyed him. "You are also a remarkably cool man, for one who claims to have lost an advantage. With your master dead, who is going to see you right, as you put it?"

Quin shrugged. "Lightly come, lightly go."

"You do not seem overly dismayed by Scalloway's death."

"Allus another way to travel, friend of Doro." He grabbed his tankard and drained it, setting it down with a thump. "Now, if yer lordship is finished with me, p'raps you'll let me go and get them buttons."

Hemp rose to let him through and watched the fellow scuttle out, still dissatisfied. What had Quin almost said? It was plain he would not budge on the matter. He reviewed what had been revealed and decided he had enough to be going on with. He could go after Mawdesley himself. The other two he'd best leave to milord.

"Hemp took it well, I thought." Lord Francis held the chair for his wife and pushed it in as she sat down to dine.

"I wish you will send at once to Mr Belchamp, Fan. This intelligence Hemp has come by through Quin must change his mind, do you not think?"

"No, I don't." Francis took his own seat and flourished a napkin onto his lap, looking over the viands on offer. He lifted a silver cover, hunting for meat. "Is there no beef today?"

"The landlady said there was a good catch of fresh fish, so I ordered that." Tillie uncovered a dish of fried fillets which looked decidedly unappetising to his yawning stomach. "Must you have beef, Fan?"

"I suppose I can endure one day without, but I like beef. What else is under there?" He stood to reach for a third cover and stared with loathing at half a roasted chicken. "Dear Lord, Tillie, chicken and fish?"

His wife handed him the carving knife. "You may give me several slices. As to the combination, I have a yen for both. Do you object?"

"Mightily." Francis laid aside the cover, took up the knife and set to his carving. "A yen? You, my bird-pecking one?" He paused in his task as Tillie began to serve herself with pieces of fried fish. "You are having them together? What in the world ails you?"

She showed him a surprised face. "I am hungry. You should be glad of that."

Francis shook his head and went on carving. "Each to his own. You want me to put this chicken on your plate now?"

"Yes, if you please."

He did so, marvelling. Having served himself with a good plateful of the chicken, he hunted about for pickled vegetables or some other side dish by way of relish, and instead spied a crusty pie. "Aha, that is more like it."

Tillie, already forking chicken into her mouth, looked up as he took up a knife and sliced into the pie. "Oh, give me a sliver of that too, Fan."

Francis complied, laughing. "I hope you won't end by being sick after all this."

She did not answer, intent now upon the fish. Francis watched in fascination as his darling wife cut a chunk of fish, larded her fork with chicken on top and shovelled both into her mouth. He was tempted to tease, but it was too heartening to see her eat well for once. Was it the resumption of hunting for a killer that had stimulated her appetite? Or, no. She had been disturbed for months over Pretty. His capitulation, however unexpected, had eased her anxiety. This might be as good an explanation as any, but it slipped out of mind as Tillie resumed discussing the case while she ate.

"Why don't you think Mr Belchamp will accept the introduction of the debt to Harbury? This whole shipping affair sounds shady, do you not think? Even Elinor Scalloway said so. Is it not enough to allow Doro to go free?"

He swallowed his portion, enjoying the pie at least, before giving an answer. "I think you may have a better chance with Belchamp once we have spoken to the gentlemen involved."

"A not unexpected turn, I must say, to find there was a debt. We need to find out more about this shipping venture."

"I agree. From what Hemp says, I am not inclined to trust this fellow Quin to be telling the truth."

"What do you say of this Ackworth, Fan? Respectable, do you think?"

Francis took a sip of wine. "According to Pymoor."

"Ah, the landlord at the Pyg & Whistle. Yes, I should much like to talk to the girl. Cherry, was it?"

Francis groaned. "I suppose you will have your way. Mama would not approve."

His wife gave the gurgling laugh he loved. "Since when did Sybilla ever approve of my activities?"

In fact, as Francis well knew, however much his mother might deprecate Tillie's tendency to beard all and sundry if it suited her, the Dowager Marchioness of Polbrook doted on her daughter-in-law and was secretly proud of her achievements. Not that she would admit as much. "Very well then, you take Cherry. But don't go there without me. After that, I had best tackle Harbury and Ackworth, I suppose."

His wife paused, her fork in the air. Francis eyed her. Had she fallen into one of her reveries? They were apt to overtake her when she was involved in one of these affairs. He waited, polishing off the remainder of his meal. As he sat back with a contented sigh, his wife spoke, still staring at the fork.

"I believe it may profit me to try Lord Radcliffe first tomorrow. His wife has likely poisoned his mind against me, but that can't be helped. I can go there on my own."

"Well, wait for me before going on to the tavern."

She blew out a breath. "To tell you the truth, Fan, I am a deal more fatigued than I thought after today's exertions. I shall leave Cherry for another day, I think." She became brisk all at once, digging into the remaining fish on her plate. "I believe the chicken was a mistake."

Francis snorted. "I could have told you that. Not feeling sick, are you?"

Tillie smiled at him. "Oh, no. I prefer the fish, but I wish I had thought of asking for fried sausages."

Francis snorted his disgust. "Now you are being absurd, woman."

"Not at all. But rest assured I will insist upon your beef for the morrow. I might have bacon for breakfast."

"You never eat bacon."

"Don't I? Well, I think I may start."

Francis took up his glass. "You've run mad. And we have barely begun with this business. It can't have addled your brain so quickly. Take care you don't scare Mrs Bertram silly when we go home."

Tillie clicked her tongue. "I cannot think why you are making such a fuss. You are always complaining of my poor appetite."

"Yes, well, true. But there are limits, my dear one. Sausages!" He got nothing by that but an enigmatic stare and sighed. "What do you want with Radcliffe?"

"Oh, I suspect he knows all there is to know of Scalloway's venture. Assuming he will deign to talk to me."

# CHAPTER THIRTEEN

Left to kick her heels in a spacious downstairs saloon in the Radcliffe establishment in Queen Square at a respectable hour on Friday morning, Ottilia grew impatient. An austere butler had shown her into the room, after having attempted to take her card up to Lady Radcliffe instead of the master of the house.

"I thank you, but it is Lord Radcliffe I wish to see. Pray ask him to grant me a moment of his time."

"I believe his lordship is occupied, my lady, but I will ascertain." He had opened a door to one side of the wide hall. "Perhaps you would care to wait in here?"

Ottilia had perforce to acquiesce. She had no intention of attempting to speak to Lady Radcliffe, whose opinion of her was tainted. It was to be hoped she had not poisoned her lord's mind against Ottilia already. She was glad of a good fire in the hearth in the marbled fireplace and moved across, holding her gloved hands to the blaze. The walk from the Ship to Queen Square had been thankfully short, the roadway and buildings glazed with a crackling frost that made the cold bite even through the laced short boots and the woollen cloak.

The butler did not return as the minutes ticked by on the case clock on the mantel. As she grew warmer, the wait became too long to be borne. Ottilia shrugged her cloak open and went to the door, stepping out onto the sunlit wood-patterned floor. What to do? She could hardly go hunting for her quarry. She toyed with the notion of opening the front door and ringing the bell for the purpose of summoning the butler back. Whether that would bring her any nearer to her goal was debatable. Had he even disturbed the wretched man to pass on her message? That he had not returned with one for her indicated otherwise.

She wandered out into the hall and headed towards the stairs. About to mount them, her attention was caught by a raised voice in the near vicinity. Turning this way and that, Ottilia sought for its source.

Someone was exceedingly put out. As she followed the sound, it grew louder and was found to be emanating from behind a closed door to the back of the hall within the confines of a small vestibule from which a stairway led down to the lower reaches of the house. Without hesitation, Ottilia crossed to the door and set her ear as close to the woodwork as she could for the brim of her tall-crowned and beribboned hat. The voice came through loud and clear.

"Dun me as much as you choose, it will avail you nothing." A murmured response was inaudible before the voice continued, "Executor? Of course I am an executor. Damnation, man, you're a lawyer! You know as well as I naught can be done before probate is granted."

Ottilia's heart gave a little fillip. Did this concern Scalloway's estate? She pressed her ear closer and was just able to hear what the other man said though he spoke quietly.

"Yet you know as well as I, my lord, that probate is immaterial. Mrs Scalloway's fortune is in no way subject to her husband's estate."

"Irrelevant, Ackworth." Ottilia fairly leapt with excitement. Ackworth here? How fortunate!

"How irrelevant? The liability —"

"That liability has no bearing upon my role as trustee. What is more —"

A throat being loudly cleared directly behind her distracted Ottilia's attention. She came away from the door to find the butler regarding her with an expression faintly pained. She took a high hand. "Ah, there you are. You did not ask him, did you?"

The man emitted one of those butlerian coughs, putting the back of his hand at his mouth. "His lordship, my lady, did not wish to be disturbed."

"Then you should have said so in the first place instead of leaving me standing about in that saloon." With which, she turned sharply about and delivered a rapid series of knocks to the door.

"My lady, I beg of you!"

Ottilia ignored him as the voices within the room ceased, immediately followed by a bellow.

"I told you I did not wish to be disturbed!"

"There, my lady. Did I not —?"

But Ottilia was not to be deterred. Grasping the handle, she turned it and pushed open the door, striding into what proved to be a well-stocked library. Two men were standing in front of a large desk that dominated the room at one end, warmed by a marbled fireplace which boasted bookshelves to either side.

A tall man of commanding aspect, whom Ottilia took to be Lord Radcliffe, strode forward, his annoyance at the interruption visible enough without his tone. "What the devil does this mean, Stowe? How dare you, madam, march in without so much as a by your leave?"

Before Ottilia could respond, the butler, who had sidled in and moved ahead of her, took a hand. "I beg your lordship's pardon. I told her ladyship you were occupied, but —"

"But I came in regardless," said Ottilia, moving to confront the man. "I am Lady Francis Fanshawe, my lord. How do you do?"

She held out a hand. Radcliffe looked from it to her and Ottilia saw recognition hit. "Fanshawe?"

"Yes, my lord. I made the acquaintance of your wife at Mrs Scalloway's home."

His face changed. "I am aware. That does not explain what gives you the right to barge into my library while I am engaged."

Ottilia tried for a soft note. "Well, that is why, you see. When I heard you were speaking to Mr Ackworth here —"

"Heard?" His lordship's already high colour deepened, almost mirroring the deep red waistcoat he wore beneath a blue frock-coat. "You were eavesdropping?"

Ottilia smiled. "But in a very good cause. I came to have speech with you, but the fortunate circumstance of Mr Ackworth being with you was an opportunity not to be lost."

It was plain Lord Radcliffe did not know whether to be angry or nonplussed. Ottilia turned her attention to the lawyer. "Mr Ackworth, well met. Just the man I need."

The other, an individual with a spare frame and an intelligent gaze, his head dressed with a moderate brown tie-wig, gave a deferential bow. "How may I serve you, my lady?"

"What? What?" Lord Radcliffe shifted back to the fray. "This is not to be borne. I will not be bearded in my own library. Lady Francis, I must request you —"

Ottilia threw up a hand. "Pray don't, sir. You will be wasting your time. I am on a mission, you must know, to save an innocent woman from the false accusation of murdering Mr Scalloway."

"Yes, I know all about that, but —"

"Then you will forgive me if I pursue enquiries which are a great deal more urgent than the business upon which you were lately engaged."

"More urgent? Who are you to —?"

Ottilia rode over him. "Although I am bound to state that your discussion with Mr Ackworth is of great relevance to my enquiry."

She then again smiled sweetly at the fulminating peer and waited for his capitulation. It came, as she knew it must. He could not be unaware of her husband's status and the instincts of his breeding were bound to come to the fore. She was after all a lady.

"Oh, very well, very well. Stowe, set a chair for her ladyship and then you may leave us."

Ottilia settled herself into a straight-backed chair with a leather seat which the butler brought to a convenient position, while Radcliffe stalked behind his desk and threw his large frame into the solid chair set there for the purpose. Mr Ackworth remained standing, shifting a little to one side of the desk. Ottilia waited for the butler to leave the room, but Radcliffe forestalled what she might have said.

"Well, ma'am, well? What do you want with Ackworth?"

Ottilia eyed the lawyer, taking in the quiet propriety of his attire, a snuff-coloured suit all of a piece, eminently suited to his calling. "I understand you acted for Mr Scalloway and Mr Harbury in the matter of their shipping venture. Have I that correctly?"

Ackworth bowed again. "I drew up the contracts, yes, my lady."

"And after the failure of the venture, you acted for Harbury against Scalloway?"

"That is so, my lady."

Radcliffe butted in. "Ha! Acted? He's still acting for the fellow. Come to batten upon me now that scoundrel is dead."

Ackworth turned to him. "It was never my desire to pursue the matter beyond that event, my lord, but my principal insists and I am pledged to serve him."

"Was insurance not taken out?" Ottilia asked, cutting in before Radcliffe could answer in a manner that promised to inflame the discussion.

"That was in the remit of the shipper, my lady."

"Scalloway himself. I take it he failed to take it out?"

"Indeed. Neither was it the only corner he cut. He employed a captain of dubious reputation and experience, added to which the vessel was undermanned."

Radcliffe burst out again. "That fool! Typical of the fellow. I had his measure from the first. I warned Carey but he would not listen. Just like that scoundrel to employ a fellow with as little moral fibre as he had himself."

Ottilia regarded him with interest. "Mr Carey is Elinor's father, is he not? The sugar baron?"

His countenance registered astonishment. "How, pray, do you come to know so much?"

Ottilia maintained a bland front. "From my steward. He was born and bred on Barbados. He knew of Carey and he also knew Scalloway. He it was who discovered that Dorote Gabon, a friend of his of old, had been accused of this murder, and he sent for me."

Now both Ackworth and Radcliffe looked utterly taken aback. The former recovered first.

"Sent for you, my lady?"

Radcliffe snorted. "Some tale of Lady Francis having solved other such killings. Not that I believe it for an instant."

Ottilia looked him in the eye. "Well, if you choose you may enquire of the justice, Mr Belchamp. He will verify it."

"Ha! He will, will he? His assurances notwithstanding, should he make them, I should like to know what you mean by implying that Elinor might herself be guilty of slaying her own husband."

A laugh escaped Ottilia. "You have that, have you? If it comforts you, I don't think she did so any more than Dorote. However, there can be no denying she had a reason far more pertinent than had the slave girl." Radcliffe's features began to suffuse again and she threw up a hand. "Pray don't rip up at me, sir, for I am sure you know as well as I why that should be."

Radcliffe humphed a little, but did not venture upon a retort. Satisfied, Ottilia turned again to the lawyer. "I believe, Mr Ackworth, that you once or twice met with Mr Scalloway at the Pyg & Whistle?"

The man's lips twisted with unmistakeable disgust. "Unavoidable, my lady. He was assiduous in finding ways to evade my requests for a meeting, so that I was obliged to run him to earth where he was most likely to be."

"Did you see him on the night he died?"

"I had not seen him for several days. The last time we met, he assured me he was in a way to raise the necessary funds."

"How, did he say?"

The lawyer's lip curled and he glanced at Radcliffe before answering. "He made no bones about revealing his wife's substantial inheritance. He did not precisely say this was his intended source, but the hint was clear."

Lord Radcliffe cut in again. "Ha! That's what brought you battening upon me, is it?"

"Mr Scalloway told me you are his wife's trustee, my lord, yes." Ackworth made a deprecating face. "I suspect even then he had it in mind that I might grow weary and apply to you." He turned again to Ottilia. "It pains me to say this, my lady, but perhaps it may be relevant to your enquiry."

"What is it, Mr Ackworth?"

"According to Harbury, Scalloway never had the slightest intention of repaying him for his loss of the merchandise. It was his contention that Harbury was responsible for the goods since he had acquired the ship — with, I may add, his wife's generous gift, for he had nothing of his own."

"You don't have to tell me," burst from Radcliffe. "Elinor begged me to advance the sum, purely in hopes it would make the wretched fellow leave her in peace. I wish I had not yielded. I knew in my bones any venture of Scalloway's must fail."

"Be that as it may, my lord," pursued Ackworth, "it is plain, for the purposes of Lady Francis's enquiry, that Harbury believed it was Scalloway's duty to take out insurance and therefore he owed him compensation. An arguable legal point, but not conclusive. Harbury, however, being a canny individual, had refused to purchase the goods without a promissory note from Scalloway to repay his costs, in the event the insurance proved insufficient to cover them should any accident befall."

"Which we see it did. Without insurance of any kind."

"As you say, my lady. Without that document, I most certainly would not have agreed to act."

Ottilia's mind had been working during this interchange and she entered a caveat. "Except, sir, that I do not see how it might profit Mr Harbury to be rid of the only hope he had of recovering his dues."

Lord Radcliffe at once took it up. "Ha! No difficulty there. Revenge, what else?"

"An empty revenge, sir, if it left him the loser by what I must suppose to be a considerable sum." A thought occurred and she put up a finger. "Unless…" Her mind flying, she fell silent and was only recalled by the lawyer's voice.

"Unless what, my lady?"

Ottilia bypassed the question. "How is it you are looking to recover this debt via Mrs Scalloway's trustee? Is it not the case that a widow cannot be held responsible for her husband's debts?"

Radcliffe snorted. "Have I not been telling this obstinate fellow the exact same thing?"

Ackworth sighed. "Very true, my lord, that is the Law. Unfortunately, by what means I know not, Mrs Scalloway was also induced to sign this promissory note."

"Nonsense! Elinor would never sign such a thing. It is a forgery!"

Ottilia put up a finger. "She might, if her husband pestered her to do so and did not give her an opportunity to read it properly." She made a mental note to discover the truth from Elinor.

Having no notion of the likely whereabouts of the Harbury fellow, Francis opted to accompany Hemp on the visit to Mawdesley. "We'll get Harbury's address from him and then I'll leave you to it. I dare say my presence may inhibit your questioning."

"Or it might aid it, milord."

"Well, we shall see. Which way?"

He had urged Hemp to guide their steps, being better acquainted with the town. Both well wrapped up in hats and great-coats, they crossed Bristol Bridge and arrived at a junction. Hemp, who had added a muffler to his attire, gestured towards an alley a little way along one lane. "Down there, milord. We may cross through to Temple Street."

The way led by a circuitous route into an area which, though largely deserted at this hour, was clearly given over to habitations of the poorer sort from the narrower lanes, the dwellings packed tightly together, ill-kept and unswept roads and a liberal stench of ordure despite the dusting of frost over all.

Francis wrinkled his nose. "Not the most salubrious location."

"No, milord. Bristol is a little like London in this respect. One might fancy oneself in another town altogether within a street or two. Or Weymouth also."

Curiosity prompted a question. "How did you fare on your visit, by the by?"

Hemp flashed a smile. "I like the town and it was pleasant to meet with acquaintances. I had hoped to convey your greetings to Colonel Tretower, but he was away on an inspection down the coast, and his lady went with him. But I met with his lieutenant and the boy."

"Ah, our key witness. He's still with the army, then?"

"And shaping well. He has grown a good deal." Hemp gave an indulgent laugh. "Very proud of his musket he is, though Lieutenant Sullivan assured me he is not permitted to use it. Sergeant Puckeridge seems to have adopted the boy more or less."

Memories of the extraordinary affair at Weymouth came flooding into Francis's head. "No theatre company at this season, I must suppose."

"No, but I hear they continue to visit and there are new performers now."

"Much needed after that debacle." Hemp had slowed his pace, checking numbers on the houses in an alley off Pipe Lane. "Are we here at last?"

"This one, milord." Hemp moved to a door and lifted the knocker, sounding a loud rat-tat.

After an interval, a shuffling sound came from within and the door was opened by an ancient with rheumy eyes and straggling wisps of grey hair. He peered up at the visitors. "Aye?"

"Is Mr Mawdesley within?"

The old man jerked his head. "Upstairs."

With which, he left the door ajar and shuffled off down a narrow corridor. Hemp stood back. "Milord?"

"You go ahead." Francis followed him in and shut the door behind him, turning in time to see the ancient disappear through a doorway at the end of the passage as Hemp began to climb the stairs. Suppressing a strong desire to be elsewhere, Francis followed suit. There were two doors at the top and Hemp knocked on both. The upper vestibule was too narrow to accommodate two men at once and Francis waited on the stairs. A door to one side opened an inch or so and an eye in a partial face showed in the aperture.

"Yes?"

"Mawdesley?"

"Who wants to know?"

"I do. Open the door."

Amusement at Hemp's blunt methods rose in Francis and he watched with interest to see how the quarry reacted. The order was not immediately obeyed.

"Who are you, then?"

Hemp's authoritarian tone did not abate. "I feel sure your friend Quin has not only informed you, but I don't doubt he told you to expect a visit from me. Open the door."

Mawdesley, assuming it was indeed he, opened a fraction more and looked past him, catching Francis's eye. "Who's this?"

Francis took a hand. "We will leave the introductions until we are within. Now do as my steward says and open that door."

The door creaked half open. "You can't come in."

Impatience got the better of Francis. "If he won't let us in, Hemp, pull him out instead."

This had the desired effect. Mawdesley removed himself from the doorway and vanished into the darkness beyond. Hemp pushed the door open and went in. Francis followed and nearly recoiled at the stale smell emanating from the chamber. "For pity's sake! Can't you even open a window, man?"

Hemp strode to the front of the room and yanking aside the curtains, threw up the sash. A gust of cold air blew in and light splashed across the small room, revealing a narrow cot bed, unmade, a washstand and dresser piled with clothing, and a small table covered higgledy-piggledy with impedimenta which equally cluttered the floor, thrown all anyhow against the walls. An untidy creature, this Mawdesley, Francis reflected. He stood blinking in the sudden brightness, in shirtsleeves and a nightcap over a bald pate. He was clearly unmarried, as evidenced by a couple of missing buttons on his waistcoat, dirty linen and a soiled neck-cloth.

Hemp was looking about in evident disgust, as well he might. He was fastidious in his own person. Francis had only once seen him in dishabille and he was otherwise always well turned out.

There was nowhere one cared to sit, so Francis settled in the least obnoxious place he could find, folded his arms and waited for Hemp to open negotiations. This was his arena.

Mawdesley regained command of himself. "What you do that for? It's freezing." He moved towards the window, but Hemp forestalled him.

"Leave it. The place needs a thorough airing."

Looking aggrieved, Mawdesley instead dragged off his nightcap, rummaged among the debris on the table, found a scratch wig and shoved it on his head. Then he picked up a coat from the end of the bed and shrugged it on, turning at last to face his unwelcome visitors. "What do you want, then?"

Hemp shifted his stance, relaxing a trifle. "First, where may his lordship find your employer Harbury?"

The fellow cast a startled glance at Francis. "Lordship?"

"He is Lord Francis Fanshawe and he is investigating the death of Mr Scalloway."

Not strictly true, but Francis let it pass. This weasel would never fathom his darling wife's role in this.

Mawdesley backed a step. "I never had nowt to do with that."

Francis's attention snapped in. Why say so? None had as yet accused him. "But you saw Scalloway the night he died, did you not? At the Pyg & Whistle."

The weasel turned surly. "What if I did? Master was danged afire with him and sent me to find him."

Hemp jumped on this. "Why was he afire with Scalloway?"

"'Cos Scalloway owed him. They was partners. Nor it weren't master's fault as the ship was drownded. It were

Scalloway as hired that ruffian. Capting, he calls hisself. More a pirate for all of me."

"Did the captain survive?"

"Got picked up by a couple of fishing boats off the Scillies. Him and a handful of his sailors. Rest of them went down to Davy Jones's locker. That's how come we heard how he steered the ship into that there reef as has done for all manner of ships. Said they watched the *Blackbird* sinking as they climbed into the boats."

Hemp turned and Francis read frowning question in his face. Was he struck by the same thought? Sabotage? Could the rescue boats have been manned by a wrecking crew? That might put a whole different complexion on the matter.

He beckoned Hemp across and lowered his voice. "Are you thinking what I'm thinking?"

"That this was no accident, milord? It is certainly suspicious. This was a favourite trick of certain rogues in the West Indies, even to luring ships in with lights judiciously placed."

"But what would it profit Scalloway to arrange it?"

Hemp frowned. "That had not occurred to me. It might account for a revenge killing if Harbury believed he had done so. Or Scalloway might indeed have planned it with the object of securing the insurance."

"Far-fetched, Hemp. Besides, he omitted to take out insurance and we know he supposed that investing in the ship would make his fortune."

Francis was intrigued to see how Hemp's lip curled with disdain and his tone roughened. "Of that devil, I would believe anything. He has no sense of right and wrong."

At this point, Francis noted the rabbit Mawdesley creeping closer as if he sought to hear better. He jerked his head towards the fellow and waved a silencing finger before his mouth.

Hemp whirled on the man. "Your master wanted Scalloway dead, didn't he?"

Mawdesley jumped back. "He didn't never!"

Was it horror or plain fear in his features? Not for the first time, Francis wished for Tillie's skill at reading nuance in a face or voice.

Hemp pursued it. "He believed Scalloway paid this captain to sink the ship, isn't that right?"

"No! No, it weren't like that!"

"What then was it like? Why didn't Harbury go after the captain, eh? Why put the blame on Scalloway?"

Mawdesley backed again, throwing his hands palm up as if to ward Hemp off. "Acos that there Capting Indigo ain't got none of the ready, has he? Whereas —"

"Indigo?" Hemp's expression altered. "That's excessively interesting, Mawdesley. None of the ready? I'll wager the fellow has those goods stashed somewhere. I'll wager he's finding buyers among his acquaintance in the thieving world at this precise moment."

Francis experienced a flicker of admiration. He might suggest Hemp took up the law instead of running a boarding house. He had the gift of driving a witness in the way of the prosecutors in court, it would seem.

Proving the truth of this, a grubby hand came up and rubbed at the little fellow's face in a frustrated fashion, dislodging the wig which was already askew. "You're mixing me up, mister. It were never nowt of that. Them goods is in the sea, gorn. Only Mr Harbury, he wants his dues, fer as he got them goods, bought and paid."

Hemp proved relentless. "How did he expect Scalloway to pay his dues? The man was all but penniless."

"*He* were. Only his missus were plump in the pocket, master says. I dunno."

"Your master must also know that Mrs Scalloway refused to pay her husband a single penny."

Mawdesley let out a mocking snort. "Well, she'll have to now, master says. Dead, ain't he?"

Francis ran the fellow Harbury to earth in a small chamber above a chandler's shop in Guinea Street, a few streets away from Pipe Lane, in an area populated with warehouses and other shops dedicated to the shipping trade. Mawdesley had alleged he used the place for an office from which to conduct his business affairs. The plaque on the door proclaimed his calling, such as it was: Thos. Harbury, Agent. Agent for what? Francis knocked and a voice from within bade him enter.

On opening the door, he spied a clerkly-looking man seated behind a desk which occupied almost half of the little room. The fellow wore a short wig with a small pigtail and was neatly clothed in a plum-coloured coat with a neckcloth tied in a plain knot. He rose upon seeing Francis, surprise in features unremarkable save for a longish nose perhaps accentuated by the spectacles perched upon it. He was not young, but Francis judged that he had not yet attained his middle years. His voice was respectful and quiet.

"Sir? May I help you?"

Could this fellow truly employ such a dubious tool as the rabbit Mawdesley? Francis wasted no time. "You are, I believe, the same Harbury who had dealings with the late Marcus Scalloway?"

The fellow's face changed. He looked both taken aback and wary. "May I have the honour of knowing to whom I speak?"

Excellent. The man had taken in the status of his visitor. "I am Lord Francis Fanshawe."

A small bow was proffered. "My lord."

No protest yet. Then let him hear what was afoot. "You may be interested to learn that I know about your dealings with Scalloway, and that you were — incensed, shall we say? — with Scalloway when he refused to pay you for the goods lost at sea."

Harbury continued wary but gave no sign. Francis waited. At length, the man dropped his gaze. "May I ask how it comes about that you interest yourself in these matters, my lord?"

"Certainly. I am acting on behalf of Scalloway's slave girl, who is accused of his murder."

That brought Harbury's head up. "What, my lord, has that to do with me?"

Now they would see. "I believe her to be innocent."

A quick frown. "How so? She was found with the dagger in her hand. Her own dagger, so I have heard."

"That is so. However, she had in fact merely drawn the dagger out. Scalloway died many hours before Dorote Gabon went near his chamber."

The frown persisted. "I still do not understand what should bring you to me, my lord."

Was he bluffing? He had not jumped to the obvious conclusion. He would not, if he was wholly innocent. Francis tried a pointed dart. "It strikes me as possible that Scalloway might be of more use to you dead than alive."

For a moment Harbury stared at him and for the second time that day, Francis wished for his wife's peculiar insight. Then a faint smile lightened the frown at last.

"I suggest, my lord, you would find it exceptionally difficult to make stick such a charge as you imply. For one thing, I was nowhere near the tavern where Scalloway met his end."

"On that night? Did you ever seek Scalloway there? I understand it was his favoured haunt."

Harbury shrugged, looking pained. "Not unless I was obliged to go there."

"Were you so obliged?"

"Occasionally."

"At any time before the murder?"

The man pondered, his eyes upon the opposite wall. Francis waited, unsure whether this was an act or Harbury was indeed casting his mind back. At length he returned his gaze to his interlocutor and gave a faint smile.

"Yes. I did seek the man there. A day or two before he met his unfortunate end, I believe. Scalloway proved as recalcitrant as ever. I resolved to leave Ackworth to settle the business, one way or another."

What did that mean? Perhaps he now sought to point a finger at the lawyer. Francis pushed. "Very well, you were not there on the fatal night. But your somewhat disreputable tool, for want of a better term, was indeed present at the Pyg & Whistle. I speak of Mawdesley, as I am sure you realise."

The brows rose and Harbury removed his spectacles. "Merely because I pay that fellow to run an errand or two for me in no way proves I employed him to rid the world of Scalloway on my behalf. Not, I must confess, my lord, that his taking off is in any way a grief to me."

Francis curled his own lip. "I had gathered as much from Mawdesley's discourse. He said specifically, if memory serves, that you were afire for Scalloway."

Harbury replaced his spectacles. "I was indeed put out when he refused to entertain responsibility for this disaster, despite having given me an undertaking to redress my losses in such an eventuality at the outset. A decision he made, I believe, upon hearing that his wife intended to leave him. Such was the message conveyed to me by his man. You may see the note if you wish." He shifted back and opened a drawer in his desk, hunting within. He brought out a slip of paper and passed it across.

Francis read aloud the succinct but telling message it contained: "*H — I am undone and can do nothing. Elinor means to desert me, aided by the Radcliffe ménage. You know my situation. Believe I tried. I plan to return to Barbados by the first passage I can secure. S.*" He looked up from the letter, surveying its recipient. "You are pretty cool, sir, for a man who has no hope of recovering severe losses."

A smile Francis could only describe as smug crossed the man's lips.

"I was far from cool at the time, I assure you, my lord. Scalloway's murderer, whether the slave girl or some other, has done me a favour. As I have stated, I set my lawyer to retrieve the needed funds. I have nothing further to do in the matter."

If this was his temper, Francis could believe him cold-hearted enough to have arranged for Scalloway's death. He evidently had no slightest sense of responsibility in the business.

"I take leave to tell you, Harbury, that it is plain you are as callous and feckless as your dead colleague."

The smile persisted. "I take it you were not acquainted with Scalloway. Moreover, I would hesitate to call him a colleague."

"You were partners."

"A business association merely. I undertook to provide him with the merchandise if he procured the means of shipping it out to the Indies. It is not the first such agreement I have made."

"That is your business, is it? Providing the goods to be shipped?"

"I have it in my power to supply such, yes. My deals are with the merchants."

A thought occurred and Francis voiced it. "You had not paid them, had you?"

Harbury raised his brows, still remarkably cool. Would nothing put him out of countenance? "That is between myself and my associates, my lord." At last a sliver of emotion showed in a tightened jaw. "I admit to an error of judgement in this instance. I took necessary precautions since I'd had no previous dealings with Scalloway. Had I known him better, I would not have entered into the agreement at all."

He fell silent and Francis mentally ran over all he had disclosed and the conclusion was obvious. "All this, sir, has no bearing upon the circumstances into which I am enquiring. The fact remains that the individual who runs your errands was at the tavern that night, and you have admitted that you expect to benefit despite Scalloway's death. Even because of it?"

The bland look returned. Was it his stock in trade? "Yet neither fact proves that I was complicit."

Francis lost patience. "You are very sure of yourself, upon my word! Know this, then. If it was indeed your doing that brought about Scalloway's demise, you will be found out."

# CHAPTER FOURTEEN

Having written a note to Sir Walter Belchamp, Ottilia consented to sit down to partake of dinner with her husband. She did not feel as much had been accomplished as she would have liked, and to her chagrin she still felt tired, but she was in hopes that the information garnered by all parties that day would prove sufficient to procure Dorote's release at last.

"If we had not been so close to the dinner hour, I should have taken the news to Mr Belchamp myself."

Francis settled her chair for her and moved to take his own seat. "There is no need to bestir yourself, my dear one. I am pretty sure he must consent now that we have supplied him with all these additional suspects." He eyed her across the table. "You still look a trifle fagged to me. Are you sure you are up to all this?"

Ottilia flashed him a rueful smile. "I will have to be, will I not? I dare say I will feel more energetic tomorrow." She returned to her examination of the viands on offer, eyeing the promised beef. "If you are about to carve that, Fan, I should be glad of some myself. Why has Hemp gone off without reporting to me, by the by?"

He took up the carving knife. "He went off on some trail of his own after we saw the fellow Mawdesley. Hemp wants to check on some detail, he said. One slice or two?"

"Two, if you please." Ottilia helped herself from a dish of artichokes. "I wonder if Hemp went to the prison?"

"What would he check on there? I doubt he would go there today if he hopes, as you do, that Belchamp will send the necessary release." Francis laid two slices of beef on her plate and proceeded to carve some for himself.

"He is anxious to get her out, but I am less happy to be sending her back into Elinor Scalloway's orbit. I don't trust that female."

Having piled his plate with beef, Francis took his seat and reached for the silver mustard pot. "Why does that trouble you, Tillie?"

Ottilia swallowed a mouthful of beef before answering. "Because she has the mind of a slave owner." She speared another portion and waved her fork. "You were right, Fan. This is exceedingly good."

Her spouse threw her an affectionate glance. "I'm pleased to see you enjoying your food."

Ottilia chewed in silence for a space, her mind revolving the various tales that had been elicited on all sides. Absently, she piled another spoonful of artichokes onto a plate already well larded, prompting a laugh from the other side of the table.

"This is becoming quite a comedy, my loved one. Are you seriously planning to eat all that?"

Mischief burgeoned as Ottilia came to herself. "Well, if I can't, I shall reply upon your good offices." She ate steadily, however, while opening her thoughts to her husband's inspection. "I am not convinced of this Harbury's being the guilty party."

"Why not? He's plainly devious, no matter that he was willing enough to tell me his part."

"Yes, and until you told me how he received you, I had used Mr Ackworth's information to set him somewhere near the top of the list."

Francis took up his wine glass and drank a little of the claret. "Then I don't see why you should drop him down."

"Because, by your account, he was not in the least bit rattled."

"But Mawdesley was. I never supposed Harbury did the deed himself."

"True, but you implied he was dismissive of that fellow. He must know the man could not be trusted to keep his secret if he had employed him to engage in murder. Hemp must have frightened him thoroughly."

A grim smile came. "He did."

"Well then?"

"Yes, an unreliable tool, I must suppose. But that leaves us with Elinor."

Ottilia polished off the last of her beef and sat back with a satisfied sigh. "I feel the better for that. Though I may indulge in a tartlet or two. Mrs Dunkeswell promised some with apricot jam were in the making." She sipped at her wine and set down the glass to find her husband regarding her with a quizzical gleam. "Well, what, Fan?"

"Are you sure you are yourself, Tillie?"

She had to laugh. "Of course, dearest. I feel remarkably well, as it happens. Although I must have drunk too much coffee today, for I am inclined to think I must nip up to our chamber before the dessert is brought in."

It did not take her many minutes to despatch the necessary errand and she returned to the parlour to find her husband disposing of cheese and an apple along with a replenished glass of claret. She scanned the table and a glow of satisfaction entered her bosom. "My tartlets! Excellent." Sitting down, she lost no time in seizing up a couple of the pastry dainties, renewing the conversation without preamble. "We also have Culverstone, don't forget."

Francis blinked. "Of what are you talking, woman?"

"Suspects. You said we were left with Elinor if we are to eliminate Harbury."

"You may eliminate him. He is most certainly still on my list. But I grant you Culverstone."

"And," pursued Ottilia through a mouthful of apricot tart, "there is this captain."

"The one Mawdesley mentioned? Why in the world should he remove Scalloway? Especially if they were in a string, colluding in this shipwreck. Which, by the by, I find too far-fetched for words."

"You do?"

"Use your intelligence, Tillie. Why should Scalloway create such an elaborate plot when his sole desire was to make his fortune in the shipping trade?"

Ottilia washed down the tart with a swallow of wine. "There is that. But what if he was not complicit?"

"You mean this captain cheated him? Well, it's more believable, but still unlikely. In fact, I can't imagine what possessed the man to employ a fellow he knew to be untrustworthy. Can Scalloway truly have been such a bad judge of character?"

Ottilia set down her glass. "According to Hemp, he was every sort of villain."

"Hemp is prejudiced."

"I grant you that. But he is level-headed enough to be able to set his jealousy aside."

Francis let out a snort. "Don't you believe it! I defy any man to keep a clear head when the woman he loves turns her attentions elsewhere."

Ottilia regarded him with a sudden thumping in her bosom. "When? Ought you not rather to say if? Do you fear I might look at another man, is that it?"

His brows snapped together. "Of course not. At least... How can I know? I don't *fear* it precisely."

She put out a hand across the table and he gripped it. "You need never think it, my darling lord. You are all in all to me, don't you know that?"

His lip twisted. "Yes." He released her hand and the brown eyes were troubled as they met her gaze. "Only there was Pretty, was there not? Oh, I know it is not the same. I felt it with her too, just before we left. Perhaps that is why." He gave one of his wry smiles. "It was unsettling, Tillie."

Ottilia leaned in, urgent to convince. "My dearest darling, it ought but to enhance our love, not change it. Affection for the child, I mean."

"Yet it still gave me a flicker of guilt, my loved one."

A relieved little laugh escaped her. "Oh, that. I will wager it was nothing to the guilt I felt when we were so much at odds over the poor little thing."

Francis had taken up his wine again but he set it down. "That too I regret. I was thinking first of the inconvenience, especially with Pretty coming from that ghastly background. But that is scarcely her fault, poor child."

The reminder was poignant and Ottilia blinked away wetness. "Don't think of it again, Fan. We are at one now and that is all that matters."

She was relieved when he said no more, but the train of thought set up by his earlier words took root. Remembrance prompted her tongue. "We may not wholly trust Hemp's judgement, Fan, but I suspect Lord Radcliffe, for all his irascibility, is a better judge. He rated Scalloway a very scoundrel, lacking in moral fibre. Mr Ackworth too, whom I take to be a sensible man, had no good word to say of the man.

I think we may safely assume him to have been all that Hemp implies."

"Then perhaps it may profit us to locate this captain."

As he spoke, a knock at the door produced Hemp himself. "I beg your pardon, milady, for my tardiness."

Ottilia smiled at him. "It makes no matter, Hemp. His lordship has given me all the relevant information."

Hemp came to the table. "All that milord knew, yes."

Ottilia exchanged a glance with her spouse, who turned a frown upon Hemp. "Your meaning?"

One of his wry looks came over Hemp's face. "I have been hunting down information concerning a certain Captain Indigo."

"The same mentioned by Mawdesley?"

"It is so, milord. I recognised the name. He is, or was, an escaped slave from one of the islands. His piracy terrorised the Caribbean for years."

# CHAPTER FIFTEEN

Every day the same. Doro had lost count of how many had passed since Hemp last visited. He had come after this Lady Fan had been, only to say she was engaged with finding out those who might have stabbed the master. Since then, Doro had had nothing to do except watch the changing sky through the window and worry at the same question. Who? Who?

Mistress Elinor hated her husband, that she knew. Mr Culverstone likewise. But the mistress had arranged to leave him. To kill him made no sense. A niggle of doubt persisted. Why had she insisted upon sending Doro to find him at the Pyg & Whistle? It would have been better to let her pack what the mistress needed. Unless she knew she need not pack at all.

Moreover, Mistress Elinor had not tried to help her maid. No word had come from her. Nothing then, nothing since. The possibility she had meant for Doro to be found, to take the blame, could not but obtrude. Better a slave with a grudge than a wife.

Doro had seen too many slaves suffer punishment for crimes they did not commit to have faith in Mrs Scalloway's intentions. Before this, she would have sworn the mistress meant her only good. She had said she would free her once she was free of the master. Recalling her own words, Doro could not but shudder. Had the mistress taken them for an omen? Neither would be free until the master was dead. Yes, she had said it, never dreaming how prophetic were those fatal words.

Yet she was anything but free. And Mistress Elinor had not put out one word to her aid.

Round and round it went. The mistress and Mr Culverstone. A plot? Was it she who took Doro's dagger and gave it to her lover? Was it he who plunged the weapon into the heart of Master Marcus?

Doro could know nothing of their comings and goings in the night hours. The letter Doro took to Mr Culverstone that day might have contained a plan to seal her own doom.

Then the darkest thought of all. If chance had not set her in Hemp's way, a ghost from days long gone, Dorote Gabon would surely have ended her days on an English gallows. Even now, one could not know that this Lady Fan would succeed. Hemp might assure her that she had never yet failed, but Doro was loath to believe in her own luck. She was cursed from the day she showed her back to a true man's love and allowed her head to be turned by a handsome face and flattery. The memories came tumbling back. The fury on both sides, the vile words exchanged…

"You go to that man, Doro, and you will end nothing but a whore!"

"How dare you use such a word to me? Marcus cares for me. He will free me from this life."

"What, and take you away from Barbados? To where?"

"I don't care where, as long as it is away from slavery. From prejudice. From people like you!"

"How like me? I am no different from you, Doro."

"You are not a slave, Hemp. You were born free. This is my chance. I will have clothes and jewels, carriages like the white women. Marcus says I will be a sensation."

"You are deluded, Doro. Can't you see he is lying? He means none of that. He wants to bed you. When he has taken you enough, he will cast you aside. Then you will be lost indeed."

"You know naught of him! Leave me be!"

"Doro, I am begging you, think!"

"Get away from me, Hemp! This is my choice."

"Then you are out of your senses. I love you. I thought you loved me."

"You don't own my heart, Hemp Roy. *You don't own my heart.*"

The image of his face upon impact had never left her. He had turned and walked away. Doro nearly called him back, but she had been too proud. When he left the island with Miss Tamasine, he had come to say goodbye. A stiff, formal, hideous moment. Doro had been haunted ever since by the pain in his eyes.

The sound of the key in the cell door roused her from the reverie. Its subject stood in the aperture as the door opened. Hemp was flashing his teeth in a wide grin and holding up a sheet of paper. "Your release, Doro! It arrived this morning at the Ship. The magistrate has set you free."

For a moment the world went still. Free? Then his meaning penetrated. Not free in the sense that she yearned to be. But free of this prison cell. Her bosom came alive and the light of hope enveloped her. "Truly? I can go?"

He was moving into the room, the gaoler, keys jangling from his fingers, taking his place in the doorway. No change in his expression. Mere boredom as he waved his keys at the letter in Hemp's hand. "Says you are bailed is all. Don't you go trying to leave Bristol. We'll send the tipstaffs after you."

Hemp was folding the paper as he turned to the man. "She's not leaving the town. Come, Doro. I'm taking you home."

Dazed, Doro allowed him to take her hand and followed as he led her from the cell. He paused in the doorway.

"Have you got everything?"

She looked fleetingly up at him, the memories pressing on her heart. "I came with nothing."

She was glad of his arm coming about her, the warmth of his body against her chilled limbs, but the sense of being undeserving of his care weighed heavily upon her.

Hemp felt Doro's withdrawal and remained silent as they negotiated the echoing stone corridors of the prison. He watched with a jerk of compassion how she blinked against the sudden light of the outside, dropping her gaze to shield her eyes. She was shivering too.

"You are cold. Here." Stripping off his great-coat, he went to set it about her shoulders.

She put her hands out to prevent him. "I am used to it, Hemp."

"Nevertheless."

Those alluring eyes studied him for a moment. Then a tiny smile flashed. "You were ever kind."

His heart warmed and he set the great-coat about her and signalled to the driver of the cab he had hired, who brought the vehicle up close. Hemp opened the door.

"Doro?"

Drowned in his great-coat, she was holding it about her, but she had turned towards the prison, gazing at its walls in a way that tore at his emotions. Her head turned and she looked at the hackney and back to Hemp, puzzlement in her voice. "For me?"

He smiled. "Why not? I thought it would be more comfortable than walking after —" He broke off. No need to labour the point.

"It is not far."

"Far enough. Come."

She got in and he gave the direction to the jarvey and followed. Inside she arranged the great-coat more comfortably about her person and he noted she relaxed a little more, her eyes flashing him a glance within the dim interior. "I thank you, Hemp."

He laughed. "You should rather thank milady. I could not have done it."

"I will thank Lady Fan. Do we go to her now?"

"Not today. We are going to the Scalloway house."

Her pose changed, becoming rigid, her hands clenching in her lap. "That is what you meant by home, then."

"For now, Doro. I can't take you away from there, not yet."

She did not speak, but her distress became clear in the shifting discomfort of her motions.

"Doro, it will be all right. Mrs Scalloway —"

"— did not help me." It was harsh and low-toned. "Do you not know what that means?"

Hemp reached out and stilled her unquiet hands. "I know. Yet the law is against us, Doro. Until I can —"

"Against me. Not against you." Then her pose fell off a little and she turned a hand and gripped his fingers. "I am grateful. You have done more than I could have hoped for."

He was tempted to unburden his heart there and then. It was the first encouragement she had shown him. Yet she was still mightily reserved, too buried in the troubled past that stood between them. He said what he hoped might ease the strain.

"Believe me, my part is minimal, Doro. You do not know milady. She has a passion for justice. Once she takes on a — well, let us call it a crusade, as the Dowager Lady Polbrook is wont to say. When milady takes on a crusade, she is indefatigable."

Doro's gaze came around to his, those blue eyes tantalising even in the gloom. "Who is that?"

"Lady Polbrook? She is milord's mother. A redoubtable old dame, she is. I like her almost as much as milady."

Doro did not turn her gaze away and he glowed with hope. "How is it you are steward to Lady Fan?"

Relief at the innocuous subject, as much as gladness at her unprecedented interest, prompted Hemp to beguile the rest of the short journey with a brief account of the circumstances of his entry into the Fanshawe household.

"Milady was sorry for me at the start, I think. But we have become friends, as far as that can be with our separate stations." The hackney was slowing. "Here we are, I think."

As the horse came to a halt, he opened the door and jumped out, turning to help Doro. Without waiting for her permission, he took her by the waist and lifted her down. After settling with the driver, he found her waiting at the top of the area steps down to the Scalloway domestic quarters. She had taken off the great-coat and held it out to him.

"I will say farewell, Hemp."

He took the garment but gestured her down the stairs. "I am coming in with you."

She hesitated. "There is no need."

"I will show your mistress the release from Justice Belchamp."

He thought she was going to argue the point, but she turned and started down the steps. It was not all his reason for wishing to speak to Mrs Scalloway, but that he preferred to keep to himself.

The cook opened the door. "Mercy me, is it you, Doro? Come you in, girl, come you in." Ushering her into the kitchen, Peg enveloped her in flesh-filled arms and hugged her. "I never thought to see you back, but I'm right glad as you are. Sit, sit, sit and I'll fetch you a coffee with lots of sugar, the way you like it. And I'll have you know I never did believe it were you as done it, never."

The softening in Doro's features cost Hemp a pang. She would not look so kindly upon him. But he was glad of it nevertheless as he listened to her thanking the cook. He accepted a cup for himself, set the great-coat in a spare chair together with his hat and took a seat at Peg's urging. Doro sipped her drink and then focused a troubled gaze upon the cook. "What has been happening here, Peg? Since..."

Peg plonked down with a flourish of her arms. "Such comings and goings as you wouldn't believe. That Lady Radcliffe has been here every day, not to mention him as the mistress is very glad to see, I'll be bound."

"Mr Culverstone? He comes here?"

"Might as well live here for all of me." The grumbling note gave way to the conspiratorial one Hemp knew from before as Peg leaned in. "You be careful, Doro. Don't you go trusting that Quin. I'll go bail he knows a deal more about this business than he's like to say. No need to look for trouble from Mr Roy. Knows all about Quin and that Mawdesley fellow, don't you?"

"More than Quin would wish, I suspect." Hemp cast Doro a reassuring glance. "It is all to do with milady's enquiries, Doro. There is naught to fear. But Peg is right. Don't tell Quin anything."

A spasm crossed Doro's face. "I have naught to tell."

"Well, you stick to that, Doro, that's all I say," advised Peg. "Drink up. You'd best go up to the mistress."

Doro looked as if her light was quenched. "Yes. How has she managed?"

"Jenny's been doing for her, don't you worry. Should think she'll be glad to have you back, though."

Doro gave a small smile. "Jenny will, perhaps. She has her own work."

"Ah, well, we've all done our part. Saul is kept to-ing and fro-ing twixt the mistress and his nibs, what with all the paperwork, Saul says. I don't know nowt of that, but it seems he's more out than in these days. Quin likewise. But he's always ready to find excuses to loaf about, he is."

Doro set down her cup in a precise fashion that alerted Hemp to her anxiety. He could not blame her. Mrs Scalloway had been palpably neglectful.

Following where Doro led up the narrow servants' stairway and along a passage towards the front of the house, Hemp was aware her steps grew slower, her silence thick with tension. He wanted to touch her, hold her, reassure her. But this was no longer the despairing Doro he had found in prison, ripe for rescue. This was a Doro closer to the woman he had first encountered on the harbour, she who tried her utmost to reject him. She was not as dismissive now, but there was a long way to go to find the warm and passionate Doro he had known and loved.

Her knock at the parlour door was tentative. At the call of 'come in' she hesitated, throwing up a glance at Hemp that caught at the affection in his breast. He spoke softly. "Open, Doro. Let us get this over with."

She let out a long breath as she turned back to the door, squared her shoulders and turned the handle. Her reception was not encouraging.

"Good heavens! Doro, is it you indeed?"

Walking in behind her, Hemp took his place at her side, casting a glance at the occupants of the room. The dark-haired woman who had spoken was seated on the sofa, her black gown and a small lace cap marking her for the widow. She was flanked by the fellow Culverstone whom Hemp had seen before. His arrival sparked instant comment.

"Why, who is this?"

Hemp stepped forward. "I beg your pardon, madame, but I am steward to Milady Francis." This information elicited a stare, accompanied by raised brows. "My name is Roy. At milady's request, I have fetched Doro from the gaol." He fished in his pocket and brought out the precious release, moving towards the sofa and holding it out as he spoke. "This is the letter from the magistrate, madame."

Mrs Scalloway took it and ran her eyes down the sheet, what time Hemp took note of the fellow Culverstone, fashionably attired in a double-breasted waistcoat with a stand collar, a blue coat with wide lapels and a neck-cloth fancifully tied in a large bow. He wore his own fair hair, tied at the neck like milord and stood stiff as a guardian by the widow's side, a challenge in both pose and features.

Mrs Scalloway looked up. "This is most gratifying."

Her tone was dry and Hemp thought the words spurious, a faint smile appearing as she turned her gaze towards Doro, still and silent before the door. The smile did not reach the woman's eyes. "I am glad to see you back, although I note that this letter does not altogether exonerate you."

Hemp would have spoken, but Doro got in first. "It is true, madame. Yet I did not do this terrible deed."

Mrs Scalloway's gaze did not falter but her eyes grew cold. "That is yet to be determined."

"I did not do it, madame."

Doro's voice was shaking and Hemp had all to do to keep his mouth shut.

"We shall see." The woman's gaze swept back, taking in Hemp. "You have done your part. You may go."

Hemp stood his ground. "I have yet a question for you, madame."

Her lips pursed. "Indeed? Are you then your mistress's deputy? You may tell her I will answer to no slave."

Hemp held her gaze. "I am not, and never was, a slave. I was born free and I am my own master."

"You are employed by the Fanshawes."

"Temporarily. My question, however, has nothing to do with this affair. If you will grant me a few moments in private, madame —"

She cut him off with a wave of her hand, turning to Doro. "Go to your room, Doro. I will speak to you later."

Willingly could Hemp have sent her to join her vile husband. But Doro stepped closer and he held his tongue on the hot words hovering there.

"Madame, shall I not see to your needs? I must wash away the prison stink and change my dress, but I am ready to resume my duties."

Mrs Scalloway looked her up and down. The disdain in her gaze battered at Hemp's control. But his need required him to remain neutral, at least within her sight. "I cannot be waited upon by a creature suspected of killing my husband."

Doro flinched and the hurt in her eyes ripped at Hemp's heart. Nevertheless, she spoke up with courage. "I am not that creature, madame."

"It may be as you say. Until this is proven, I will not have you about me, is that understood? You may relieve Jenny of her duties. She has learned to understand my needs and will serve me very well in your place."

Doro looked crestfallen. Why would she not? But there was yet a touch of defiance in those speaking eyes of hers. "If this is your wish, madame." She bobbed a curtsey, turned and left the room, closing the door softly behind her.

Hemp longed to follow, to offer comfort, but this was his chance. He could not afford to relinquish it. He brought his gaze back to find both Mrs Scalloway and Culverstone regarding him, she with wariness, he with suspicion.

"Well? What do you want with me, steward?"

For the first time the man Culverstone spoke up, a threat in his voice as well as his words. "You will keep a civil tongue in your head when you speak to Mrs Scalloway, if you know what's good for you."

Hemp eyed him. "I do not believe I have been uncivil, sir."

"I misliked your tone. Mend it."

For a brief moment, Hemp held his gaze, letting his rage slip through. The man did not back down but he blinked rapidly. Hemp dropped his gaze, exhorted himself to control, and raised it again to the lady of the house. "Madame, this is my question. Who owns Doro now?"

Ottilia watched Hemp's agitated pacing with a breast awash with compassion. For once, Hemp had come to her with an overburdened heart and she was relieved Francis had opted to see what he could find out from the lawyer Ackworth, albeit with an injunction to his wife not to overtire herself, although she was feeling a degree more rested today. His presence at this moment, however, would have kept her friend from speaking out.

"Tell me it all, Hemp. Mrs Scalloway was shocked that you asked. What then happened?"

Hemp paused in his perambulations, staring out of the window. "She was more than shocked, milady. I believe she thought it presumptuous in me even to enquire." He turned, bleakness in his features. "I fear my cause is hopeless. She is so much against Doro, I think she cannot condone the possibility of a future for her."

"Did she say as much?"

Hemp let out a defeated breath. "She said Doro's circumstances were nothing to do with me, that she would not discuss such a matter with a person of my origins —"

"She said that?"

"She used a pejorative term. I will not soil my lips with it, milady. I heard it too often in Barbados."

Wrath swept away the compassion. "Only wait until I question her again!"

Hemp came across, agitation in his face. "I beg you not to speak of it with her, milady."

"Oh, I shall not speak of that, but I will not spare her either."

A slight smile showed for an instant. "I hope you won't. I cannot forgive her for her treatment of Doro."

Ottilia's heart stirred. "Is she very distressed?"

"What would you, milady? I saw her before I left, briefly. She had been weeping, I know. She told me the mistress and she had been close. Doro shared all her secrets, helped her against Scalloway whenever he was cruel or they quarrelled. She was trusted, even loved. So she thought. She believed in Mrs Scalloway's care, and she is utterly betrayed."

Ottilia felt his frustration, his anger, futile though it was. She sought a way to soothe. "Let us not waste a moment upon Elinor Scalloway. She has shown herself callous, although I suspect her prejudice is ingrained. Children learn from their parents. My brother Patrick and I were fortunate in ours, for my father taught us tolerance for all men, and my mother, an Irishwoman with a vast knowledge and interest in folklore and things unexplained, would have it we must keep an open mind. We did not, she insisted, know everything. I learned humility at her knee and Papa trained me in observation. Look, he said. You cannot know unless you look." She stopped, conscious of talking too much to a man who needed comfort rather than the pattering of a pointless tongue. She smiled. "I am running on to no purpose."

But Hemp was studying her, she thought, an intent expression in his eyes. "This influence is well seen in you, milady. I was similarly fortunate for all my ill beginning. My education I had from my father. From my mother I learned the value of affection."

Ottilia's mind flew. "You tried to pass on both to Doro! Oh, Hemp, you cannot be father, mother and lover too, to the same woman."

He looked discomfited, cleared his throat. "You see too much, milady." She waited as he paused, seeming to make up his mind. Then he lifted an agonised gaze. "What should I do?"

Ottilia could not help smiling. "Show her how you love her, Hemp. Don't talk. Just show her."

He let out a huge laugh. "You make it sound so easy, milady."

"Well, it is not very difficult, is it?" She eyed him. "You mean to try to buy her freedom."

This produced a taut breath. "I must. I wish there was another way."

"Why?"

"Because Doro will take it for a different sort of slavery, if she owes her freedom to me."

"She will think herself obliged to accept of your offer, you mean?" Ottilia caught a faint look of anguish. "You do intend to marry her, do you not?"

Hemp's shoulders shifted. "If I can persuade her to accept me out of affection. Not from a sense of obligation. I don't want her on such terms." He threw up a hand and ran it over his face in a sort of suppressed agitation. "That is a lie. I want her on any terms."

"But you would prefer a love match to a bargain. I do not blame you." Ottilia rose and went to him, setting a hand on his arm. "Take heart, Hemp. She loved you once. There is no reason to suppose the fire is not there still, even if it is a trifle obscured. You may — you *will* rekindle it."

He gave a decisive nod. "You give me hope, milady." She released him and he struck his hands together. "But first we must ensure she is vindicated. That woman insists upon holding the suspicion over Doro's head."

"Of course she does," Ottilia said, as she moved to the mantel and picked up the bell. "Elinor Scalloway is herself under suspicion and she knows it. I think I will go and remind her of this fact." She rang the bell. "But first, coffee!"

She was pleased to see Hemp's mood lighten as he laughed. "Naturally, milady. No one would expect you to proceed without your customary dose of coffee."

"You know me so well."

Ottilia went to resume her seat and Hemp headed for the door. He paused there and turned. "Do you wish me to accompany you, milady?"

"If you please, Hemp." A thought occurred. "Or, stay! Let us leave that for later, or tomorrow perhaps. His lordship has gone to find Mr Ackworth and I do not know when he may return. While I have your escort instead, I think it better I seize the opportunity to visit the Pyg & Whistle. I need not fear to enter such a place if you are with me."

# CHAPTER SIXTEEN

It had proved no great feat for Francis to track down John Ackworth. The lawyer turned out to be well known in the town, just as Pymoor of the Pyg & Whistle had stated. Dunkeswell, landlord of the Ship, where he and Tillie were staying, was able to furnish him with the direction to the fellow's office, which entailed a walk via Baldwin Street to The Back where the other side of the floating harbour was situated. Thankful for a dry day with a scattering of sunlight, Francis crossed the Bristol Bridge and found his way down to the end of Redcliff Street.

Francis shed his great-coat and hat in the outer office and left them in the charge of one of Ackworth's clerks, entering the man's sanctum at the lawyer's invitation. The place was a good deal better appointed than Harbury's poky premises. More spacious, better furnished with a large desk, with a stack of papers and a pair of unfolded spectacles laid down on top — Francis had clearly disturbed the lawyer in the midst of his work — and shelves behind filled with ribbon-tied scrolls and legal boxes. To one side there was a seating area with comfortable chairs into which Ackworth gestured him.

"Pray take a chair, my lord. I had a notion I might be receiving a visit from you."

Francis sank into a leather-covered armchair. "Did you indeed? After meeting my wife at Radcliffe's, I take it?"

Ackworth took a chair opposite, crossing one leg over the other in a negligent fashion. He was perfectly at ease, exuding a more bonhomous air than had the agent. "That is so, my lord.

Given her ladyship's enquiry, I thought she must wish for more particulars."

"You are willing to give them, then?"

Ackworth spread his hands. "Why should I not, my lord? It is in my interests to have this affair settled."

To what end? Francis eyed him for signs of duplicity and found none. "Are you acting for the deceased Mr Scalloway?"

"In the matter of his will? No, my lord. That is in the hands of Lord Radcliffe and his own lawyer."

"Then how does it benefit you to have the murder resolved?"

Ackworth's features took on a look of distaste. "Until it is so, I cannot abrogate those responsibilities I so regretfully took on in acting for Mr Harbury."

Francis believed he meant it. He went straight to the point of his visit. "What do you know of a certain Captain Indigo?"

From his expression, Ackworth was startled. "Captain Indigo? The fellow who lost the ship?"

"Precisely. Did you ever meet him?"

Ackworth blew out a breath. "Never. But I've read his account as he told it to the harbourmaster. He refused to speak to anyone else and Scalloway failed to find him, or so he claimed."

"What was Indigo's account?"

"He hit the rocks on the Seven Stones Reef. I admit it is not an uncommon occurrence with that particular shipping hazard. However —" Ackworth wrinkled his nose as if at a bad smell — "one would have supposed an experienced captain must know how to navigate these waters, but it seems he misjudged the way in fog, which is not altogether unlikely at this season."

Francis took note of the modifier. "Not *altogether* unlikely. Why the caveat, sir?"

Ackworth pursed his lips. "I took care to enquire of two other seamen who had been out that particular night. Neither encountered fog."

"Ah!"

Ackworth held up a staying hand. "It is scarcely conclusive. They were sailing further north than the Scillies. It is true that fogs do not come up uniformly and have certainly been known to cause other vessels to founder on the reef. One cannot discount the possibility the seamen I spoke to were more fortunate than Indigo."

"Or more truthful," said Francis with deliberation.

A faint smile crossed the lawyer's lips. "Possibly."

Francis pursued it. "Had you any other reason to doubt the veracity of Indigo's account?"

"Only his reputation. He has not been known long in these parts. I believe he was used to captain a ship in the Indies but he fell upon hard times, or so the story goes. He lost his ship, and —"

"What, another?"

"Not by a wreck. His ventures failed and he was obliged to sell. He took passage for England in a bid to find better fortune where the shipping trade is more robust."

"Who told you all this history?"

"Why, Scalloway. He knew the man, it seems. Which is why he employed him to captain the *Blackbird*."

The whiff of collusion grew stronger. Sold his ship forsooth! Not according to Hemp's account. Nor had these failed "ventures" any association with the legitimate shipping trade. Francis chose to refrain for the present from revealing his better knowledge. "I understand several members of the crew also survived the wreck?"

Ackworth's brows rose. "It would certainly be remarkable if all had perished."

"Why so?"

"Seven Stones is a popular fishing area with Scilly Isles locals. The chances of being picked up are high."

"I wonder if Indigo knew that?"

Ackworth's brows drew together. "You suggest he is a better sailor than we give him credit for? You are proposing the possibility of criminal intent?" He paused, eyes narrowed.

Francis had to smile. "Now you look like an advocate."

Ackworth's brow flickered but he made no answer, his attitude expectant. The lawyer at work?

Francis dropped his bombshell. "Scalloway pulled the wool over your eyes, Ackworth. He must have known perfectly well that Indigo is in fact a pirate."

"A pirate? Good God!"

"The news startles you?"

For the first time, a look of indignation overspread the man's face. "Do you imagine I am familiar with any such? Where had you this? How do you know if it is the truth?"

Francis raised a hand. "Peace, sir. I meant no offence. I had it from my Barbadian servant, a man of integrity whose word I have no hesitation in taking."

Ackworth was visibly impatient. "Very well, but what of Indigo?"

"It seems he is an escaped slave, not from Barbados but from another of the West Indian islands. Somehow, he acquired a ship and took to piracy all over the Caribbean. There can be no doubt he is indeed an experienced sailor. He was captured, forfeited his ship and was imprisoned, awaiting trial, when my fellow left Barbados for England. How Indigo managed to escape a second time remains a mystery, but if he is here masquerading as a ship's captain for hire, I leave it to you to draw the likely conclusion."

Ackworth heard him out in silence and then rose, shifting to the back of his chair and seizing hold of the wooden frame there. Francis read dismay in the keen gaze.

"If you are correct, my lord, this raises grave questions in my mind."

"Mine too, Ackworth. Chief amongst them being, how could a man who was wanted across the Caribbean steer a ship to the Indies without running afoul of the law?"

"That indeed leaps to the eye, my lord. Scalloway cannot have been ignorant of this fact."

"You are reading my thoughts."

Ackworth released his hold on the chair and paced across the room and back, clasping unquiet hands together behind his back. Francis awaited his dictum. He was the legal expert. He must know what was next to be done.

At last the man returned. "Before seeking to institute criminal proceedings, I must first test the veracity of these accusations."

Francis rose. "How, pray?"

Ackworth made an impatient gesture. "Discreet questions in certain quarters. I have contacts who are familiar with the shipping world. They may have heard such tales. Or at least may know more of Indigo's activities."

Francis could not forbear a derisive look. "You have such persons in your pocket, I dare say. I am ready to believe it. My man of business likewise has a string of rapscallions at his beck."

Ackworth acknowledged this with a faint smile. "One is obliged, in my profession, to consort with men of all sorts and conditions. One must make use of what tools there are to hand."

"No doubt." Francis bethought him of his darling wife's tendency to approach any and every person she might wish to question, regardless of station. He made up his mind. "Would you object to it if I accompanied you, sir?"

"I think perhaps you had best wait in here, my lady, while I find the landlady."

Ottilia looked with disfavour around the unprepossessing hallway, thick with grime and smelling of must, gloomy after the brightness outside. "I thank you, Hemp, but I am not remaining alone in this environment. I will come in with you."

"If you insist, milady."

"I do. Come, it is hardly the worst place I have been in."

Hemp laughed. "True. May I request that you stay close behind?"

Ottilia smiled at him. "Lead on, my stout protector."

She followed him into a long taproom, hot from a blazing fire, with blackened walls and emanating odours of stale sweat and liquor, where some half a dozen patrons occupied the available settles and stools. Why in the world did no one think to open one of the casement windows? Hard upon her entrance, the murmur of voices died as one after another fell silent, staring. Ottilia was seized with an inane desire to giggle. She was herself wholly out of place, but it was evident her escort was attracting as much attention. Or was it merely the fact of their being obviously together?

Hemp headed directly for the counter, upon which an individual was leaning, exchanging desultory talk with a fellow standing on the other side. He was heavy-set, with scant grey locks and sporting an apron as unkempt as his establishment, worn over shirtsleeves and a waistcoat. He straightened at Hemp's approach, looking from him to Ottilia and back again.

"You do not remember me, Pymoor?"

Another glance from one to the other. "You, mebbe."

Hemp gestured. "Lady Francis wishes a word with your wife."

"My wife?"

"Your wife, yes."

At that, a female figure Ottilia had not noticed came bustling up from the back of the room. She was small but sturdy, wearing with confidence her old-fashioned chemise gown of brown serge covered over with a large apron, and looked to be formidable from the sharp glances she cast from Hemp's face to Ottilia's as she reached the counter.

"I'm Mrs Pymoor. Who is it wants me?"

"This is Lady Francis Fanshawe. She would like to speak with you in private."

The surname name had evidently jogged the landlord's memory. "Here, if this is about that there Scalloway again —"

"Ah, you are the fellow who spoke to my husband, I think," Ottilia cut in.

The man looked taken aback to have been thus addressed. He bobbed his head. "Aye, ma'am — my lady — if so be as it were he who come arsting all manner of questions t'other day."

"Just so. Now it is my turn to enquire a little of Mrs Pymoor, if she will be so obliging." She cast a smile at the landlady, who at once assumed a servile mien.

"Pleased to oblige, my lady. How can I help you?"

"In private, if you please."

Mrs Pymoor hesitated. "Well, there's only the one parlour, my lady. Nor it ain't fitting for the likes of you."

"Thank you, it will serve well enough, I make no doubt."

The woman came out from behind the counter. "I'll show you where, shall I, my lady?"

"Pray do." Ottilia lowered her voice as the landlady started out towards the door. "Come with us, Hemp, but perhaps wait outside the door."

"Will you leave it a little ajar, milady?"

Ottilia paused in the doorway, noting where Mrs Pymoor crossed to a door at the back of the little hall. The murmuring behind, which had started up again, subsided, all eyes back on Ottilia and Hemp. She was relieved when Hemp took a moment to pass his glance across the company, inducing them to turn away and pretend immediate interest in a neighbour or tankard.

"Do you wish to hear what is said? Or do you think I shall not be safe?"

Hemp looked a trifle sheepish. "Both had crossed my mind, milady."

She had to laugh, but softly. "Very well, I will not wholly close it."

The landlady was waiting by an open door. Ottilia crossed and entered the parlour. It was small but clean, although its furnishings were simple. Mrs Pymoor had nothing to blush for. She began to feel hopeful. If the woman kept a neat house, it was probable her mind was similarly so. She had a keen look about her.

Ottilia moved into the room and turned to face her. "Pray leave the door a little ajar, if you will."

Mrs Pymoor glanced out into the passage and back at Ottilia with a slight frown. She hesitated, but at length put the door to but did not fully close it. Before Ottilia could frame any sort of question, the woman opened negotiations. "You've come about the murder then, my lady?"

"Just so. I am hoping you may be able to give me a more coherent account than I have so far heard."

Came a toss of the head. "Ain't as if I've not given it over and over. Such goings-on in a house don't do it no favours, my lady."

"I have no doubt you have been severely tried, Mrs Pymoor," Ottilia said, on a sympathetic note. "It is no pleasant thing to have such an event happen in one's establishment."

"Terrible it were and no mistake." The woman became confiding. "I don't mind telling you, my lady, it give me palpitations even to think of it."

"I am not surprised. I am sorry to oblige you to think of it all over again."

But palpitations notwithstanding, Mrs Pymoor showed no reluctance to repeat her story, which she did with embellishments referring to her emotions at the time. It did not differ greatly from what her husband had told Francis, except in one particular.

"I believe the slave girl was locked into one of your chambers until the constable came. Was it you who led her there?"

"I never, my lady. I told him where to take her, but I had my hands full with that Cherry falling into hysterics, silly girl."

"You told whom where to take her?"

"That fellow what was in the dead man's service. A regular here, he is. Or he was."

"Quin?"

"That's the one. Always hanging about. Waiting for his master, he said. Taking any excuse to tip drink down himself is what I thought. Still, he paid his way. That's all I cared for."

Ottilia's senses prickled. "Was he — what is it they say? — plump in the pocket?"

"I don't know that. Never short, that's all I know. And I'd swear I've seen him slip a silver bit to Cherry now and now."

For services rendered? Was the woman as willing to bed the boots as she was his master? Or did Quin merely act on Scalloway's behalf? It was evident he was a go-between in the man's business dealings. Why not in his amorous affairs too? "I wonder, might I speak with Cherry?"

Mrs Pymoor looked severely shocked. "Speak with that —! Well, I don't want to say in front of your ladyship."

"Ah, I understand. Pray be under no illusions, my dear Mrs Pymoor. I am quite aware Cherry was with Mr Scalloway in his bed that night."

The landlady reddened, more with annoyance than embarrassment, Ottilia guessed. "No better than she should be, she isn't. I wish your ladyship won't think the worse of me for keeping such a female on, for I've wished to be rid of her long since. Only Pymoor won't have me send her off. I can't deny she's a comely girl and the customers like her making sheep's eyes at them, but..." She sighed in a frustrated way. "Well, there. What is a body to do? It's business when all is said and done."

Ottilia could sympathise with her dichotomy, but she grew impatient. "Nevertheless, I should wish to speak to her."

Mrs Pymoor shrugged. "I'll fetch her to you, my lady, but I'd best warn you as she's a pert young madam and there's no saying she'll be respectful."

She went out on the words and Ottilia ran over in her head the matters upon which she required clarification, assuming the allegedly impertinent barmaid could be persuaded to talk.

Cherry proved to be indeed a most comely girl, with a quantity of black curls escaping from an inadequate cap, a lively pair of long-lashed inquisitive brown eyes and pouting lips of a colour to match her name. She was dressed in a somewhat gaudy gown of printed cotton, the bodice cut low enough to expose a good deal of bosom. She came in on a bounce, eyed Ottilia with avid interest and bobbed a curtsey, wholly ignoring the landlady trailing in her wake.

Dispensing with that lady's presence was of the first importance. Ottilia had no wish for interruptions that might stop the barmaid's tongue. "Thank you, Mrs Pymoor. I will not keep you from your duties. You must have a thousand things to do."

Looking chagrined, the woman threw a warning glance at Cherry, who tossed a defiant head, and departed. The barmaid turned on the instant to the visitor and produced a sly-eyed grin. "That your big black feller out in the hall?"

A trifle taken aback, Ottilia responded on a repressive note. "He is my steward, if that is what you mean."

"Prime, he is. Better nor old scallywag for all of me." She gave a bright smile that Ottilia suspected was feigned. "That's what you come about, is it? You'll be wanting to know about Marcus?"

Nothing servile about this woman. Her pertness was only equalled by her insouciance. One could guess at the significance of her remarks concerning Hemp. But the opening must not be neglected. "You addressed Mr Scalloway by his name?"

"It's what he liked. They all do. Makes them feel special, men."

A cynical observation in one so young, despite the implication of an unsavoury side-line to her career serving in the tap. Ottilia found it hard not to judge her harshly. "Can you tell me a little of what happened on the night Mr Scalloway died?"

Cherry's mouth formed a moue of distaste. "I don't like to think of it, ma'am. Fair give me the shivers to think as I'd been with him only hours before that black girl did for him."

Ottilia hit back hard. "It happens, Cherry, that Doro did not do for him, as you put it."

Cherry's eyes popped. "She didn't? But I saw her meself!"

"You saw her holding the dagger and jumped to a false conclusion. By then Mr Scalloway had been dead for several hours."

Cherry did not look particularly struck by this information. Had she heard it before? Was this all an act?

A heavy frown descended. "If so be as he died afore, she must've crept in during the night and done it."

"How did she get in, do you suppose? Is not the house locked up at night?"

"'Course it is. Old Pymoor don't want no marauders coming in, do he?"

"Then it is hardly possible Doro got in, is it?"

Cherry lifted her chin. "She could've come in while the place were open and hid, waiting fer everyone to go to sleep. No one wouldn't see her in the dark. Black as the ace of spades, she is."

Ottilia seized on this. "You know Doro?"

Another head toss. "I seen her. Ain't the first time she come to find him. She says as her mistress sent her, but that's a fib."

"How do you know it's a fib?"

Here a note of indignation crept in. "'Cos old scallywag couldn't do nowt but talk of her, could he? Doro this and Doro that till you wanted to scream. He had it bad for that Doro, had Marcus. Only give it to me for as his missus wouldn't let him give it to Doro. Nor her neither, he said."

Crude as this history was, it set Ottilia's mind streaking through new possibilities. "But Doro herself did not reciprocate Marcus's desire."

"That's what he said." Cherry's expressive gaze became bright with excitement. "I knew all about that dagger of hers. Many's the time she brandished it at Marcus, he said, threatening to stick him with it if he come near."

"Perhaps so, but a man of his stature could readily overpower her, could he not?"

The fervour grew. "Scallywag wouldn't risk it. For why? 'Cos Doro's a witch!"

With difficulty Ottilia refrained from a scoffing retort. "What makes you think so?"

"'Cos Marcus said she cursed him in that outlandish tongue, muttering them spells of hers all the time. He never come near her but she started up, he said, making weird signs with her hands, giving him evil with them eyes, and that ain't natural, is it? Them eyes. Never seen no black with blue eyes and they comes in here often and often. Chock full of blacks is Bristol, but I ain't never see a single one who don't have black eyes, 'cepting her, the witch girl. Good thing if they hangs her, afore she can curse us all!"

Ottilia nearly slapped the silly female's face. Instead, she drew on her authoritative voice. "Stop talking arrant nonsense, Cherry, and attend to me!"

The sharp tone had the effect of making the barmaid jerk back, blinking as if she had lost herself in her own rodomontade. Ottilia took instant advantage. "That is better. I have heard quite enough of the rubbish Scalloway saw fit to pour into your ears. What I wish to know is, which of his acquaintances came to the tavern that night?"

Cherry turned surly. "How do I know? Kept too busy nights to see who come and go."

"Yet I feel sure you noticed. Come, don't you wish to know who killed your Marcus?"

"He weren't mine. Nor I wouldn't want him. Mean, he were. Never buy me nowt, spite as I did all to please him."

Impatience gnawed at Ottilia. "Who was here, Cherry? Mr Harbury, perhaps?"

Cherry looked a trifle taken aback. "Him? Not that night he weren't."

"But he was used to visit here?"

"Now and now." She eyed Ottilia in an odd manner she could not interpret. "Seeing Marcus mostly."

Was there some detail she was withholding? Had Harbury been another who bought her extra services? Ottilia let it go. "Very well, thank you. Let us concentrate on the night in question. Pray try to remember who was indeed here. I am sure you can if you make an effort."

Cherry pouted, but the answer came, if grudgingly. "Well, there was that Quin, but he were allus coming after Marcus, case Marcus needed a message sending."

"Very well, thank you. Who else?"

Cherry hesitated, puckering her brow. Then her face cleared and a bright, hard look entered her face. "Mawdesley! I remember him, for as he tried to have a feel while he were waiting on Marcus, what was having an argy-bargy with that other feller. I give that little toad a piece of my mind and the back of my hand too."

Ottilia cut through this adjunct. "Who was the fellow having an argument with Marcus?"

Cherry snorted. "The one what he said was after his missus. He come with them on the same ship. I forget his name. He don't come in here mostly."

This became interesting. "Are you talking of Mr Culverstone?"

Recognition came into Cherry's eyes. "That's him. Marcus were hot agin him. Worse that night, though he never said why. Never talked like he was used to, now I think of it. All he wanted were to grind into me till he fell to sleep and I were able to scarper."

Despite the crudity, which Ottilia found offensive, this was valuable at last. One question yet nagged. "How was it you went into Scalloway's room so early?"

The barmaid made a scornful face. "'Cos he give me the office to wake him, didn't he? Said he had to get home afore the missus broke her fast or he wouldn't be in time."

In time to prevent her from leaving? That was plausible. Nor, having heard Cherry's version of Scalloway's rumblings about Dorote, could one be surprised at the song and dance she set up upon finding the slave holding the dagger. Indeed, it was to be expected of such a credulous female, clearly given to histrionics. But the remembrance of the cynicism Cherry had displayed could not but niggle.

# CHAPTER SEVENTEEN

The Ostrich tavern was seedy in the extreme. Situated in the Bathurst Basin on the harbourside, it drew its patrons, according to Ackworth, from those concerned in the main Bristol trade — sailors, sailmakers, chandlers, ropemakers, porters and others engaged in all the paraphernalia pertaining to shipping. As with everywhere in the town, dark-skinned individuals were dotted amongst the clientele, but it was difficult to judge whether one might be Captain Indigo. By Hemp's account, the pirate was said to be a huge man with thick limbs, a barrel of a chest and voice to match. Not that Francis had come here in the expectation of encountering the man.

Beyond a couple of cursory glances when he entered the large taproom with Ackworth, none paid them much heed. There was a buzz of conversation, the occasional burst of raucous laughter and much clinking of drinking vessels within the fug of smoke from a number of pipes and a smouldering fire.

He raised his voice to be heard over the general noise. "For whom are you searching?"

Ackworth was looking this way and that, his head poking forward as if he pierced to see through the smoky atmosphere. "A particular snitch of mine. Mordecai is one of these fellows who get everywhere. Not much he doesn't hear. If anyone has wind of Indigo's true origins, it will be he." He cast another searching glance around and shrugged. "It looks as if we are out of luck on this occasion."

He gestured to the door and Francis was just about to shoulder a route through when a fellow of no great stature sidled up. His voice was a whine and his mouth wore an ingratiating leer.

"Is it you, Mr Ackworth? Long days since you put a bit o' business in my way." He cast darting glances up at Francis as he spoke, although reserving his most eager gaze for Ackworth.

Ackworth produced a silver coin. A mittened hand snaked out, seized and pocketed it so fast that Francis was half inclined to think he had imagined the transaction. Was it done thus to avoid drawing attention from some other who might relieve the little man of the coin the moment Ackworth was out of sight?

"On account, Mordecai."

The fellow twinkled up at him in an engaging way. "Seen, sir, seen. Finger pointing, is it? A little job done?"

"Merely information."

Mordecai tapped the side of his nose. "Ah. You knows me, mister. Keeps me eyes and ears open."

Ackworth shifted closer to a latticed window where a small space had opened up as two men vacated it and swung out through the main door.

Francis followed suit and the informant slipped between them to the window, effectively shielding his person from the general view. A cunning fellow, this Mordecai. He eyed Ackworth in an expectant way and the lawyer kept his voice low.

"Heard of Captain Indigo?"

Mordecai grinned. "Who ain't?"

"What do you know of him?"

"Lost a ship, din't he? Yer honour had an interest there, no?"

Not strictly accurate, but Ackworth let this pass. "What else?"

Mordecai glanced from him to Francis and back again. "Summat afoot? Ain't the first as comes askin'."

Francis cut in swiftly. "Who has asked you?"

For the first time the fellow looked up at him directly with inquisitive eyes. "T'other one were black too. Barbados, he says."

Ah, so this is where Hemp came when he checked on this same matter. "My steward. He asked you about Indigo?"

"He asked around. I heard him."

"You told him you knew the fellow?"

An uncouth cackle escaped Mordecai. "Not to say know him, not personal."

"But clearly you know of him?"

"Of him, of his gang too."

"Gang?" Ackworth was evidently startled. "What sort of gang?"

Mordecai made use of his finger tapping gesture once more.

Francis grew impatient. "What exactly did you tell my steward?"

Mordecai looked aggrieved. "Ain't a man of violence, your honour. I'm telling you, aren't I?"

"I have no intention of laying hands on you, Mordecai, but I wish you will answer questions instead of asking them."

A hand was laid on his arm and Francis turned to find Ackworth giving him a meaning look. A murmur reached him. "He has his methods, my lord. Best to let him tell it in his own way." The implication being that they would get further faster.

Francis curbed his irritation, turning again to the man. "Very well, Mordecai. Pray what else can you tell us of Captain Indigo?"

The little fellow had evidently not missed the interchange, his sharp gaze flitting from one to the other. The leer came back. "That feller arst where he's from. I told him, same as you, I said. West Indies."

Now they were getting somewhere. "Capital. Now tell us of this gang of his, if you will."

Another of those peculiar laughs escaped the man. "Word is Indigo's gang don't boggle at nowt. I'm a peaceable man, sir. I keeps outta the way of cutthroats with cutlasses, I do. Special as there's goods as is fer sale, and there's goods as ain't never seen again."

Ackworth threw a glance at Francis. "It looks as though you may be right, my lord."

Mordecai raised his hands palm up. "Never said nowt, me. All I say is there's goods as changed hands, and there's goods as didn't."

The suspicion could not but obtrude. Why not ask it straight out? This Mordecai seemed remarkably well informed. If there had been other nefarious doings, it was likely he had heard of them too. "Does this gang deal in wrecking, Mordecai?"

The blunt question appeared to offend the fellow. He shifted back, the keen gaze fixed on Francis's face. "See this head? It's the only one I got."

Did that mean the guess was sound? "Can you nod or shake it merely?"

"Not less'n I'm of a mind to lose it. Which I ain't."

Francis eyed him. Hard to know exactly what he meant to indicate, but his reluctance was tantamount to a positive response.

"Well, my lord? Is it enough?" Ackworth sounded a trifle anxious, and not a little disturbed.

Francis kept his gaze on Mordecai, who did not, to his admiration, buckle under it. "I understand you, I believe."

A grin came, accompanied by the nose tapping. "Ah, a leery one, eh?" He leaned close, dropping his voice to a croak. "If so be you was wishful to find a body what you wants to know about, it might suit yer honour to take a noggin at the Full Moon up North Street." He then twisted his arm, cupping a hand towards Ackworth. Francis caught a flash of silver and then the hand vanished, along with its owner who sidled out of sight as silently and swiftly as he'd arrived.

Outside, Francis paused perforce as Ackworth stopped short within a few paces away from the Ostrich.

"I am appalled, my lord. This raises so many questions, not to mention the urgent need for investigations. I had better inform the magistrate at once."

Francis held up a hand. "Hold for a space, Ackworth. We have only Mordecai's word for it that there has been mischief afoot, and a cryptic word it is. You don't imagine he will repeat any of that to an officer of the law, do you?"

Ackworth let out a frustrated sound. "Only under duress. Damnation!"

Francis glanced at the sky. The earlier sun had escaped within the clouds, but there was no sign of rain. "I believe we would do better to repair to this Full Moon."

"To what purpose? Even if we discover this piratical fellow there, you cannot suppose he will admit to having intentionally sunk the ship and stolen its cargo?"

"Of course not. But we may at least verify his whereabouts and that we have the right man. There is no saying but we may glean something useful too."

Ackworth blew out a breath. "I don't like it, my lord. Moreover, the afternoon will be well advanced by the time we get there. One does not wish to be walking such streets in the dark."

"Then go back to your office and leave me to reconnoitre."

Ackworth threw up a hand. "Under no circumstances. If you will go, I shall accompany you."

"Good God, man, do you think I cannot give a good account of myself? I am not such a fool as to enter the lion's den unarmed."

A reluctant smile dawned. "You speak as a man of experience."

"I was a soldier, sir, in war time. It is not an education one forgets."

With Ackworth's knowledge of the town, after crossing back over Bristol Bridge and proceeding northwards by a somewhat circuitous route, Francis at length found himself in an unsavoury neighbourhood with narrow cobbled streets, replete with shadowed lanes and filth running through the kennels.

Ackworth halted at length, gesturing towards a shoddy building, both weathered and dirty on the outside walls, and sporting a sign depicting a moon in a night sky. "This looks like the place, my lord."

"You've not been here before, I take it."

Ackworth gave a grimace. "It is not an area I care to frequent unless I must."

"Yes, I can appreciate your reluctance. Nevertheless, I think we must at least take a look." He would have moved on, but Ackworth hung back.

"We will be conspicuous, my lord."

"No doubt. Wait here if you prefer."

That galvanised the fellow. "By no means. I would much prefer to trust to a military man than remain on my own out here."

Francis laughed. "I like your candour. Let us see what we may discover."

If the Ostrich was not to his taste, this place struck Francis as noxious. The door creaked, opening directly into a gloomy taproom with low beams and walls blackened by smoke, an inglenook fireplace spilling ash, the odd gleam of brass hangings and a pervading smell of burning tallow. The windows were too small to permit of much light, even had the street outside been wide enough to provide it. From booths in darkened corners, shifty-eyed patrons took note of the newcomers and a surly-looking fellow in a greasy waistcoat peered at them from between the two barrels mounted on either end of a counter. No one spoke. Francis found the hush eerie. Was it a mistake to have come?

Ackworth plucked at his sleeve, his voice a whisper. "We should leave at once, my lord."

Francis's resolve stiffened. "No. We are here. We may as well make use of it." There was no sense in pretending to be other than they were. No one here would believe this was a casual visit. He made for the counter. "I believe a man called Indigo is to be found here. Is that correct?"

The fellow did not answer, only casting a glance behind into the recesses at the back of the room. A gravelly, accented voice spoke out of the darkness there. "Who wants him?"

Beside Francis, Ackworth fairly started, shifting back. Francis moved out into the room, his gaze piercing the gloom. "Captain Indigo?"

"Who wants him?"

The repetition rankled. "If you are he, come out and show yourself."

"My lord, I beg of you!"

Francis ignored the frantic plea, still trying to see into the space from where the voice had come. A figure rose up and began to move towards them, becoming clearer as it hit the beginnings of such light as there was in the well about the counter. If this was Indigo, report had exaggerated. Clad in dark garments from head to foot, the fellow was equally dark complexioned, thick-bodied with a bull-like head, but he was not of a height with Hemp. He reminded Francis of Cuffy, the other older footman from Willow Court where Hemp had originally been employed. This man's tight curls were grizzled, his jaw square, his countenance flat and stamped with age. He had, however, a commanding presence and a magnetic eye. It was easy to see how he had carved himself a career once he had thrown off the shackles of slavery. Villain he might be, but one could yet admire his confident stance.

He did not speak, instead holding his gaze on Francis. Waiting for him to open negotiations? So be it.

"I'm glad to have tracked you down, Indigo. I am looking into the death of Marcus Scalloway."

The fellow did not speak, a mere jerk of his chin indicating he had heard. Francis could readily believe a man of this type might have disposed of the victim, if he had reason. He tried a throw. "You captained his ship." A nod confirmed it. "Which went down." Another nod. "What happened to the goods?"

For the first time, Indigo looked past him to Ackworth hovering behind. "What's he want here?"

"He is assisting me. What happened to the goods?"

"Lost 'em."

"Succinct, but scarcely a satisfactory reply."

Indigo's mouth slashed open in a sudden grin. "All there is."

Francis raised his brows. "I sincerely doubt that, but let it pass for now. Tell me this instead. Did Scalloway cheat you?"

It was an impulsive fly at a catch, but it hit home. "No mourning here. Rats belong in the sewer."

"Do they? Now why?"

The dark features gave nothing away, but Indigo's gaze flicked from one to the other. Francis waited, not unhopeful.

Indigo gestured with his chin towards his companion. "He a merchant?"

"I am a lawyer, acting for Mr Harbury." Ackworth's voice was a trifle higher than usual and Francis cut in again, moving in a position to intercept at need.

"Leave him be, Indigo. He is not involved in this business. What had you against Scalloway?"

The black gaze, stark against the white of his eyes, came back to Francis. "Should have been a special crate. Weren't there. Opened 'em all once clear to sea. Naught."

Ackworth started forward. "What, no goods at all?"

Francis put out a hand to hold him. "Steady, man. I think he means there was meant to be some prize for himself. Is that it, Indigo? Scalloway promised you a boon and did not deliver?"

Indigo brought his now inimical gaze to bear on Francis. "He came to me. His deal. His promise. He reneged. His blame."

"Ah, I see." Had Indigo scuppered the ship to revenge himself? For what prize, or for how much? "I am tempted to ask just what was promised, but —"

A thick finger jerked up, cutting Francis off. "Between him and me."

"Very well, but it would seem he knew you of old."

"Didn't know him. Knew his snivelling rascal."

"Quin?"

Indigo scowled. "Name no names, me. Threw him off my ship, that one, years gone."

This became interesting. An odd history for a boot boy. Was Quin then Scalloway's informant? A go-between? "Scalloway knew your ways from Quin, then? I presume that is why he sought you out?"

Indigo emitted an explosive sound, redolent of scorn. "Why? Renown is why."

Francis eyed him, wary as he noted a glistening in the dark cheeks, fire burning in the eyes. But this needed sifting. Best not to speak of piracy. "I take it Scalloway wanted more than for you to captain the ship?"

The voice deepened further. "What he wanted I left behind long time gone. Rats try to use me. Wise to 'em now."

"Then why take the deal?"

A glimmer of yellow showed against the blue-black skin as Indigo grinned. "Have to live." His expression darkened. "Near lost myself well as the ship. Thanks to the rat. Said it before, his blame."

It was the longest speech he had so far made, and Francis was tempted to believe in his innocence — of pirating the goods at least. If his story were true, he had reason enough to rid the world of Scalloway. Could he safely bring up the question of Indigo's reputation in the West Indies? How could he phrase it without raising the man's ire?

"One thing more," he said carefully. "If you have left that life behind, how was it possible for you to sail to Barbados?"

The eyes burned. "Accusing, is it?"

"Not at all. I am merely curious."

Indigo hesitated, his stare eminently disconcerting. Francis was tempted to edge a hand to the pocket where his pistol was secreted. Then a hack of a laugh escaped the man and a set of broken, blackened and yellowing teeth showed briefly. "Ways and means, mister, ways and means. Old seadog, me."

There was no getting his secrets out of the man. A flicker of reluctant admiration caught at Francis. "So I perceive. I thank you, Indigo. That is all I need."

The man's attention had shifted. He was eyeing Ackworth again, a speculative gleam appearing. "Lawyer?" Ackworth nodded, staying well back, Francis noted. "Compensation for that other?"

Did he think to seek a share? Ackworth spoke low. "Perhaps. It depends."

Indigo stepped in, bullish head thrust forward. "Get mine!"

Francis could have laughed at the expression on Ackworth's face, except that the situation was growing too precipitous. He deemed it best to answer himself. "I doubt he is authorised to attempt to obtain whatever it was Scalloway promised you, Indigo."

"I say it. Let him do it." Indigo's eyes never left Ackworth's face.

Time to depart. If they could get out without let or hindrance. Prevaricate? What else was there? "Let us see if he can succeed on Harbury's behalf, and then perhaps we will talk again."

"Talk now best."

How to deflect him? Francis seized on the one thing that might deter the man. "I'm afraid that is not feasible, Indigo. We are dealing with a murder investigation. Until that is settled, there will be no funds forthcoming for anyone." To his relief, this tack gave the fellow food for thought. He rocked back, thrusting his chin upward. Francis took immediate advantage. "My thanks. You've been of help." He did not wait for an answer, but eased Ackworth before him and made as dignified an exit as was possible.

Outside, where it was at least a little less gloomy despite the approaching dusk, he breathed more easily. Ackworth was not similarly relieved. Freed of the oppressive presence of the intimidating Indigo, he gave rein to his indignation. "This passes all bounds! Can he truly suppose I would consent to act for a man of his stamp?"

"I doubt he supposes anything beyond getting his dues, whatever they are."

"Ha! If you ask me, he has had them. What would you wager against the odds those goods are stashed away somewhere?"

"I would not take you. But let us waste no words here." Francis urged Ackworth onward. It would soon be growing dark and as Ackworth had himself said, this was an environment to be avoided in the night hours. "I don't much care for our captain's attitude, my friend. We should make all speed to remove from this neighbourhood."

Ackworth fairly shuddered as he hurried along. "By heaven, yes! The fellow frightened me to death."

As Francis had observed, but he refrained from saying so, instead voicing an increasingly urgent misgiving. "I hope you are familiar with the area, for I have no notion where we are."

"I know it, but not well. This way is shorter." Ackworth steered them into a lane more an alley than a street and Francis took care to avoid the stinking kennel. Each turn brought them into just such another insalubrious lane, worse for the growing shadows on the walls as the light faded. He began to wish Ackworth had not taken this alleged shortcut.

Before they had penetrated too far into the maze of unpleasant streets, movement up ahead caught his eye. Two men were entering the alley they were now in at its other end, one from each side. Instinct put Francis on alert and he put out a hand to grasp Ackworth's arm. "Hold!"

The muttered command brought Ackworth to a standstill just as each of the two newcomers took a stance that effectually blocked the exit from the alley. Each had a cudgel, swiftly brought up and cradled suggestively in both hands.

Blood surging, Francis dug a hand into his pocket and brought out his pistol. Without hesitation, he cocked the gun and aimed the weapon at one of the would-be assailants. "Don't move, Ackworth!"

A single glance at the lawyer's frozen figure told him the command was superfluous. The man was rigid. Francis could hear his rasping breath. If he was going to be of help, he would need kicking back to his senses. "Ackworth!"

"Y-yes?" It was the veriest whisper.

"Come, man, this was not entirely unexpected. Take a quick look behind in case there are more of them."

Ackworth fairly whipped about, uttering a cry of alarm. Then his breath sighed out. "No, thank the Lord!"

"Excellent. Now listen to me."

"Yes?" He sounded a little less immobilised but still fearful. It was a start.

"I have only one shot. I can likely put one out of action, but the racket will bring others out upon us."

"Do it! They might help."

"And they might side with these."

Ackworth's breath rasped the more. "What then? This is Indigo's work. Because I would not act for him, I would guess. These are his men, I make no doubt."

"Very likely." Notwithstanding the pistol, which they must be able to see despite the darkening skies, the men took a couple of slow steps forward. "Here we go."

"Shoot, for heaven's sake!"

"Not yet. Once I fire, we need to be in a position to run. Back up slowly. That will bring them on."

Francis kept his gaze on the adversaries as he began to retreat, Ackworth following suit. Francis could feel the man's rising panic as their would-be assailants kept pace. Heaven send he did not run ahead of the command! The threat of two of them, even if one was going to prove worse than useless, must at least give the men pause. Thoughts reefed through Francis's mind as he assessed his options, the speeding beat of his pulse keeping his senses acute.

Were they spoiling for more than a fight? Persuasion? Beat the lawyer into submission? Unlikely. Indigo was shrewd. He would hardly risk an attack upon a man of rank, would he? This close to his own ground, when the crime could be brought home to him? He'd left no traces with Scalloway. If he'd had a hand in that. These of his gang were armed with cudgels. A threat? Indigo must have smelled Ackworth's fear. Or did he mean to warn them off from returning to his hidey-hole? One couldn't rely on it. Nothing for it but to protect Ackworth as well as save himself.

They were still several yards away. The same distance as the start. Capital. If the pace was maintained, there was a good chance of reaching the corner unmolested. Foolish of them not to attack now when it would be easier to trap their quarry.

Even as the thought left his mind, one of the men made a sudden spring, closing the gap by half. A whimper came from the side.

"Get behind me," Francis growled, taking a firmer grasp of his pistol.

Nothing loath, Ackworth scrambled to relative safety.

"Keep moving."

Guided by the man's steps, Francis backed. Ackworth's soft tones came from behind. "We are nearly at the corner."

"Praise be. Here's the plan. I need you to pay attention, man."

"Say on."

"I'll take the first one down. When I grapple the other, get out of sight around the corner. Wait for me there. Understand?"

"I understand."

A measure of relief entered Francis's breast. Ackworth's fear had abated somewhat. A few more steps did the trick.

"We are at the corner."

Wasting no words, Francis aimed at his first opponent's legs and fired. The ear-shattering report was followed on the instant by a scream of pain. The first man dropped his cudgel, seized his thigh and keeled over, squirming in the dirty cobbles.

No time to waste. Francis upended the pistol and seized it by the barrel as the remaining assailant pounded his way towards him, covering the yards between at an alarming pace. Devoutly hoping Ackworth had followed instructions, Francis wielded the pistol hard as the fellow bored in. He got one crack at the man's head before he went down under their combined weight.

The attacker was a big man and the air whooshed out of Francis's chest. He struggled to free his pistol hand, which had become entangled with his opponent's body. A blow cracked into his face. Searing pain blinded him for an instant. Then sheer rage consumed him. Heaving upwards, he succeeded in shifting the man's body enough to get an arm free. Grabbing at the nearest part of the head above him, he found an ear and twisted, hard. His attacker squealed, turning his head, what time Francis hit him again with the pistol butt.

An undirected fist caught Francis again, but the violent eyes were rolling and the fellow was struggling to raise himself. Seizing his chance, Francis gathered his strength to throw the body off. As he did so, there came a heavy thump. His assailant's mouth fell open, his eyes glazed and he collapsed, still half covering Francis.

Above them both stood Ackworth, a cudgel poised to strike again.

A wild laugh escaped Francis. "Good man! Now help me get this ugly customer off me and let's get to blazes out of here."

Twice had the waiter come in to state that dinner was ready to be served. Ottilia was hungry, but she did not wish to begin without Francis.

Where in the world could he be? She and Hemp had come back from the Pyg & Whistle over an hour since and more. All her husband had meant to do was to see what he might discover from the lawyer Ackworth. She had expected to find him in the parlour, no doubt growing impatient for his dinner. But here it was, long past the appointed hour and no sign of him.

Ottilia gave over watching from the window — not that she could see much of the harbour below despite the glow of a lantern here and there — and went to the mantel for the bell. Her impatient ring brought the waiter again.

"Are you ready, my lady?"

"I fear not. Pray ask Mrs Dunkeswell to hold a little longer. Send my steward to me, if you please."

While she waited for Hemp, Ottilia began to fret. It was not like Francis to be late. Even had he been detained, his ready stomach would bring him in a good hour from wherever he had gone. She pounced on Hemp the moment he entered the room. "Hemp, where is he? His lordship, I mean. Where can he have got to?"

Hemp preserved his calm. "I can go and look for him, milady."

"How?" Ottilia did not know whether to be soothed or irritated. "There is no saying where he might have gone."

"I may begin where he began."

"Yes, true." Hemp made for the door, but she stopped him. "No, wait! Have you dined?"

"An hour ago, milady."

"Then go." Again, she called out as he opened the door. "Stay! You might ask Tyler if Francis came back."

"I have already done so. His lordship has not been seen here since he went to find Mr Ackworth."

Ottilia let him go, half inclined to go out into the hallway and call him back again. Waiting alone was decidedly uncomfortable. She let out a breath and moved determinedly to a chair. Of what use to fret? It would not bring him back any the quicker. She sat, trying to concentrate on the ramifications of the murder, but she could not help taking frequent glances at the wooden clock on the mantel. The hands did not appear to move at all.

At last a murmur of voices and footsteps beyond the door rewarded her vigil. She jumped up as the door opened. Francis entered, supported on one side by Hemp.

"I found him just arriving, milady."

Ottilia's gaze was riveted on her husband's face. Blood oozed from his lip and an ugly patch of violent red decorated his cheek. "Fan! Dear heaven, what in the world happened to you?"

She was moving on the words as he answered, his tone cheerful enough. "I got in a fight."

Ottilia reached him, putting a finger gently to his wounded face. "You are injured, my darling!"

He grimaced. "I doubt it's as bad as it looks. Let me sit awhile."

Ottilia started, realising he was still leaning heavily into Hemp's supporting shoulder. "Heavens, yes! Bring him to the fire, Hemp. Sit, Fan, sit."

She stood back while Hemp helped Francis into the chair she had just vacated. He sighed as he sank into it, leaning back and closing his eyes. Ottilia did not take her gaze off him, her bosom tight with a horrid sensation of dull terror. She recognised it. The suppressed wish to make it undone, as though it had never happened.

Common sense came to her rescue. "Hemp, fetch a bowl of warm water, if you please. Also beg a clean cloth from the landlady."

Hemp departed on the errand without a word and Ottilia sank to her knees before Francis, reaching for his hand. He hissed in a breath and she relaxed her hold.

"Does it pain you? Did you hurt your hand too?"

Francis opened his eyes. "I am pretty well broke to pieces. I'm too old for this game." He grinned and then winced, putting up a hand to his jaw. "Wretched fellow got in a flush hit."

"I perceive as much. My poor darling, who was it?"

He was flexing his jaw between his fingers in an experimental fashion. "I have no notion. At least, I suspect he and his confederate were members of Indigo's gang."

Ottilia's mind leapt. "That's where you went? To find this Captain Indigo?"

"We found him all right. And you may usefully add him to your suspects. I'll tell you it all presently."

She patted his knee. "Yes, let it wait. But two men attacked you?"

He put his hand down and Ottilia slipped hers into it, trying for a calm she did not feel.

"I don't think Indigo relished our visit. Especially when I told him Ackworth could not act on his behalf. I thought the man was going to prove the weak link, but he did for the fellow who had me on the ground." The words conjured up a hideous picture in Ottilia's mind and she could not speak. "I had wounded the other. Ackworth had the sense to pick up one of the discarded cudgels and use it. As well, because as we ran, we could hear the hue and cry raised by the pistol shot."

Ottilia's heart gave a sickening thud. "You used your pistol?"

His gaze widened. "What would you have had me do, for pity's sake? I didn't kill the fellow."

She hastened to soothe. "Of course not, dearest. I was only shocked to realise you were in so much danger." She brought his hand to her lips and kissed it, swallowing on threatening tears. The opening of the door brought her head round. "Ah, here is Hemp with the water. Now I may clean these wounds."

He gave her a frowning look and Ottilia made haste to push herself up, turning away from his too keen gaze. She moved with the intention of fetching a small table when another voice stayed her.

"I'll do that, my lady."

Ottilia saw the footman for the first time. "Oh, thank you, Tyler. By the chair, if you please."

He placed it and Ottilia bade Hemp set down the bowl. He did as she asked and then stood back. Ottilia gave him an agonised glance and then took the cloth, ready to set about repairing the damage to her spouse's face.

She dabbed carefully at his lip, but Francis pushed her hand away. "Food, Tillie. I am devilish hungry."

She hesitated, her nerves still a-jangle. "Do you not wish to change first? I must see to the blood, Fan."

He set his elbows on the chair arms and pushed forward. "Tyler, help me get this coat off."

Ottilia kept out of the way as the footman eased her spouse out of the great-coat. Once free, Francis leaned back again with a sigh. "Take it away. I will dine as I am."

"Certainly, my lord. Is there aught else I can do?"

"Tell them to bring dinner."

The footman bowed and made to leave the room, but Ottilia stayed him. "Brandy, Tyler. Bring his lordship a glass."

As she moved in again, her spouse jerked his head up. "Hold a moment! Hemp, take care of my pistol. In the pocket. The ball is spent, but make sure it is safe in my dressing case."

Hemp was already rummaging in the pockets of the coat that Tyler held out to him. "Shall I prime and load it for you, my lord?"

Francis glanced at the pistol now in his hand. "Thank you, but I prefer to do it myself."

Hemp's rare smile flashed. "A man should always see to his own weapon."

Francis laughed and winced, making Ottilia's heart flip. "Indeed."

Both servants retired at last and Ottilia dipped the cloth in the water again, squeezed the worst of the wet out and approached her spouse once more. "Will you please let me attend to your wounds, Fan?"

A quirk of an eyebrow came, together with a mischievous look. "You may kiss them better if you choose."

A chuckle escaped her, albeit a trifle watery. "When you are no longer bleeding. Besides which, there is dirt on your face."

"I'm not surprised."

His voice was muffled as Ottilia dabbed carefully at the blood on his lip. He closed his eyes and she devoured his damaged features as she continued her ministrations. In the years they had been together he had never looked other than comely, strong and capable. The red splash across one side of his face rose almost to the eye and was already showing blue in spots. The lean, high-boned cheek was a trifle swollen, giving him a slightly misshapen look. His hair was dishevelled, his neck-cloth disarranged and spotted with dirt. Ottilia's heart cracked and tears slipped down her cheeks.

Not wishing Francis to see how she wept, she held back the threatening sniffs and finished her task in silence. Setting aside the cloth, she straightened. "There, that is better."

Francis opened his eyes and Ottilia quickly turned away, picking up the bowl and the cloth. She looked about the room for somewhere to set it down, keeping her back to him only so he might not spy her distress.

"Tillie?"

She moved away. "You are going to have a hideous bruise." Spying the table near the window, she went towards it.

His voice came, light, as if the incident was a mere bagatelle. "Not a black eye, I hope."

"Quite likely," she managed, setting down the bowl. "You will have a swollen face for a day or two." She struggled for control but the tears would keep falling and she could not face him.

"Well, that's a bit rich. I very much hope the wretch has a violent headache."

"So do I, Fan. I wish you had…" Her voice broke.

"Wish I had what?"

She could not answer. There was no keeping back the moistures and she sniffed, diving a hand into her pocket for a handkerchief.

"Tillie?" His tone had changed. "Are you weeping?"

Impelled, Ottilia turned and swept back to the chair, dropping down before him and seizing his hands. "Oh, my dearest darling, how can I help it? This is all my fault!"

He rolled his eyes. "I might have known it! I wish you won't be absurd, my dear one. You didn't injure me."

"I might as well have done." Once begun, the words poured out. "I brought you here. I am forever involving you in these horrible affairs and see what has come of it. Well, enough. This is the end of it. I shall never, ever allow myself to be dragged into —"

She broke off as her spouse gave a burst of mirth. He released one of his hands from her clutch, hissing a breath and putting his fingers to his wound.

"Don't make me laugh, you wretch!"

"It is not funny, Fan. I mean it."

His eyes were still brimming with amusement. "Now, I dare say. Tillie, my foolish dear, you are not responsible for what I may do."

"I am, I am. If we had not come here —"

He sat up, cradling her face with his free hand. "Don't do this, sweetheart. You know as well as I that you could not and would not have refused to help Hemp."

"This time perhaps, but another time —"

"Another time it will be some other imperative. Don't make foolish promises you can't keep."

Ottilia sighed, striving to regain her common sense. "I know you are right, but I want to make it. So many times I have driven you…" Her voice failed again.

"I know what you would say." His gaze was tender and her heart melted. "Yes, I have decried your putting yourself in danger many times, but —"

"And here the tables are turned, Fan, and I feel quite dreadfully that I put you through what I am feeling now. If that wretched villain had killed you!"

"But he didn't. Nor do I think either assailant had any intention of going so far. I dare say their orders were merely to frighten us. Besides, I had the pistol, remember."

She drew in an overwrought breath and let it out again. "Small consolation."

He smiled at her, notwithstanding the cut at his lip. "Where, wife, is my consolation, by the by? I thought you were going to kiss me better."

That did elicit a giggle. But she rose up. Bracing her hands on the arms of the chair, she set her lips, as gently as she could, below his eye, then to his cheek in several places and at last to the cut upon his lip. Pulling back, she met his gaze. "Better?"

"Much." Francis pulled her to him and planted a kiss on her lips. "But I feel sure I shall require a repetition in the very near future."

"As many as you wish, my dearest dear."

"I'll hold you to that."

There was time for no more, the opening door giving warning of the arrival of dinner. Ottilia hurriedly straightened and moved away, feeling a little less oppressed. She tried for a cheerful note.

"We will both be the better for some food, I dare say. Do you think you will be able to manage?"

"I shall have a damn good try."

Francis was rising as the waiter and Tyler, bearing trays, set out the accoutrements for dinner. Watchful, Ottilia saw how he took hold of the mantel. To steady himself? She lowered her voice to be heard only between them. "You are worse than you would have me believe."

"Stop fretting and fuming, woman. A tot of brandy will soon make me feel more the thing."

"Heavens, I forgot!" Ottilia shifted into the room. "Tyler, the brandy?"

"Here, my lady."

The footman brought across a glass with a measure of the golden liquid inside. Francis took it with a word of thanks and tossed it off, handing the empty glass back. He blew out a breath. "That was much needed."

Satisfied, Ottilia ushered him to the table where Tyler was holding out a chair. Francis waved her to her own seat and took his, allowing the footman to shunt it in for him.

Ottilia was already lifting the silver covers in search of viands that would satisfy him. The waiter left, but Tyler remained, ready to serve. For once, Ottilia was relieved to note, her husband did not dismiss him. She was happy to see that his plate was piled much as usual and as he began, somewhat gingerly, to eat, it occurred to her that she had not yet heard the full story of his adventure. One could not speak of it before the footman.

"Thank you, Tyler, we will manage now." He bowed and departed. "Are you up to giving me an account, Fan?"

As he ate, with far less of his usual appetite and taking small portions, the tale he unfolded gave Ottilia furiously to think. What had Scalloway promised? Gold, perhaps. Or some special sort of cargo. Did Indigo indeed intentionally pilot his ship onto the rocks? If so, it might be to obtain the goods for himself. Or simple revenge. Then he had no need to dispose of Scalloway. Why should he, when perhaps he might have frightened the man into giving him his due?

The description of the encounter with Indigo's bully boys momentarily revived her distress, though Francis made light of it.

"At least I managed to deflect his blow with the cudgel." He chewed a moment, a frown appearing. "Come to think of it, I have no notion what happened to the thing. He must have dropped it when I hit him with the pistol butt."

"Perhaps that is the one Ackworth used?" Ottilia felt hollow as she said it, the idea of a cudgel blow taking hold. What if Francis had been knocked unconscious instead?

"No matter. I was grateful to the man for finishing the fellow off. We've put two members of Indigo's gang out of action, which can't be a bad thing."

Ottilia did not give voice to the instant thought of a possible and dreadful revenge. This brought her mind back to the murder. "Well, if this Indigo is prepared to send his bravos after you, I cannot imagine he would boggle at contriving Scalloway's death. Assuming he did not feel the loss of the ship and all its cargo sufficient punishment."

Francis was cutting up the remainder of his meat small. "If he did contrive it. If, moreover, the cargo was indeed lost."

"It was lost to Scalloway."

"Even so, if Indigo did for him, I doubt he would do the thing himself."

"Interesting." A random thought crossed Ottilia's mind and vanished again before she could catch it.

Her spouse speared one of his portions of beef. "How many do we have on the list now, if we add him?"

Ottilia belatedly recalled her visit to the Pyg & Whistle. "Culverstone must be there, for I found out he had an argument with Scalloway that night, in the tavern."

"Then who do we have? Culverstone, Indigo, Mawdesley or Harbury."

"We cannot yet discount Elinor either."

"What of that fellow Quin?"

Ottilia held a forkful of ham pie poised in the air as the notion filtered through. "Why, though? Scalloway was his passport to gratuities. What would it profit him to cut off his master?"

Her spouse regarded his plate, another small piece of meat ready on his fork as he chewed. He was evidently managing better as the meal went on and Ottilia breathed a little more freely.

"Bribery? He was on Indigo's ship at one time. What if he paid Quin a sum greater than any he could hope to amass by running errands for Scalloway? He had access to the dagger."

"From your account, I must question whether this pirate would employ so unreliable a tool." Ottilia set down her fork, replete for the moment. "A little far-fetched, I think."

"We've had far-fetched before, Tillie."

"True. Let us not discount him altogether, then."

Her husband likewise set his fork down and pushed the plate away. "That was more painful than I thought for."

Ottilia's conscience rose up again, but she refrained from referring to it. "Have you had enough?"

He gave a faint grimace. "To tell you the truth, I feel a degree under the weather."

"A degree! The wonder is you are not laid down upon your bed."

He produced a grin. "Devil a bit. I'm not dead yet."

She put out an impulsive hand. "Don't! You know I cannot bear that thought."

He took the hand and touched it to his lips without a full kiss. "I do know, my loved one. Don't let it trouble you. It is over."

For now. But she did not say it. "Thank heavens it is Sunday tomorrow. You may rest with a clear conscience."

The words felt spurious. She was more shaken than she had ever thought to be, and tears were not far from the surface. Foolish, and unlike her. Where was her calm good sense? Francis was right, after all. It had been a brush, and he was suffering, but it had not ended as badly as it might have done. To her relief, he resumed the earlier discussion as he took up his glass of wine.

"What else did you discover at the tavern?"

As she told him of her visit to the Pyg & Whistle, a tingle of having heard or noted a detail she now could not recall beset her. That random thought again, but it proved recalcitrant. Was it one of the barmaid Cherry's disclosures? It eluded her and Ottilia abandoned the present attempt to find it, instead telling her husband of Hemp's desire to purchase Doro's freedom. But the niggle persisted at the back of her mind.

# CHAPTER EIGHTEEN

The morning fires were not going well. For so long Doro had been a lady's maid, she had lost the knack. She had crept into the mistress's room while the widow was still asleep, working so stealthily it had taken an age to get the fire alight.

Just being there felt alien. The change from trusted confidante to despised skivvy hurt her more than she had allowed Hemp to see. He had known she was distressed. Had he not ever been able to discern her moods? Almost from the first moment of setting foot in the sugarcane fields, he had been her solace, her comfort, her friend. She had not seen him that day she arrived at the plantation, but he later told her he had seen her, and divined at once her despair.

"I did not see you," she'd told him.

"Because you saw nobody, *ma reine*. Your eyes were looking inward." He'd smiled that special smile, reserved for her, she knew. "I came to find you in the fields."

That was when she first saw him. He'd helped her with the cutting, shown her how to wield the knife to make it easier on the arm. Treated her with kindness she had not known since the terrible day of capture. He never asked, not then. Years went by before she told him: how her father resisted until they cut him dead with a machete; how her mother fell upon the body and would not leave him, and had to be dragged away, screaming; how she then fell sick and died in the terrible confines of the slave ship, her carcase thrown over the side to float away in an alien sea.

Hemp had let her say it all. Then he held her while the pent-up rage and grief was spent. They never talked of it more. From that day, she began to live again.

"Daydreaming, Doro girl?"

Doro jumped with shock, almost falling as she turned on her haunches. "Quin! Why must you do this?"

He was regarding her from the middle of the carpet, the leer she both feared and hated in his face. "Do what?"

"Creep up behind me."

He set his arms akimbo. "What's taking you so long? Jenny would have had the whole lot going by this time."

"Jenny is used to doing it."

"Come down in the world, haven't you?" The jeer made her cringe inside. "Shouldn't have stuck that dagger in the master's chest."

Doro flung herself up in one fluid movement. "I did not!"

"Can't prove it though, can you?"

"I need not prove anything. The magistrate knows I am innocent."

"Maybe he does and maybe he don't?" Quin came closer and Doro backed. "What if I could tell him summat that'd change his mind?"

Fury leapt in Doro's breast. "Do you threaten me?"

He threw his hands palm up. "Me? No, girl, I'm aiming to help you."

A faint hope warred with her natural suspicion of Quin. "How?"

He advanced again and Doro forced herself to hold her ground. She must not show fear, though she was conscious of a blip in her heart rate.

Quin's tone became wheedling. "Ah, now see, it don't go that way, Doro girl. I don't give nowt for nowt, know what I mean?"

The implication made her shudder inwardly. But what if he truly had information that might exonerate her? "What is it you want?"

He leered again. "I'd guess you know, Doro girl. You be kind to me and I'd be willing to maybe give a little something in return."

Disgust roiled through her and she could no longer pretend. "Rather will I swing on the rope!"

His expression changed and he shrugged. "Suit yourself. If you don't want to know..."

"An honest man would tell me. Without such a bargain attached."

He shrugged again and made to leave the saloon. Doro's intense need intervened.

"Wait!"

He turned, with a look of satisfaction that made Doro feel physically ill. "Thought you'd change your mind."

She ignored this. "Do you truly know something?"

"Would I say I did if I didn't?"

"That is no answer. Why should I believe you?"

He strolled back towards her. "Gotta trust someone, Doro. The mistress won't help you. Jenny won't for as she's happy not to be doing the chores no more. Saul don't care long as he keeps in with the mistress. Who else is there?"

The catalogue was painful to her, but he had omitted the one light that shone for her in this house. "Peg. She will look out for me."

He made a scoffing sound. "Peg! How much influence d'you s'pose Peg's got? The mistress don't care for Peg. Nor none of 'em. It's you and me, Doro, what came with them from Barbados. If the magistrate was to say as you sure hadn't done it, the mistress would take you back like lightning, she would."

For an instant, Doro was tempted. To be reinstated? Once more to have those privileges attendant upon the intimacies she had shared with the mistress? Yet it could never be the same. The betrayal must ever stand between them. Then there was Hemp. The secret half-acknowledged hope snaked into her bosom. If there was to be forgiveness, let it come from a worthy breast.

The thought of Hemp threw a different slant into the maelstrom of question. Where had he said? He had shifted his lodging from the Rummer where he first stayed, to be at hand in the inn with his employers. The Ship? If she had it wrong, it would not be hard to find where they were staying. They must surely be there on a Sunday, and Hemp also therefore.

But first she must be rid of Quin and finish her morning's work. He was waiting, his look one of satisfied expectation. Did he suppose she meant to capitulate?

She drew herself up. "No. You may keep your secret. I will take my chance."

He scowled. "You'll regret that decision, Doro girl. Come crying to me you will, when that magistrate turns up to arrest you again."

She watched him leave the room and turned, with a newly determined will, to her task of renewing the fire.

Hemp chafed. Milady had once again postponed her promised visit to the Scalloway home. He had hoped the Sabbath would not interfere with the progress of the investigation. But today it seemed nothing would be done to further his urgent desire to clear Doro's name.

"His lordship is aching today, Hemp, and I must stay with him."

Another option with which he had been toying crept into Hemp's mind. "Does milord mean to come down today?"

"Later, perhaps. I persuaded him to break his fast in bed. I came to the parlour myself only to confer with Tyler. His lordship does not wish a physician to attend him, but I want Tyler to find an apothecary for an ointment. I must trust there will be one who is willing to do business on a Sunday. The bruise is severe and the jaw pains Francis a great deal."

Hemp hesitated, watching her cross to the mantel for the bell. He might as well be occupied. "Shall I do that for you, milady?"

She rang the bell and turned. "Thank you, no. I may need you. When his lordship is feeling more the thing, I hope to talk over our findings. We began over dinner, but Francis was too debilitated to trouble over it for long."

Ah, this was more hopeful. Yet the thought of standing idle was anathema. "Is there aught I may be doing in the meanwhile, milady?"

She gave him one of those warm smiles, but Hemp deemed her distrait. "To be truthful with you, my head is too full of my husband's condition to think how to act. Once I am satisfied he is recovering, I will give it my full attention, I promise you."

At this moment Tyler entered and Hemp was obliged to be content. He waited while she gave her instruction to the footman for the precise recipe she wanted, but milady had no further word for him. She left the parlour on Tyler's heels, saying she must return to the bedchamber.

For a short while, he paced about the parlour, unable to settle. Should he seize the opportunity to visit Doro? Except that milady had spoken of needing him when Lord Francis should be ready. Who knew how long that might be? Inaction had become a burden to him. As long as there was progress towards the end goal, he was able to possess his soul in patience. This hiatus was intolerable.

Then there was the question of the future. There was no letting Doro out of his life now he had found her again. His scheme of finding somewhere to settle must wait. Indeed, if he could persuade Doro to take him, it would not be a matter only for his choosing. If, that was, he succeeded in delivering her from the clutches of Elinor Scalloway. This reminded him of the notion he had taken which resulted in his resolve to confer with Lord Francis. He must speak to him face to face. This was not a matter to be relayed by a go-between, although he did not doubt milady would act for him if he asked her. As for Doro herself…

His imagination balked. He had seen his queen in the full flood of protest and it was not a sight to be provoked. Doro became like a wild thing, showing her ancestry in the violence of eye rolling and strange mutterings, the jittery dance of her limbs. The first time he had feared she was suffering a fit of some kind. But she came out of it none the worse, unable to recall what had been said to throw her into that condition. She'd told him of it one evening, while the moonlight hid her expression from his gaze, her face a silhouette, leaving only the eyes a-glitter.

"They say, the others from my village in Gabon, that my grandmother was a witch. I do not remember. She was used to go into a kind of trance and they say I do the same. That is why they do not like me, *mon roi.* They are afraid I may cast spells upon them."

He had tried to mitigate the hurt. "But they have known witch doctors. They should rather welcome you as a healer."

Light glistened on her lashes. "She was not that kind of witch. Her magic was evil. Blue charm, they call it, for that my grandmother's eyes were the same as mine. We are not looked upon kindly, we of this affliction."

Hemp had taken her into his arms. "It is not an affliction to me. If it is a charm, it is one I cherish, not only for its beauty. I bask in your spell, *ma reine.*"

She had dissolved into laughter, letting him hold her longer than she usually did until he had not been able to resist her lips. That was the first time he had kissed her. Doro had not rejected the overture. When he drew back, he found the blue eyes glowing and knew then she was his destiny.

Perhaps he had been right even then, he reflected, as his mind returned to the mundane parlour again, with its white-washed walls, dark wood furniture and leaded casements. He had thought it ended with Scalloway's triumph. But perhaps she was a witch, her blue charm drawing him here because she was here, and in trouble, needing him.

Hemp shook his mind free of such thoughts. Thus had Doro always made of him a dreamer flying at the stars, instead of the pragmatist he had been taught to be. His feet had been firmly on the ground these three years, apart from the personal tragedy that could never wholly leave a corner of his heart. Now here he was, enslaved again to a slave. Which she would not be for long, if he had his wish.

He came to himself with a jerk. What was he doing, wasting time in this fashion? Indulgence. Let him arrive at the end of the journey before he allowed himself that liberty.

Spying the desk, he went across. Pens there were in the standish, and ink. Paper? A drawer opened rewarded him. Either his lordship's or a supply left by the Dunkeswells for the convenience of their guests. Hemp took the chair and brought out a sheet, laying it on the blotter. He chose a sharpened pen, dipped it in ink and began to jot names, adding such information as had been gleaned of their movements, associates and possible reasons for wishing Scalloway underground.

That done, he wrote down: *Dagger. Who took it?* He followed this with a list of the inhabitants of the Scalloway home. Not that he supposed either Peg or the maid Jenny could have perpetrated the theft. Saul? Had he any reason to wish his master dead? More to the point, why would he try to implicate Doro? No, the most obvious was Quin. Only his dislike of the fellow made Hemp cautious. Milady never took the most likely culprit for gospel unless she had eliminated every other possibility. Even though it had indeed proved to be the likely solution once.

A knock at the door brought his head round. "Come in." One of the waiters slipped into the aperture and Hemp rose.

"Milord and milady are in the bedchamber. What is it?"

The fellow came in. "It's you, Mr Roy, as I was looking for."

"Me?"

"There's a female asking for you." He nodded towards Hemp. "One of your kind, she is."

*Doro!* His mind leaping with conjecture, he moved swiftly towards the door, and then checked. No privacy to be had down in the lobby, and he could not take her to his room. "Will you bring her up here, if you please?"

The waiter looked doubtful, but he shrugged and left. Hemp did not feel it behoved him to inform the man that milady would not object to him using the parlour. The whole business was in her hands, after all, and Doro would not be seeking him for other than the resolution of the murder. Had a new fact come to light?

It was not many minutes before a soft footfall sounded without, along with the heavier tread Hemp recognised as the waiter's. He opened the door himself.

Doro, dressed in a gown of more sober hue than that in which he had first seen her, with the same spencer and bonnet atop, stopped short, a look of anxious surprise in her face. The very sight of her set off a jolt in his pulse.

"Thank you, that will do. Miss Gabon, please come in." No need for the waiter to know upon what terms they stood. He stepped aside to allow her to enter and she passed him with head lowered, what time the waiter stood waiting expectantly. Hemp found a coin and dropped it into his ready palm. Then he followed Doro into the parlour.

She was standing in the space before the fire, looking about her. "You can afford a parlour?"

He grinned as he shut the door. "Yes, but this one is hired by Lord Francis and his lady."

Doro's look became hunted. "I should not be in here."

"Have no fear. My employers are keeping to their chamber for the moment. In any event, neither would be troubled to know we use their parlour." He crossed to join her. "What brings you, Doro? What has happened?"

She dropped her gaze from his, fidgeting with her ungloved fingers. "I am not sure it is of use, but it may be."

"Tell me."

She turned away from him, shifting to the window. Sensing her discomfort at being closeted with him, Hemp remained where he was, giving her space.

Doro looked back. "Quin caught me while I was lighting the fire in the saloon."

A cold feeling crept through Hemp. "What did he do to you?"

She turned fully then, fluttering a hand. "Naught. At least, he made a — a proposition."

Hemp made a silent resolve to find the perfidious Quin and choke him. He controlled the rising rage. "What proposition?"

A little quiver shook her. "This is not the first time he has made suggestions. But it was different this time." The blue gaze came up to meet Hemp's. "He hinted he has information which might make the magistrate believe me innocent."

Hemp did not leap on this. If anything, he distrusted what came out of Quin's mouth. "I take it he would not tell you the substance?"

With pain he saw the shudder that went through her. "Not without payment."

The inflexion on the word told Hemp just what Quin had demanded for his trouble. His murderous resolve strengthened. But Doro was not done.

"At first I thought he knew a thing to prove me guilty. That he meant me to satisfy him so he would not speak of it. But when I taxed him with that, he denied it. Rather he implied it was to my advantage."

"Do you believe him?"

"Oh, he meant it, Hemp." Her disgust was unmistakeable.

"I was asking if you believe he knows something."

She spread her hands, turning a little away again. "I do not know. When I refused to play this game of his, he said I will regret it, that the magistrate will come to arrest me again. I do not know what to believe."

He could not refrain from saying it. "But you came to me."

One of those fleeting smiles crossed her lips as she looked back at him, those eyes lighting in a way that caught at his heartstrings. "It was all I thought of."

He fought the urge to go to her, to crush her in his arms. "You did right. Will you be missed?"

"Only Peg knows I am out of the house. I cannot go and come now as freely as I did."

That was to change. But mum for that for now. "Only let me tell her ladyship and fetch my coat and I will be ready to accompany you. Is it cold out?"

"There is a little wind, but the sun is out. Wait!" She came across before he could reach the door, seizing his arm. "What will you do, Hemp?"

He nearly ground his teeth. "Choke it out of him if I have to."

She did not release her hold, her gaze searching his. "I do not want you to be hurt, *mon roi*. Not on my account."

He could not prevent himself from taking the hand and bringing it to his lips. "On no better account, *ma reine*." He released her, aware the blue eyes dimmed a trifle. She was still shy of him, wary. It would not be easy to reclaim her to him. "Wait here."

Seated on the edge of the bed, Ottilia surveyed with a critical eye her husband's face as he sipped at the hot black liquid in his cup. He was propped against a bank of pillows, high enough to rest his head, the lush brown locks framing his face. He looked up and caught her gaze.

"Aren't you having any?"

"Any?"

"Coffee, Tillie."

"Oh. No, I did not fancy it." To her own surprise, Ottilia had eschewed the brew. Strangely, the aroma had failed for once of its magic. About to pour herself a cup, she had felt abruptly repulsed and set the pot down again.

Francis was staring at her. "Did not fancy it? What in the world is the matter with you, my dear one?"

"Nothing. I probably drank my fill at breakfast."

"You had tea at breakfast."

"Did I?" She spoke vaguely, preoccupied with the condition of the wounds Francis had received. "The swelling has already reduced, but the bruise is beginning to darken."

Francis put up his free hand and touched his fingers to his cheek. "It still feels tender."

"It will do for a few days."

"Capital." He ran his fingers over his chin. "I need a shave."

Ottilia tutted. "Cannot you manage without for one day at least? Give it a chance to heal, Fan."

One eyebrow flicked up. "You won't care for it when I kiss you."

"I shall always care for it when you kiss me."

"I mean the rough edge, woman."

She regarded him with a fillip of mischief. "I don't know that, my dearest. If I am honest, I am rather taken with the look of you."

Both brows flew up. "What, with a night's growth of beard and a battered countenance? Have you acquired a sudden taste for a ruffian, wife of mine?"

She gave way to giggling. "You do not know everything about me, dear husband."

"Indeed? Who is this secret self, then?"

Ottilia reached for his hand. "One who is enjoying not being the victim for once. And having the opportunity to care for you instead of the other way about." She smiled as he cast his eyes heavenwards. "No, I did not know it was in me either."

"Last night you were grovelling in guilt, you wretch."

"I was not grovelling!"

"Grovelling," he repeated with emphasis. "Now you tell me it gives you pleasure to see me thus damaged."

"It just shows one cannot always be certain of one's feelings, do you not think?"

"What it shows, and I've said it countless times before, is that you are ripe for bedlam." His lips twitched. "On the other hand, you tempt me to drag you back into this bed and —"

A knock at the chamber door made him break off with a muttered curse. Ottilia, feeling distinctly warm, echoed it in her mind, but called out to whoever had disturbed them to enter.

Tyler's head popped round the door as it opened and he came in, holding out a small pot. "Your ointment, my lady."

Ottilia jumped up. "Excellent, you found an apothecary!"

"At his home, my lady, but I persuaded him your need was urgent."

"Was he able to make it up as I requested?"

"Just as you told me, my lady."

She took the pot and opened the lid, sniffing at the contents, what time Francis intervened. "Tyler, fetch up hot water for washing, will you?"

The footman bowed and withdrew. Satisfied with her purchase, Ottilia slipped the pot into her pocket through the slit in her petticoats.

Her spouse eyed the hand as she withdrew it. "What the deuce is that you have acquired? Some foul potion or other?"

Ottilia sighed as she came back to his side. "I knew you would object." Which was why she had not given Tyler her instructions in the bedchamber. "It is merely an ointment to make your wounds more comfortable. They will heal quicker."

"Why in the world had I to light upon the sister of a doctor for my wife?"

She tutted. "Do stop being a child, my darling. I won't put it on you until you are done with washing and dressing."

"Thank heaven for small mercies."

She ignored this. "Are you sure you are recovered enough to get up, Fan?"

"I can't languish here all day." He set down the empty coffee cup on the cabinet beside the bed and glinted at her. "Unless that is an invitation?"

Ottilia could feel warmth rising to her face again. "Don't make me blush, you fiend. Besides, Tyler will be back in a moment with your water."

Francis gave an elaborate sigh. "Pity. I was preparing to turn myself into a very tiger for you."

She dissolved into laughter, picking up the cup and taking it across to the tray set on a small table by the window. She was oddly exhilarated by the silly exchange, which surprised her. Such banter was like to set off her innate prudery, except that her years with Francis, coupled with the widening of her horizons, had made her more tolerant. Consorting with all sorts and conditions of individuals, as she must when engaged in these enquiries, had done much to adjust her outlook.

Disapprove she might of such creatures as Cherry at the Pyg & Whistle, but she acknowledged that life did not always provide the choice of a better form of survival.

"You have grown quiet, my dear one. What's to do?"

She turned, looking across at her spouse. "I was thinking of Cherry and her ilk."

"Who is Cherry?"

"The barmaid, Fan, remember? I told you I spoke to her when I visited the tavern where Scalloway was killed yesterday."

He frowned. "My brains must have been more addled than I knew. How dared you go there without me?"

She threw out a hand. "Don't scold. I had Hemp for my escort."

"So I should hope. Not that it makes it much better."

"Come, Fan, you know how well he looks out for me. I was never out of his sight, I promise you. At least, I was in a stuffy parlour, but the door was open and he was outside it." She glided towards the bed again. "Moreover, I don't see why you should see fit to censure me when you managed to get yourself almost slaughtered by a pirate's bullies."

He lifted a warning finger, but she was saved from retaliation by Tyler's arrival with a jug of steaming hot water. Francis threw off the covers. "My razors, Tyler. And a fresh shirt and neck-cloth."

Ottilia moved to the door. "I will leave you to your ablutions, dearest."

He was already hunting for the chamberpot in the bedside cabinet. "I will find you in the parlour."

Shaking out her blue petticoats, Ottilia left the room on a relieved sigh. By the time he was dressed, he would have forgotten all about the little contretemps. As she entered the parlour, she recollected the ointment in her pocket. She would apply it when her spouse came in. Despite his recalcitrance, he would be glad of its soothing properties if he truly meant to shave.

She had barely settled into a chair by the fire when a servant knocked, entering on her word to present a silver salver with a sealed missive upon it addressed to her husband. What now? She dismissed the fellow, rose and moved across to the window to examine the unknown handwriting in the better light. A flash of white on the desk caught at the periphery of her vision.

Why, what was this? A sheet of paper lay on the blotter, decorated with jottings in a neat hand. She set down the sealed letter and picked up the paper. A list of names with notes beside each coalesced into a pattern. The suspects? The writing became familiar. She had seen it a couple of times before. Hemp had been busy, had he? Written before he had gone off on his errand with his Dorote, in all likelihood. Taking the thing with her, she began to read with more care.

Hemp's quarry was lounging in the kitchen when he entered on Doro's heels. He caught the apprehensive glance she threw at him as she spied Quin at the table. The fellow spoke before either could say a word, his sharp gaze going from one to the other.

"Well, well, what's this then? Consorting with the enemy camp, eh, Doro girl?"

He would regret that tone presently, but Hemp kept his own even. "Miss Gabon had a message for milady, that is all."

Quin's lip curled. "Miss Gabon, is it? La-dee-dah. You was easy enough with your Doro this and Doro that when you first come, friend of Doro."

At this point, Peg came bustling in from the pantry, carrying a joint of meat on a platter and Hemp was obliged to keep his tongue. She exclaimed at his presence and at once offered a brew from the pot.

"I thank you, no. I came only for a word with Quin here."

Doro had not spoken, but her lips were tight and she had kept her gaze lowered. She raised it now, addressing the newcomer. "Not for me either, Peg. I must put off my outer garments. I will come down to help you in a few moments."

"No hurry, my dear. Them pans are soaking in the tub."

Hemp watched Doro slip through the door leading to the servants' stairway and turned back to Quin. The fellow was watching him, a wary look in his face. Was there a touch of fear too?

"Outside, Mr Quin, if you please."

The man made no move to get up. "I don't please, Mr Roy. What d'you want with me?"

"That you shall discover."

"What if I don't wish to?"

Hemp allowed his teeth to show, but without mirth. "Then I shall remain until such time as you acquiesce."

Quin made a face. "Acquiesce? Ooh, now there's education for you."

Peg had chosen a large knife from her collection in a drawer in the sideboard and was preparing to cut a hunk off the joint. At this, she ceased her labours and looked from one to the other. "What is this?"

Hemp gave her a cool glance. "Nothing to concern you, Peg. Merely, I have a strong desire for a word with Quin alone."

"To do with the master's murder, is it?"

"It has a bearing on the business."

Peg eyed Quin. "Well, what's your objection, then? You want it sorted, don't you?"

"I don't answer to no one, least of all him." A thumb jerked at Hemp. He got up at last. "'Sides, I've work to do."

Hemp lost patience. "You will come outside with me, Quin, or I shall take you by the scruff of the neck and drag you out." He made a move towards the man, who backed off, throwing up his hands.

"All right, all right. Since you're so insistent…" Quin hesitated, and the light of fear was stronger in his eyes.

Hemp stood aside, leaving him access to the back door, and gestured. "After you."

Under Peg's puzzled gaze, Quin fairly scuttled to the door, opened it and was through almost before Hemp could follow. He caught the man as he grabbed the rail and set a foot on the first of the metal steps.

"Not up there on the road. We'll talk down here." He pulled Quin back as he spoke.

The area was narrow and long. Quin pushed past him, ran to the raised bulk of the coal hole, seized a shovel from among a collection of implements and turned, standing at bay with the shovel poised for attack.

Hemp regarded this defensive pose with grim humour. "Have no fear. I am not going to set about you, Quin. Not this time."

The rider caused his opponent to take a stronger hold of his improvised weapon and make a stabbing gesture. "You try it is all!"

No sense in attempting to persuade him to set the thing down. "If you are comfortable, may we now commence our discussion?"

For a moment the man said no word, eyeing Hemp from under his brows. "Ain't nothing to discuss for all of me. What do you want?"

Hemp kept a surreptitious eye on the movement of the shovel, but took a careless leaning pose against the wall, folding his arms over his great-coat which he had left hanging open, the day being a degree warmer than hitherto. "I have two things to say to you, Quin."

Suspicion and fear deepened. "Say 'em quick, then."

Hemp ignored this. "One." He tried, but the rage would creep into his voice. "If you ever again make advances to Doro, I will beat you to a pulp."

Quin made no reply, but Hemp could see the rise and fall of his thin chest and the quiver in his limbs. That threat had gone home.

"Two. You will tell me now exactly what little piece of information you have which induced you to hold a threat over Doro's head."

Defiance leapt in Quin's eyes. "I'm telling you nowt! You can't make me."

In one fluid motion, Hemp straightened, closed the distance between them, pushed the fellow back with one hand and seized the weapon with the other. Quin squealed, losing balance and making violent efforts to retain his hold. Hemp let him go so he could use his other hand to wrench the shovel away by main force. Quin let go, shrinking back into the corner.

Hemp discarded the shovel out of the fellow's reach. "Now, are you going to tell me or aren't you?"

Quin snivelled. "You're a bully, you are."

"And you are a sneaking rascal. Cut line!"

Hemp saw the capitulation as the fellow's shoulders drooped. Quin's tone turned sullen. "I'm saying nowt, but since you make such a point of it, I'll show you."

He made a move towards the door and Hemp stepped back to allow him to push past, following him into the kitchen, where Peg stood round-eyed. Had she heard the exchange? Quin did not speak, but his pace quickened as he walked through into the passage. Hemp kept right on his tail as they climbed the stairs. He was surprised when Quin passed the main downstairs rooms and went on up. Where was he headed?

"You had best not be taking me on a wild goose chase."

Quin did not answer, only casting a resentful glance over his shoulder as he carried on past the first-floor landing. He did not stop until they reached the attics. What in the world could he have to show up here?

In another surprising move, the boots halted at Doro's door and knocked. "Doro's chamber? What do you want in here?"

Quin looked up at him. "You want to see or not?"

The door opened, revealing Doro's astonished features. Hemp made haste to soothe. "No need to concern yourself. Quin is about to show us what it was he spoke about."

"In here?"

"He says so."

Doro did not pull the door open. "I do not want him in my room."

"I'll go then, shall I?"

Hemp grabbed him. "No, you don't. Doro, this is his answer to the information he told you he has."

"In my room?"

"Apparently. Well, Quin?"

The fellow eyed Doro in a way that made Hemp itch to slap his head for him. "Can't show nowt if you won't let me in."

She looked at Hemp and he nodded. At last she stepped back. Quin went in, heading for the bed. Hemp waited in the doorway. He was acutely aware of Doro, who looked dismayed and poised for flight, but he kept his eyes on Quin's actions.

The little man lifted the mattress, shoved his arm under and swept an arc. A grunt escaped him and he brought his arm out, allowing the mattress to fall back into place.

Doro gave a gasp and Hemp's gaze became riveted, his mind alive with conjecture. Quin was holding Doro's dagger.

# CHAPTER NINETEEN

At her husband's urging, once he had submitted to have his wounds smeared with her ointment, Ottilia had sent for a snack of more sustaining viands than he had consumed at breakfast. Tyler having supervised the selection, Francis was disposing, with more care than usual and in smaller bites, of a gargantuan portion of beef liberally laced with mustard and slapped between two slices of bread. A jug of ale was at his elbow where they sat together at the table, poring over Hemp's notations.

Ottilia sipped at her coffee, having succumbed to her addiction after all, and nibbled at a macaroon. "He has noted everyone down, including what they have said and their movements as far as we know them. Did I not say Hemp is efficient?"

The response came a trifle muffled. "Huh! Solved it all too, I dare say."

"How should he? Pray don't be petty, my dearest. Although it looks to me as though he favours this Mawdesley. What is your mind on him?"

A grunt was all the answer she received until he had swallowed down his mouthful. "Too fearful. Hemp would do better to look to Captain Indigo."

"You maintained Indigo would not do his own dirty work."

"Nothing to stop the fellow sending one of his ruffians to do the business."

"But how would the fellow get in? The tavern is locked up at night, so Cherry said."

Francis took a pull from his tankard. "A break-in?"

"An excessively clever one if the Pymoors did not discover any sign." Absently, Ottilia reached for another macaroon, her concentration on the list, running over the details. "Cherry suggested the murderer could have hidden himself before Pymoor locked up."

"And then escaped how? No door was found unlocked in the morning as far as we have heard."

"True. No doubt Mrs Pymoor would have complained bitterly and at length of any such damage."

Francis was about to take another bite of his improvised meal, but he paused. "It is not beyond the bounds of probability that the murderer waited in his hiding place —"

"After doing the deed."

"— and strolled out once the place was buzzing in the morning."

Ottilia smiled at him. "Your adventure has not entirely addled your wits, my brave hero."

She received a comical look. "An appellation I shall remind you of any time you seek to crow over my inability to guess at the truth."

She laughed. "Do I crow?"

He declined to answer, instead tapping a finger on the paper. "Concentrate, woman. Who of this motley crew could have hidden in the tavern and waited for Scalloway to fall asleep?"

Ottilia studied the list again and sighed. "Any, I must suppose. Both Mawdesley and Culverstone were there that night."

"But both left again."

"Just so. I cannot see Culverstone sneaking back. I submit too that this factor rules out Elinor. Doro attended her to bed, so unless she got up, dressed herself again and crept out of the house unobserved, I cannot think she had the opportunity to conceal herself in the Pyg & Whistle."

"No, and she must have been noticed if she had."

Ottilia finished the last of her macaroon and picked up her cup. "Which leaves us with Mawdesley and Indigo."

"There is Harbury too, although his involvement must include Mawdesley. Plus, he claims not to have been at the tavern that night."

"True. It is becoming quite a puzzle, Fan, in spite of Hemp's meticulous work here." Ottilia recalled the letter that had arrived earlier, which had proved to be from Mr Ackworth, requesting Francis to be ready to bear witness about the attack since he had the intention of laying the affair before Mr Belchamp, along with the suspicion of criminality. "I hope that magistrate does not come calling too quickly. We are not far enough forward with this."

Her spouse was laying down the remains of his snack, the bread somewhat mangled from the difficulty of chewing. "I dare say he will turn up tomorrow. Ackworth's note indicates a high degree of anxiety on his part. I recall he was voluble upon the subject even as he assisted me to get back here last night. Not that I paid his tirade a great deal of attention, what with concentrating on remaining on my own two feet. I doubt the fellow will feel safe until Indigo's ruffians are under lock and key. Which, by the by, means Belchamp must inevitably hear of Indigo, so we may as well add him to the list of suspects you gave him before."

Ottilia inwardly chafed. "It will not do. I cannot get a grip on this business at all. Do you get the feeling we are being led something of a dance, Fan?"

"By whom?"

"I wish I knew. One of them must be lying, do you not think? Only see how we are wandering from one to the other with no firm conclusions."

"On the contrary." Francis drank off a draught of ale and set the tankard down. "You have eliminated Elinor and Culverstone."

Ottilia got up. "Not entirely. Well, Elinor perhaps, but I am by no means certain of Culverstone's innocence. He had so much to gain."

"But getting into the inn again?"

"He might slip in unseen if he went directly upstairs from the hallway."

"Then so might Elinor." Francis followed her across to the fireplace, sinking into his previously vacated chair, his unbuttoned green coat falling wide to reveal his striped waistcoat. He had been obliged to give Tyler the task of brushing and cleaning his second set which had suffered from yesterday's contretemps.

Ottilia remained where she was, one hand on the mantel as she looked down at him, not really seeing him as she drew images in her mind's eye. "Culverstone was there. What if Cherry's suggestion is correct and he never left?"

The question remained unanswered as a knock at the door was followed by the immediate entrance of Hemp, still dressed for the street in his great-coat and the round hat with a large brim, his aspect one of anxious bewilderment.

"Milady, I beg your pardon for coming in directly, but there is a matter you should know of at once."

Disturbed by his manner, Ottilia moved out into the room. "What is it, Hemp?"

For answer, he opened his coat. Only now did Ottilia see that he had been concealing something inside with one hand tucked into the folds. "This was under Doro's mattress."

He was holding a dagger by the hilt. Ottilia stared at the thing in silence, struggling with incomprehensibility. She was aroused by her spouse's voice.

"Dear Lord, is it the same one?"

He had sprung up from the chair and now went across to take the weapon from Hemp's hand, examining it closely as Hemp responded.

"It cannot be, milord. The magistrate has the one that was used for the murder." He turned his gaze to Ottilia. "We searched that room, milady. It was not there."

She moved to Francis, her gaze fixed on the blade. "Why did you think to look again?"

"I did not, milady. I made Quin tell me what he knew that he tried to use to force Doro's consent."

"Consent?" Ottilia glanced at Hemp as she spoke, and thought she heard him grind his teeth.

"He told her he might prove her innocence with the magistrate if she … co-operated."

"Scoundrel," came from Francis, still preoccupied with the dagger. "Is this Doro's, then? I thought she claimed the other."

"It is very similar. They were made by a slave on the plantation. Buck had been used to do ironwork at his home, making knives and other implements. His style was distinctive. I bought this one for Doro."

Ottilia surveyed the dagger's ornate curlicue. "It is intricate work on the hilt. Are you certain this one is Doro's and not the other?"

"I never saw the other. Doro swears it was very like." Hemp held out a hand. "If I may, milord." Francis gave up the weapon to him and Hemp ran a finger across the metal at the base of the blade where it fitted into the handle. "Here are her initials. I had Buck engrave them. I could not mistake."

Ottilia was sifting possibilities. "This alters things indeed. Do we take it Quin put it there himself?"

"I got him to admit as much, milady."

"Why did he have it?"

Francis snorted. "Isn't it obvious? The scoundrel must have stolen it. Did you not say at the outset, my love, that someone had taken it for the purpose of putting the blame upon Doro?"

"Ah, but this is not the dagger that was used, Fan."

He cursed. Hemp, who had set aside his hat, did not speak, but his concentrated gaze upon Ottilia was disconcerting. She smiled.

"Are you expecting me to fathom the solution? I fear you will be disappointed. We have been sifting over all this evidence you wrote down." She gestured to the paper still lying on the table. "I confess I am as baffled as are you, Hemp." She became brisk. "However, we may establish a few things from this. Whoever chose the weapon for the purpose had either been to Barbados or knew someone from the island."

"Well reasoned," said Francis, cocking an eyebrow. "And?"

"And this Quin has a trifle of explaining to do."

Hemp came alive. "I have already questioned him closely. He claims he found the dagger among his master's effects. He says Scalloway was afraid Doro would use it to stab him and thus confiscated the dagger."

"Interesting. Cherry spoke of Marcus fearing to be attacked with Doro's dagger." Ottilia regarded the smoulder at his eyes. "I take it you do not believe Quin's story?"

"I believe naught that little —" Hemp broke off, tightened his lips for a moment, and then resumed. "If Scalloway had it, then he took it without Doro's knowledge. She had no notion it was missing. Yet it seems far more likely to me that Scalloway would have instructed Quin to take it, if he was involved at all in removing it from Doro's possession."

Francis took hold of the dagger again, observing as he did so, "That is all very well, but Quin was never a suspect. Isn't that so, Tillie?"

"Not directly."

"Why is he not, milady?" Hemp was looking quite murderous himself. "He is hand in glove with Mawdesley. He, we know, went to the Pyg & Whistle."

"Added to which, he was there in the early hours of the morning," put in Francis, abruptly changing his tune, "so he may well have hidden."

"Exactly so, milord. Moreover, he produces this dagger now when he was the one who handed it to the constable, claiming it was Doro's."

Ottilia touched his sleeve in a calming gesture. "All that proves, Hemp, is that he recognised the dagger, or thought he did. The theft may have occurred after the murder, for all we know."

"Tillie, that doesn't make sense. If Quin thought the dagger was Doro's, why trouble to look for it?"

"He may not have been looking for it. He may merely have been snooping." A growl from Hemp made her hide a smile. "Let us suppose for a moment that he did indeed find the dagger among his master's effects, realised he had made a mistake, and purloined it."

Francis looked sceptical. "To what end?"

"That I do not know. He might have had an idea even then that he could use it for gain with Doro."

"But she was in prison then. Why should he think he might have such a chance?"

Hemp took this. "Because he knew the day of the murder, milord, that I was doing my utmost to set Doro free." His face changed and he cast an agonised glance from Francis to Ottilia and back again. "In that regard, milord, I have been wishing for the opportunity to speak with you."

Wondering, Ottilia looked at Francis, whose brows had drawn together. "In what regard?"

Hemp drew a visible breath. "Doro's freedom. I am talking of manumission." He glanced at Ottilia. "Milady will have told you I asked about Doro's ownership, but Mrs Scalloway refused to discuss the matter with me. She said that until the murder is resolved, there was nothing to be done."

"Well, that seems logical."

Hemp's tone became the more even. Suppressing agitation? "Milord, I am anxious to get her out of that house. I had thought of approaching Lord Radcliffe, who is no doubt familiar with the procedures required, but I am certain he would refuse to entertain my request."

Francis set the dagger down and leaned against the table's edge. "What, you want me to talk to the fellow on your behalf?"

"Yes, milord. Also — and I ask this only because I do not have a draft on my bankers for the purpose — to lend me the purchase price."

Ottilia heard this with rising emotion. Not of sympathy, but of indignation. Francis was speaking, however, before she could give voice to her thoughts.

"How much is it likely to be? I have limited funds on my person. Though I could give Radcliffe a draft on my bankers, of course."

"I cannot say precisely how much, milord. A female slave is worth more than a male. But when you seek to buy a slave's freedom, the seller is apt to raise the price. If you apply direct to the courts in Barbados, it is clearer. A female slave may receive manumission for three hundred, assuming you can show cause to satisfy the courts."

"Then I imagine I had best first see Radcliffe and discuss terms."

Ottilia found her voice. "Not while I live!"

"Ottilia!"

She was too angry to care for the admonishing tone, nor had she room at this moment for the shock of hurt in Hemp's face.

"Milady?"

"You expect me to consent to be a party to trafficking a human being? No, Hemp, I will not!"

He looked altogether crestfallen, but Ottilia's disgust was too great to care. Her husband intervened, speaking with urgency.

"Tillie, this is not like you. I thought you must jump at the chance to see Doro freed. You are as much an opponent of the trade as my mother."

"Opponent? I loathe and despise it. Oh, do not look at me like that, the pair of you! Cannot you see what you would be at? To make such a bargain is but perpetuating the disgrace."

Francis's tone grew angry too. "That is enough! I choose to assist Hemp and I am frankly astonished that you should take up this intransigent attitude."

Ottilia struggled to control the demon riding her that urged her to fight back. "Fan, pray listen to me a moment."

"Well?"

It was not encouraging. Ottilia took a painful breath. "I am as anxious to see Doro free as is Hemp, but not like this."

"How, then?"

Hemp's voice shook as he cut in. "Milady, I do not like it any more than you, but there is no other way. We spoke of this, remember?"

"We spoke of your wish to buy Doro's freedom. That is your privilege. We did not say that either myself or his lordship would become involved in such a transaction."

"Ottilia, be silent! You do not speak for me."

She threw Francis a violent glance. "Then allow me to speak only for myself." He made no answer, and she pressed on, turning to Hemp. "I have given this matter some thought, Hemp. Since you spoke to me, I mean." She cast another, more moderate, look towards her husband. "This took me too much by surprise. I apologise for my ill temper, to both of you."

Francis still looked sombre. "Very well, but the issue remains."

She threw up a hand. "It need not. Hemp, there is another way. A better way."

"What way?"

She disregarded the scepticism in her husband's tone and addressed herself to Hemp. "Doro told me that Elinor promised to free her, as soon as they were both free of Scalloway. She must be made to honour that promise. No money need change hands, and we may all be satisfied."

Neither man spoke for a moment, Francis evidently ruminating on her words while Hemp chewed at his lower lip. He broke the silence first. "Milady, I do not think Mrs Scalloway is in a mood to do so much."

In a musing tone, which lightened Ottilia's heart a little, Francis spoke. "You said she refused to discuss it while the matter was unresolved. But Doro's innocence is no longer in doubt. Her dagger was not used."

"Just so." Ottilia pressed her advantage. "She must — she *will* — agree. Moreover, we will have it in writing."

Hemp, she was relieved to see, was beginning to look more hopeful. "A particular document is needed, milady, a manumission deed. I do not know if we can get that from Lord Radcliffe, but he may write the substance of the same in a letter. Then I will need to take it to London to put it to the Lord Mayor for the necessary certificate."

"Very well, we will do whatever is needed as soon as Elinor capitulates."

She received a shrewd glance from Francis. "And who, may I ask, is going to force her to capitulate?"

Ottilia's lips quivered on a smile. "Do you truly need to ask?"

A grin lightened his features and Ottilia breathed more easily. "I ought to have known better than to trouble my head with the business in the first place."

She went to him then, setting a hand to his chest. "No, you were right to respond the way you did. Forgive me, my dearest. I cannot think why I flew up into the boughs." A throat clearing behind her reminded Ottilia they were not alone. She broke away and turned. "Leave it to me, Hemp. Tomorrow I shall repair to Charlotte Street. I swear I shall derive a great deal of enjoyment in bending Elinor Scalloway to my will."

At last Hemp's features relaxed and he flashed his teeth in a grin. "I am half inclined to pity Mrs Scalloway, but that her treatment of Doro made me furious. Not to mention this business with Quin…"

"Have no fear. We will have Doro out of there in short order."

"Thank you, milady. You have relieved my mind of a great weight." He bowed, snatched up his hat and left the room in a bit of a hurry.

It crossed Ottilia's mind that his emotions were about to get the better of him, but she was too anxious to make her peace with Francis to give it much attention. She went to him the instant the door closed. "My darling, will you forgive me? That was badly done of me and I am so very sorry."

"I had not thought I married a termagant." He captured her to him and she was gratified by his kiss. "You are absolved."

She grimaced, setting both hands to his chest. "Yes, but I am not a termagant, Fan. What is the matter with me?"

He raised an eyebrow. "You are asking me?"

She let out a gurgle of laughter. "Well, I don't recall ever before losing control in quite such a manner. Poor Hemp must have been shocked to see it."

"Poor Hemp? What of poor Francis?"

Ottilia leaned in to him and reached up to touch his face. "Poor wounded Francis at that. What a shrew I am!"

He grasped her fingers and brought them to his lips. "Never a shrew, my loved one. But I wish you will tell me by what means you intend to coerce Elinor Scalloway."

# CHAPTER TWENTY

True to her promise to Hemp, on Monday, Ottilia betook herself to the Scalloway home. She was later than she might have been, taking time first after she had broken her fast to ensure her husband was suitably fed and settled in comfort with his feet up and a news journal for company. She noted with satisfaction that he was feeling a good deal better, his bruises now having turned distinctly blue and the swelling having reduced. Nevertheless, she subjected him to a further application of her ointment before consenting to leave him in peace and depart upon her errand. An overcast sky threatened rain but Hemp, who accompanied her at her behest, given under her husband's admonition not to go alone, had taken the precaution of bringing an umbrella. He saw her to the front door before retiring, as he said, to the domestic regions via the area steps.

"Send to me, milady, when you are ready to leave. I will meet you outside here. I do not think Mrs Scalloway would wish to see me."

Ottilia laughed. "I doubt she will be pleased to see me either."

To her surprise, the widow exhibited a modicum of welcome in her greeting. When Ottilia entered, having shed her cloak in the hall, worn with the hood up in place of a hat, Elinor Scalloway was found to be engaged in writing at a desk in the big front parlour where Ottilia had met her before.

She rose at once. "Ah, Lady Francis, how glad I am to see you at last. Have you any news?"

If she was complicit in her husband's death, one would not know it, so assured was her manner. Ottilia avoided taking her hand by bowing merely from the neck. "If you mean, Mrs Scalloway, do I know who killed your husband, I am afraid I must answer in the negative."

"I am sorry to hear it." Elinor gestured to the sofa. "Will you be seated?"

Ottilia settled, taking up a central position so that the widow might not join her. After a moment's hesitation, Elinor sat down in a chair opposite.

"Well, ma'am?"

"Well what, Mrs Scalloway?"

A spurious smile flickered. "I presume you are not come merely to pass the time of day."

Gloves off? That suited well with Ottilia. She smiled back, with equal insincerity. "I am here for a sufficient purpose. Before we come to that, however, allow me to put a few questions to you."

Elinor made a graceful gesture of consent. "By all means, ma'am. I have nothing to hide."

"Did you know that Laurence Culverstone went to see your husband at the Pyg & Whistle upon the fatal night?"

A shade of wariness came into Elinor's eyes. "Not at the time, but he has since told me so."

Ottilia tried a throw. "Has it occurred to you that he might not have left? That he could have remained hidden in the tavern, waiting his moment?"

There was no mistaking the consternation that leapt in her face, and was as swiftly banished. "Pho! A nonsensical notion."

"Is it? It did pass through my mind that you might have done the same, but —" ignoring the indignant sound that came from her victim — "it seems unlikely you would have allowed your maid to undress you, necessitating the inconvenience of dressing yourself again, if you meant to go out into the night."

"Not to mention," returned Elinor on a mocking note, "the difficulty of slipping out of the house unseen, the danger of walking through the streets unescorted, and concealing myself from all at Marcus's disgusting tavern."

Ottilia nearly laughed aloud. "I see you have considered the matter in some detail."

"Of course I have not. But I am not a fool, Lady Francis. These things leap to the eye. Besides, if you had ever lived in Barbados, you would know a lady would never dare to venture forth alone in such a nefarious fashion."

"Not even cloaked and masked for disguise?"

Elinor made a scoffing sound. "That would be infinitely worse. My papa taught me always to secure a guard for escort. A female is never safe among slaves."

Ottilia's amusement evaporated. This was not the impression she had gained from Hemp and his colleague Cuffy with regard to Flora Sugars. Young Tamasine, daughter of the owner, had run free among the slaves, who all looked out for her. Was it the arrogance of ownership that made Elinor afraid? Or had she reason to fear from the way her father's slaves were treated? From one or two things Hemp had occasionally let fall, Ottilia knew there were slave owners guilty of cruelty. But mum for all that for the moment.

"But Culverstone is not similarly burdened. Do you think he killed your husband?"

The direct question disconcerted the woman. She looked away, fidgeted a while, and then her gaze returned to Ottilia's. "I did wonder."

She said no more. Ottilia waited, regarding her without, she hoped, any sign of judgement in her face. Elinor abruptly rose up, paced to the fire and turned there, setting a hand on the mantel. The knuckles whitened as she gripped its edge. Her gaze returned to Ottilia's face. "I hoped you would have settled this. I do not believe Laurence would stoop to murder. He knew I meant to leave Marcus. Why ruin everything?"

"Because the procedure for separation and divorce is lengthy and complicated? Because he was impatient to secure your wealth?"

Elinor's face changed, flying fury. "How dare you suggest such a thing? There is no question of… If that were all, Laurence would have abandoned me once I married Marcus. But he did not. He insisted we might be friends, if we could not be man and wife. Though it went against the grain with him, he tried to cultivate a friendship with Marcus." A quiver went through her. "He did not then know, any more than I, with what sort of man he had to deal." She swept back to stand before Ottilia. "I do not hesitate to tell you the truth, for you will discover it in any event. You are famed for that, as I have learned. Laurence and I were sweethearts long before my father chose to ally me to Marcus Scalloway. Laurence has neither money nor birth, not to satisfy my father's ambition at least."

Ottilia was glad of her loosened tongue, which must make her task easier, but here she entered a caveat. "But Scalloway had no money either. Nor is his birth of any great note."

Elinor made a despairing gesture and threw herself into the chair she had vacated. "What did we know, we colonials? Besides, eligible males were few and far between. Marcus had not then embarked upon a career of dissipation. Or at least, he behaved impeccably within our limited social circle. I have no knowledge of how he conducted himself outside it. He was handsome, he had address. In a word, he was plausible. Only Lord Radcliffe had doubts. My father would not listen to him."

"Yes, so his lordship said."

"You have spoken with him? To what purpose?"

"I needed particular information. But you were telling me of Laurence Culverstone. He chose to accompany you back to England?"

Elinor sighed. "He knew by then how unhappy I was. When I told him we were sailing, he arranged matters with his father for a temporary leave of absence and took a passage on the same ship."

Ottilia pressed for more. "You had it in mind even then to leave Marcus?"

Elinor had the grace to blush. "I could not have done it in Barbados. My father would never have permitted me to cause such a scandal."

"Which meant you were obliged to rely upon Lord Radcliffe?"

Elinor shifted her shoulders. "I did not know if he would support me. But he is my trustee. I hoped, if I could show him how badly Marcus treated me…"

Ottilia did not spare her. "You will scarcely deny, I hope, that your husband's murder is highly convenient for you and Mr Culverstone."

Elinor threw up her hands. "How can I deny it? It is of all things the best outcome I could have hoped for." In an abrupt fashion, she stopped, staring across at Ottilia with an earnest look. "I told Marcus I would kill him, you know, when he threatened to beat Doro."

"Was that his habit?"

"The wretch was apt to raise his hand to the girl whenever he lost his temper and could not take it out on me as he was wont to do in the early days. But I swear to you I did not mean it, though I confess I had thought of it often. If I had killed him, I would have chosen to use a pistol. I keep one. We all did in Barbados."

The candour appealed to Ottilia, but she held to the possibility it might well instead be a clever ploy. Collusion could not be ruled out. She might test it out a little. "Do you know the substance of the discourse between Culverstone and your husband when he spoke to Marcus at the tavern?"

Elinor bit her lip, then spread her hands. "Why conceal it? Laurence told him our marriage was at an end. He knew I had agreed to wait upon the morrow instead of leaving that day. Laurence was afraid, I think, that I might capitulate, change my mind."

"Afraid enough to make certain?"

Elinor's bosom rose and fell sharply, but she did not look away. "You are forgetting that the dagger belongs to Doro."

Ottilia played her ace. "It happens, Mrs Scalloway, that it was not Doro's dagger that was used. Your own fellow Quin found her dagger, decorated with her initials, among your husband's personal effects, from where he stole it and himself put it back under Doro's mattress. The murder weapon is in the possession of the magistrate."

Elinor looked to be thoroughly taken aback. And a little fearful too? "That is not possible!"

"Why not?"

She did not answer this. "You are saying Doro is innocent of the deed?"

"That I knew from the first, but this is proof, yes. Moreover, the dagger that killed your husband could only have been acquired by someone who has been to Barbados. Like Doro's dagger, it is unique to a slave who made such weapons there."

If Elinor was red before, she was now perfectly white. "How can you know that?"

"My steward is acquainted with the maker, a man called Buck, who lives on the Flora Sugars plantation."

Elinor looked dazed, a sort of dull horror creeping into her eyes. Did she suspect Culverstone after all?

Ottilia relented a little. "Do not be dismayed, Mrs Scalloway. It happens there are others, associates of your husband's in this shipping venture, who may equally have acquired a dagger of this type. Moreover, their reasons for wishing your husband dead are as valid, if not more so, than Mr Culverstone's."

Elinor let out a series of gasping breaths, throwing a hand to her bosom. "Oh, how you frightened me!"

She might be the more so shortly. "On another matter, were you in the habit of signing papers your husband put before you? Without reading them fully?"

Elinor stared. "I do not understand you."

"Yet the question is simple enough."

"What has this to do with his demise?"

"Oh, it may have a bearing." Ottilia softened her tone. "Mr Harbury claims you signed an undertaking to reimburse him should anything untoward happen with this shipping venture."

For a moment, Elinor looked dismayed, then nonplussed, her brows drawn together. Which was real? Then her brow cleared and she gave vent to a breathless laugh. "Oh, that was merely for the purpose of Marcus securing the contract. He destroyed it, he told me."

Ottilia felt almost sorry for her as she shattered this illusion. "He lied."

Elinor's features became first white, and then red. "That blackguard! Is there no end to the deceits he practised upon me?"

Ottilia judged the moment ripe for the bringing forward of her chief mission. She chose not to beat about the bush. Catching Elinor unawares was a bonus.

"You will recall, I hope, Mrs Scalloway, that you promised Doro her freedom?"

Elinor blinked in an uncomprehending manner. "I beg your pardon?"

"On the day you told your husband you were leaving," Ottilia pursued, unrelenting, "you told Doro that you would take her with you and would free her as soon as you were yourself free."

Elinor waved a vague hand. "What of it?"

"You are now free."

"True, but —"

"And Doro is no longer under suspicion."

"That is only your word."

"Not at all. The dagger is clear evidence. If she meant to kill her master, she would have taken the only weapon she knew of, her own dagger. You will find, I believe, that the magistrate will accept this as proof of her innocence."

Elinor was regaining her senses, as evidenced by the frown. "Yet you would blame Laurence, with far less cause. Doro was holding the dagger."

"Yes, and Quin took it from her and handed it to the constable, saying it was Doro's. But he now knows very well it is not hers, and so he may testify."

"Even so —"

Ottilia rose, allowing her tone to alter. "There is no even so, Mrs Scalloway. A promise is a promise. You have no reason in the world not to do as you said you would. Free her, Elinor! You owe her no less."

Elinor was still balking, that was plain. She fidgeted. "I need her."

Ottilia demolished this without hesitation. "You don't need a slave! Besides, you dismissed her services as your maid."

"That was because I thought she had killed Marcus."

"Now you know she did not."

"Yes, and I will reinstate her. Jenny is not nearly as useful to me. Doro and I —"

Ottilia lost patience. "There is not going to be any more Doro and you, Elinor. There is a far better future awaiting her, and it is not in your household."

Elinor stared. "I don't know what you mean. She is mine. I own her. Marcus bought her for me as a bride gift."

Ottilia's emotions threatened to overcome her again. With difficulty, she suppressed the violence of feeling in her bosom and spoke with what calm she could command. "Pray do not talk of owning a person to me, Mrs Scalloway. I will not trouble to express my views to one of your ilk, for I can see it would be useless. I will remind you once again, you made a promise to Doro. If you do not make it good, and in short order, it shall be my business to make known to the world at large the events of these past few days." She saw that these words had gone home and lost no time in driving in the message. "Do not imagine I cannot do it. I have a great deal of influence. Moreover, my mother-in-law is a dowager marchioness and her views on slavery are a good deal more forthright than my own."

Elinor was almost cowering, but she rallied enough to fight back. "You would blacken my name? Well, I will not be remaining in England, so it matters little to me."

Ottilia smiled, though she felt far from amused or friendly. "News travels far, Mrs Scalloway. I do not suppose your social circle in Barbados is immune to gossip. Do you?"

Walter Belchamp, arriving with Ackworth not ten minutes after Tillie's departure, was surveying Francis's countenance in a way he found somewhat embarrassing.

"That must have been a nasty blow, my lord, very nasty indeed. Did the villain catch you with a cudgel? Mr Ackworth here tells me both assailants were thus armed."

Francis ran his fingers across the damage. "I thought so. We were on the ground at that point and I was occupied with attempting to throw him off, so I can't tell just what happened. It hurt like the blazes afterwards. That's all I know."

"It was the cudgel," put in Ackworth. "I saw it."

Belchamp threw his head back in a gesture of shock. "I am astonished he did not break your jaw, my lord."

"Oh, he could not put the full force of his arm behind it, for Lord Francis had him almost pinioned." Ackworth demonstrated as he went on, "He must have struck from the elbow. Insufficient power there, you see."

Both men were standing in the middle of the parlour while Francis, having set aside his footstool and risen to meet them, took his favourite stance by the fire. He was thus able to rest an elbow on the mantel, supporting his maltreated body. He was still sore, despite his assurances to his darling wife, and remaining upon his feet for any length of time was difficult. He brought the discussion of his injuries to a close. "I can give you a statement as you ask, sir. Of more importance, can you do anything?"

"Do, my lord? I've done it." Belchamp waved his arms about in excitement. "An initial foray at least. I have sent Pucklechurch off to see what he may discover. Mr Ackworth having given me an excellent description —" Turning to the lawyer, "Most detailed, sir, very helpful." And back to Francis. "Having that, as I say, the constable may ask around."

Francis grimaced. "Take care he does not receive much the same treatment. You did not send him in search of Indigo, I trust?"

Belchamp threw up a hand. "Ah, now there, my lord, we must take a different approach. With what Mr Ackworth here has imparted, it might profit us to investigate further. If indeed the fellow deliberately sunk that ship. Although I do not think it behoves us to tackle the fellow at this juncture."

"Well, when you do, I suggest you take the militia with you."

Even Ackworth looked astounded by this suggestion. "The militia?"

"The man's a dangerous pirate. I dare say he is wanted in every island in the Caribbean. I cannot suppose he would have crossed to England else."

Belchamp put his hands behind his back and ruminated for a space. "Hm. You paint a pretty picture, my lord. However, I cannot have him arrested for piracy here. As regards the lost ship, it may well prove a tricky piece of work to make a case against him."

Francis spoke without thinking. "Unless he proves to be the man behind Scalloway's murder."

Belchamp stared. "Gracious me, my lord! Have you any reason to suppose it?"

Francis turned on Ackworth. "You didn't tell him?"

"The matter of those ruffians setting upon us was more pressing, my lord," said Ackworth in an apologetic tone.

"But that was my whole purpose in seeking the fellow out!"

Belchamp drew his attention back. "What made you suppose he might be involved, my lord?"

"Mawdesley alerted us. He mentioned the name and my steward recognised it. I believe I told you he is from Barbados."

"Who is this Mawdesley?" Belchamp had begun to look bewildered.

Francis grew impatient. "My wife mentioned him when she gave you a list of suspects other than the slave girl. Who, by the by," he added, recalling the duplicate dagger, "is now successfully exonerated."

Both men stared. Belchamp found his tongue first. "You don't say so, my lord. By what means?"

Francis related the story of the discovery Hemp had made through Quin. He retrieved Doro's dagger from the desk where he had secreted it and showed the magistrate the initials on the blade.

Belchamp was much shocked and much inclined to revile the boots for not reporting his find immediately. "But so it is with these rascally petty thieves. Never an ounce of responsibility or thought for the invidious situation of another."

"As it chances, Quin thought to use it to coerce Doro into lying with him. He was not likely to give up such an advantage."

"An unconscionable rogue."

"You had best take this into your charge, Belchamp. I assume you will take it as proof of Doro's innocence?"

Belchamp agreed at once. "Indeed, my lord, indeed. It must form part of the evidence. But I must protest at the perfidy of this fellow Quin of the Scalloway household. I do not think much of the judgement of the deceased."

"It is worse than you know. Scalloway used him as go-between in all his nefarious dealings. It was he who led Scalloway to Indigo."

"You don't say so? You astonish me, my lord, indeed you do."

"Prepare to be even more astonished. Indigo claims he threw Quin off his ship in the old days."

For a moment, Belchamp could do nothing but splutter. "But — this is —! Good gracious me, my lord!"

Francis suppressed a laugh. "So much for Scalloway's judgement, sir."

Ackworth cut in. "Assuming he knew his fellow had been a pirate too."

"Quin? I doubt it, artful though he has proved himself to be. More like he was employed to swab the decks. He has no physical valour." Francis turned back to Belchamp. "Nor indeed has this Mawdesley, of whom we heard, incidentally, through Quin."

Belchamp recovered from his amazement. "Ah, yes, you were about to tell me of him."

"Mawdesley works for Harbury, who was joined with Scalloway in the transaction with the ship. Ackworth knows all about that. He is attempting to recover Harbury's losses through Mrs Scalloway's trustee."

"A commission I now regret accepting. Especially now that this wretched pirate is involved. It is he and his sailors whose story of the shipwreck prevails. No one else was there."

Francis took this up. "We first supposed Indigo was in a string with Scalloway to scupper the ship for gain. Indigo maintains, however, that Scalloway cheated him of a promised prize. Which makes me strongly suspect he did scupper the ship."

"For revenge?"

"So I should imagine, Belchamp. Unless he offloaded the goods first and has them stashed somewhere."

Belchamp balked. "The whole thing is fantastic. Really, one does not know what to believe."

"Then you will have to entrust the business to us. I speak of the murder. Our interest in the matter ends with that. Any criminal proceedings regarding the lost cargo is within your province, sir. As to Scalloway's assailant, if anyone can unravel that, my wife can."

Belchamp's natural jollity resurfaced. "Ah, the incomparable Lady Fan. You have admirable confidence in her abilities, my lord."

Francis laughed. "I assure you I have often been sceptical during the proceedings. But I have seen her succeed too many times to doubt her abilities in this line."

"Such a pity one is not able to appoint her to a position of authority."

"It has been said before."

"I am not surprised. We do not give our womenfolk their due, my lord."

Throughout, Francis had been vaguely aware of Ackworth chafing in the background. He gave tongue at this point.

"May we stick to the matter at hand, gentleman?"

Belchamp laughed and gave the man a buffet on the shoulder. "There speaks the lawyer. Very well, sir. I suggest we repair to my home, for I would have your written statement of the attack. I shall require yours also, my lord, in due time."

Ackworth hesitated. "I wonder, Mr Belchamp, if it is worth your speaking to Harbury with regard to this agreement between Scalloway and Indigo?"

"You mean to discover if he knew?"

Francis cut in. "He won't admit it if he does." Although it would certainly help Tillie if such a motive could be proven. He was about to suggest they instead tackle Mawdesley when it occurred to him that he and Hemp might have better success with the little man. Hemp had intimidated him the last time.

His visitors having departed, Francis settled back into his chair and took up his interrupted reading of the *Bristol Journal* brought up by Tyler. He had been catching up on the progress of the Anglo-French hostilities. No engagements had as yet occurred, but the threat to the Low Countries was under discussion, along with Pitt's determination to protect the realm from invasion after reciprocating France's declaration of war. Having moved on to local news, Francis had just chanced upon a passage referring to the loss on the Seven Stones Reef of vessels other than the *Blackbird* when the door opened to admit his wife. Tillie came in with a jaunty step, a mischievous smile leaping to her face as her eyes met his.

"You look decidedly triumphant, wife of mine. I take it you carried the day?"

"I did." Tillie threw off her cloak and slung it over a straight chair by the table, moving immediately to join him at the fire and, shaking out the blue dimity petticoats, dropping into the armchair opposite. "I was obliged to resort to blackmail."

Francis lifted an eyebrow. "When have you ever balked at using any such means?"

She laughed. "Well, as a rule I prefer persuasion, but the woman has no moral fibre. Would you believe it? She dared to say she could not do without Doro and would reinstate her. As if such a pitiful concession could benefit her."

"What threat did you use, my ruthless one?"

Tillie looked a trifle sheepish. "You will laugh at me, but I laid claim to a great deal of influence and touted Sybilla's rank."

"Ha! I've noticed you use it when it suits you."

"Well, but the creature tried even to brush that off. She thought herself safe from gossip in Barbados, silly woman."

Francis regarded her in some amusement. "Do you suppose your word will carry so far?"

The delicious gurgle that never failed to delight him came. "I highly doubt it. Although I dare say Hemp's connections might do the trick. But it sufficed to frighten her into submission when she was brought to believe I might ruin her reputation in her homeland."

"She will free Doro, then? I imagine Hemp is cock-a-hoop."

The light in her face dimmed. "He is glad, yes. But I think he will not be truly convinced until he has this manumission certificate in his hand and may give it to Doro."

"Will he tell her?"

Tillie made a gesture in the negative. "He does not wish to get her hopes up. I think he is afraid Elinor will renege when it comes to the point." Francis received a speculative look. "In which regard —"

Francis threw up a hand. "You need not say it. You want me to see Radcliffe to arrange the business."

Her warm smile appeared. "You know me so well, my dearest dear."

Francis grunted. "You need not waste your cajolery. I'll do it. Hemp had best come with me."

"Soon?"

He smiled at the anxious note. "Tomorrow. I've no doubt I'll be steadier on my feet by then. Though I don't imagine Radcliffe will comply before talking to Mrs Scalloway."

"But you will set the wheels in motion."

"Indeed. Then, when we've seen Radcliffe, I want to seek out that fellow Mawdesley again and I need Hemp for that."

"Can you do as much? Pray be careful of your health, Fan!"

"I might say the same to you. I had forgotten how fatigued you were."

She made a gesture as if to brush this off. "I will do, Fan. I have not been obliged to work nearly as hard as you on this occasion, my poor darling. You have borne the brunt of it."

Francis could not withhold a comical look. "We'll reckon it up one of these days."

The characteristic gurgle escaped her but when she spoke, Francis heard that note in her voice she ever had when interest in a case caught her attention.

"What do you want with Mawdesley?"

He gave her an account of Belchamp's visit and his wish to tackle the little man concerning the agreement between Scalloway and Indigo, which might well bear upon the murder.

Tillie became thoughtful. Going off into one of her reveries? What had she latched on to this time? Francis did not disturb her train of thought, even when his stomach began to inform him that the dinner hour must be approaching. He glanced at the clock and the movement served to jerk Tillie's attention back.

"Sustenance," he said, rising to pick up the bell. His wife did not answer as he rang it, but when he set it down, she spoke. Her words struck oddly.

"It cannot have been so simple."

Francis leaned an arm along the mantel and grinned at her. "As cryptic as usual. Of what are you talking, woman?"

Her gaze remained upon him, but Francis was sure she had her attention on some inner thought. "The dagger."

"Which one?"

"Both. But in particular the one Quin had in his possession."

"You mean Doro's."

"Not necessarily." Her head tipped a little to one side as she gave him a speculative look. "Quin came with Scalloway from Barbados."

Francis made the jump. "He might have had a dagger of his own!"

"Just so. Why then take the one belonging to Doro?"

"For the purpose of incriminating her." Francis frowned over this. "But do you suggest Quin killed his own master?"

Before his wife could answer, a knock produced Tyler. Francis put in his order for a snack to be served directly which might sustain him until they dined.

"But not too much, Tyler," Tillie cut in. "The dinner hour is not far off."

Francis nodded. "Speaking of which, make sure they take hot water to the chamber in good time. Her ladyship and I will repair there in an hour."

"Do you wish me to lay out a fresh neck-cloth, my lord?"

Francis waved him away. "No, this one will do. I have but sat in the chair all day. But we will freshen up before dinner."

Tyler withdrew and Tillie got up. "I must go to the chamber for a space, Fan."

Francis put out a hand to stay her. "Hold a moment. Do you seriously suspect Quin?"

She hesitated. "It is a possibility."

He cursed. "Now you are being provocative. What aren't you saying, Tillie?"

She touched a hand to his chest. "My darling lord, I am but just in the process of ruminating." Her brows drew together. "You said Quin and this Mawdesley are hand in glove?"

"I don't know that. Hemp knew of the other from Quin. They were messengers between their respective masters."

"But which masters?"

"Harbury and Scalloway, of course."

Tillie produced a secretive smile and touched a finger to his injured lip. "It is mending quite well now, Fan."

"Tillie!"

She showed him an innocent face. "What, my dearest dear?"

Francis exploded into laughter. "You are the most infuriating female, wife of mine. I don't know why I bear with you."

# CHAPTER TWENTY-ONE

A degree of trepidation attacked Doro as she answered the mistress's summons. She knew from the footman Saul that both Lady Radcliffe and Mr Culverstone were with Mrs Scalloway in the parlour this morning. Since the mistress, in her widowhood, was no longer participating in the social life of the City, doubtless her ladyship would be bringing the latest gossip attendant upon the master's murder. There had been a deal of talk of this kind as Doro had heard Jenny telling Peg. Just as had been the case before all this trouble, when she was privy to such chattering discussion. Slave owners thought of their human property as so many pieces of furniture. A humiliation, but not as hard to bear as the one she now endured.

She was feeling vulnerable and alone, although she had seen Hemp briefly upon the previous day when he came with milady. He'd had little to report. He only asked how Doro did and would not reveal why Milady Fan had come here.

"She is still making enquiries. The real culprit must be found."

Doro had searched his face. "Does she think my mistress killed her husband?"

Hemp shrugged. "As to that, I do not know. Milady does not reveal all her thinking to me."

All? Some, then. She did not ask the question, sensing reticence in Hemp. Her duties were pressing and she left him in the kitchen being regaled with coffee by the cook. Yet an inexplicable disquiet persisted. She was no longer a suspect, but she did not feel the comfort of that. Indeed, it was hard to believe the constable would not after all arrive to set her in manacles again, a horrid reminder of her early captivity.

When Jenny found her in the midst of polishing the dining table after clearing the remains of madame's late breakfast, she was dismayed to hear she was wanted.

"The mistress said you are to go up straight."

Doro eyed the maid. Jenny had taken a superior tone with her ever since her elevation to lady's maid. "What does she want?"

"How should I know?" Jenny stuck her nose in the air. "Go as you're asked and you'll find out."

Doro cast a glance down her own person. Her apron was spotted with dirt and she was aware of dampness where she had perspired from her exertions. "I am not fit for it. I shall have to wash and change my apron."

"Suit yourself." Jenny shrugged and made for the door, halting there with a parting shot. "She's not in the best of moods, so I'd make it quick if I was you."

Alarm struck at Doro. Following upon the maid's exit, she began untying her apron as she went, heading not for her chamber but for the kitchen. She might wash her face and hands in the pantry and, with luck, find a clean apron in the freshly done laundry.

Revived a little by these small preparations, and sped on her way with an encouraging word from Peg, Doro hurried up the stairs and along the corridor. She straightened the colourful chintz gown, once more fit to wear, as she hesitated outside the door, listening to the voices within.

"For my part," came clearly to her ears from the one she recognised as Lady Radcliffe, "I think you should refuse to answer any questions, Laurence. What authority has this Lady Fan, as she calls herself?"

A low-voiced response from Mr Culverstone went unheard. Then Lady Radcliffe again. "If that is so, the magistrate is derelict in his duty. Radcliffe thinks it disgraceful that he should be permitting this female to undermine him."

This time the mistress responded. "Believe me, Caroline, I am in agreement. She is a forceful woman, however. She seems to think her rank makes her unassailable."

"Yes, it is a pity she is so highly placed. One might otherwise cut her for impertinence. How dared she make such representations to you, Elinor? I hope you will pay no heed to that nonsense. She has no power to coerce you into doing as she demanded, be her mother-in-law the Queen of Sheba!"

Mr Culverstone here spoke up, loud enough to be heard. "You would not suppose her to be of such rank as she claims. She does not know how to keep a proper distance. She consorts with people of all conditions. She even entered the Pyg & Whistle, as I have heard."

A noise of disgust escaped Lady Radcliffe. "One might hope her husband could control her starts, but on the contrary, Lord Francis actively encourages her."

"Oh, he has been questioning around on his own account. I met that fellow Harbury — your husband's partner, Elinor, if you recall — and he had a visit from Lord Francis, who was himself making enquiries."

The mistress cut into these animadversions, her tone both cutting and irritated. "I am glad *someone* is trying to find out who killed Marcus. So also should you be, Laurence, for as you are quite as suspect as I am, if not more so."

"Curse that woman! If she had not interfered, no one would have questioned that girl's guilt."

Shock set Doro into such a panic, she was knocking on the door before she could question the wisdom of making her entrance at this juncture. The sudden silence beyond the door brought it home and her spirits plummeted.

"Come."

Doro drew a painful breath, willed her unruly knees to strength and turned the handle. She pushed open the door and entered to the stare of three pairs of eyes. A swift glance showed Mr Culverstone to be reddening, as if he realised he had been overheard. Lady Radcliffe's eyes filled with disdain and the mistress straightened her spine, her features assembling into an expression Doro knew of old. It was not the moody one Jenny's words had led her to anticipate. Thus had she ever looked when she meant to be gracious. It was a look not always to be trusted. What was afoot?

"Ah, there you are, Doro. Come here, my dear, for I have something to say to you."

Her dear? She had not used that caressing note since the terrible day of Doro's discovery. Avoiding the gazes of the other two, she moved closer, halting some feet away and dropping a curtsey. "Madame?"

The mistress produced a smile. It was not the one with which Doro was familiar. It had a brittle quality that set her nerves on edge. "You will be aware that your friend's mistress, Lady Francis, was with me yesterday."

Should she admit as much? It was scarcely phrased as a question. "I heard so, madame."

Mrs Scalloway's smile slipped a little. "No doubt." Doro remained silent as she paused. "I understand there is now some doubt as to the ownership of the dagger that was used on Mr Scalloway."

An impulse to respond with eagerness came over Doro, but caution urged her to hold her tongue. She no longer trusted the mistress. Where was this tending?

"Well? Have you nothing to say?"

What should she say? She fell back upon repetition. "I did not do it, madame."

"As indeed the magistrate has been led to believe." Another smile. "That being so, my dear Doro, I have decided to reinstate you to your proper position in my household. You may take up your duties once more as my personal maid."

Doro willed herself to thank her, but thoughts battered at her mind. Elinor's maid again? When her trust was shattered? When the mistress had betrayed her vaunted care, left her to ignominy, disgrace and death? Without compassion. Without a word or sign of aid. Had Hemp not found her, Elinor Scalloway would have left her to rot in gaol, to end her miserable life on the rope.

Long-buried resentment rose up from the depths of her humiliation. She tried to hold back, but the words escaped, out of control. "I cannot, madame, I cannot. Let me work as I have done these many days. I had rather scrub and rake out ashes than serve you close again." She saw shock and incredulity in the mistress's face, but the devil that used to ride her in the old days had too strong a hold. "Do not ask it of me. After what has passed, I can no longer trust your caressing ways, madame."

Mrs Scalloway found her tongue. "How dare you speak to me in this fashion?"

Doro drew in a painful breath, but her breast was too full to keep from speaking out of turn. "I dare because you hurt me. You made of me a friend, as I thought, a confidante. But it was false, all false!"

"Great heavens above, Elinor! Are you going to sit there while this slave reviles you?"

Doro threw a glance at the other woman who had spoken with contempt, but the implication passed her by, her tongue once loosened unable to stop. "Why did you not send to me one little word, madame? Why did you at once believe I could do such a terrible thing? Have I not been your friend, not merely your maid? Have I not comforted you, cared for you when he hurt you? Have I not —?"

"That is enough, girl!" Mr Culverstone was standing over her, fury in his face. "Shut your mouth! You will not speak to your mistress in that manner, with such vile words, not in my presence."

Doro shrank away, the old fear of the blows that the master had not hesitated to let fall penetrating the urgency of her need to say it all. She was glad to hear the mistress's voice.

"Stand aside, Laurence. Let me deal with this, if you please."

Relief washed over Doro. The mistress would not allow him to hurt her, just as she had ever protected her maid from the cruelty of Marcus Scalloway. Mr Culverstone stepped back and the mistress took his place. There was time for only an instant of realisation that she had mistaken Elinor's intent before a hand swung, catching her a violent slap across the face.

Doro staggered under the blow and nearly fell. In horrified shock, for Elinor had never before raised a hand to her, she gazed at her assailant, an avenging fury. The fine eyes flashed fire, the voice lashing as painfully as the sting at her cheek.

"You ungrateful baggage! I took you to my bosom and this is how you repay me? Very well, if you are minded to be obstinate, let us see how you fare in the gutter. I don't want you here. Take your things and go."

The words made no sense. "Go?"

"Go. Get out. You are no longer welcome in my house."

The floor seemed to vanish under Doro's feet. "Where shall I go?"

Where could she go? She was wholly dependent upon this woman's charity. Slave she might be, but she had no other home, no other life. No money, no means. What hope had she if she left this house?

There was no softening in Elinor Scalloway's features. They were colder than Doro had ever seen them, her voice likewise. "I have no slightest interest in where you choose to go."

Despair seized Doro. "But you own me."

Iron entered those eyes. "You wanted your freedom. Take it. Now. Leave this house and never let me see your face again."

Numbness settled over Doro's mind. Freedom? What manner of freedom was this? Not knowing what else to do, she turned from the woman's frozen stare and found herself on the other side of the door. Voices from within penetrated through the wood, but they failed to rouse her from the deadness.

"Bravo, Elinor!"

"Yes, well done. I did not expect that, I must say. Though I believe in law it cannot end there, Elinor."

"Oh, don't fret, Laurence. She will be begging back here in five minutes, mark my words."

From somewhere inside the cloud, Doro found the sense in this. Begging back? She almost opened the door again there and then, but a streak of rebellion stayed her and the numbness began to dissipate. Had they been still in Barbados, she might expect a whipping for such impertinence. The slap was a bagatelle compared to what some owners would do. Did the mistress use her less harshly because she expected capitulation? Was Doro to sue for forgiveness with abject and grovelling apology? She was within an ace of doing precisely that. What, after all, did it matter compared to the terror of finding herself unsheltered and alone? A random thought snaked into her mind. Her king, proud man that he was, would never abase himself in such a fashion. The implication leapt in her head. Hemp! He had loved her once, and he had saved her. She was not alone. She had a champion.

Ottilia cogitated as she sipped her coffee and nibbled at a morsel of cheese. What her mother-in-law would have to say to her new-found predilection for the hard cheese generally favoured by working men, she dared not think. She could just hear Sybilla's sarcastic tones.

"*Why I should be surprised I really do not know, Ottilia, considering the way you make no bones about penetrating into low taverns and such. I cannot think how you come to have such ungenteel notions.*"

A giggle escaped Ottilia. Although she ought to reconsider her dietary habits. She was putting on flesh, as she had discovered that morning after dismissing the chambermaid who had tied her stay-laces.

"Fan, that dratted girl has done these too tight. I can scarce breathe. Pray play lady's maid and loosen them for me, will you?"

He had been willing enough, though he teased. "It must be all this extra eating, Tillie. I shall take to hiding tartlets from you in future. I can't endure a fat-bottomed wife."

"Fiend! Fat-bottomed indeed!"

But when he had loosened the stays to her better comfort, Ottilia spent a few moments, before dressing herself in petticoats and bodice, in examining her outline as she was, in her stays and under-petticoat, in the long mirror standing in a corner of the chamber. "Am I thickening indeed, Fan, do you think?"

He cast her an amused glance. "You're as plump as a pudding, my dear one."

"No, be serious. Do but look, if you please."

Francis had turned fully from his ministrations to the queue in his hair, looking her up and down. "Not that I've noticed."

Ottilia ran her hands up her stays and tugged at them. "My bosom looks bigger."

An eyebrow lifted. "All to the good, say I."

Ottilia gave it up. "You are impossible, wretch of a husband."

She had thought no more about it as she resumed dressing herself in the only gown she had brought with her other than the blue. She pinned the sprigged poplin bodice, glad of the material's warmth, then shook out her petticoats and did not think of looking again for any increase of girth as she checked in the mirror whether her appearance would pass muster. But when hunger rose up even after an adequate, if not substantial breakfast, the matter crept back into her mind. Not that it stopped her from sending for her favoured cheese along with the coffee Tyler brought up for her.

Realising she had strayed far from the questions raised in her head about the daggers, she bent her mind upon them again. If the fellow Quin had appropriated Doro's dagger, then whose was it that was plunged into Scalloway's heart?

It narrowed the field somewhat, if one was to take it the perpetrator had acquired the dagger himself. Or herself — let her not rule out a female in the case as yet. Who had been in Barbados to have been able to purchase one from Buck? Quin. Culverstone, Captain Indigo. Also Elinor and the Radcliffes. But Ottilia did not suppose the latter could have any reason to kill Elinor's husband. Both were involved in arranging for her to leave Scalloway. While Lord Radcliffe clearly disapproved of the man, it was unlikely he would take such a drastic step on behalf of Elinor, be she never so much his friend's daughter.

But wait. Indigo had not been enslaved upon Barbados. Suppose the killer was given the dagger by another? Had not Francis claimed that Indigo would not do his own dirty work? Which had given her furiously to think. By the same token, Harbury had his go-between in this man Mawdesley, the same who Francis and Hemp meant to accost today after seeing Radcliffe. What if either Harbury or Indigo acquired a dagger made by the slave Buck through some other avenue? Stolen, borrowed or been given it for a gift, like Doro. Or was she to give serious consideration to Quin?

Why would he slaughter his master? By all accounts, Scalloway used him to advantage and he must have earned himself gratuities far in excess of his pay as the boot boy. Why kill the golden goose? The possibility remained that Indigo, with whom he'd had early acquaintance according to the pirate, had either bribed or blackmailed him into doing the deed, but Ottilia found it unsatisfactory. Which was why she had not mentioned it to Francis. Too tenuous. It did not sit right. She was just shifting her thoughts to Culverstone when she was interrupted by a knock at the door.

Tyler entered on her permission and closed the door behind him. "Your pardon, my lady."

"What is it, Tyler?"

He moved into the room, lowering his voice. "There is a female wishing to speak to you, my lady."

Surprised at his manner, Ottilia eyed him in a puzzled fashion. "What sort of female?"

"It's that girl of Hemp's, my lady." He coughed. "I mean, that friend of his."

But Ottilia was already setting aside her cup and plate. "Doro? What in the world can have happened to bring her to me, I wonder?"

The question was rhetorical, but the footman answered before she could tell him to admit the slave girl. "As to that, my lady, she asked for Hemp at first. When I told her he was out with his lordship, she looked pretty blue, my lady. Then she asked for you."

Ottilia was rising. "Where is she?"

"Just out in the hall, my lady."

"Well, bring her in, Tyler."

The footman hesitated, emitting another discreet cough. "I should tell you, my lady, as she has a portmanteau with her."

Dismay swept through Ottilia. "Oh, heavens! I hope she has not run away."

"She was out of breath and hardly coherent, my lady, that I will say."

Ottilia had heard enough. "Fetch her in at once, Tyler. Pray also take charge of her portmanteau."

"Yes, my lady."

He departed and Ottilia moved to the middle of the room, conjecture filling her mind. She heard a murmur of voices without, and in a moment the door opened again and Dorote Gabon slipped into the room and stood just inside as the door shut behind her.

Ottilia took in only peripherally the untidy aspect she presented, her great-coat, of black stuff and reaching only to the knee, buttoned awry and her bonnet askew, but her attention caught on the distraught look on Doro's face. She was indeed "blue" as Tyler had put it.

"My dear Doro, what is amiss? Come in, do." Sweeping up to her, Ottilia took hold of one of her hands. "Heavens, you are ice cold! Come to the fire."

She would have drawn Doro to the hearth, but that she resisted, hanging back, although she did not try to pull away her hand.

"I am sorry, milady. I did not mean to trouble you. I wanted to find Hemp."

"You are not troubling me in the slightest. Come, my dear. We cannot have you shivering like this."

Doro allowed herself to be drawn through the room. "It is not the cold, milady."

"Very well. You shall tell me presently what the trouble is, but let us get you warmed up first." Once at the fire, she tried to make Dorote sit, but she would not.

"It is not fitting, milady."

"Fiddle! Bring that chair closer and you may warm your hands."

Instead, Doro squatted on the rug, consenting at last to set her hands to the blaze. Ottilia picked up the bell.

"Let me send for a warming drink. Which you do prefer, coffee or tea? Or no, perhaps chocolate?"

The startling blue eyes looked up at her, astonishment in them. "For me, milady?"

"Of course, for you, my dear. Which is it to be?"

Doro made no answer, but as Ottilia waited, a film of moisture gathered in the blue gaze and spilled, tracing a path down the ebony cheeks. Moved, Ottilia rang the bell and sat down, reaching to pat Doro's shoulder.

"Come now. Whatever it is, we will take care of it."

Doro sniffed back the tears, wiping the back of her hand across her face. Her voice was husky. "It is not that, my lady. It is — no one has ever — only Hemp…"

It did not take much imagination to fill in the blanks. Pity filled Ottilia's heart. Had this poor woman been so starved of kindness? Thinking of Elinor Scalloway, she could readily believe it. She did not refer to it, however, but spoke in a light manner to give Dorote a chance to compose herself.

"I am sorry Hemp is not here just at this moment. He and my husband have gone upon a couple of errands. We are still enquiring into your late master's death, you must know."

"Yes, Hemp told me." She sounded a trifle less distressed. "He did not say what enquiries you are making, milady."

There was a faint question in it, but Ottilia chose to ignore it. Of more urgency to find out what had brought her here, burdened, as one must suppose by the portmanteau, with her possessions. But that could wait until she was warmed up and calmer.

The arrival of the waiter, plainly agog at sight of her visitor on the floor by the fire, provided a distraction. Without again referring to Doro, Ottilia ordered a cup of chocolate and a plate of whatever cakes or tartlets might be available.

With the departure of the servant, she turned to Doro again and found her gazing into the fire. Ottilia watched her for a moment, noting the faraway look and the gradual relaxing of Doro's pose. She had slipped to a seated position, her knees folded under her, the flowered chintz of her petticoats billowing about her. She looked, Ottilia thought, like a beautiful statuette, so still and silent was she.

Presently Doro stirred, seeming to come to herself and glancing round in a bewildered way. Had she forgotten where she was? Her gaze met Ottilia's and she let out a gasping breath. "Forgive me, milady. I was thinking…"

"What were you thinking, Dorote?" Ottilia prompted as she faded out.

The extraordinary eyes clouded. "Of Barbados. Before."

"Before Scalloway?"

The head dipped, hiding the blue gaze. "Yes, milady."

Recalling what Hemp had told her, Ottilia ventured a question. "You had no thought of anyone but Hemp then, I dare say?"

Doro gave a brief shake of the head. "He was all in all to me: father, mother, brother." Her lips parted on one further word and closed.

Ottilia supplied it. "And lover?"

She looked up, misery in the depths of those eyes. "I did not know how much. I was foolish, blind."

"Hemp does not blame you, Doro. He made excuses for you." Should she say more? Or leave Hemp to make his own peace? Ottilia could not resist a hint. "I think you may find he is more afraid of your response to him than you are of his."

"How can I be as I was to him? I am not worthy."

"If he believes you are?" Doro was silent. "Why do you suppose he has moved heaven and earth for your sake?"

A knock at the door put an end to her saying more. Ottilia greeted the entrance of the waiter bearing refreshments with a modicum of relief. She had likely said too much. It was Hemp's task to persuade Doro. Not perhaps as difficult as he supposed, for Doro's heart was plainly still engaged.

She busied herself with supplying Doro with the promised treat. "Here we are, drink this. It will warm you."

Doro took the tall cup, holding it between her hands. A smile came. "It is hot to my palms."

Ottilia laughed. "Excellent. But don't neglect to drink it too."

She watched Doro sip with caution, taking pleasure in the obvious enjoyment she exhibited as the sweet tang took hold. Ottilia proffered the plate of macaroons that had arrived along with the drink, but Doro gave a small shake of the head, intent upon the chocolate. Ottilia set the plate down on the hearth within her reach and sat back, content to watch the exquisite features until Doro had drunk her fill.

She reflected that Hemp was more fortunate than he knew, through a lucky chance to recover one of the two females who meant the most to him. Strange that both should be so beautiful, each in her own style. Tamasine, in every way opposite, that pale beauty with golden locks and the china-blue eyes that were apt to turn malevolent, poor afflicted child. There was no recovering Tamasine. Yet here sat the love of his life, dark-skinned and blessed with an aberrant gaze, quite as blue, yet expressive with emotions real and true.

When Doro at last set down the tall cup and reached, absently Ottilia thought, for one of the little cakes, she judged it time to discover just what had occurred at the Scalloway home to bring Doro to seek refuge with Hemp.

"Do you feel up to telling me what happened, Dorote?"

The interview with Radcliffe had not gone well. In the first place, he saw fit to comment upon the bruise disfiguring Francis's face.

"One would suppose you had been in a brawl, my lord."

"I have been, thanks to the machinations of your friend Scalloway."

"He was no friend of mine, sir."

"Be that as it may —"

"What brawl, Lord Francis?"

Francis stared him out. "I decline to tell you. Moreover, it is irrelevant to my purpose here."

At this point, Hemp, evidently growing impatient for his own concerns, butted in. "My lord Radcliffe, we are here to ask you for the papers which may grant manumission to Dorote Gabon."

The interruption was at once productive of a worsening of the atmosphere as Radcliffe plainly took an affront at the Barbadian steward entering the discussion.

"I do not negotiate with slaves."

Aware of Hemp's stiffening and conscious of umbrage himself, Francis took it head on. "Hemp Roy is not and never has been a slave. He was born a free man on the island of Barbados and, what is more, he is a man of substance in his own right."

Lord Radcliffe spared a contemptuous glance for Hemp before returning his gaze to Francis. "I am perfectly aware of what that means. I knew Matthew Roy well. Not that I had much to do with that family, Flora Sugars being what it is."

Before Francis could answer this, Hemp interjected, an edge to his voice. "Is that a reference to the late Mrs Roy's condition, my lord?"

Francis threw up a hand as Radcliffe's features suffused. "Let it go, sir. You too, Hemp. We are not here to rake up old scores."

To his relief, Hemp dropped back, though his eyes still smouldered. Radcliffe champed a moment but refrained from taking up the challenge, instead reverting to the matter at hand. "It is of no use to refer to me with regard to that girl. She is the property of Mrs Scalloway."

"That is so." Francis primed his guns. "What we need from you is the legalities in the business. Mrs Scalloway has promised to free Dorote Gabon, but I am reliably informed that there are particular documents that must be drawn up. You being her trustee —"

"I am not a lawyer, sir. You had best engage the services of that fellow Ackworth."

"I shall do so if needs be. You are, however, in a position to advise exactly what is required. I imagine you must have acted, or perhaps been yourself in need of such deeds of manumission in the past."

Radcliffe, with an apparent disregard now of Hemp's presence, moved back to the desk from where he had risen upon their entrance. "I have naught to do with those matters. It is all handled by my agents in Barbados."

Francis could have cursed the man. "That may be so, but I beg you will not attempt to persuade me that you are not perfectly au fait with the proceedings in such cases."

The fellow turned on him a look of prideful mockery. "I have no intention of persuading you of any such, Lord Francis. I am merely pointing out that you have come to the wrong shop."

"I don't believe you."

"Good God, sir, do you dare to give me the lie?"

Francis refused to back down. "I make no doubt, sir, that were Mrs Scalloway to request your aid in the making up of such documents, you would not hesitate to assist her."

Radcliffe sniffed. "That, sir, is another matter altogether."

"Ah, is it? In that case, we know where we stand. I will address myself to the lady in the first place. Good day to you, sir."

He turned on his heel and made for the door, gesturing to Hemp to follow. Radcliffe's voice arrested him before he could leave the room.

"Lord Francis!"

He halted, turning. "What now, my lord?"

The man took a few steps towards him. "Do I take it your lady wife has abandoned this business now that the slave is no longer suspect?"

Francis stared at him in some suspicion. "How did you know that?"

"My wife heard it from Elinor."

Outrage overtook Francis. "Then you must also already have known Mrs Scalloway meant to free her!"

"I did not. Elinor said no such thing to Caroline, if you must have it."

Hemp spoke again. "She means to renege!"

Francis seethed as he eyed Radcliffe. "I don't know what game you are playing, the three of you, but know this. Dorote Gabon will be freed if I have to take her case through the courts. Or indeed Parliament, if it should come to that. Moreover, nothing in this world will stop my wife until the real murderer of Marcus Scalloway is identified."

With which, he left the man gobbling from the sounds which followed him into the corridor. Once outside on the Queen Square pavement, he was halted by the unexpected sight of Hemp, holding the railing that ran along the front of the property, doubled up with laughter.

"What the deuce ails you, Hemp?"

Hemp straightened, hiccupping on his paroxysms, but the dark eyes were alight still. "Your pardon, milord, but his face!"

His temper rapidly dissipating, Francis quirked an eyebrow. "I was in no condition to notice, but I'm surprised you aren't railing, Hemp."

Hemp sobered. "It was a close-run thing, milord. I must thank you for taking so bold a stance." He looked rueful. "Also for keeping me from doing what could only prejudice our case."

"Quite so. Besides, it would not have done to have fallen into a wrangle. There is no point talking to men of that persuasion. The day will come when these things change."

"I hope you may be right, milord, but what are we to do if Mrs Scalloway refuses to keep her word?"

Francis blew out a frustrated breath. "The woman is a snake, but we'll find a way. On that I am resolved. Meanwhile, let us go and see if we can get information concerning this prize Indigo expected to receive from Scalloway from this Mawdesley fellow." He glanced at the sky, for once cloudless. "At least we are fortunate in the weather."

Hemp gestured in a direction that must lead them towards Bristol Bridge. "Mawdesley had best give us what we want, milord, with the mood I am in at this present."

Francis laughed. "He has no cause to love you. I am relying on your methods of persuasion."

When, after negotiating for a second time the ill-kept narrow streets around Pipe Lane, they reached the house where Mawdesley lived, Francis was chagrined to suffer a setback.

"He ain't here," said the ancient who answered the door. "Ain't seen nowt of him fer the last four and twenty hour what's more."

Inwardly cursing, Francis pressed on. "That is extremely inconvenient. Have you checked his room?"

The ancient shrugged. "Ain't his keeper."

Annoyance rising again, Francis gestured to him to move out of the way. "We'll take a look."

"Suit yerself." With which, he shuffled off towards the back regions as he had done before, leaving the door wide.

"Go ahead, Hemp. I'll follow."

By the time he reached the landing, Hemp was already rapping on the door. "Mawdesley! Mawdesley, are you in there?" He waited a moment, and then turned with a resigned look. "No use, milord."

An odd determination overcame Francis. He could not have said why, but he was reluctant to leave it. "Let me come there." Hemp shifted out of the way and Francis took his place. He did not trouble with knocking, but grasped the handle and turned it. "It's not locked." He pushed the door inward.

Darkness pervaded the room, the familiar stale smell augmented by a stink that sent a streak of suspicion through Francis. He knew that odour too well. "Hemp!"

"Milord?"

Francis made a cautious shift into the room, making space as he cast a glance about the shadows that indicated the meagre furniture seen last time. The light from the doorway helped to enable him to make out the various shapes. "See if you can make your way across to the window. But take care where you tread."

Hemp hesitated on the threshold, blinking. "What is it, milord?"

"I'm not sure, but we need those curtains opened."

Francis watched Hemp's form turn into a silhouette as he made his careful way towards the outline about the edges of the curtain where light seeped through. An odd bump sounded and Hemp stopped.

"There's something on the floor, milord."

Francis drew a breath. "That's what I'm afraid of. Go on."

A shadow was materialising on the floor near the bed. Francis kept his gaze planted on the vague shape as Hemp eased his way to the window. It seemed an age until the sound of the drapes being drawn back flooded the room with sudden light. Hemp turned as Francis started forward.

"Hell and the devil confound it!"

Mawdesley was sprawled face down, the handle of a weapon protruding from his back.

Francis dropped to his haunches beside the still form, but there was no mistaking his condition. "Looks like he's been dead for some hours."

Hemp opened the second half of the window curtains and the picture became clearer still. He joined Francis on the other side of the corpse, gave a muttered exclamation and pointed to the handle. "Look, milord."

"I see it."

The ornate signature curl told its own tale. Mawdesley had been slain with the same type of weapon that had killed Scalloway.

"For pity's sake, it's another of these blasted daggers! That makes three of them."

# CHAPTER TWENTY-TWO

Hemp entered the parlour on the echo of his knock, swept a glance across to find Ottilia and stopped dead. "Doro!"

She turned her head from where she sat on the rug before the fire, one hand resting in milady's. "You have come at last."

His brain, stupidly thickened and full with the recent discovery, refused to work. "How came you here? Why? I mean, what happened to bring you?"

Her hand was released and Ottilia rose, moving into the room. "It is rather a tangle, Hemp, but pray where is my husband?"

As he spoke, Hemp's gaze remained on Doro, who had dropped her own, hiding the blue orbs from his sight and looking shamefaced. "His lordship has gone for Mr Belchamp. He sent me to tell you, milady…" He faded out, caught by the earlier words. "What tangle?"

Ottilia's tone grew tart. "Presently, Hemp. Tell me what?"

His attention snapped in and he brought his gaze to bear upon Ottilia. "We found Mawdesley dead."

Doro's head came up, drawing his glance, but Ottilia's question forced it to return to her.

"Dead how?"

"Murdered. A dagger in the back."

Ottilia clicked her tongue. "Oh, this is too much!"

"Milady?"

"The business is beyond complicated already." Her features became thoughtful. "It does tend to shift the focus, however. A dagger, you say?"

The memory of his lordship's response caused Hemp to flash a grin. "The third, milady. Milord is excessively put out."

"I'll warrant he is."

Ottilia's laugh brought a sense of normality back and Hemp was better able to take in the oddity of Doro's presence. It was indeed odd, but undeniably welcome. He could no longer hold back, moving a little towards her.

"Doro, tell me what has occurred."

She was on her feet though she remained by the fireside. "The mistress threw me out." He must have shown his inner fire for she put out a hand. "I brought it on myself. Madame said she would reinstate me and I … I forgot my position."

Hemp had no difficulty in interpreting this. "You lost that fiery temper of yours, *ma reine*, is that it?"

A tiny smile crossed her lips and vanished again. "It was foolish. She grew enraged. She said I might be free and should go at once." Distress entered in. "She did not mean it, for I heard her from the corridor. She prophesied I would beg to come back. I could not endure it, Hemp. I packed as she bade me and I came to find you." Her voice cracked. "I do not know why. You cannot help me."

Ottilia spoke before Hemp could answer. "But I can. You did right to come, did she not, Hemp?"

His eyes were on Doro. "Very right, milady." Then the memory of the earlier interview surfaced, before Mawdesley was found. He turned to Ottilia. "We did not fare well, milady. Lord Radcliffe would not co-operate."

"Objectionable man. We shall persevere, however. I will see Mrs Scalloway myself, but first we had best find out how this new murder alters our enquiries."

Hemp hesitated, wishing he might change his immediate plans to engage with Doro's needs, but it was of no use. His lordship was depending upon him. "Milord wished me to return to the house. We left an aged fellow to guard the scene and I doubt he can be trusted."

"Yes, go. And pray take note of anything that may be of use in identifying the killer."

"What shall I look for, milady?"

"Ask at the house, and of any round about, if anyone has been seen. Try and see if you can find anything out of place, anything unusual. Was there a struggle? Note, if you please, the angle of the dagger, which may tell us whether the killer was taller."

Hemp let out a frustrated breath. "Almost certainly he would have been, milady. Mawdesley was a small man."

"But one cannot take it for granted." She frowned. "I wonder if I should come with you?"

The suggestion was anathema. "I doubt milord would wish it. The area is particularly insalubrious and the house is worse."

Ottilia's smile came. "Worse than the Pyg & Whistle?"

"Much."

"If you are with me?"

Hemp raised his hands. "If you insist, milady, but to be truthful, I doubt there is much to find there that will materially help us."

"And we cannot leave Doro alone here. Very well, I will rely upon your good offices."

Hemp was tempted to take Doro with him instead, but she was safer here with milady, who could be depended upon to repel any attempt to retrieve her that might be made from the Scalloway household. He was at one with Doro in disbelieving Elinor Scalloway's true intentions. She clearly did not think Doro would have dared to leave the ménage. He went across to her. "You are never going back there, Doro. I have been wanting to get you out of that house."

Those magnificent eyes searched his. "But what is to become of me?"

He smiled. "We will secure your freedom with all necessary documents."

"And then?"

"Then it is as you wish, Doro." He saw in her face the truth of her plight. "Do not trouble your head about the future. We will take care of you until you decide what it is you want."

She veiled her eyes from him, her voice a whisper. "*Merci, mon roi.*"

He longed to catch her into his embrace, but that would be to force her. It would not be easy but he wanted her willing. Besides, milady was standing there. He contented himself with a smile and turned, addressing himself to Ottilia. "I will do my best, milady, and report to you whatever I find."

"This is most distressing, most indeed."

That the magistrate was upset came as no surprise to Ottilia. She was not best pleased herself. The complications were mounting, the more so since her spouse had returned, bringing Walter Belchamp with him. He came later than Hemp, having accompanied the Justice of the Peace to Harbury's office.

"He thinks to rattle that man with a report of Mawdesley's death, milady."

"Because he employed him? Yes, that fits. Does my husband think Harbury did it?"

Hemp shrugged. "I cannot say, milady. I fear the business of the extra dagger is baffling to milord as well as I."

Ottilia glanced to where Doro was seated in a straight chair at the table. Ottilia had not succeeded in persuading her to one of the easy chairs at the fire. Like Hemp, she would not violate protocol. Was the habit ingrained in both? "We have been talking while you were gone. Doro wondered if the boot boy Quin might have his own dagger."

Hemp's gaze had slipped to his inamorata and back again. "Then why take Doro's, milady?"

"Just so."

"Unless it was indeed his that he used on Scalloway, knowing Doro had one also?"

Ottilia smiled. "It is a good theory, Hemp, but it falls down when we add Mawdesley's death into the equation."

"How so, milady?"

"Quin would need yet another dagger. One he returned to Doro, the other is with Mr Belchamp."

For the first time, Doro cut in. "You are saying the same person killed my master?"

Ottilia returned to the table and re-seated herself in the chair she had vacated when Hemp came in with his news. "It looks very much like it."

"The same method, same weapon."

"Similar weapon, Hemp. It cannot be the same one. But yes, the method suggests the same hand. By the by, did you notice the angle of entry?"

Hemp rested a hand on a chairback where he stood at the other side of the table. "It looked straight, but on closer inspection I thought there was a slight downward slant."

As expected. "Anything else?"

"I asked at the houses round about, milady, as you requested, but no one heard or saw anything. Nor would they if the murder happened at night, although Mawdesley was still fully dressed."

"The doctor's account will help with that, once we have the time of death. Did you notice any other little detail at the scene that may help us?"

Hemp shifted with discomfort. "I could not tell much. There had been no struggle, I think. The killer took him unawares."

"He knew the killer."

"Because he turned his back on him?"

"Or her. Do not let us forget it might yet prove to be a woman."

Doro let out a gasp. "But not I! And how could my mistress know that man?"

"Quin knew him," said Hemp.

"But Quin was my master's man, through and through. The mistress does not like him."

Ottilia intervened. "I am reasonably certain Elinor Scalloway committed neither murder. Yet it is of interest that you say the angle downward was only slight, Hemp. It suggests a man, or woman, of a similar height to the deceased."

She saw Hemp and Doro exchange puzzled glances. Hemp took the point. "But what woman, milady?"

"Ah, that I don't know. I am simply saying we should not rule out the possibility."

Something was nagging at her. One of those elusive little snippets that had no meaning at the time, but had somehow taken on significance. If only she could place it. She recalled a stray thought she'd had a couple of days since which she could not catch. This felt much the same. Insistent and niggling. Whether that was the cause of her determination to keep the option of a female perpetrator open she did not know. On the other hand, there was one male she had not yet tackled. "I think tomorrow I must corner Laurence Culverstone.

Preferably before he has a chance to incarcerate himself at the Scalloway house."

"If you wish to catch him early, milady, Doro knows where he lives." Hemp glanced at Doro. "I followed her there, but I do not remember it precisely."

"Excellent. We will go there together at an early hour, Doro, if you are willing."

"If the mistress does not come to fetch me back before then."

Ottilia gathered her forces. "She may come, though I doubt it, but she won't be removing you anywhere. Hemp, take Dorote and arrange for her accommodation, if you please. Tyler took care of her portmanteau." She went to Doro, who was rising. "Go with Hemp. He will see to your needs." She cut short Doro's flustered expressions of thanks for her kindness. "There is no need of thanks. I am sure you deserve a great deal more consideration than I am able to supply."

To Ottilia's relief, Hemp drew his inamorata out of the parlour. Doro's extreme reticence and her crushed spirit made her a difficult companion. She would do a deal better with Hemp, and it would give him the opportunity to further his cause with her.

Ottilia had little time to mull over the various possibilities in her mind before Francis arrived with Belchamp in tow. The magistrate, she was informed, had left his constable at the scene until such time as Belchamp's surgeon, accustomed to deal with these matters, had been to certify the death and arrange for undertakers to remove the body.

"As to who did this terrible deed, I am utterly at a loss, I don't mind telling you, my lady." He cast a hopeful glance towards Ottilia as he spoke and she could not prevent a gurgle of mirth from escaping.

"Forgive me, sir, but I do trust you are not looking to me for an instant solution, for I fear I have none."

Belchamp sighed. "Well, I did hope you might have formed an opinion."

"Several, but they take us no further forward at this juncture."

Belchamp became eager. "I am ready to hear whatever you have, my lady."

Before Ottilia could answer, her spouse took this, casting her one of his wry looks. "You'll be lucky, Belchamp. My wife has a habit of keeping her notions close to her chest until she is certain."

Ottilia had to smile. "True, but in this instance I have little in my head." With a gesture she invited Belchamp to sit at the table where she had been cogitating over a cup of coffee. "I am quite willing to share what I have."

Belchamp fairly threw himself into the chair, setting his folded hands on the table and sitting forward, a keen look in his face. "Fire away, my lady Fan."

Ottilia threw a glance at her husband and received a comical grimace in response. She was obliged to suppress a strong desire to laugh and made haste to relate her thoughts concerning the daggers and her conclusions mulled over with Hemp.

Francis took it up when she had done. "These daggers are a cursed nuisance, for my part."

"Yes, but at least we may deduce that whoever did the killing had access to a weapon specific to Barbados. Indeed, more specific to this Buck, a slave known to make these with those particularly ornate handles." She looked from Francis to Belchamp. "You have the dagger?"

"I left it in situ, my lady, until the doctor should have seen it."

"That is a pity. But I take it you will impound it?"

"Oh, yes. Pucklechurch will bring it to me."

"Then I suggest you look closely to see if there are any initials carved near the handle, as there are on Doro's dagger."

"I did look for that," her spouse cut in, "but the place is too gloomy to be able to see properly."

"The dagger was not in to the hilt?"

"Not at all. There were a good couple of inches still visible. Why?"

"It suggests the perpetrator was not necessarily strong."

"I don't see that," Francis objected. "It takes some doing to stab through the ribcage, I'll give you that, but it's by no means necessary to drive a dagger right in to do enough damage to kill."

Belchamp threw up a fist. "Aha! There speaks the soldier."

Ottilia ignored this. "Even so, Fan. Would not a strong person thrust harder as a matter of course?"

He frowned. "What are you getting at, Tillie? Who is it you suspect?"

"I don't know. I am trying to establish some notion of the size and strength of Mawdesley's adversary, that is all."

Belchamp leapt on this. "So you may compare it to those we think may have done it?"

"Well, it is little enough, but it could be of help." She looked from one to the other. "What of this man Harbury? How did he react?"

Francis snorted. "As he does always, I imagine. He exhibited no sort of emotion whatsoever, which is just how he acted the last time I spoke to the fellow. Belchamp even asked him if it did not come as a shock to him, and he answered that he had always felt Mawdesley would come to a bad end."

Ottilia looked across at Belchamp. "Could he have done it? Physically?"

"Oh, readily, my lady, readily. He is not a large man, but he has brawn enough."

"What of his movements?"

"He claims he was at his home last night," Francis cut in. "Belchamp means to enquire of members of his household."

"Who may well lie on their master's behalf." Belchamp sighed. "It is ever so, I fear."

Ottilia was following a train of thought. "The victim had been dead some hours, then?"

"Undoubtedly." Francis eyed her. "You are thinking the time of death is similar to Scalloway's?"

Ottilia hesitated, but why withhold such a thought? "It would shorten the list if it turns out to be so."

Belchamp leaned in, eager again. "How so, my lady?"

"Those who could have done Scalloway to death in the Pyg & Whistle in the night hours are few. If we then assume the same procedure with Mawdesley, the field is similarly narrowed. The more so when we may be sure from how this murder was done, that the victim knew his killer."

Her spouse adopted his sceptical note. "Which means what exactly?"

Ottilia threw him a mischievous glance. "It means that I must talk to Culverstone as I intended. But I must also revisit the tavern."

# CHAPTER TWENTY-THREE

Rising early on Wednesday, Ottilia left her husband discussing a hearty breakfast in bed and sallied forth with Dorote. A cold wind bit, but her woollen cloak with its substantial hood kept the worst at bay. Doro, also well wrapped in the worn great-coat in which she had arrived at the Ship, was observably a trifle less anxious, but it was evident she had little belief that the widow would not come for her in the end.

"The mistress means me to sweat, milady," Doro said as she guided Ottilia along the Broad Quay, already beginning to be busy with porters, shoremen and sailors going about their labours. "She is copying the master."

"How so?" Ottilia narrowly avoided collision with a fellow burdened with a large trunk carried on his back, head down as he went.

Doro paused to admonish the man before answering. "Take care where you tread!" The fellow looked up, saw Ottilia and muttered an apology, shifting out of her way. "The master was apt to hold off delivering a reprimand, or a beating. He liked to prolong the waiting, for as his victim — myself or another slave when we were in Barbados still — might be more malleable for living in fear for a day or so. Unless he lost his temper. Then there was no waiting."

Ottilia clicked her tongue. "Really, this Scalloway sounds to have been a most unpleasant person. If it was not in your interests to find his killer, I declare I would be inclined to cheer the deed."

A tiny laugh escaped Doro. "I cannot believe this, milady. Hemp says you are a stickler for justice."

Ottilia threw her a rueful look. "True. But that does not mean I cannot also be glad such a man has met his end."

A little shiver shook Doro. "I am ashamed, milady."

"Because he beguiled you? My dear Dorote, you were an innocent. I am sure he would not have shown his true colours until he had you in his power."

"He fooled the mistress also."

"Oh, I don't think he did, Doro. She told me her father was the instrument of her marrying. Mr Culverstone was ever her choice."

Doro was silent as she directed Ottilia's steps past Stone Bridge and up the Quays towards Nelson Street. Was she mulling the matter? Had Elinor kept the truth from her maid? It was plain Doro had believed her mistress to be more sympathetic than she was. Was there convenience in having Doro's loyalty? Could she thus have fostered a breach, knowing her husband wished to make the maid his mistress? Ottilia had not yet divined whether he had succeeded, but it was possible Elinor chose to use her as a shield, or a weapon to wield against Marcus Scalloway. Touch the maid and he forfeited his marital rights? Every attempt might then become a potential for argument to keep the battle alive. And to keep him from her bed? She waited to be free of her father's influence before she could carry out her design to leave him. Now she was free to marry Culverstone and return to Barbados. Her father could not act against a fait accompli if her first husband was dead. Which furnished an excellent reason for Culverstone to carry out the killing and to make Doro his scapegoat by using a dagger similar to one she was known to possess.

Doro halted by an establishment of respectable size, though situated a little out of the way of the main drag of the City and with its outside paint plainly in need of refreshment. Was this the unfashionable quarter?

"This is the house, milady."

Feeling primed, Ottilia walked down the short pathway and knocked on a plain wooden door. It was opened by a blousy female in a mob cap.

"Mr Culverstone, if you please."

The woman looked past her, evidently noting Doro. "Oh, this again, is it?"

Ottilia became tart. "Do you mean to keep me standing on the doorstep?"

The matron looked her up and down. It was evident she took in the condition of the visitor as her expression altered and she bobbed a curtsey. "Begging your pardon, ma'am. If you will please to step into the parlour, I'll go up and fetch the gentleman."

"Thank you. Dorote, come in out of the cold." She waited outside the open parlour door for the landlady to go off up the stairs before turning to Doro. "It is better if I see him alone, I think. Would you mind waiting in the hall?"

The ghost of a naughty smile flickered on Doro's face. "I will listen at the door, milady."

Startled at the brief change, Ottilia yet could not forbear a smile. "I have no objection, my dear, and I am delighted to see you indulging in a little merriment."

Doro's face clouded. "There was a time when I could laugh."

Ottilia pressed her shoulder. "It will come again." Then she dropped her hood back and walked into the parlour, a large term for a poky room overstuffed with old-fashioned furnishings, the damask upholstery to the straight chairs and sofa faded and worn, the tables heavily ornate, with Rococo over-decorated paper to the walls.

She had not long to wait. A few moments saw Laurence Culverstone hesitating on the threshold, surveying Ottilia in a manner with which he might well have regarded a dangerous animal. He looked to have dressed in haste, a few strands of his blond locks escaping from the tied ribbon at his neck, and his neck-cloth done up in a loose bow. "Do come in and shut the door, Mr Culverstone."

He did so, whether from an automatic response to her tone of command or a reluctance to be overheard by the landlady. "What is it you want with me, Lady Francis?"

Ottilia remained by the meagre fire, one hand steady on the mantel. "I think you know, sir."

He stiffened. "If you mean to accuse me —"

"I do not. There are, however, one or two questions I would wish to put to you."

His chin, freshly shaved by the look of him, lifted. "I see no reason why I should answer."

"That is as you choose. I cannot compel you. I might point out that it is in your interests to do so, since I know that you were in the Pyg & Whistle the night Scalloway was killed."

His colour deepened. "How do you know that?"

Ottilia kept her tone steady and cool. "It is my business to discover these things. I cannot else make an accounting to Mr Belchamp."

His tone became mocking. "Do you tell me a magistrate employs you to make these enquiries of yours, Lady Francis?"

"I don't tell you so. But you are fully aware that I have taken it upon myself to find the killer only for the purpose of clearing suspicion from Dorote Gabon. I have Mr Belchamp's blessing, if that helps."

Mr Culverstone did not look as if he relished this information. He was clearly trying to take a high hand, but

Ottilia noted a slight shift in his stance as if he was not quite comfortable. At least he had not the temerity to sit in her presence uninvited. She took his silence for assent.

"Tell me, if you please, what was the subject of your discourse with Marcus Scalloway on the night you accosted him at the tavern."

She thought he was not going to answer, for his jaw tightened and a hard look came into his eyes. He spoke as if the words were forced from him. "If you insist upon it, I told him Elinor would leave him as arranged on the Monday and that nothing he could say would change that."

So far, the words agreed with what Elinor had told her. "Did he accept your words?"

A short and bitter laugh escaped him. "What do you suppose? The liar threw it at me that she had agreed to a reconciliation. I knew he was lying, for Elinor sent to me immediately after the argument. Moreover, we met at —" He broke off, and continued smoothly, "At a venue we were used to use, and she told me word for word what had been said."

"Did you tell him so?"

"Certainly not. He was ignorant of our meetings."

"But you gave him the lie?"

"I said I did not believe him, that I knew from the Radcliffes what arrangements were in hand. Scalloway pretended all that had changed. Said he'd been to Radcliffe and settled with him." He snorted. "As if he was capable of settling with Radcliffe. The man was a consummate coward, capable only of bullying tactics towards those weaker than himself."

Ottilia eyed him. "Elinor does not strike me as being weak."

He glared. "She is a female. Marcus was not above using his superior strength to chastise her."

"You mean he beat her?"

"With his fists." The words seemed to choke him and his own hands curled into weapons. "I wish to God I *had* plunged that dagger into his heart! It is no less than he deserved."

Ottilia eyed him. "Do you happen to possess a dagger of that type, Mr Culverstone?"

The man's shock was patent. His cheeks darkened. "I said I wished I had done it. I did not say I did."

"But you do have one of this man Buck's daggers with the ornamental handle, do you not?" His lips compressed and his eyes flared. Ottilia smiled. "Come, Mr Culverstone, it is of no use to lie. Elinor gave you away days since."

Was it fear now? Disbelief? Horror? His expression changed so rapidly, Ottilia could not be sure. At length he spoke, rasping a little. "I don't believe you."

"We were talking of Quin having found the maid Doro's dagger among Mr Scalloway's effects," Ottilia pursued doggedly. "When I said the true murder weapon, another dagger, was with the magistrate, Elinor became decidedly agitated."

"That is nothing to the purpose."

"Pardon me, but I fear I must contradict you. It is very much to the purpose if Elinor knows you possess such a dagger and feared upon the instant that you had indeed stabbed Marcus Scalloway."

Culverstone rose in a bang. "I had no hand in it! I shall prove it to you. Wait!" With which, he fairly ran from the room.

Ottilia listened to the pound of his steps on the stairs with a mixture of triumph and relief. Her deductions were not at fault. She was at last getting somewhere. The steps were heard returning in short order and Ottilia was unsurprised when Culverstone burst back into the room and raised his hand, showing that he was grasping a dagger much in the same style as all the rest.

"There! Yes, I have one, but I did not use it to kill Scalloway."

Ottilia relaxed back. "Thank you, Mr Culverstone. You may set it down. You have made my task a deal easier."

A bewildered look overspread his features. "I beg your pardon?"

She smiled. "Besides the dagger, your vehemence against Scalloway was potent."

"Oh." A sheepish grin slipped onto his face, his erstwhile anxiety diminishing. "I can't talk of Marcus with any moderation, I admit."

Ottilia made up her mind. "Let us sit down a moment, sir." She crossed to one of the overstuffed chairs, threw her cloak back to her shoulders and sat, gesturing him to one opposite. He hesitated, puzzlement evident, and then did as she asked, setting the dagger on a convenient table beside the chair. Ottilia looked across at him. "You may be able to help me."

"Yes?"

Ottilia tutted. "You need not sound so wary, sir. When you went to accost Scalloway, did you see his servant Quin there?"

"That fellow?" His disgust was unmistakeable. "As devious as Marcus himself. He was there, yes. Usually hung about waiting when Marcus drank. Elinor says his task was to help him home, unless he chose to remain there for the night."

"Did he do that often?"

"Not often enough for Elinor's sake. But yes, he was apt to drink and debauch whenever things went awry. As they usually did."

Ottilia's attention pricked. "You are thinking of the shipping venture?"

Another snort escaped Culverstone. "Who but Scalloway would hire a renegade slave to captain his ship?"

"Indigo?"

Surprise came into his face. "Do you know everything?"

Ottilia chose not to answer. "You knew he was a pirate?"

"Everyone knew it. Elinor guessed at once the venture would founder. She was infuriated to have agreed to give Marcus the money for it. She had hoped it would give him independence enough to enable her to leave him."

"Which she resolved to do in any event, I take it?"

"What would you? The man ruined himself and put that fellow Harbury into debt into the bargain."

Could that have been enough to cause Harbury to revenge himself upon Scalloway? Or might there be a different reason to be rid of the man? But Culverstone's words begged a question. "How is it you are so well informed, sir?"

He looked away. "Since the death, we have heard a good deal about the business."

Ottilia jumped on this. "Through Lady Radcliffe?"

His colour mounted as his gaze returned to her. "Caroline is a close friend. She and her lord tried their utmost for us — for Elinor and me — while Mr Carey was insisting upon her marriage to Scalloway."

"Yes, and there is matter for surprise. How was it Mr Carey did not recognise Marcus Scalloway's true character?"

Culverstone shrugged. "He was blinded by the fellow's looks and address, I must suppose. He had what Carey called polish, the stamp of a true gentleman. Whereas I…" He faded out.

Curiosity overcame Ottilia. "What is your background, if I may ask, Mr Culverstone?"

He gave a short laugh, laced with self-mockery. "I am a nobody, ma'am. My father was an overseer until he married my mother. To Carey, that was bad enough. Add to it my mother's family of merchants, supplying the island with English goods, and the fact that both my father and I are involved in that business, and you must see my unworthiness. I had as well fly to the moon as aspire to the hand of a sugar princess."

Worse and worse. Ottilia could not forbear a smile. "I am glad you showed me that dagger, sir. A more cogent reason to be rid of Scalloway can scarcely be imagined."

"It was not I, as I have told you. If you would have more reason to trust my word, know that Scalloway meant those goods for the West Indies. He had a ready-made customer in my father, who has agents across several islands. Why should I take the bread out of my family's mouths?"

"It would certainly seem foolish to do so, except for the fact that Scalloway had lost the goods by the time he was killed." Culverstone was effectively silenced, and Ottilia changed tack. "You will not have heard, I dare say, that Harbury's man Mawdesley was found dead yesterday?"

He looked blank. "I've never heard of the fellow."

"Are you certain? He seems to have been acquainted with the boot boy Quin."

"Boot boy forsooth! Anyone Quin knew must of necessity have had dealings with Scalloway. If he is Harbury's man, that would explain it. Quin was ever running to and fro on his master's behalf."

"You saw him that night, you said. Was he still there when you departed?"

"At the Pyg & Whistle? I suppose so. I did not look for him particularly. Since Marcus was still drinking, I imagine so."

She changed tack. "What do you know of the barmaid Cherry?"

He scowled. "Only that she warmed Marcus's bed for him. So she did any man's, by all accounts."

"Yours?"

His cheeks suffused. "Certainly not! Nor did I frequent the Pyg & Whistle."

"Except to find Scalloway."

Culverstone looked positively outraged. "What are you trying to say? If you wish to imply I was in the habit of seeking Marcus out, you should know I had no need. I visited the house. Marcus could not gainsay my welcome. He knew Elinor and I had been friends from childhood up. Besides, he needed my good will for the success of his venture, had it succeeded."

"Did he know you and Elinor were more than friends?"

He bit his lip, resentment in his gaze. "If he did, he never accused me directly. We were always circumspect in their home, and before the slaves or servants."

Except for Doro, who carried letters between them. But Ottilia refrained from saying so.

Francis regarded the outside of the Hatchet Inn with disfavour. It was one of the oldest buildings he had seen in Bristol, made somewhat in the Tudor style, but of such dingy aspect even from the outside that he was wholly reluctant to set foot in the place.

He turned to Ackworth, who had come to the Ship in some urgency, demanding his attendance. Since he had but just dressed, Francis was not in the least inclined to oblige the man. Except that the lawyer's manner, as well as his words, indicated the information might be important to the enquiry. He was not, however, in the best of tempers for being dragged away from his comfortable parlour into a biting wind.

"This better be worthwhile, my friend. I have had enough of these foul places."

"You will not regret it, I promise you. I would have relayed the information but that it would then be hearsay."

Francis suppressed a sigh. "Very well, let us go in."

The interior proved as repulsive as he had feared, though perhaps not quite as gloomy as the Full Moon had been. With the grimy casement windows firmly closed, the heat from a substantial fire made the place stuffy and too hot, even for March. Ackworth took the lead, making for a booth in a far corner, away from the few patrons hardy enough to be drinking at this early hour. As he rounded the edge of the back bench of the booth, Francis spied the fellow already seated there, tucked into the far side of the booth against the wall.

"Mordecai?"

Ackworth nudged him. "Hush, my lord!"

The little fellow produced a leer, peering up at the two of them out of those sly, darting eyes. "Name no names, mister."

Francis lowered his voice, slipping into the booth beside Ackworth. "Are you telling me this fellow has more to add to the puzzle?"

"He will tell you himself." Ackworth signed to Mordecai. "Go on. Tell him all you told me."

Mordecai's mouth twisted in a cunning look as he sidled his cupped hand towards Ackworth. "Summat fer summat."

"I'll deal with this." Francis dove a hand into his pocket and brought out a shilling, which he held up. "When you've spoken."

A grin appeared. "I said you was a leery one, yer honour, only I ain't trusting, see."

The hand remained cupped. Francis dropped the coin into it and it vanished. "You'd best make it good, Mordecai."

The little fellow drew in a sharp breath, tapping his nose in the way he had. "Hist! Don't yer be sayin' it, not here."

Francis's patience snapped. "Cut line, man!"

Ackworth set a hand on his arm. "Patience, my lord. We'll get further if we let him alone."

The murmur was nevertheless heard by Mordecai, for he showed his remaining teeth in another leer. "Yer knows me, Mr Ackworth."

"I do, but his lordship does not. Come, your story, if you please."

The little man reared up, peered over the back of the bench and cast his eyes about the taproom. Then he dropped back down and with an odd stretch of his neck, shoved his head towards Francis. "It's this way, see. I were at Pyg & Whistle."

"When?"

Mordecai tapped his nose again. "A night in which yer honour got an interest, as I hear it."

Francis began to be intrigued and his annoyance dissipated. "You mean the night of Scalloway's murder?"

The snitch hissed through his teeth again, drawing back. "That's a bad habit you got, yer honour, sayin' things out straight."

Francis allowed his expression to speak for him. It did not appear to have any more effect on the little man than to produce another grin. But at last he pressed on with his tale.

"Seen 'em, together they was, hugger-mugger in a corner. Speakin' low they was, but me ears is good. Heard 'em too, din' I?"

"Who?"

"Tellin' yer, aren' I? It were that feller as gorn same way as t'other."

Francis was about to say it when he remembered the wretched little man's dislike of naming names. Instead, he looked to Ackworth. "Does he mean who I think he means? Our friend who was stabbed in the back?"

Ackworth nodded. "As you say, my lord. But listen on."

"Who was he talking to?"

Francis directed his question towards Mordecai, whose sharp eyes had gone from one to the other during this exchange. He returned Francis's regard for a moment and then ducked his head, speaking out of the side of his mouth. "'Twas that there barmaid, she as lifts her petticoats fer all sorts."

Mawdesley and Cherry? But Mordecai had more to say.

"Hear as yer honour's rib were wantin' ter know more of her." He produced an engaging grin and winked, sliding his cupped hand towards Francis this time. "If so be as yer honour wants ter know it too."

Francis sighed and dug a hand into his pocket, bringing out a second coin. "I want to know about this conversation you overheard, but you may as well tell me." He held the coin between finger and thumb. "When you've done. Say on."

Mordecai snickered. "Right downy one, you are." He sniffed but Francis made no sign and the fellow capitulated. "Remember as you was arsting after a certain darkie? Time was, afore she come to the Pyg & Whistle, this same barmaid took and give him what she give any man."

Good Lord, Indigo? "She was his mistress?"

"Not to say allus, fer as she won't be beholden to nobody. More, she's one to pick and choose, if'n yer honour take my meaning, and 'tis said as she'd pick a darkie over any."

This was all grist to the mill and placed Indigo nicely in the running. But more important was the exchange between the barmaid and Mawdesley, whose death was lacking both suspect and reason.

The coin dropped into the fellow's still cupped palm, which he promptly withdrew from sight, and Francis lowered his voice. "I thank you for that. But let us return to the girl and the man who was stabbed."

Mordecai grinned and cocked his head. "Fer another?"

"If it proves worth it. What did you hear between those two? Word for word, if you please."

# CHAPTER TWENTY-FOUR

At this early hour the Pyg & Whistle was quieter than it had been upon the last occasion. Keeping Doro close, Ottilia walked straight into the tap, which smelled of stale liquor and dead wood. She wrinkled her nose, ignored the stares of two ancients in a nook near the fire and accosted the greasy landlord.

"Good day to you, Pymoor. I wish to see your girl Cherry again, if you will be so good as to find her for me."

He looked decidedly taken aback. "My lady?"

"You heard me."

"I don't know as she's up and about yet, my lady."

"Then have Mrs Pymoor get her up and be quick about it."

The authoritative tone had its effect. The landlord slipped off via a door to the nether regions in the depths of the taproom and called out for his wife. An answering call came, sounding particularly grumpy. The muttered voices went on for a moment or two. Pymoor explaining her advent and request? Presently, Mrs Pymoor emerged, smoothing her apron and peering towards Ottilia.

"It is you, my lady! I thought as Pymoor were bleary-eyed like he is of a morning, saying you was here at a time like this. What can I do for you?"

Glad of the co-operative attitude, Ottilia repeated her need. "I'd like to speak to Cherry once more."

The attitude altered at once. "That fussock! I tell you straight, my lady, I'm of a mind to throw her out, bag and baggage. Which there is apt, if you like, for as it's a baggage she is and no mistake, peacocking about, gowned like the lady she isn't, not by a long chalk."

Ottilia's senses prickled. "She has bought a new gown?"

"Aye, and fit for a pantomime it is, all frills and furbelows. If she didn't look the part she played before, she does now." Mrs Pymoor then coloured up, putting a hand to her mouth. "Begging your pardon, my lady, for saying such to you, but that trollop has me fair riled. Nor it ain't the only thing she's bought neither."

"What else?" Where had the barmaid the wherewithal for such extravagance?

Mrs Pymoor drew in her cheeks. "A cloak, my lady. Not one like yours as might warm a body in these March winds, oh no. A thin, gauzy thing it is, all spangles. When and where she thinks to wear such a thing is beyond me."

Distracted, Ottilia followed this up. "Did you ask her?"

"That I did. What do you think, my lady? Cherry ups and says she's off to take her talents to the stage. Talents! I know what talents she's got, and they ain't nowt to do with no theatricals, that I will swear to."

Ottilia was amused by Mrs Pymoor's affronted manner, but the matter was too important for laughter. "Has Cherry then left your establishment?"

"Not she. Knows where her bread is buttered. Pymoor's even more besotted now, like they all are. I'd have her out straight if it wasn't as this wretched gown of hers has brought them in, eyes popping at that disgusting display."

This was clear enough. Cherry's bosomy charms were much to be admired. But Ottilia's need became paramount. "If it not too much of a trouble to you, Mrs Pymoor, I am doubly anxious to have a word with Cherry."

Mrs Pymoor huffed a little. "It's asking a deal of me, but seeing it's you, my lady, I'll go and rout out the wretched little slugabed."

Ottilia thanked her, watched her retreat into the hall and turned to Doro, a round-eyed spectator of the exchange. "Tell me what you know of Quin, if you please."

Doro's brows drew together. "Only that he was a favourite with the master. I cannot abide him and his sneaking ways."

"You have reason. But I am asking if you have any information about his past history."

Doro gave a little shrug. "I have never heard of that, milady." Which would indicate his early association with Indigo was not generally known in the household. "The mistress is certain he spied upon her for the master."

"I imagine that might well be so. He appears to have been deep in his master's confidence."

"Not so, milady. What he knew he found out by listening at doors. I have done so myself, but Quin would often be found where he had no business to be. I doubt the master trusted him."

"Enough to use him for his messenger, however."

"It was so, but Quin cannot read or write. Thus, he did not learn from reading what he carried." Doro's tone hardened. "Quin knew more than he ought. Just as he found and purloined my dagger, he sneaked around everywhere in the house, poking and prying. Several times I caught him. He pretended to be on the master's business, but what business had the master in my mistress's clothes press or her dressing table?"

None at all. Unless he hoped to find money? Or had it in mind to sell her jewellery? If Scalloway were short of funds, he might well send his man, like a sneak thief, to do his dirty work for him. Then he could conveniently lay the blame elsewhere. It was certain that Quin, having been once under Indigo's tutelage, would not boggle at any nefarious task.

Ottilia's cogitations were interrupted by the abrupt return of Mrs Pymoor, who swept into the taproom in a bang, throwing her hands in the air. "Would you believe it? That worthless wench has absconded!"

Her mind leaping, Ottilia started forward. "Cherry? She has gone?"

"Decamped in the night, it looks like. Her chamber's a mess, but she's took the lot, new clothes an' all."

Imperative to see for herself. "Would you object to it if I looked at her chamber, Mrs Pymoor?"

The landlady bridled. "It ain't fit to be seen, my lady, special by the likes of you."

"Nevertheless, it may be of use to me."

Mrs Pymoor shrugged. "Well, if you insist, my lady, I can't gainsay you, but I'll beg as you'll note it ain't the way I keep my house."

Ottilia found words to soothe as she followed the woman upstairs, signing to Doro to follow. Doro hesitated at the stairs. Fearful of returning too close to the scene of the murder? "Come, my dear, there is nothing to alarm you now."

Mrs Pymoor halted on the landing. "Afeared, is she? Can't blame her. Nasty business, it were."

Doro, however, gave a short nod and dropping her gaze, began to mount the stairs. Satisfied, Ottilia continued on up.

The barmaid's chamber was not, as she anticipated, situated in the attics. Cherry had occupied an upper room, not large, but properly furnished, as far as one could tell under the shambles left by a hasty departure.

The bed, of a good size though lacking posts and a tester, was unmade, the quilt half-falling to the floor, the sheets tangled and thrown all anyhow to one side, the pillows in disarray. Two of the drawers of a plain commode stood open, their remaining contents spilling out or jumbled together within. An old robe sprawled over a stool before a mirrored washstand, also with an open drawer wherein lay an empty pot of face paint, a broken fan smeared with rouge and a sprinkling of coloured powders. The jug and ewer were on the floor, the latter full of dirty water, displaced by a clutter of paste jewellery and ribbons piled on the washstand surface, and a stinking chamber pot near the window set the seal on as unkempt a scene as Ottilia had ever witnessed. Small wonder Mrs Pymoor had been reluctant to permit her entry.

She stood in the middle of the limited space remaining, Doro and the landlady hovering by the door, and circled slowly, checking for she knew not what anomaly. Nothing surfaced. Cherry had packed in haste, that was all one could tell.

Feeling deflated, Ottilia crossed to the commode and lifted out the spilled garments. She held a faded dimity petticoat up, showing it to the landlady. "She seems to have discarded her older clothes."

Mrs Pymoor drew near, peering at the petticoat. "That's a working day dress, that is. Huh! Too high and mighty now, is she, to be wearing such? And where's she gone, I'd like to know?"

"We may both desire that information, Mrs Pymoor." As she spoke, Ottilia's gaze flitted across the chamber and was caught by something in the fireplace that was neither ash, nor half-burned coal. She moved across and dropped down to look more closely.

"What have you found, milady?"

Ottilia glanced up to find Doro at her shoulder. "I don't yet know, but this fire has been out some time."

"Then Cherry went from here last night?"

Ottilia was feeling the remains of the coal, her attention focused on the object poking through from beneath. "Or in the early hours of this morning. The hearth is still warm." Her fingers moved to the so far unidentifiable thing buried in the ashes. Cloth? It was soft and malleable, burned as it was. Taking hold, she gave it a tug. It shifted, but did not come out. "Dorote, pray pick up the poker and see if you can dislodge this cloth. Careful now. We don't want to bring the ashes out upon the rug."

"Let me, milady. I am used to such work." In proof of her statement, deft and quick with the poker, Doro shifted ash and half-burnt coal to each side, scraping at the cloth until it began to come free.

Ottilia had moved back, but she leaned in and took hold of the cloth, tugging gently. It proved to be much larger than she had supposed as she drew it forth, Doro clearing its path as it came. "It looks like a shift." Rising with it in her hands, she met the startled gaze of Mrs Pymoor.

"Mercy! Do you say Cherry has gone and burned that all up?"

"Not all." Ottilia shook it free of debris into the hearth and held it up, letting the rest fall free. It was only partially destroyed, its bulk too great to fully burn. There were large patches of brown, a few holes with blackened edges, but its original use was clear. "It is a nightgown. How very interesting."

Mrs Pymoor exclaimed again, blessing herself. "Why in the world should Cherry take and burn a perfectly good nightgown?"

Doro's blue gaze was alight with conjecture. "What does it mean?"

"Mean?" Mrs Pymoor responded. "Nowt, for all of me. It don't make no sense at all."

"Oh, I think there is a reason." Ottilia spoke absently, engaged in a minute examination of a brown stain she had discovered on the remaining sleeve, the other half burned away. A thorough examination exposed several more on the body of the garment, spots and splashes, different in both colour and shape from the burns. "This I will take, if you do not object."

Mrs Pymoor watched her as she bundled the ruined nightgown up, taking care to keep the relevant parts folded within.

"Well, I don't know why you'd want it, my lady, but you're welcome if you do."

"I do. Moreover, I am glad you are here to stand witness as to where I found it."

Mrs Pymoor's eyes grew round. "Witness? Why, whatever do you mean?"

Ottilia smiled. "Pardon me for that at this present, Mrs Pymoor. I have an idea, but I prefer to keep the matter to myself until I am certain."

"Well, I never did!"

"Have no fear. As soon as I am able, I will admit you into my confidence. But I must thank you, for I believe you may have solved a little puzzle for me. Come, Dorote. I am much in need of my breakfast."

Arriving back in the private parlour at the Fanshawe's temporary lodging presently, Ottilia discovered it had been invaded. Elinor Scalloway rose from a chair at the table and flung out an accusing finger.

"I knew it! You, madam, have stolen my slave!"

For a moment, Ottilia stared stupidly. From nowhere, a gust of blinding rage overtook her. Thrusting the cloth she carried at Doro, she advanced upon the widow, her hand rising almost of its own volition.

"How dare you speak so to me?" She struck out, her palm connecting with Elinor's cheek. "You have the gall to come here in this guise after you hurled abuse at Doro and threw her out in the street? She came to me for succour, shaking and miserable. You, Mrs Scalloway, are inhuman. Have you no compassion at all? I despise you!"

Awareness returned in a bang as she took in the stunned expression on Elinor's face. What in the world was the matter with her? This was not her way. One got nowhere by flying into a pelter. She struggled for calm, stepping back. "Well, I have said enough, I think."

Elinor Scalloway's eyes were watering. "You hit me!"

Ottilia drew a breath. "I did and I ought to apologise, but I am afraid I cannot bring myself to do so. Tit for tat, Elinor. Did you not strike Doro for daring to speak her mind?"

Elinor sniffed, drawing herself up even as her hand moved to rub at her reddened cheek. "I will not tolerate such language from a slave."

Ottilia's ire threatened again but she was able this time to control it. "Then you may tolerate it from me instead. I did not *steal* Doro. *You* reneged on your word and told her to leave your house. She did so. You did not expect that, did you?"

To her surprise, Elinor took this up. "No, I did not. Slaves know well that running away brings the harshest penalties upon them. I may have spoken in a fury, but of course I did not imagine she would go." She shifted out into the room and looked past Ottilia to where Doro was standing, pressed against the wall near the door, hugging Cherry's nightgown to her midriff. "You will return with me, Doro. You need not fear a whipping, my dear. Let us forget this episode."

Ottilia moved quickly between them as Elinor started forward. "She is going nowhere, Mrs Scalloway. If you think I will release her into your clutches again, you are mightily mistaken."

Elinor turned on her. "You have no rights in the matter, Lady Francis. Pray don't again threaten me with scandalous gossip, for I care naught what anyone thinks."

"Indeed?" Ottilia prepared for battle. "Will you care for a charge of murder, then?"

It was a bow drawn at a venture but the widow started back. "What? You cannot bring that home to me!"

"Oh, I think I can at least lodge an accusation. Not quite equivalent with the one you have thrown at me, but I hardly think your reputation will survive, even if the matter did not come to trial."

"That is ridiculous." But Elinor began to look uncertain.

"Is it? I have no doubt there are whisperings already among the gentry hereabouts. Do you truly care to carry the stigma of suspicion back with you to Barbados? People are never quite sure, are they? There is no smoke without fire, they will say, and recall how you were always seen in company with Laurence Culverstone prior to your marriage. Especially damning when you return with him still in your train, do you not think? Worse, if you have the intention to take him as your husband before you leave. Is that not your plan? To present your father with a fait accompli?"

Elinor's lip trembled and her gaze grew dark with fury. "You are a witch!"

Ottilia gave a spurious smile. "I prefer magician, if you must call me names."

Elinor's bosom rose and fell as she struggled for words, finding them at length. "What is it you want of me?"

Ottilia concealed her triumph. "Speak to your friend Lord Radcliffe and sign whatever papers are necessary to obtain manumission for Dorote Gabon. Meanwhile, she remains in my charge."

"And when she is free? What then?"

"That is Doro's choice. She may remain with me until she has time to look about her and decide what she wishes to do with her life. I dare say it will be for the first time since she was brutally deprived of all she knew and taken from her rightful home in Gabon."

Ottilia was glad to see that Elinor Scalloway had the grace to look a trifle shamefaced at this reference to Doro's origins. Perhaps there was hope for her after all.

It lasted only a moment. Ottilia was obliged to own she had backbone as she resumed her habitual prideful air. "Have you in fact made any progress in your alleged hunt for my husband's killer?"

Ottilia likewise dropped into an echo, somewhat in pretence, of her customary manner. "Why, yes. I believe I am closing in upon the truth. I shall, however, wish to question your fellow Quin shortly."

Elinor stared. "Quin? You think Quin did it? But he was devoted to Marcus. Disgustingly so, for my part."

Ottilia bypassed the question. "You are behind the times, Mrs Scalloway. There is a second murder to be accounted for now."

For an instant, Elinor looked utterly fearful. "Who?" Hoarse and anxious.

"I doubt you would know of Mawdesley. But Quin does." Elinor's features had relaxed again, but Ottilia regarded her, curiosity to the fore. "Whom did you suppose it might be?"

A shrug came. "Who can say? The business is too sordid."

"Were you afraid for Culverstone? You need not be. He is alive and well, for I met with him not two hours ago." She saw from Elinor's expression she had hit home. "Why should anyone wish to dispose of Laurence Culverstone?"

Elinor shuddered. "You spoke of Quin. Laurence went to see Marcus that night. If Quin had seen him there, he might seek vengeance, supposing Laurence to have been responsible."

"You believe his loyalty to Marcus was so great?"

"He was fully my husband's man." Elinor spat the words. "I know not how many times he spied upon me, for Marcus could only have found out … certain things of which he accused me, had Quin followed me."

Why the hesitation? Had Elinor cuckolded her husband while he was still alive? To Ottilia's surprise, Doro put her oar in.

"It is true, milady. Quin was used to try and follow me also. I took pains to put him off the scent and take a roundabout route to my destination."

Elinor gave a pathetic smile. "You were a boon to me, Doro. I wish you will think better of leaving me."

Ottilia quashed this without hesitation. "Well, she will not. That time is over, Elinor."

"Can you not let the girl speak for herself?"

"As she was permitted to live for herself? Choose for herself? Don't try to turn the matter to your account. You betrayed her loyalty and there's an end."

Ignoring her, Elinor turned on Doro a winning smile. "We can be friends again. It will be different. I will change towards you, you'll see."

Doro looked Elinor straight in the eyes. "Did you believe the master, madame, when he said the same to you?"

Chagrin spilled across Elinor's face. "You would throw that back at me, would you? Very well, so be it. I should have known better than to expect gratitude."

Ottilia nearly laughed in her face. Elinor stalked to the door and Ottilia spoke as she opened it. "By the by, Elinor, you may be relieved to hear that I have ticked your Laurence off my list. He did not kill Marcus."

A flash of some kind showed in Elinor's eyes and then she was gone, leaving the door open behind her. Doro moved to close it and Ottilia looked for the hand bell, her hunger reviving with the departure of her uninvited guest.

"Milady, I must thank you."

"No need, Doro. I pledged you my protection. Besides, you must know Hemp has been baying for your freedom all along." She rang the bell as realisation set in. "Where is Hemp? Francis too. I left him breakfasting in bed but he should have risen by this time."

The question was rhetorical, but Doro took it up. "I shall go and find Hemp, milady. But first, where would you wish me to put this?"

Ottilia glanced across, for the first time realising what she had done with her evidence. "Heavens, I forgot it! Set it on the writing bureau, if you please, my dear."

She ought to find a hiding place, but her brain refused to work. Food! Where was that waiter?

The door opened as Doro reached it, producing the servant himself. Ottilia put in her request for a belated breakfast, realised that Doro had left the room and sat down in her accustomed chair by the fire to wait, feeling filleted all at once.

She had just time for the thought that she had done too much on an empty stomach before unconsciousness claimed her.

# CHAPTER TWENTY-FIVE

Swimming back to the real world from a hazy dream, Ottilia found her husband bending over her, concern in his bruised features.

"Tillie, are you all right?"

She blinked uncomprehendingly. "Yes." Then memory hit. "I sat down … I swooned, I think."

"I think you must have done. You are dreadfully pale." His hand tipped her face up. "What ails you, sweetheart? I said you were overdoing it!"

"A little, perhaps. I am tired."

"You are not ill, are you?"

"Ill? No!" A vague memory surfaced. "Hungry. I hadn't eaten." She looked about. "Did they bring it?"

"Bring what?"

"Breakfast."

"They've not had time. I met the waiter on the stairs. That's how I knew you were back. It could not have been many minutes, my dear one, but I found you like this."

The mists were dispersing. "I will do, Fan. I need food, that is all."

He straightened. "Well, if you say so. I wish you will stay put for a while, though. You clearly need rest."

Recollection was growing. "I remember. Elinor!"

Ottilia put out a hand and he took it in his, perching on the arm of her chair in a position that enabled him to face her. "What of Elinor?"

"She was here. Fan, she made me so angry. I slapped her."

His brows flew up. "That is not like you, Tillie."

"I know. I can't think what came over me. My temper was too quick for me."

"Again? You *are* sickening for something."

"I am not, I promise you. Perhaps it was the shock of what she said, that I had stolen her slave. Stolen forsooth! As if she had not done so in the first place."

"Did she take Doro back?"

Ottilia tossed her head. "Certainly not. I would not allow it. She is going to free her."

Francis was openly grinning. "I'll go bail you threatened her with dire consequences if she didn't, you unscrupulous female."

A chuckle escaped Ottilia. "I did. I said I would accuse her of murder so that the suspicion would follow her to Barbados."

He gave a shout of laughter. "Wretch! Is there nothing to which you will not stoop?"

"Not in such a cause, Fan."

They were interrupted by the entrance of a waiter bearing a tray, and Ottilia's interest veered to whatever might be concealed beneath the covers of the silver dishes. "I hope there may be bacon. I asked for it. And coffee, of course."

"Of course." Francis glinted at her as he rose, offering his hand to help her up. "I might share your bacon."

"You may count yourself lucky if I leave any, my dearest dear. Besides, you already broke your fast."

"That was hours ago."

But when Francis had removed his outer garments and they sat down at the table, Ottilia was gratified to see him pile her plate with almost as much bacon as he was wont to supply himself. She took the cover off the second dish and an agreeable aroma of roasted cheese assailed her nostrils. Her fatigue vanished. She seized a serving spoon and dug into the crust, slicing through the softened mound.

"Roasted cheese for breakfast?"

"Mm, why not? Butter a roll for me, Fan, if you please."

She began upon the bacon, larding each piece with a sliver of cheese. "Delicious."

Francis, busy with the roll, began to laugh. "I have no notion who you are, woman. What have you done with my wife?"

She twinkled at him, but concentrated on the food. As her hunger began to be assuaged, she sighed with satisfaction and picked up the prepared roll. "That was perfect. You should try it, Fan."

He had taken up a fork and was already working through the remainder of the bacon in the dish. "I'll stick to my meats, I thank you."

Her mind at leisure to think of other things, Ottilia recalled her husband's initial absence. "Where were you, Fan, that Elinor was able to park herself in here to wait for me?"

"Ackworth arrived with an urgent entreaty to accompany him to another of these appalling noisome inns that abound in this City. You remember I met his informant, the one who led us to Indigo? Well, this same Mordecai was at the Hatchet Inn and had an interesting tale to relate."

Ottilia had reached the stage of pouring coffee and did not look up. "What tale?"

"He overheard an exchange between Mawdesley and the barmaid."

Ottilia's attention snapped in and she almost dropped the coffee pot. "Cherry?"

"That's the one."

"Where?"

"At the Pyg & Whistle, of course. This wretched Mordecai seems to find his way anywhere there is a possibility of his making an advantage out of it."

"But what was said, Fan?" She set the coffee pot down, intent now.

"Mordecai did not hear precisely at first as they were speaking low, but he's an inquisitive little rascal — to our advantage in this case — and he closed in to eavesdrop. Mawdesley then said something like 'It's for tonight'. She didn't speak, but only nodded. Then he handed her a package which she slipped under her apron."

"When was this?"

"On the night of the murder. When else if I remarked it as pertinent?"

Ottilia's mind positively fizzed. "That is all that occurred?"

"Well, it's not much, but I thought it might be of use."

"Of use? Fan, it is practically conclusive!"

Having despatched Francis, upon request, to relate the result of her activities to Walter Belchamp, Ottilia left Doro with the mundane task of seeing to the laundering of items in her wardrobe and, feeling a great deal more able after her excellent breakfast, made the walk across Stone Bridge and up Park Street towards the Scalloway home, accompanied by Hemp.

"I think it best if you find the fellow and bring him before me."

"Will not Mrs Scalloway send for him, milady?"

"Thank you, but I prefer to rely upon your good offices, Hemp. I am not best pleased with Elinor Scalloway. Nor do I trust her to adhere to the business in hand."

She had no need to relate the events of the morning since Hemp had heard them from Doro, except for one or two points upon which he asked for enlightenment. "Doro did not know why you took that nightgown, milady."

There was a hint of question in it, but Ottilia refused to be drawn. "I will reveal it all presently. I must speak to Quin before I say more."

But Hemp was not quite done with queries. "What of Mr Culverstone?"

Ottilia glanced round. "He is not guilty. To his good fortune, I may say. It would not have served him to do the deed, no matter the temptation."

"You believe he thought of it, milady?"

She laughed out. "I imagine he did so many times, but not with any serious intent. He was prepared to wait for his Elinor through all the gamut of separation and divorce." She was about to add that she did not doubt the pair would have lived in sin, or at least taken their pleasure together regardless, when she recalled the possibility of Marcus Scalloway having defiled Doro. There could be little advantage in bringing this painful notion to Hemp's mind by speaking of Elinor's potential adultery.

Arriving at the Scalloway residence, Hemp headed for the area steps. "Where will you be, milady?"

"A good question. I am tempted to come down to the domestic offices with you, but I don't wish to alarm the servants." Hemp made no response to this, which Ottilia took for agreement. "I suppose it is too much to ask if there is a housekeeper's room?"

Hemp looked wry. "They do not even keep a butler, milady."

Ottilia capitulated. "Well then, I must ask Elinor for a suitable chamber."

She let him go and trod up the steps to the front door. The footman let her in. "Madam is resting, my lady."

Hope reared. "In her bedchamber? Then show me to the parlour, if you please." After all, if Elinor could invade her private parlour, she might do the same here.

The footman looked taken aback. "But madam is not in there, my lady."

"So you have said. It makes no matter. My errand is to Quin. Pray inform my steward that he will find me in the parlour." With which, she passed the man and began to mount the stairs. From the corner of her eye, she saw him hovering below. He would scarcely lay hands upon her. No doubt Elinor had behaved in just such a high-handed fashion at the Ship. As she reached the upper floor, she saw him shrug and move off towards the back of the house. Ottilia hid a smile and made her way along the corridor to the parlour door.

It was not unoccupied. On her entrance, Laurence Culverstone rose from a chair set at a small bureau to one side, dismay writ plain in his features. "You here, Lady Francis?"

Ottilia came fully in and closed the door. "As you see."

"Elinor is resting. She has developed the headache."

Secretly amused, Ottilia raised her brows. "Indeed? Then perhaps she should take a tisane."

Had Elinor not told him of the slap? Neither she nor her adversary had come off unscathed from the encounter, it would seem. At least the disorientation from her own swoon had proved temporary.

"She has taken a powder." Culverstone was still regarding her with wariness. "Elinor cannot see you now."

Ottilia moved to take a seat on the sofa. "I have no wish to see her. I am come to speak to the boots."

He stared. "Quin?"

"Just so. Elinor knows I had that intention. Did she not tell you of her visit?"

Culverstone shrugged. "We had a bare moment to speak. She was disturbed and in pain. I did not wish to detain her."

"You intend to wait for her?"

"I was writing a letter." He gestured to the bureau.

Ottilia regarded him in a speculative way. "Might you finish it in some other room?"

His brows drew together. "You want to use this one?"

"That would seem to be a fair inference."

Her dry tone hit home. "I dare say I might go elsewhere." He hesitated. "Why do you wish to question Quin?"

Ottilia raised her brows. "Have you some objection?"

"No, why should I?"

He hovered, clearly uncertain. A knock at the door brought Hemp, thrusting Quin ahead of him. "Get in!"

Quin fairly stumbled into the room, cast a resentful glance at its occupants and turned back on Hemp, his tone surly. "Ain't no need to bully them as is smaller than you, friend Roy."

"I am not your friend and there is every need." Hemp closed the door and looked from Culverstone to Ottilia. "Is it inconvenient, milady?"

Ottilia was eyeing Quin. "Not at all. Mr Culverstone is just leaving." She shifted her gaze to Culverstone, who gave a grunt, went to pick up the sheet upon which he had been writing, and crossed to the door where Hemp opened it for him and gave place. Culverstone did not even trouble to thank him, much to Ottilia's disgust, but went through and left it to Hemp to shut it behind him. Really, the manners of these colonials were atrocious. She turned her attention to the clearly recalcitrant boot boy. She tried a soft approach. "Do pray come in where I can see you, Quin."

His chin went up, but he shuffled to a position in the centre of the room facing the sofa, casting a hate-filled glance at

Hemp who took his station to one side, conveniently between Quin and the door.

Ottilia opened negotiations on a forthright note. "It was you, was it not, Quin, who told your master Captain Indigo would demand a high price to take a ship to the West Indies?"

The man visibly blanched. "I didn't never!"

"Come, let us be frank. You worked for Indigo in your youth. You knew he could not enter Caribbean waters without risk. Or indeed at all, was that it?"

Hemp cut in, his tone sharp. "That's what he wouldn't tell me, milady?"

"I imagine so. Too risky. You were less afraid of your master than of Indigo, were you not?"

Quin's eyes shifted this way and that. "I dunno what you mean, missus."

"Don't you? Well, let us leave that and move on to the other matter." Quin looked decidedly ill at ease now. Ottilia opted for another attack direct. "You have been with the barmaid at the Pyg & Whistle, have you not?"

"What if I have?" Shock registered on Quin's face. At her speaking so plain?

"You had no qualms to go where your master had been?"

"With that Cherry?" He emitted a vulgar sound. "Who ain't been there?"

"Do you know her well?"

Quin shrugged. "Jawed now and now. She ain't one to waste words, if you take me." A leer crossed his face. "Give you a sixpenny flyer soon as open her gab."

A growl came from Hemp. "Mind your tongue before milady!"

Quin became truculent. "Why should I when she don't? Never heard such out of a gentrymort's mouth afore!"

Hemp strode forward. "If you don't want my fist in your teeth, you'll mend your manners this instant!"

Ottilia intervened as Quin cringed away. "Peace, Hemp! Let him alone."

Hemp held his glare on the man's face for a moment, and then broke away to resume his former stance. Ottilia saw Quin's shoulders sink. Relief? Not for long, poor fool.

"Did you know your friend Mawdesley also had truck with Cherry?"

At mention of the name there was an instant change. Quin's gaze turned shifty and his body shrank into itself.

Intensely alert, Ottilia pressed him. "Well?"

"What if he did?" It came out almost a croak. "Nowt to me."

Time to turn the screw. "I am not talking of the fellow bedding her, nor do I care whether or not he did. The two of them were overheard on the night of Scalloway's death, plotting."

Now Quin looked merely confused. "Plotting? Plotting how?"

Ottilia presented an innocent front. "I was hoping you might tell me. The outcome, you see, has been unfortunate. For Mawdesley, you know."

The shiftiness returned. "Don't know what you mean, missus."

"Oh, I think you do, Quin."

She waited, keeping her gaze upon him. He brought up a hand and bit at the tips of his fingers. He glanced with longing at the door, but Hemp's stalwart form was in the way. At length, a horrible sort of gargle escaped him and out it burst.

"I never done for him, I swear it!"

Ottilia leaned back. "How do you know Mawdesley was done for?"

Again, he plainly struggled. Wishing he might escape, yet burdened with the knowledge? It came. "'Cos I seen him, din't I?"

"How did you come to see him dead?"

The word made him shudder. "He were to meet me at the Cock down Temple Street, only he never come. I went to the house. The old 'un ope the door and up I went. Yelled at Mawdesley to come on out of it, but he never answered, so I go in, don't I?" A grimace twisted his face. "He were lyin' there. One of they daggers in his back. Stabbed he were, like the master."

Ottilia was inclined to believe the story. Reliving it had infected his pallor. "Was he warm still?"

"How should I know, missus? I weren't nowise goin' to touch him." There was no mistaking the recoiling horror.

Ottilia tried another tack. "What time was this?"

"Five, six, I dunno. It were light still just about, I know that."

Ottilia pounced on this. "But the curtains were closed."

"Not when I went in, they weren't. I closed 'em afore I left."

"Why?"

"So's no one wouldn't think to wonder is why. I scarpered, missus, double quick."

Ottilia sighed. "I suppose I need not ask why you did not think to report his death?"

"Who to? They'd have thought I done it, wouldn't they?"

"Could you not at least have told Mr Harbury?"

Quin emitted a scoffing noise. "Harbury? Haul me before the magistrate, he would, and I'd have been in gaol before the cat could lick her ear, and I never done it. I swear it, missus. I never touched him. I ain't got one of they knives as Buck makes. Couldn't afford it nohow."

Ottilia eyed him. "Oh, you knew it was Buck who made them, then?"

"Everyone knows it. Even Harbury. Dessay he got his from one of them traders."

On her return to the Ship, Ottilia was glad to find Francis had but just returned from his errand. She began upon her urgent question even as she threw off her cloak and laid it aside. "What said Belchamp, Fan?"

Her husband, having set aside his hat and stripped off his gloves, was divesting himself of his great-coat. "He is beyond gleeful, although incredulous at your assertion that the barmaid wielded the weapon."

"Is that what you told him?"

"Of course not." He moved to the mantel and picked up the handbell. "He made the inference from your story. I related it exactly as you gave it to me. Why, don't you think it was this Cherry?"

A trifle disturbed, Ottilia paced to the window. "She was bought."

"By whom? I must tell you Belchamp drew his own conclusions and has sent his constable off to the tavern where we found Captain Indigo."

Startled, she turned. "He thinks to find Cherry there?"

"He is convinced Indigo is behind both murders."

"How so?"

"Out of a general suspicion that a known criminal is the most likely to be guilty, I expect. He says Indigo has the most telling reason to kill Scalloway."

Ottilia let out an exasperated sound. "It occurred to me also, but I have since changed my mind. Belchamp has fixated on this notion of Indigo thinking he was cheated. Yet if he deliberately sunk that ship, he had his revenge. Why risk hanging when he must know none can prove it was not an accident?"

Francis rang the bell he had all the time been holding. "Or indeed, why should he kill Mawdesley?"

Smiling, she moved to join him. "I ought to have known you would seize on that one. But why seek for Cherry there?"

"It would seem he may not be far wrong, if our friend Mordecai is to be believed. He claims she was used to distribute her favours in that quarter before she came to work at the Pyg & Whistle. According to Mordecai — although he speaks in such riddles one cannot be sure — Cherry has a penchant for a dark skin."

Ottilia recalled Cherry's somewhat crude reference to Hemp. "That may well be true." She took her customary chair, looking up at her spouse. "It would be too bad if Cherry were obliged to take the full blame."

His brows drew together. "But you believe she did stab Scalloway?"

"At the instigation of another."

"Indigo?"

"I believe not. Moreover, I am not absolutely certain whether Mawdesley also died by Cherry's hand. Tell me, is Harbury a man of stature?"

She received an amazed stare. "You think he is behind all this?"

Ottilia spread her hands. "I cannot think any other fits the facts. Only consider. Mawdesley is Harbury's man. He and Cherry made an arrangement which one could take to be the signal for doing the deed. Doro happens by at precisely the right moment, giving Cherry the perfect scapegoat."

"Of which she takes full advantage."

"Just so. All three conspirators are safe. They think. Enter the Fanshawe avengers —"

"You include me, do you, my woman of wonder?"

She gurgled. "I could not manage without you, my dearest dear. More so this time, as you must admit. But do concentrate, Fan."

She would have continued but that a knock at the door produced Tyler, who was armed with a tray. Francis silenced her with a gesture. "Ah, good man! Coffee and ale, I trust?"

The footman smirked as he set the tray down on the table. "Indeed, my lord." He made to prepare Ottilia's coffee, but her spouse intervened.

"Leave it. I will do the honours. But remove all these to the chamber, if you please." He gestured to the discarded outer garments and crossed to the table, busying himself with the coffee while Tyler collected everything up. As soon as the burdened footman retired, he threw a glance at Ottilia. "You were saying?"

She sighed. "What was I saying? That very welcome aroma has made me forget."

"Enter the Fanshawe avengers," he quoted, making an exaggeration of the words with a flourish and a bow.

Ottilia had to laugh. "Just so, O play-actor husband of mine."

He dropped two lumps of sugar in her coffee cup and brought it across. "Cut line, woman. Where were we?"

Ottilia took the brew and sipped, emitting a satisfied sound. "That is a deal better. Where were we, yes. With the release of Doro and the plethora of questions, I suspect Harbury may have begun to fret over the possibility his accomplices would fail to stand firm."

Having poured himself a glass of ale from the jug, Francis brought it across and took his seat opposite. "So he rids himself of both?"

Ottilia considered for a moment, sipping her favourite beverage. "Cherry began peacocking about in new finery."

"He paid her off?"

"Or paid her again. With, I imagine, the proviso that she made herself scarce. She was talking glibly of going upon the stage, but I dare say that was a blind."

"To conceal her intention to go to Indigo?"

"By no means. She's a cunning piece. Amoral, too. I should think she had her plans well laid. She is likely far away from Bristol by this time. She may even have taken ship. Indeed, I should not be at all surprised to find it was a condition of Harbury's that she left the country."

Francis was frowning. "But I don't yet see how this helps us with Mawdesley. Did she kill him?"

"This is the question, Fan. Did you not gain the impression that Harbury does not dirty his own hands?"

"Ah. Yes, I see. He pays Cherry to dispose of Mawdesley and sees to it she vanishes in short order. But how in the world will you prove it?"

Ottilia was prevented from answering this impossible question as a knock at the door produced a harassed-looking Walter Belchamp, who broke into complaint before any greeting could be exchanged.

"A wild goose chase, my lord, a wild goose chase is what we have been on." Spying Ottilia, he threw out a hand. "My lady Fan, thank the Lord! Forgive my impatience and know that I am very glad to see you, very glad indeed."

Rising, Francis cut in before Ottilia could respond. "What ails you, man? Did your fellow not find the girl?"

"Nothing of the sort, my lord." Belchamp threw up exasperated hands as he marched over. "Not only was this Cherry absent, but Pucklechurch reports that Captain Indigo has also taken off, bag and baggage. I have sent for the militia, but I highly doubt any sign of them will be found, search as we might from now until Doomsday."

Ottilia at last managed to edge in a word. "I fear you are in the right of it, Mr Belchamp. However —"

"What is more —" He recollected himself. "Beg pardon, my lady, for butting in again, but this I must say: that blackguard left one of these infernal daggers embedded in the panelling of his chamber."

"Another?" The exclamation, in disgusted accents, came from Francis, almost oversetting Ottilia's gravity.

"Indeed, my lord, indeed. Cocking a snook at us all, I'll be bound. Impertinence! It has set me in such a fume, saving your presence, my lady Fan, as I have not experienced this age."

Francis rolled his eyes. "I'm not in the least surprised. Is it initialled?"

"See for yourself, my lord." Belchamp dove a hand into a pocket of his great-coat and extracted a package wrapped in cloth, which he handed across. "I have not yet had an opportunity to examine it."

Ottilia watched as her spouse unwrapped the thing, reserving any further contribution she might make until the magistrate should have exhausted his indignation.

"It's the same design," said Francis as the dagger emerged. He peered closely at the hilt, checking both sides of the blade. He lowered it, looking up. "Nothing. How disappointing. I suppose there is no doubt it belonged to Indigo?"

"What else is one to infer?"

Ottilia spoke up at last. "But it was not used to kill Mawdesley, that is plain."

The dissatisfaction in Belchamp's features grew and his tone was sour. "True. I have that in my desk."

"Had it any initial?"

"Not that I saw," came from Francis. "But I did not see it once it had been removed from the body."

Belchamp sighed. "No, nothing there either."

Francis shifted into the room. "Let us understand this. You now have possession of four daggers, only one of which has any identification mark, that belonging to Dorote Gabon."

"That is indeed the case, my lord." Belchamp's gaze swung to Ottilia. "It is most frustrating."

"But not for Doro, sir. If any further proof were needed that she had naught to do with Scalloway's murder, this lack of markings on any of the other daggers supplies it."

Belchamp let out a grunt. "Of more importance, if you will forgive me, my lady, this latest find proves Indigo is indeed our man."

"Pardon me, Mr Belchamp, but it does no such thing. Merely because Indigo had a dagger of this type tells us no more than that. Culverstone is also in possession of one. Moreover, unless your fellow Pucklechurch heard at the Full Moon that Cherry went there, we don't know if that is so either. Did he hear of her being there?"

"No." Belchamp sounded regretful. "But she might have met him elsewhere according to a prior arrangement."

"She might, of course, but I fear it may be mere coincidence that Captain Indigo departed this morning. It was this morning, I take it?" A stray thought crossed Ottilia's mind, distracting her for an instant as Belchamp shifted his shoulders. His next words drew her attention back.

"Last night. Which in itself is suspicious. Who sets out upon a journey at night, except for some nefarious purpose?"

A snort emanated from Ottilia's spouse. "You are talking of a pirate, Belchamp. Of course, his purpose was nefarious. But not, as my wife is convinced, in order to evade the law. Unless it be, he has taken my visit there with Ackworth as a warning that investigations might be undertaken concerning the sinking of the *Blackbird*."

The magistrate's brows drew together. "I don't follow, my lord. From all that you told me, I took it this barmaid acted under Indigo's direction."

Ottilia intervened. "Not Indigo's, sir. The man you want, if I can find a way to show his guilt, is Scalloway's partner, Harbury."

At first incredulous, Belchamp became eager by the time he had listened to Ottilia's reasoning. "He instigated both killings? Good God! A pretty revenge, I must say."

"Oh, it is not revenge, sir." Ottilia put up a staying finger. "Observe the facts. Scalloway refuses to pay up. Harbury presses him to ask his wife. Scalloway does so, but is obliged to report failure, especially faced with the prospect that his goldmine is preparing to leave him. A clever man, I surmise, this Harbury. He knows from Scalloway that it is his wife who holds the purse-strings and that he expects to benefit when she inherits her fortune on the death of her father. He holds a note of hand signed by both. With Scalloway alive and about to be thrown to the dogs, he may never retrieve his money. With Scalloway dead, he is certain of getting it."

"So, knowing this Cherry to be one of Scalloway's — er — flirts, he employs her to do the deed?"

"Not at all, although he might well have done. He entrusts the business to Mawdesley, possibly with the suggestion that such a solution is workable."

"Leaving him out of it altogether, the scoundrel!" Belchamp was growing indignant again, but he frowned. "But he must certainly have done for Mawdesley."

Ottilia spread her hands. "It is possible, but I am inclined to believe he chose to use Cherry once more."

"How might he do so, my lady, if he used this Mawdesley fellow as go-between?"

"Because Cherry knew him better, I suspect, than she would admit. It has been niggling at me for an age, and I could not fathom why until I found the nightgown. My husband mentioned that, I take it? I recalled then, that when I first spoke to Cherry she said that Harbury had ventured into the Pyg & Whistle in the past. She was oddly reticent when I mentioned him and she took care to intimate he was only there to meet Scalloway, but I am of the opinion she was quite in the habit of sharing her favours with Harbury as well as any other."

Belchamp coughed. "You suggest he took the opportunity to use such an occasion to engage her services to slay Mawdesley?"

"Just so. I am sure Cherry was perfectly aware it was Harbury behind the first murder. And he was most certainly in her room at some point." She held off from mentioning why she was so sure of this.

Francis took up the point. "Indeed, and on this occasion, he must have ensured her silence by buying her off, with the proviso that she vanished. That, at least, is how my wife sees it."

Ottilia smiled at him. "Thank you, Fan. I might add that if I were Cherry, I would have obeyed the man's dictum to disappear, for fear he might decide to take my life into the bargain if I did not."

Belchamp became suddenly impatient. "Well, great heavens, let us be after the fellow before he also has a chance to escape!"

"Hold hard, Belchamp!" Francis caught the man's sleeve as he made towards the door, seeming ready to hurtle off on the instant. "Proof, sir. Harbury will merely deny it, and there is as yet nothing with which to gainsay him."

Belchamp let out an explosive sound. "This is intolerable!" He looked to Ottilia. "What are we to do, my lady?"

# CHAPTER TWENTY-SIX

Ottilia waited outside the door while her husband ascertained that Harbury was indeed in his small office. She heard him greet Francis in a manner entirely free from any sign of nervousness.

"Ah, my lord Francis, is it you indeed? I trust you are come with solid news this time?"

"Not quite. There are a few points yet requiring clarification." Francis pushed the door wide. "You will not object to it if my wife asks you one or two questions?"

Ottilia entered on the words and saw the man rise, with a sharp motion, to his feet. He was deceptively ordinary in both looks and stature, even to his dress and manner, which grew immediately respectful as he perceived her. As well she had certainty to counteract a temptation to suppose she must be mistaken.

"How do you do, Mr Harbury?"

He executed an awkward bow without lowering his head, his gaze holding on Ottilia. "My lady."

She moved forward as Francis stood aside and set the one chair before the desk for her to sit. Instead she rested her gloved hands on the back, looking across at Harbury. "This concerns your fellow Mawdesley, poor man."

"Ah, yes." She thought she detected, even through the spectacles, a wary look in his eye. "I doubt I can help you, my lady. I had not seen anything of the man for some days."

"He worked for you, I believe?"

Harbury shrugged. "Odd tasks only. He was not in my employ as such."

Trying to distance himself? Ottilia produced a tone of sympathy. "Nevertheless, I am persuaded you must miss his usefulness."

"Not since the tragic event."

"Which tragic event? Or don't you consider Mawdesley's death to warrant the term?"

Harbury's cool manner was not dented. "Naturally I am sorry for it. I was speaking of Scalloway's demise. Mawdesley being acquainted with my colleague's fellow Quin marks the extent of his usefulness to me."

The inherent callousness of this remark was not lost on Ottilia. She pressed the matter. "Because he might carry messages? Or did you hope to gain thereby such information as Scalloway would not give you directly?"

Was there a faint colour in his cheek? His lip curled. "I had no desire to converse with Scalloway more than was strictly necessary."

Francis intervened, his tone sceptical. "That won't fadge, Harbury. You may not have been to the Pyg & Whistle on the night Scalloway was killed, but Mawdesley was certainly there, and he was your messenger."

A little click of the teeth indicated a certain disquiet. "I sent Mawdesley because Scalloway wrote to me a ridiculous excuse. You saw the note, my lord. There was no end to his excuses."

The underlying rage was creeping through. Seeking to keep him unsuspicious, Ottilia affected a light manner as she at last moved to take her seat. "Well, his venture appears to have ended in a disastrous fashion."

"No surprise there, my lady. Scalloway had no head for business. I should never have agreed to his proposal. One lives and learns."

"One does indeed." Ottilia could feel her spouse's growing frustration. She cast him a reassuring smile and was relieved to see him take a leaning stance against the wall, one hand in his pocket. Since he kept a pistol there, she did not suppose for a moment that his nonchalant pose was real. She returned her attention to Harbury. "Do sit down, sir. You are giving me a crick in the neck."

He gave a slight bow. "With your permission then, my lady."

She watched him take his seat behind the desk and set folded hands on the leather pad, having pushed aside some papers upon which he had evidently been engaged on their entrance. He removed his spectacles and set them down on top of the papers in a precise manner. Playing for time? Then he looked across, tipping his head slightly to one side in an expectant way. "Was there anything further?"

Ottilia gave a spurious smile. "Why, yes, Mr Harbury. Had you any dealings yourself with the barmaid Cherry?"

A flash at his eyes, quickly veiled. "You are very forward, my lady, to be asking me such a question."

"I have that reputation upon occasion. Had you?"

"Had I what?"

"Dealings with Cherry."

His complexion darkened, his lips compressing. Ottilia waited, holding his gaze. At last he looked away. "That is my business."

"Perhaps."

The gaze returned, faintly glaring. "What has the barmaid to do with this?"

"That is what I am endeavouring to find out."

He regarded her in a considering way. Trying to work out what she might know? The certainty she had it right grew upon her. She would not speak. Let him find his own way out of it, if he could. His lips pursed. "It is not my habit to indulge where too many men have been. I am a married man, my lady."

"So was Scalloway. Married indeed to a rich woman. Or she will be, once her father's fortune devolves upon her."

Harbury's nerve, if he had one, held. "The more fool he to be playing fast and loose with a potential fortune." A scoffing sound emerged. "Scalloway had not the brain to see where his bread was buttered. Anyone who knew him might know he would fail."

"At any enterprise, perhaps?"

"He was a fool."

Ottilia seized an advantage. "Not such a tragedy then, his death."

Harbury reared back, as if she had struck him. "What do you mean?"

She did not back down. "You had no good opinion of him. One might almost suppose you to be glad he is dead."

"Glad? Of course not. Merely because I disliked the man?"

Ottilia struck. "Because his death virtually guarantees that you will get the compensation you claim he owed you, in time."

Harbury slammed his hands flat down on the desk. "So that is it. What do you imply, my lady? I hope to be paid, yes. Perhaps. If Lord Radcliffe —" He stopped, seemed to pull himself in, removed his hands and began in a more moderate tone. "So far Lord Radcliffe has proved obdurate, so Ackworth says."

Ottilia did not let up. "But he cannot continue so once probate is granted. Your investment is safe."

"I do not consider it in quite that light."

"No? Yet you did not hesitate to send Mr Ackworth to Lord Radcliffe within days of the death."

"Why should I not? I had waited long enough!"

He was growing belligerent. Excellent. Ottilia turned the screw. "You became impatient, I dare say?"

"What would you? Scalloway evaded me. The whole affair was his fault. Employing a pirate for a captain? Who would be so stupid?"

Francis beat Ottilia to the post. "Ah, so you knew he was a pirate?"

"Anyone who has to do with shipping must know it. Even now, I dare say the authorities are within an ace of catching up with him. Good riddance when they do! The man is a menace and I will never believe he did not scupper that ship on purpose."

Was there a scent here? Ottilia followed it, for the notion she'd had earlier might well have substance. "Is it possible, Mr Harbury, that you alerted the authorities?"

He gazed at her fixedly. "I? Why should I?"

"To make of him a convenient scapegoat?"

"I cannot imagine what you mean, my lady." But the timbre of his voice had risen a notch.

"With Indigo on the run, the authorities might shift their attention elsewhere." He did not venture a word. Ottilia softened her tone. "Or perhaps it was merely to have your revenge upon Indigo as he had his upon Scalloway."

His stare grew rigid. "Revenge? I do not indulge in pettish games, my lady. I am a businessman. I operate always for expediency."

"It was highly expedient for Scalloway to die."

Did he flinch? His gaze remained fixed upon her as his lips worked. Wondering how to reply? At length he spoke, his tone cutting, but Ottilia detected a quiver behind it. "I see what you would be at. You are mistaken. I did not stab Scalloway."

Ottilia raised her brows. "Did I say you did?"

"You said — the implication —" He broke off. In a goaded voice, he repeated his assertion. "I did not stab him."

"Did you stab Mawdesley?"

"Of course not. I sent —" He cut off the words in a throaty grunt. "I meant…" Then his lips came together, shut tight. Yet his eyes belied him, the consternation visible.

Ottilia hit home. "You did not stab him. You sent Cherry to do it for you, did you not? Even provided her with the dagger. I wonder how many of these exclusive Barbadian daggers you have acquired in your career, Mr Harbury?"

His lips unfolded, but the quiver had become a shake. "I d-don't know what you are t-talking about."

She piled on the torment. "Souvenirs, perhaps? Gifts from grateful clients?"

"I know naught of such."

"Come, come, sir, this will not do. Anyone who has truck with traders from Barbados knows of Buck's daggers, with those ornately curved hilts. If you do not, you are singularly ignorant."

Harbury drew himself up, but his voice came out even higher. "I possess no such daggers, madam."

"What, you mean you have none left? You have used them all?"

His eyes grew a little wild, veering to Francis, to his desk, back to Ottilia. "Search if you choose. You will find nothing."

"I believe you. You are adept at foisting off your crimes upon others, are you not?"

"You are insulting!" He spat the words.

Ottilia pursued him, relentless. "Let us be clear, sir. You supplied Cherry with a dagger to kill Mawdesley. You paid her when the deed was done, and told her to leave the City, expecting the hue and cry to follow her. Then you doubled your insurance by pointing the finger to Indigo so that he fled likewise." She waited, but Harbury had no words, his features hard and set. Ottilia played her concealed ace. "Cherry is not stupid. I could not understand why she would leave so obvious a clue as a half-burned nightgown."

This tack brought his hands up, and he folded his arms, tucking them away. But Ottilia had seen their tremor. It also drew her husband's frowning glance, which she had expected. He mouthed "What?" at her and she gave a quick shake of the head to silence him.

"You are gibbering," Harbury said, hoarse now. "Nightgown? What have I to do with nightgowns?"

"A great deal, since you planted the thing, seizing a moment alone in her chamber where you had most certainly spent time upon several occasions. It was inexpertly done, Mr Harbury. But I dare say you don't know that the act of stabbing does not produce random spots of blood on the perpetrator in the way they were placed on that nightgown, especially when the weapon is left in situ. What is more, the fire had died down too much to have been responsible for the burning. Very likely, in her haste to pack and be gone, Cherry did not notice the edge of the nightgown poking out."

Harbury pushed himself up. Snatching at his spectacles, he thrust them onto his nose. A shield? He looked to have regained command of himself. "I wish you to leave."

"Why, because I have hit upon the truth?"

"It's not the truth! You are suggesting I had Cherry murder Scalloway. Well, I didn't. You can't prove it because it isn't true."

Ottilia rose too. "No, it is not true."

"Well, then?"

"You were careful not to appear in the matter. You employed Mawdesley to make the arrangements."

"Balderdash!"

"Just as you employed Cherry to rid you of him when he became expendable and a danger to you."

"A fairy tale! No jury would convict on such flimsy evidence."

"But you know and I know that it is what happened, do we not?"

Harbury came out from behind the desk. "Get out of my way!"

"Oh, no, you don't!"

Ottilia found herself shifted to one side with Francis in her place, his pistol in his hand.

"Stand where you are!" He cocked the gun.

Harbury hesitated, his gaze veering from one to the other. Then he jumped at Francis, knocking his pistol hand down with one fist and spoiling his aim. The gun went off, the bullet embedding itself in the desk.

In the confined space, the explosion was thunderous and Ottilia clapped her hands over her ears. Her spouse growled a curse as Harbury sprinted for the door and disappeared through it.

"Damnation!"

Ottilia lowered her hands. "It makes no matter, Fan. Belchamp's men will get him."

Francis was blowing at the barrel of his pistol. "Good thing you advised him to bring the militia."

"He had called them out already, Fan."

He pocketed the pistol. "Harbury didn't actually confess."

"Very nearly. He damned himself by trying to make a run for it."

"You rattled him finely, you wretch."

"He deserves it. So callous, Fan."

He eyed her. "What now? Have we to run the gamut of the courts?"

"By no means. We will leave all that to Belchamp, together with the pursuit of Indigo and Cherry, if he wishes to attempt to recover either one. But we cannot return home until we have secured Doro's freedom."

# CHAPTER TWENTY-SEVEN

Rejoicing to feel Doro's hand creep into his own, Hemp cast her a quick smile of reassurance and, holding her fingers tight, returned his attention to Lord Radcliffe. With the murder successfully resolved, and Doro finally and fully exonerated, Hemp could not have been happier to find that milady had no use for delay, taking immediate opportunity on the day following her triumph to beard Lord Radcliffe in person.

For Hemp's money, the peer was not best pleased to be invaded by the deputation. If milady had not dragged Mrs Scalloway along, would he have refused to see them?

"Elinor, what is this? Are you here upon this mission of your own free will?"

Ottilia cut in before Mrs Scalloway could reply. "Never mind Elinor's free will, sir. The only freedom in question here is that of Dorote Gabon."

Lord Racliffe's cheeks suffused. "Will you allow Elinor to speak for herself, madam?"

"Here, Radcliffe!" said Francis, angered. "You use that tone to my wife at your peril, I warn you."

"Be content, Fan. I care naught for his tone." Ottilia turned to Mrs Scalloway. "Elinor, you made a promise, remember?"

Elinor tossed her head. "It is immaterial to me. I don't want the girl. I will sign a document to say that I am willing to grant manumission, Edward, if you will draw it up."

Lord Radcliffe hesitated, looking from her to Ottilia and Francis, and thence to Doro. Hemp braced. Let him say one word amiss! Thankfully, his gaze returned to the widow.

"Are you sure about this, Elinor? Once it is done, there is no changing it."

She shrugged. "There will be other slaves. Doro has ceased to be of use to me. Besides, she has grown insolent. I have no use for an insolent slave."

Hemp tightened his hold on Doro's hand, likewise keeping his lips as tight closed upon the harsh words hovering on his tongue. For Doro's sake, he must bury his rage. When she was his in truth, it would be different. Then Ottilia spoke for him.

"Elinor, if you don't wish to receive another blow from me, I suggest you mind your tongue in my presence."

"How dare you speak to her in that fashion, madam?"

Ottilia turned on Lord Radcliffe. "Don't you madam me, sir! I have had quite enough from both of you. I am not such a fool as to expect gratitude for saving Elinor and her paramour from the gallows. But at the least, I demand to be spared hearing the sort of language that ought long ago to have been consigned to history."

"Bravo, Tillie!"

But Francis's praise was overborne as Mrs Scalloway bridled. "I was never in danger of the gallows. What is more, your threats are empty now that the real culprit has been apprehended."

"Oh, be silent, woman!" Francis strode forward. "Radcliffe, for pity's sake let us have an end to this! No more wrangling. Write the necessary documents. I will vouch for it that my wife will not stir from your house until it is done."

Elinor flounced to the chair before the desk, waving at the one opposite. "Sit down, Edward. The sooner it is done, the sooner I can be rid of this menace."

Lord Radcliffe harrumphed a little, but at last moved to his place behind the desk, opened a drawer and took out a sheet of parchment. He eyed Francis. "I take it you will be responsible for securing the deed of manumission? It must be done in London. I cannot complete the business here."

"We will do whatever is necessary. All I ask is that you do your part."

Lord Radcliffe grunted again, but at last, to Hemp's relief, he reached to his silver standish and picked up the quill there. "Have you a seal, Elinor? If not, I will use mine."

Dipping the sharpened point into the inkwell, he began to write, what time Mrs Scalloway pulled at her glove. A whisper from Doro reached Hemp's ears. "She has one on a ring."

"A seal?"

"It is the Carey seal."

"Even better," Hemp murmured in her ear. "Not long now and you will be free."

Doro said no word and he glanced down. Her gaze was fixed on Lord Radcliffe's moving hand. "What does he write?"

"I do not know the exact wording. Master Roy used a wording of his own at Flora Sugars. It will enable you to obtain your certificate of manumission to say that henceforth you are no longer a slave." He did not add that he intended to pay the fee and would himself escort her to the Capital for the purpose of securing the certificate from the Lord Mayor of London. That duty was his alone. He would not trouble milord on the matter.

"It feels like a miracle."

"That is milady's province. She deals in miracles." Hemp looked towards Ottilia as he spoke and saw she was in low-voiced conversation with her husband. It occurred to him that his plans might best be put on hold for a space. He was not going to change his life thus soon if Doro meant to remain with the Fanshawes. That would give him time to woo her and win back her love.

Feeling as if she was held in suspension, Doro became aware of her heart pumping in anticipation as she watched Lord Radcliffe melt the end of his stick of sealing wax at the candle flame. Her mistress — still so? Or was that over? — stood next to him, her ring held ready. Doro had watched the ink appear as she signed her name to the document.

The red waxen droplets fell upon the paper, like blood, dripping out her old life. The ring came down, the seal stamping its message into the hot wax.

It was done. It was over. She was free.

Thought blanked as she let go of Hemp's hand and stepped forward in response to madame's beckoning finger. She felt oddly detached, unreal. The paper was held out towards her.

"Take it. Keep it safe until you can obtain your certificate."

Doro put out her hand, a little surprised to see how her fingers quivered. The parchment felt rough. She held it between both hands, read the words. They made no sense, failing to penetrate the blanketing unreality.

Running on a long-practised habit, Doro dropped a curtsey. "I thank you, madame."

The mistress's face held disdain. Was there disappointment too? "Is that all you have to say?"

Confused, Doro pulled the parchment closer, half fearing it might be snatched away from her. "What should I say, madame?"

Elinor shrugged. "Naught, since you choose to forget all we have been to each other."

Doro met her gaze. "I do not forget."

The sense of standing outside herself grew as Elinor's eyes filled. She came out from behind the desk. One hand came up and caressed Doro's cheek. "We were friends, were we not?"

Doro tried to respond suitably, but her tongue would not say the words. She curtsied again, dropping her gaze. "I am grateful, madame," was all she could manage.

Then Lady Fan was there, and an arm came about her shoulders. "There, that is done. You are your own woman now, my dear. Come, let us go." She turned away from Elinor. "Hemp!"

Then he was there, taking her hand, leading her out of the room. Doro found her legs weakening and she stumbled. Hemp's arm came about her, halting her. He put out his free hand. "Let me roll it up for you, Doro."

She held it away from him, reluctant to let it out of her grasp. "Not yet." She held it so he might read it. "What does it say?"

His voice came, a tease within it. "Have you forgotten how to read?"

"*Mon roi*, please. I cannot see. I am blind at this moment."

His hug was both comforting and productive of a drag at her heart. She listened as he read the words. She heard them but only the word "freedom" registered.

"It does not seem real."

"It will be real soon, Doro, you will see. But let us be gone from here."

She let him draw her to the door where a porter was holding it open. The cold hit as she walked out into the familiar street, effectually pulling her out of the numbing sensation that had her in thrall. Yet to Doro, it was quite as if the sun shone brightly. As Hemp mercifully guided her uncertain steps, a bubble of some long gone feeling burgeoned in her breast. Happiness? She drew in a huge breath and let it out again.

She stopped walking and turned to Hemp. "Is it true?"

He set his hands either side of her face and held it so that she must look straight into his eyes. "It is true, *ma reine*. Your life begins anew."

# CHAPTER TWENTY-EIGHT

Ottilia had barely stepped down from the coach when her nephews tumbled out of the front door, besieging her with an overlapping commentary.

"We saw you from the window, Auntilla."

"Auntilla, you must come and see Pretty on her hobby horse. She loves it."

"Was it a murder again, Auntilla? Did you find out who did it?"

Tom seized her hand and shook it. "You've got to come, Auntilla. You won't believe how fast Pretty goes."

Feeling battered, and still a trifle queasy from the journey, Ottilia was grateful to her spouse when he intervened.

"Have done, you imps, you'll deafen her. Let your aunt at least get into the house."

"Beg pardon, sir," said Ben, contrite. Then his tone changed. "Good grief, Uncle Fan, you are bruised all to pieces! What happened?"

Tom's gaze veered, fixing upon Francis's wounds. He became gleeful. "Fisticuffs! Did you do for the other fellow?"

"I did indeed, Tom, with a little help from a friend. But that story can wait. Will you let go of your poor aunt's person, wretched boy?"

Unlike his brother, Tom made no apology. Nor did he release Ottilia's hand. "Thing is, we've so much to tell her, Uncle Fan."

Ottilia found her tongue. "I shall be glad to hear it all, Tom, but presently, if you please."

Ben nudged his brother. "Leave her be, Tom."

But his younger sibling, oblivious as usual to restraint, began to tug at the hand. "Well, we'll tell you, but you must come and see Pretty first."

Ottilia threw a helpless look at her spouse, who was settling with the post-boys. "I am overborne, Fan."

He threw up his eyes, handed his purse to the butler with an admonition to see to the fellow's needs and came to the rescue. "Don't drag her, Tom, for pity's sake! Be gentle."

Thus adjured, Tom curbed his pace and Ottilia yet found herself drawn willy-nilly to the front door. Tom released her at last as they reached it and darted inside.

"There she is! See, Auntilla?"

Ottilia walked into the hall and at once saw the little girl, sat astride on the seat of the wooden toy and galloping around the chequered floor. She looked to be enjoying the game, and Ottilia's heart warmed to the sight. Hovering close by was Hepsie, and following the progress of the hobby horse, though more slowly, was Mr Madeley.

"She's expert already," said Ben, with a prideful air that sat oddly on his youth.

Ottilia watched the child, who had not yet noticed the augmented company, so absorbed in the game was she. "It seems so indeed."

"We made it," announced Tom. "With Mr Madeley's help, of course."

Ben snorted. "What you mean is Mr Madeley made it. We did help a bit, Auntilla."

"That sounds much more likely. How do you do, Mr Madeley?"

Pretty's grandfather had ceased to follow the child. He looked across at Ottilia and gave a small bow. "Well, my lady. I am glad to see you safely returned."

The additional voice evidently attracted Pretty's attention. She came to a stop and Ottilia was gratified to see recognition in the big blue eyes as they rested upon her. Then the gaze shifted away and Pretty gave a little shriek, dropping the hobby horse where she stood. Stepping over it, she ran towards the group by the door, her crowing delight cutting a nick in Ottilia's bosom.

"Papa! Papa!"

With an odd mixture of pain and pleasure, Ottilia watched her husband start forward, stooping, his arms out to catch the child. "There's my little sweetheart! Up you come then!" Francis swung her up into his embrace, cuddling her close and making soothing noises as she continued with her cry of "Papa".

Ottilia was brought back from contemplation with a jerk. "Why doesn't she call you Mama, Auntilla?"

She answered without thought. "Because she has not yet accepted me in place of her own mother, Ben."

He met her gaze, his face now almost level with her own so much had he grown. "Will she some day?"

"I hope so." Strangely, Ottilia found the yearning that had accompanied this thought had lessened. Because of the new-found closeness between Pretty and her husband?

She had no time to indulge the thought for at this moment the servants were seen to be seeking entry, burdened with portmanteaux and the impedimenta involved with a sojourn away from home. Seeing among them Dorote and Hemp, who had travelled in a second post-chaise, Ottilia dragged her gaze away from Francis, who had set Pretty down and was squatting next to the hobby horse while she explained to him its purpose, in an excitable treble. Mr Madeley had joined the pair, his deeper tones mingling with Pretty's to throw light upon obscure phrases. He had apparently learned to understand his granddaughter's babyish speech. Ottilia captured her nephews by one shoulder each. "Boys, I would like you to meet someone who has joined our household for the time being."

"Who is it?"

"A friend of Hemp's from Barbados, Tom." She raised her voice. "Doro!"

The former slave girl, catching her name, turned her head towards them. Ottilia heard a gasp from Ben, and a muttered exclamation from Tom.

"She's got blue eyes!"

"Be quiet, you ape," growled his brother. Ben glanced at Ottilia, and an awed whisper came. "She's pretty fetching, Auntilla."

"Yes, very beautiful." Ottilia spoke more normally as Doro came up. "These are my nephews, Doro. Ben, Tom, this is Dorote Gabon, although perhaps she will allow you to call her Doro, as Hemp does."

Doro dropped a curtsey. "Master Ben, Master Tom."

"Oh, we ain't masters, miss," piped up Tom. "Were you on the plantation like Hemp? Were you a slave?"

"Tom, that's rude," scolded his brother. "Beg pardon, ma'am. He doesn't think before he opens his mouth."

Doro, to Ottilia's secret amusement, looked thoroughly taken aback. One of her rare smiles peeped out and Ottilia rejoiced. Hemp's smiles had been rare too when first he had joined the household. Perhaps Doro would likewise relax and begin to enjoy her freedom.

"Ah, here is Hemp. He will explain, boys. I will leave you to become acquainted, Dorote. Pray don't stand upon ceremony. These two never do. And they are simply Ben and Tom. You will find no masters here."

She left them, conscious of an urgent need to rest and was relieved to see her maid awaiting her at the bottom of the stairs. "Joanie! Just the person I need. Fan, I am off to the chamber. Mr Madeley, we will talk anon."

Curiously, she felt no urgency for the discussion. After all, Francis had been adamant he would not allow Pretty to be removed from their care and if she could trust anyone, she could trust her darling lord.

As she mounted the stairs, it occurred to her that she was overtired. They had remained only one further night at Bristol, Francis having invited Mr Belchamp to dine at Ottilia's request. She felt a little guilty for leaving him with the aftermath, but he had assured he was more than capable of finishing up the business, having already despatched the militia in search of the missing Cherry.

"As for Captain Indigo, I propose to send my best thief-taker after him. Moreover, I intend to institute a search in the Scilly Isles for this missing cargo. Not that I dare hope it may be found. But one must do everything in one's power to carry out the workings of the Law."

The roads being less troublesome on the return journey, they made good time, nevertheless breaking for the night at Calne once more. Today's journey had been equally swift and Ottilia was at a loss to account for her extreme exhaustion. The reflection could not but obtrude that she had been tired all along, but this felt exceptional. Unless it was the drop after all the excitement? At the top of the stairs, she began to feel light-headed. "Lend me your arm, Joanie. I fear I am going to swoon."

The maid jumped to her need. "Lean on me, my lady. It is only a short way to the bedchamber. You can lie down and I'll fetch you a glass of water."

Ottilia managed to hold herself together until the chamber was gained, but she had not strength enough even to remove her cloak, sliding to the bed and well-nigh falling to the pillow, her head swimming. She felt her legs lifted and sighed as they stretched out. Sliding into a state half sleeping, half waking, she lay in a sort of stupor, hardly aware of much beyond the gentle murmur of Joanie's voice.

"There now, my lady, you rest. Let me take off your bonnet. There, that's better. Never mind your cloak. It will keep you warm. But let's have these boots off and you'll be a deal more comfortable. Now then, my lady, just you say where you are. I won't be a moment."

The next thing she knew was the housekeeper's clucking. "Dearie me, whatever has come over her?" She opened her eyes to find Mrs Bertram's motherly features bending over her. "Ah, she's come round. Let me raise you, my lady, so Joanie can help you sip the water."

Ottilia made no objection and obediently drank when the glass was put to her lips. Presently the lassitude possessing her began to recede and the fogging died away from her brain. "Help me to sit up, if you please, Mrs Bertram."

The housekeeper clicked her tongue. "Had you ought to get up so soon, my lady? You've been in a swoon."

Ottilia managed a smile. "Yes, I realise that. It happened in Bristol too. I dare say I am merely tired. I felt quite fatigued throughout. It has been a strenuous time."

"Then should you not remain —?"

"I need to get these things off, then Joanie can loosen my stays."

The exercise of removing her outer clothing, and then her bodice proved exhausting and Ottilia lost patience as the maid began to work upon her petticoats. "Leave them, Joanie! My stays. Untie my stays. I fear I have gained flesh, for they irk me unbearably if they are too tight."

Mrs Bertram busied herself with removing the discarded clothing while Joanie wrestled with the knot on the bodice. "It is tied a trifle tight, my lady, but don't you worry. I'll have you free in a jiffy."

Ottilia endured while Joanie worked, but at last the strings were loose and the stays came away. The maid lifted them off and Ottilia sighed with relief as her held-in muscles were permitted to sag. Joanie then insisted upon removing both petticoats and under-petticoats, Mrs Bertram supporting Ottilia as she stood for the garments to be tugged down to her feet. She stepped out of them and sat down again, relieved to be clad only in her shift.

"I'll fetch you a shawl, my lady. You'll take cold. Mrs Bertram, ma'am, could you poke that fire a bit, if you please?"

Ottilia drifted a little, smoothing the shift over her midriff and massaging where the stays had been. Her hands stilled as she became aware of Joanie, standing before her, a warm wool shawl hanging from her hands, gaping at her stroking hands.

"What in the world are you gawping at, Joanie?"

The maid's gaze came up. "My lady, it's not flesh as you've gained."

Irritation seized Ottilia. "Of what are you talking, Joanie?" But even as she spoke, the maid's meaning dawned on her. "Oh, dear Lord, I've been a fool!"

"No, my lady, you've not. Last time you was sick as a parrot! Have you not been sick?"

Her mind felt sluggish. "Not sick, no. But I did faint before. And I was so tired! I have been eating like a horse too. Yes, and my breasts have got bigger." She cupped them in her hands, looking down. "Don't you think so, Joanie?"

Mrs Bertram, eyes popping over the maid's shoulder, answered for her. "I don't know about that, my lady, but you sure as sure have a little bump there."

Ottilia cradled her stomach. She did have a bump! "How could I have missed this? To be sure, I had my mind on other matters, but…" Her voice died as the implication sank into her brain. The answering joy began to swell in her bosom, just like the new life that must be growing inside her.

The tiredness vanished. Ottilia drew a deep breath and let it out again, trying for a measure of calm. "Thank you both. Keep mum for this for the moment, if you please." Her heart cried out with love. "Pray fetch his lordship to me, as fast as you can."

Pausing only to set the shawl around her mistress's shoulders, Joanie hurried away. Ottilia watched the two women leave the room, exchanging excited whispers. Then she rose, found her knees a little shaky and grasped the nearest bed post, waiting until her legs felt stable enough to carry her. She went to the long mirror, dropped the shawl and stood there in her shift, turning sideways on to check that her senses had not deceived her. Yes, there was a bump. Slight as yet, but the memory of the last time leapt in her head and she knew it was real.

Ottilia was weeping silent tears by the time Francis came, at a run, for she heard his steps pounding before the door burst open.

"Tillie, what is it? I knew you were doing too much! Are you ill?"

"Not ill, no." Ottilia half stumbled towards him, holding out her arms.

He caught her, but held her off, his gaze frantic as he searched her face. "If you are not ill, what is the matter? Joanie said I must come at once. You are weeping! For pity's sake, my loved one, tell me!"

Ottilia's lips were trembling, but she put her hands to his chest. "Oh, Fan, my darling lord, I don't know how. I have been unforgivably slow, perfectly stupid and blind."

His face changed. "What? You don't mean we had the wrong man back there? You can't have made a mistake, surely?"

Ottilia grasped his lapels and shook them, sniffing back her tears. "Not that, Fan. Do you remember how I've been eating and eating? Of course you do, you spoke of it enough times. And then I was tired and swooned, and I nagged at you that I was putting on flesh. And lost my temper for no real reason. You remember? I never thought, Fan, for I was so ill the last time, but I have not felt so, not at all, except a little in the coach."

A kind of light was dawning in his eyes and he became still, his voice little more than a croak. "Don't keep me in suspense, Tillie! It can't be, can it?"

Ottilia's tears spilled over again as her lips broke apart, the smile uncontrollable. "Yes, Fan, I do believe I am *enceinte*."

# A NOTE TO THE READER

Dear Reader

When I took Hemp to Bristol, I had no idea what I would find by way of research material. I chose this City because I found out that in the $18^{th}$ Century it was the main seaport for trade with the West Indies, although ships also travelled from there to America. Bristol's main trades were in sugar, coffee, tobacco and chocolate which were produced in the Caribbean by the slave trade. This made it the perfect setting for the rescue of my slave girl, Dorote Gabon.

One of the best resources I found was a map of Bristol, very close to the period, which had been photographed and turned digital by a French university. To my joy, I could not only trace routes through the centre, but was also treated to lists of buildings with numbers to show me exactly where they were. Thus, the Bridewell, the streets around the floating harbour, the location of various inns like the Full Moon, are as accurate as the map could make them.

I took one or two liberties for convenience to the needs of my story, but on the whole, the setting of the tale is as it would have been at the time.

Unusually, Ottilia and Fan were not accompanied by other members of the family on this adventure. But with the resolution of Pretty's future and the gradual reveal of Ottilia's condition, I felt a time of privacy between them was appropriate. It enabled them to renew and strengthen their relationship, finding again the joy in each other unmarred by the troubled chafing that often accompanies dealing with importunate relatives.

As for Hemp, I have known about Doro for some time and was only waiting for the right moment to tell their story. What I didn't know until I started writing was that Doro would turn out to possess the anomaly of those extraordinary eyes. I was relieved to find that I was quite right when I discovered a stunning model with just that combination of ebony and deep blue. Placing Doro's origins in Gabon, with its strong French history, added an unexpected dimension to the tale of these star-crossed lovers: she was *ma reine* to Hemp, while to Dorote he became *mon roi.*

Such touches that flip out from one's subconscious are a boon to the writer. I hope you enjoyed reading about their love story as much as I enjoyed writing it.

If you would consider leaving a review, it would be much appreciated and very helpful. Do feel free to contact me on **elizabeth@elizabethbailey.co.uk** or find me on **Facebook**, **Twitter**, **Goodreads** or my website **elizabethbailey.co.uk**.

Elizabeth Bailey

SAPERE
BOOKS